GLORIOUS

GLORIOUS

Book One

EBB TIDE

Fergus Dunlop

First published in Guernsey by Hollenden House 2025

ISBN 978-1-8383663-2-2 (hbk)
ISBN 978-1-8383663-3-9 (ebk)

Cover design © Fergus Dunlop
Typeset by www.shakspeareeditorial.org

To My Wife

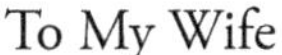

By the same author

Fiction

Glorious trilogy – ISBNs 978-1-8383663-8-4 (hbk); 978-1-8383663-9-1 (ebk)
  Book 1 – *Ebb Tide* ISBNs 978-1-8383663-2-2 (hbk); 978-1-8383663-3-9 (ebk)
  Book 2 – *Flood Tide* ISBNs 978-1-8383663-4-6 (hbk); 978-1-8383663-5-3 (ebk)
  Book 3 – *Tidal Race* ISBNs 978-1-8383663-6-0 (hbk); 978-1-8383663-7-7 (ebk)

Non-fiction

Available in hardback through local bookshops or online retailers.
Available as an ebook on Amazon, Apple iBooks, Kobo and other ebook retailers.

Borderline Pass – 5 maps, 5 line drawings, 693 pages
  Second edition (2024): ISBN 978-1-0369-020-1-1 (hbk)
  First edition (2020): ISBNs 978-1-5272239-8-1 (hbk); 978-1-5272396-0-9 (ebk)

The Lady with no Name (2021) – 14 colour photographs, map and line drawing, 319 pages
  ISBNs 978-1-8383663-0-8 (hbk); 978-1-8383663-1-5 (ebk)

Discount available when you buy direct from the author
www.fergusdunlop.com

Go online at www.fergusdunlop.com/glorious for supporting resources:

Maps

Epilogues of historical characters

Index of historical characters

Invented characters

Sources, including bibliography and tide tables

Miller MS

Miller Journal

Miller-Gwyn Papers

Contents

Prologue

The word 'glorious' was invoked five times in the sermon at the coronation of William and Mary in 1689. The ceremony was indeed the climax of an extraordinary series of changes. A Catholic king of England and Wales, Scotland and Ireland, James II, was officially removed, and his half-Dutch, Protestant, nephew-cum-son-in-law installed.

Yet the full name for those events, *The Glorious Revolution of 1688*, does not emerge in written form until 1713, in another church sermon. It seems that English men and women learnt of the glory of the revolution of 1688 only gradually; and from the pulpits of the established church.

Religion in late-seventeenth-century England took centre stage. The Great Plague of 1665 still loomed large in the collective memory. Infant mortality was brutal. No one was safe. Of King James II's twenty-seven progeny, eighteen were stillborn or died in childhood. Faith in a Hereafter was the sole consolation.

A surge in printing had spread English-language Bibles far and wide. Literate households had one. People knew the Good Book far better than today, a few even from cover to cover. Yet secular research, news, plays and novels also flourished. Which other generation was so quick to believe in fantastical Popish Plots, while searching so hard for scientific truth, and still trying to enjoy itself? This Pepysian paradox of sanctity, gravity and levity is part of the appeal of the late Stuarts.

Such sanctity is hard for us to grasp. Such gravity we may glimpse in others. Such levity reminds us of ourselves.

The two weeks covered are a watershed in Anglo-Saxon history. Yes, England turned towards centuries of large-scale overseas military engagement, but also squirearchy, misogyny, a rampant slave trade and a divided Ireland.

This novel is factual for King James II and his family, for William of Orange, for their soldiers, the Council of Peers, the newssheets, the riots and the populace in the Irish Night panic. Fictional additions are noted in the Afterword. More is at www.fergusdunlop.com/glorious – with details of what happened next to the historical figures mentioned, also tide tables, maps, a bibliography and the chance to download facsimiles of the *Miller MS* and *Journal*, key sources for this book.

The timeline is accurate. The liberties and little inventions are acknowledged. The rest is true, plausible, or at least possible.

Glorious it was not.

Simplified tree of the Kings and Queens of England 1485–1714

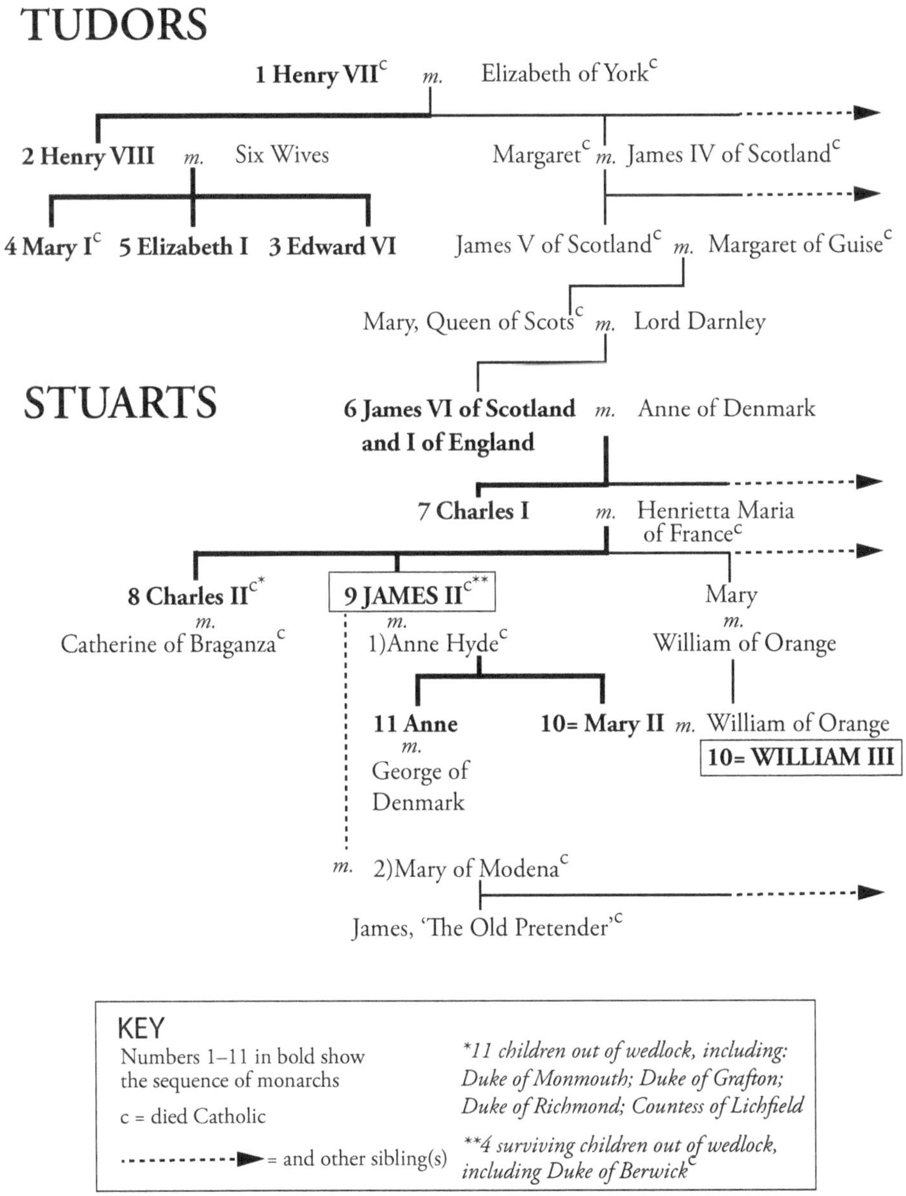

TUDORS

1 Henry VII[c] *m.* Elizabeth of York[c]

2 Henry VIII *m.* Six Wives   Margaret[c] *m.* James IV of Scotland[c]

4 Mary I[c] **5 Elizabeth I** **3 Edward VI**   James V of Scotland[c] *m.* Margaret of Guise[c]

Mary, Queen of Scots[c] *m.* Lord Darnley

STUARTS

6 James VI of Scotland and I of England *m.* Anne of Denmark

7 Charles I *m.* Henrietta Maria of France[c]

8 Charles II[c*]   **9 JAMES II**[c**]   Mary
m.   *m.*   *m.*
Catherine of Braganza[c]   1) Anne Hyde[c]   William of Orange

11 Anne   **10= Mary II** *m.* William of Orange
m.   **10= WILLIAM III**
George of
Denmark

m. 2) Mary of Modena[c]

James, 'The Old Pretender'[c]

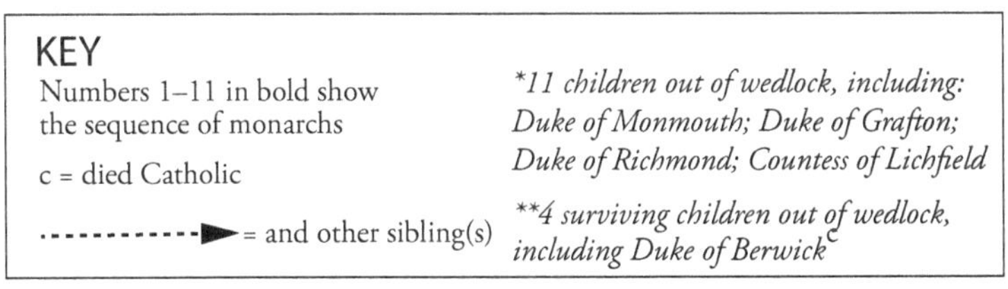

KEY

Numbers 1–11 in bold show the sequence of monarchs

c = died Catholic

-----------▶ = and other sibling(s)

11 children out of wedlock, including: Duke of Monmouth; Duke of Grafton; Duke of Richmond; Countess of Lichfield

**4 surviving children out of wedlock, including Duke of Berwick[c]*

Day 1. Sunday 9 December 1688

Kitty: 04:00

Johanna Catherine Jones, also known as Kitty, was in bed at her parents' home in a corner of the City of London. She had slept on her right side and pinched that arm, which had woken her up. With her left hand she scooped her hair to the top of her head and rolled over. The blood came tingling back.

The night was dark. Winter swart. Blackfriars black.

Adults would say, when she was small, 'penny for your thoughts', and she would have none. But somewhere along the way, long before this her nineteenth year, the canvas of her mind had begun to fill with images, the scroll to swim with words. Nowadays, if asked what she was thinking, she would wonder where to start.

As the only child of the house, the tutors and books which would normally have been lavished on an eldest son, had come to her. No sibling rivals had competed for her parents' resources or affection. In consequence, she was happy in the company of adults, and unsure of herself with her peers.

The quieter she seemed, the more was going on inside. The problem was expressing it, which she did with music and, most of all, drawing. Plants were her speciality.

With both her hands now good again, from old habit she rubbed her face. Her two palms moved in tandem either side of her nose, smoothing her forehead, eyebrows, cheeks and jaw, careful not to scratch. In the final upstroke, her thumbs slipped behind her ears, to seek the fine skin which she liked to sniff for freshness, holding the knuckles together under her nose.

Sunday before dawn was the moment in the week when the metropolis held its breath, even here, within earshot of the Thames. But tonight, rain pattered steadily on her window and drowned out the silence.

A rain-swept night made her glad to be in her warm, dry bed. But she had another reason to smile: whatever weather the Lord's Sabbath threw at them, the Joneses need not go out.

It was their family secret.

Kitty gave a small grunt of satisfaction and went back to sleep.

Jack, 07:00

Jack Wilson stirred on his bedroll. He liked to gather his wits before the twin horns sounded. A reveille tucket was the Colonel's idea of fun. Sir Henry had picked this up in his decade in Tangier, he said, from the Moors' competing pre-dawn calls to prayer from their surrounding camps. But today being a Christian Sunday after a month marching through England, they could look forward to an added hour's rest. Tension was down. Everyone, from the Commissary of Ammunition to the wheelwright's servant, would have their first uninterrupted chance for weeks to clear drainplugs, rebalance loads, grease bearings, tighten axles, shoe horses, mend tack and otherwise take stock.

Jack's billet was dry, the wooden floorboards warm, and he had slept well – a soldier's trick. Also a young man's. After so long on the road, he took his sleep where he could. Any roof was better than striking wet canvas the next morning. And here he was in a windmill, a childhood dream, for tonight as well, two nights in a row, with the best view for miles around.

The rain ceased drumming on the dome above, but still trickled into a butt by the ground floor entrance. Jack sat back against the ladder which led up to the gear loft and listened. It was the best moment of what should prove an easy day. Nevertheless, from childhood habit, he offered a silent prayer for a steady mind, adding, in case unrequited love was allowed, *and Kitty Jones*. Two more days' trudge to the city, Monday and Tuesday. Then on Wednesday the Royal Artillery's horse-drawn caravan, or train, extending over a mile, would be home where it belonged, in the Tower of London. Then, give him amber-blonde Kitty too.

Terry Jones, no relation, the other occupant of the narrow second floor room, breathed with the regularity of deep sleep. Technically, Jones, as a gunner's mate, was junior to Jack, who was a firemaster. However, with scores of different ranks in the cannon train, sanity had prevailed – Terry was simply Corporal Jones and Jack was Lieutenant Wilson.

No similar unit in England had ever attempted a winter march like this. Nor would the experiment be repeated. Yes, half a century earlier, in high summer, Charles I had ordered a bigger weight of guns all the way from London to Scotland. And it was true that three years ago a short train of eight light cannon under this same Henry Shere had marched seventeen miles in one day, from Dorchester to Sherborne, before the Battle of Sedgemoor, to suppress the last rebellion. But that too had been in June. Nevertheless, on 10 November, 280 men of the Royal Ordnance in their blue and scarlet coats had set off from London for Salisbury in south Wiltshire, eighty-five miles away. With them had gone 250 horses pulling twenty-six cannon and sixty wagons, including limbers, ration carts, field kitchens, farriers and a smithy. And as many again of other personnel – cooks, carters and boys. Furthermore, the enterprise had been guarded by 400 Royal Fusiliers – flintlock musket, knee-length red coat with silver buttons – with their own quartermaster and supply wagons. To travel eighty-five miles in fifteen days would have required the artillery train to cover six miles in a day. Once moving, the single-file procession had managed fewer than three.

Luck had been against King James II from the start. Prince William of Orange's Dutch invasion fleet had been expected in the northeast – his frigates had cruised the Yorkshire coast for months. The Royal Navy had positioned itself at anchor in the mouth of the Thames, waiting to pounce as the enemy sailed north from Holland. In the event, starting on 2nd November, an easterly wind had carried the enormous convoy, roughly twice the size of the Spanish Armada a century before, down the English Channel to Devon. The same wind had trapped the King's warships in the estuary until the Dutch were ashore. It had then swung to the southwest, releasing the royal men-of-war but delaying their chase down the Channel.

The King's land-based great guns had set off westwards from London on the day that news of the Devon landing reached them. They had pressed forward, with the gale now in their faces, toiling in limited light, on sunken roads, at best rutted, at worst deep in mud, without pause for God's Day of Rest. The last cannon had just crested Jenkins' Hill, the ridge after Bagshot, a third of the way to the Salisbury camp, when His Majesty and retinue had sped through in the same direction. That was twenty-one days ago. To Jack it had been an enviable sight. The royal cavalcade, with its detachment of Horse Guards and Irish Dragoons travelled as far in half an hour as the ordnance train did in a day.

It had been reported through the camp at nightfall that King James had conferred from his carriage window with Colonel Shere. Neither had seemed best pleased. They should have ordered up cannon from the arsenal at Portsmouth, as they had before Sedgemoor. Everyone else was aware of the blunder. Portsmouth to Salisbury Plain was the distance Sir Henry's men had by then covered from London. Moreover, the way was more level. To have a few big guns in the royal camp by the time His Majesty arrived would have made all the difference to morale. Instead, King James, the former admiral, more interested in artillery than even Henry VIII, would find himself out-gunned by an invader who had come over the sea, of necessity with few heavy weapons.

A week later, on another Sunday, the artillerymen had stopped after dusk on the expansive common at Hartley Wintney, halfway to Salisbury. Jack had calculated they could be there in ten days if they kept up this improved rate, as the inexperienced gained the measure of the task. But the King's cortège met them again, coming the other way. His Majesty had even roughed it for the night, sleeping in St Mary's Church. Tolerant Catholic that he was, he said he preferred that to asking a weary convoy to pitch the regal tabernacle it was bringing, for just one night; or to imposing himself unannounced on the nearby gentry at Bramshill. Glad to be occupied with something more than a dead-slow march, the fusiliers, the regiment James himself had founded, had mounted enthusiastic guard around the village. The next morning, King James II had ordered the train to retreat. Back to the Tower, 'turning aside neither to the right hand nor the left.' Numbers 20 and Deuteronomy 5, Jack had thought. Also Proverbs.

The order had come at the right time to be executed – a cannon train could not reverse direction once on the move. The Colonel had dispatched a troop of four lighter guns with minimal supplies ahead to London, no need to hold them back and they might be needed. An ensign had ridden the other way to recall the advanced party, which had been strengthening the span over the River Whitewater at Hook. These had retired last to camp that night, and led off the next morning. The sixty pioneers and six engineers always made a fine sight in red jackets, red capes and leather caps. Captain of the pioneers was a stepping stone to seniority, even colonel. Jack had been offered the job because he looked the part, tall and well-knit. But the pioneers were a Hell-raising, fist-fighting pack. You needed some of that wild spirit in your own blood to tame such a crew. Jack was of printer stock – his father and both his grandfathers in their day. Printers usually had their noses in a book. He knew himself well enough not to accept.

The return journey should have been quicker, thanks to the pioneers' previous reinforcement work – at least some good had come of their labours. Also, the sou'wester was no longer in the men's faces. But still they had struggled. The magic of having guarded the King for a night evaporated and with it any sense of urgency. Downhill slopes became more fearsome with the wind blowing from behind, while on the flat, the problems mounted. The horses were in worse shape than at the start and showed a new tendency to graze or gawp at every roadside distraction. The wagons broke down more often.

An axle had sheared on a baggage cart in a narrow cutting on Star Hill, spilling its load and blocking the road. Although Sir Henry had spaced out the convoy in anticipation of trouble, the clotpoll Comptroller of the Train, Captain Exe, panicked and the slope behind became clogged. Jack had taken the initiative, calmed the horses, trebled-up teams and dragged the wreckage to the top.

Exe was now on the lookout for any slip Jack might make.

After this hiccough, the men sank low. The prospect of a dry barracks in London was still too distant. Only fear of the bedlam should the royal army retreating from Salisbury catch them on the same road, spurred them on. Or, perish the thought, the Dutch. The guns had crawled across the bridge over the Blackwater to camp at Camberley, then back up to the Bagshot ridge for a night, and down the old Roman road to the River Bourne by Breakheart Hill for their next stop.

Breakheart. Ah Kitty, don't you do that to me. She had waved him off. Smiled as he marched past. It had looked like eighteen-year-old insouciance. Was she brave or just content with life? Did she know the danger he faced? Did she foresee that it would all be for nothing and that battle would be avoided? Or did she just not care? What could he offer a girl so self-possessed?

Dry in his lofty perch, Jack made the most of the morning's peace. The dripping in the water butt had stopped. A few more minutes, he thought, and the Colonel's cornets would pounce. Groans would rise from hay barn to bakehouse, as the non-commissioned officers bullied the slugabeds. Better to be up and washed before all that.

He'd greased his boots well last night, especially on their soles and seams, and now reached across and drew out their straw stuffing. Blisters and lesions had to be avoided on long marches, at all costs. The wet came from the roads in winter and from sweaty feet in summer. Good boots were the infantryman's most precious possession. He pulled on his clean socks, donned his britches, laced up the footwear, slung his tunic jacket across his bare shoulders and went to the little window to enjoy the view.

Then he was scrambling down the ladder shouting, 'Stand to, stand to, the rabble is at the baggage train,' and pandemonium reigned.

No one, least of all Jack, had thought much about placing sentries on Hounslow Heath. The artillery train was so close to London and well away from the enemy. After three years of summer training camps this was home from home. But on a wet Saturday night, almost the longest of the year, that was too much trust. The men had trusted the officers. The officers had trusted Sir Henry. And Sir Henry had trusted the locals. The gunners and fusiliers were not used to thinking for themselves. They were only as good as their orders. Those to mount guard had been insufficient. And now the locals had jumped the few sentries in the night.

Jack ran into the fusiliers' barn. 'I need men,' he called. 'Grab some clothes, muskets, powder and flint. Now! Forget topcoats, forget headdress. No swords, bayonets or bullets. Just the flintlocks and the powder.'

'What is it, Lieutenant?' asked their sergeant.

'They're looting the baggage train.'

To widespread curses, soldiers in various states of undress stepped forward, or hopped as they pulled on boots.

'Let's go,' shouted Jack. 'Double-time, run. Not a second to lose.' From a peg near a dazed fellow officer he grabbed a brace of pistols and a powder flask and sprinted for the wagons. He did not look back.

At the end of the windbreak hedge he saw a sentry on the ground, bound and gagged; and then what looked like all of Hounslow and surrounding villages, maybe 200 men, women and children, spread across as many yards, crawling over the supply tumbrels, handing down trunks and barrels, the best-organised of them hitching their horses between cart shafts, harnessing traces, others already whipping up and moving off.

'Now listen,' he said quietly as the dozen or so soldiers caught him up. 'I want a line of us over the heath on either side of me, here,' and he gestured wide to his left and right.

'Ten paces between you. Load with powder, no bullet, aim straight ahead, look like you are shooting to kill. You lot go that way. You rest, that. Fire on my command, then advance twenty paces while reloading, count them out, then fire again, and so on until they run. Use your musket butts if you have to, but these are our countrymen, unarmed. So powder only – and reloading will be twice as fast. Twenty paces before each volley, wait for my word to fire. Now go.'

Miraculously, the group jogged away on either side. The plunderers still had not spied them. This was a surprise, but not as Jack had long imagined. As his line formed, over 100 yards across, he primed his borrowed pistols from the powder horn and pressed the bung back into its neck. Carts were slipping from his grasp, away over the scrub. A glance up and down and he saw the men were ready.

'Aim!' he shouted and counted to three. Several looters looked over, startled.

'Fire!' That breathless pause held while the sparks caught. Fourteen muskets and two pistols rattled out flame and smoke in the space of seconds.

'Advance and load,' yelled Jack and pulled the stopper back out with his teeth, leaving the horn to swing. Like a line of guns in a snipe shoot, the fusiliers set off across the rough grass, muzzle loading as they walked. After twenty paces Jack halted. So did the row to his right and left. With a deeper voice he shouted at the gaggle of humanity.

'Drop what you have and leave. You are stealing from the King. Go now and you will not be harmed. Now!' He belted it out. He had everyone's attention, but no one moved. Perhaps they thought it was a trick, which of course it was. Also, they outnumbered the soldiers a score to one. Perhaps they knew that too.

'Aim,' he counted to himself up to three. 'Fire!' He let off his two pistols directly at the wagoner in front of him. The man dropped from his high seat and bolted. Ransackers became the ransacked.

'Advance and load,' and this time he called out the paces, loudly, and his comrades picked up the refrain, 'Three, four, five…'

Carts were still trotting away, but no new ones set off. Instead, trembling hands were unloosing horses they had just hitched, fumbling with buckles. Men, women and children were running. Some stout hearts with wheelbarrows were still making off across the heath, trundling bales and sacks from the quartermaster's stores.

At twenty, Jack bellowed again, 'Drop everything and leave', to little effect. 'Aim,' he yelled at the top of his voice, 'Fire.' Again, that long ripping sound and the white moustache of gun smoke spread either side of him.

'Advance and load.' The last of the stolen wagons was disappearing over the open heathland, followed by the villagers who had fled early, and those men and women who had now mounted and were galloping away, some lying low on their horse's neck, depending on the degree of flexibility and panic in the rider.

Jack's scratch was among the nearest wagons now. The wheelbarrow mob had abandoned their pushcarts and were running for their lives, falling over their feet.

'Aim…,' and again at the top of his voice, as the last villagers, now seventy yards away, dived for cover, he yelled, 'Fire.'

A light breeze from behind drifted musket smoke down the range, over the scene of Jack's victory. The last straggler hopped away on a twisted ankle. Ten strange horses and twice as many unfamiliar carts and barrows remained among the litter of abandoned supplies around each wagon. Casks and kit trailed out over the heath where they had been dropped. It was Sedgemoor, without the bodies.

'Cease fire,' he called up and down the line. 'To me all of you.' And he blew on his firemaster's whistle for good measure. The rout was complete and the rest of the regiment was just arriving.

'Still alive and still together,' said Jack to the men. They gathered around, grinning eagerly into his face. From behind them, the reveille sounded. They laughed. 'Someone else can clear up this mess,' he continued. 'Let's go and get dressed.' And they looked at each other in their shirtsleeves and guffawed again.

'Form up,' shouted one of them, the sergeant reverting to type. 'Slope arms. Quick march.' They swung away, back to the heath's strange billet, the cluster of mill, barns and homestead, two abreast. The sight of these tough fusiliers in their britches and smocks, with muskets shouldered, made Jack a little proud and raised cheers from their correctly presented comrades hurrying up.

Jack's paternal granddad had been in Cromwell's army in the Civil War. Jack had met a few of Poppa's old comrades, but had never asked, 'Did you kill anyone you knew?' Those questions are not heard in families after a civil war, he thought.

The old soldiers had said, 'We weren't paid to think. Let the commanders do that, strategy and tactics, loyalty and betrayal, right and wrong. Nah. You just march, pray and fight.' But in his army career Jack seemed to do more than that.

At Sedgemoor, too, he had helped save his regiment's reputation. 'Initiative and skill,' Shere had acknowledged afterwards. The Colonel had received a knighthood for it, Sir Henry, which Jack hadn't minded, he liked the man, although Lord Feversham's garter was an outrage. And now Jack had done it again, in a minor way, but more obviously alone.

He felt a hand on his shoulder. It was Shere himself.

'Sir,' he said, and saluted stiffly.

'Our casualties?' asked Shere, looking him closely in the eye.

'None, Sir.'

'*Matériel?*'

'Depends, Sir. We were lucky. They can't have been at it for long. One night past the full moon. Should have been good. But it was raining. Bad for torches.

They must've jumped the sentries just before dawn to have light to see what they were doing. Still hard to spot. Part of the King's tent is gone. And your own wagon, I fear, Sir. Altogether, I'd say fifteen. But they have left almost as many of their own. It took them time to find the food. But chests, valuables, small items they could run with, we will only know in a while. We were almost too late, Sir.'

Shere looked out over the heath. 'What about civilian dead?'

'None, Sir.'

'None? But I heard four fusillades.'

'Smoke, Sir, fireworks. We left the bullets behind. Final civilian casualties: one turned ankle and probably some cracked ribs from diving on the count of three.'

The Colonel put his hand back on Jack's shoulder and smiled for the first time, saying, 'Bless you, Jack Wilson. Now, give me a leg up.'

As he re-mounted his fine white horse, other officers arrived. 'I want these supplies re-stowed and an inventory of what's missing,' Shere barked. 'And a fusilier guard around the clock, Major St Clair. And scout me out secure campsites for tomorrow and Tuesday night. We misjudged the mood of the people, Major. There is rebellion in the air, more than we thought.'

Captain Exe, as Comptroller of the Train, puffed, 'What about the villagers, Sir? We'd recognise our own carts, our own stuff. Yours too, apparently.'

'No, leave them. A search would probably turn nasty and certainly slow us up. We've been lucky here. I want no retribution. No tit-for-tat. Nothing newsworthy. Every man is to stay in camp. We may be on the edge of something bigger than we know. These people are our own flesh and blood. They cheered us on the way out. It is hardly their fault that law and order is collapsing, armies foraging, deserters stealing. They don't even know who'll be planting in the spring.

'Mr Willoughby,' he continued to the Adjutant, 'Sunday prayers are still at noon and the mess sergeants are to feed us at one. I want the sentries changed every hour. Get laundry done. We will hold a full parade at four for those not on guard duty. Then I want all officers to me in the miller's parlour directly after that. How we conduct ourselves in the next few days… Well, we are going to have to think that through. Meanwhile, get a written report from Lieutenant Wilson here. We head on to London at sunrise tomorrow. So it's spit and polish today and an early night tonight.'

Jack was well pleased with that. He returned the borrowed pistols to their owner who had come up with Exe and set off back to his windmill.

Elizabeth, 07:30

Elizabeth Forrester woke early. The silence below her window was wrong. The square outside the home of the twenty-three-year-old Duke of Ormonde, Lord Ossary until his grandfather's recent death, was normally busy, even on a Sunday. Yet not a voice, not a hoof, not a carriage wheel could be heard. Then she remembered. Yesterday, another wave of well-heeled refugees had fled, leaving workmen to nail planks over some of London's newest, smartest front doors. Here, a stone's throw from St James' Palace, across the park from Whitehall Palace and Parliament, fear had turned to panic. Foreign troops were advancing on London unopposed. Could the Dutchman really reach the heart of government?

Once awake, Elizabeth rarely dozed. Today she had more than her normal inventory to consider. She moved her thoughts from one mental cuddy to the next, opening them in turn, resolving whether to take action and resealing each.

First was the awful gamble at court. Her next few days would decide her place in society for the rest of her life. As a Paget great-grandchild, with what might be called Royalist Puritan blood, she could jump either way. Her great-uncle William, the fifth Baron, had switched sides twice in the Civil War. Now, a few decades later, with nobles and gentry flocking daily to the invader, fate again seemed equally balanced. A small slip by either party could hand the other the victory.

Elizabeth's first sympathy as a Protestant was for the Prince of Orange, but one look at his bedfellows cooled that impulse. To be lumped in with the fanatics around him ran against all her patrician instincts. Inflammatory preachers of revolution like that thin-jawed Scotsman, Robert Ferguson, for Heaven's sake. He had frothed about 'taking half a dozen rich old London citizens from their homes, hanging them from sign-posts and giving their houses as plunder to the mobile.' Did he think such a circus would end there? Had he any idea what young radical apprentices wanted? How they ached to finish the job their Leveller grandfathers had started, to upset the whole apple cart and introduce one-man-one-vote – birth, rank and property be damned?

Also, Elizabeth was by nature a procrastinator. Not giving an answer had worked well for her so far, in her twenty-one years. Intelligent, presentable, independent but opaque. Nevertheless, a choice of sovereign was close. Just not today.

Carefully, she closed that lid.

Then she reflected on her day-job as companion to the Duke's mother, the still-sprightly Emelia, Dowager Countess of Ossary. Elizabeth had held the role for three years now. Emelia was Dutch, which had become quite a twist in itself. To have a Dutch employer during a Dutch invasion created possibilities. Not that this former lady-in-waiting to Catherine of Braganza, King Charles II's childless Portuguese queen, now widowed, was anything but a royalist.

Most of Emelia's own eleven children had died in infancy, and she was a widow herself at the age of forty-two. After a respectable period of mourning, she had decided to 'launch out once more', as she had put it. She still fancied her chances, as once one of the once-sensational Windsor Beauties who had lit up Restoration England, having married into the aristocracy a quarter of a century before. So she had employed Elizabeth Forrester to be her companion and to watch over her youngest daughter, Lady Henrietta, then ten. In exchange, she had given Elizabeth the finish she merited: a certain bearing; courtly manners; a sense of when to show vivacity and coquetry, when to feign vacuity, and when to deploy a biting wit.

Now Elizabeth needed to put these assets to work. At twenty-one she was getting on, which was why this morning she pondered her successor. She must find a replacement as Emelia's helpmeet. She had one in mind and would sound out Kitty Jones later today. It remained only to captivate her. Or did she mean capture?

Click, she shut that second box.

Those two issues were her main concern, but older ones also needed thought. For example, what about boys? Men, she should say. Almost since she could remember, she had found her power over them both invigorating and absurd. As her grandmother used to scoff, 'Men hold all the cards, but show their hand so easily.' Nevertheless, however coolly Miss Forrester expected to control her admirers, she would soon need a mate. Meanwhile, some passion would be welcome. Discreetly of course, she must not stain her reputation or limit her choices.

She also knew that a husband took all his wife's assets upon marriage, to manage as he wished. And she had an asset – the farm. She saw the humiliating betrothal which her older sister, Beryl, seemed to have fallen into with Ridley Despart, an arrogant courtier who quickly bored of her. As far as Elizabeth knew, Beryl's wedding day had been the last time her sibling had had a say in anything. The event itself had been a masterclass in pretension, conducted by the Bishop of London for goodness sake, their mother's old friend, Henry Compton. Rebuilding St Paul's Cathedral had barely begun, so the wedding took place in his chapel at Fulham Palace with a grand reception in the principal rooms. Ridley had even managed to lose his temper coming down the aisle. He and Beryl were ten years older than Elizabeth, children of the Commonwealth austerity, a different generation. Elizabeth would not let such a marriage happen to her.

Nevertheless, a man was needed. Not a volcano, that would be too much – but more than the spouting oil lamps she found at court, or the academic amorists, flashing their intellects like fireworks on Guy Fawkes night, gushing starshine, burning out so fast. She wanted someone who cared less about her 500 acres, or being seen with her on his arm, than about the next twenty years for his country. A man who could think fast and act. He could be her own age, or perhaps older. Perhaps in uniform – although not a man of the cloth. Or he might be educated, a gentleman of course, maybe an aristocrat. Or a merchant, so long as he stuck to his side of the bargain and did not mortgage her land for his ventures. That would require firmness on her part.

While she sought such a man, she needed to learn. A short affair would be ideal, an illicit liaison, with a swain who knew the world, who had more experience of love than her. It would be easier in London, with its large population and non-overlapping circles. She had a candidate for that too, but again, time was short.

Enough. Her mind moved on.

The other perennial topic was her farm in Suffolk, a sealed trunk which Elizabeth opened less often. It was complicated, but it was also the reason why she approached life as she did, in compartments, a cabinet of curiosities. She had done so since she was sixteen.

Suffolk should have been her mother Isabelle's, or at least Beryl's. Elizabeth remembered herself as a small girl, watching mama become forgetful, little by little, to the point of defencelessness. The doctors had no word for the disease, if that it was, even less a cure. Senile did not quite capture it, because Isabelle could perfectly well wash and feed herself. Nevertheless, the forgetfulness had made the Forresters leave London after Beryl had married. They had retreated from Blackfriars to Suffolk to live with Isabelle's widowed mother and bachelor uncle, Lady Penelope Foley and the Hon. Andrew Paget. Isabelle still recognised her uncle's home and would be found more easily when she wandered off. As for Elizabeth, it was a chance to be near her grandmother, Grannam, of whom she was in awe, and great-uncle Andrew, although she thought him rather a grump.

The young Elizabeth discovered that country people could turn their hands to anything. A carter might also be a thatcher, a butcher, a sidesman in church and the man who burnt the village rubbish. Children did valuable work from an early age, were unafraid to speak up and were listened to. Everyone at a barn dance would sing and join in the quadrille, while most could play an instrument. The adults showed pride in what they did. Amour-propre was absent – country people were ready to lead one moment and follow the next, without having their feelings hurt. They also helped each other out, forming a social and financial safety net if someone was lamed or ruined. This self-sufficient self-esteem seeped into little Elizabeth's soul.

When she was not at Grannam's harpsichord or lessons with her governess, the girl had the freedom of the Suffolk manor, farmhouse and tied cottages. Isabelle would inherit the estate and eventually Beryl, as the oldest great-niece. So, Elizabeth's affections were lightly attached. It would soon be gone, she would be excluded, and she must not hurt too much when the day came; whereas those friendships she attracted were the more genuine because she was not the future chatelaine. Nevertheless, every corner soon held a poignant memory: a harmless-looking hedge where, taking a shortcut, she had been caught by her hair and had kept calm and freed herself lock by lock; the fallen tree trunk upon which she had been lying when a fox trotted by; the sunny slope where she buried small animals, not only dead pets but also songbirds she found that sparrowhawks had killed for their hearts.

Great-uncle Andrew Paget had welcomed his niece, Isabelle, into his home, just as he had taken in his beloved sister Penelope when she was widowed. He had even been willing to treat Isabelle's husband, Major Forrester, as a son. However, he saw Isabelle drifting into empty-headedness and how little a retired soldier might incline to agriculture. Gradually, the old bachelor realised that his part of the ancestral Paget estate must jump a generation. However, he could not abide Ridley and suspected the fop had married Beryl solely for this land.

So, sometime in those happy years, Andrew had changed his will in favour of Elizabeth, giving his sister a life interest. Only Lady Foley knew.

After Andrew died, Grannam sailed into her seventies with iron dignity, determined to live until Elizabeth was at least of age before telling her about her inheritance. Too much responsibility, too early, could scar the inside, however pretty the packaging. And Paget girls were always gorgeous.

Penelope Foley made many improvements to the manor farm during her stewardship. She introduced manuring and hoeing. She adopted an idea from Norfolk friends that a four-season rotation of crops, including one for clover or turnips, obviated the need to leave fields fallow one year in three. The yields rose and the farm animals had more winter fodder.

She conjured up a wavy brick garden wall, facing southwest, to grow fruit against. It ran from the front gatepost towards the corner of the house. The wall's serpentine, corrugated shape made it strong – as if buttressed – and the westward concavities focused any afternoon warmth. This novelty had been introduced by itinerant Dutch labourers, hired to drain the Norfolk Fens for the Earl of Bedford. The now-redundant Dutchmen had been working their way south to Ipswich and passage home, along with fen dwellers whose way of life was destroyed by the canalisation, when Lady Penelope had spotted them. Elizabeth called it 'Grannam's crinkle-crankle wall' (said with a gentle Suffolk burr) and it became her highlight of the estate. Together they had planted soft-fruit bushes, peaches and apricots, in the dimples to be out of the east wind. Even delicate lemons ripened there.

Elizabeth had also kept a New Forest pony, and later a horse, a Suffolk Sorrel. Although neither was built for speed, she nevertheless rode like fury, in britches, astride like a boy. Aged ten, she had begged her father to let her accompany him to the Newmarket race festival. After that, their shared interest had bonded them. They both had an eye for a winner and would stalk the paddock and enclosure discussing the form, the going, the jockeys, indeed all the finer points of the Sport of Kings. The July race meeting was attended by Charles II and his brother James, Duke of York. The courts of Whitehall and St James' would empty, the sun would gleam on the flanks of the racehorses, and politics (Whigs and Tories and all that nonsense) was forgotten. Elizabeth felt herself in very Heaven. In those years, Newmarket was where Patrick met his old friends from army days, and former Blackfriars neighbours like the Joneses, who would travel out to Cambridgeshire just for fear of missing out. No one could resist her father's charm.

In the summer of 1683, shortly after Elizabeth was sixteen, her grandmother had slipped on the top front step of the manor house. She had been carried white-faced to her room, her pelvis shattered. Before she died, she had summoned Elizabeth from the fields to her bedside and breathed the news of the latter's imminent responsibilities. Through the grim, stoic mask her grandmother's eyes shone undefeated and Elizabeth felt the awful abyss of her own inexperience.

Her girlish sobs were countered by Lady Foley's unwavering voice, 'All this is yours, dear one. It is what my brother wanted. Do not be afraid. Take life as it comes. Wear many faces. You are well equipped to do this. If I can, so can you. Trust your own judgement. Choose your man at leisure. We are quicker and brighter than them.'

In the silence which followed, Elizabeth calmed herself. Trees stirred and birds sang beyond the leaded windows, as if life would go on. Eventually, the old woman drew Elizabeth's hand to her mouth and kissed the back of the girl's fingers. Then she asked for the priest. She died that evening.

Elizabeth had understood. After the funeral, she took her grandmother's bed and bedroom as her own. From now on, starting with this one air-tight box in Suffolk, she must be Penelope. And suddenly she was. She was the new Paget to 500 acres, a rancid steward in the farmhouse, five families in tied cottages and more in the village, sixteen labourers in all, plus the livestock. The latest in a line that had been there forever. People who thought they understood Elizabeth, now found they did not. And she found she did not know them either. Beryl and Ridley left in high dudgeon after the will was read and would not speak with her. The farm became mysteriously unprofitable. Elizabeth challenged the figures and they changed back. The steward, Obadiah Faken, was impossible to dismiss, although he clearly deserved it. The man ignored any woman younger than him. But for Grannam's other investments, she'd have been in trouble.

After her first harvest was in and the planting for next year decided, Elizabeth could not wait to return to London for the winter. Isabelle had taken her mother's sudden absence hard. She still managed her toilette and recognised Patrick and her two children, but appeared disinclined to leave any house she came into, or even any room. Settling her in the carriage from Parham to London took several attempts – and in this she was probably right, you had to be careful which coach company you picked. But when Isabelle left Suffolk for the last time, a place she had loved almost as much as Queen's College, Oxford, within hours she had no recollection of having visited for those last months, or even of her own mother's death.

That was when Elizabeth had resolved to keep all her relatives physically away from the farm. Conveniently, it was off the senior Pagets' beaten track between London and the principal patrimony in Staffordshire; and two days' journey from London in its own right. Her kith and kin never asked to accompany her on her flying visits (Elizabeth liked to appear unannounced). Nor did they seem to understand. Her parents held part of her love, but even they could not treat her as her own woman. They became a separate heredity. Her mother had no memory, her father would rather forget, and her sister offered only hate.

With a sigh, Elizabeth shut the lid on that box. She had not meant to go there this morning.

The stillness outside was even stranger now the day had broken. She raised the shutters' iron bar to gaze upon the day and was bent over her basin when a soft knock came at her door.

It was Hendriksen, Emelia's Dutch butler.

'Her Ladyship likes not ze qviet. She asks you go out for news.'

Simon, 08:45

Simon Speke had dropped onto his cot in Clerkenwell, muttering the word 'Sunday' with a contented smile, and fallen sound asleep.

It had been a long night drinking with his fellow apprentices in the Tower Hamlets. As chief of their three newly elected 'Colonels', he had been expected to stay to the end. Afterwards, he had faced the long circuitous walk home. Clerkenwell was a northern suburb, whereas the two wards of the Hamlets, namely St Botolph-without-Aldgate and St Mary Whitechapel, were to the east, not only 'without', but 'Beyond the Tower'. However, Simon had found the Aldgate open, which had cut the journey on foot to forty minutes. Once inside the City, he had veered away from the night watch in the fashionable area around Royal Exchange. Instead, he had hugged inside the Roman wall – Camomile Street, Wormwood Street, Allhallow on the Wall – until he came out through Cripplegate. After that he cut north, past the recently ransacked convent of the Order of St John (a brutal victory, with dead on both sides) and reached his lodgings on the Green.

Now the bells of St James' Clerkenwell woke him. Its stumpy tower was behind his boarding house and level with his garret. He lay in bed, listening to the peals, finding pleasure in skipping church. It was still a criminal offence, but in London few checked. Simon smiled as he dozed and dreamt of power. He would take command for the common good, wealth for the many, which made him feel happy. Self-enrichment, greed, such things still came into it, of course, and the criminal element would be key to success. He was not opposed to that –

the means were justified by the noble end. But he also enjoyed power for its own sake, as self-fulfilment. He particularly enjoyed the trick of using the darker side of human nature, while aiming for the light. Yes, dreaming of power was his thing – and soon to be more than a dream.

'With the mob,' he had said last night, 'one must attack while their blood is up. Otherwise each of us, of them, goes back to our private fears and hopes, our individual dreads and fantasies, life and love and all that hogwash. The lonely, frightened soul in each of us must not regain command, not until victory.' They had clapped him, hypocrite that he was.

Their hour had come, he told them. Now they must strike. It was a priceless chance for the common man to dictate terms. A glint of gold in the babbling brook of history, seen but once in many lifetimes, lasting just a few hours, a week at most.

They had cheered him to the rafters.

But time was so tight.

Lying in his cot, he now asked himself, how? How could a leader hope to grasp the moment, without time to prepare?

Simon Speke – Spike to his growing legion of admirers, Pesky Speke to his detractors – was sensitive to history, that tide in the affairs of men. He could feel it running with him. The people, the lower orders, the mob, in the modern parlance, were turning to his view of things. They had begun to think, to speak, as a pack. This was the shift he needed, from dumb participants to witting protagonists. During last month's practice riot here in Clerkenwell, they had moved as one, thought as one. Now, perhaps, they would also speak as one, put their case as one, argue back as one. King and Prince would bow to the common people.

He kept telling them these were not new ideas, only dangerous ones: the compact between servant and master had broken long ago; monarchy had become an unnatural state; private ownership of vast estates was ill-gotten; common land should be given back to those who had worked it; churches, those pulpits of patronage, should be stripped of treasure and their territory returned to the poor; and likewise the universities, incurably royalist, hatcheries of elites, sentinels of sophistication, should be purged of all but practical subjects; every adult male should have the vote, which would equip parliaments, meeting annually, to confiscate and redirect the wealth fairly, to house and feed the needy and to educate their children.

'We must organise,' Spike told his fellow apprentices. 'Our mobile must be disciplined. With discipline we will be impossible to stop, even a row of muskets can be swamped by a mob. In our grandfathers' day, the Levellers in the New Model Army had it right. They organised, were disciplined. They came so close. But they were owed months of back pay. Their officers did that deliberately. The paymasters held everything far in arrears to keep the troops in fear of being cashiered. Why should an honest soldier kiss goodbye to what he has justly earned? It played on the rank and file, individually, alone, in the night.

'And then there were the selective executions. Of ten ringleaders, they shot one at random in front of each battalion.' ('Shame,' a Speke plant would cry from the crowd.) 'It worked a treat. And the delays, the procrastination, the false promises. Look at the Putney Debates of forty-seven. Two weeks to discuss one-man-one-vote! Such a beautiful idea, for free men who had fought for a better world, and won, and deserved it; an idea talked out of time by the grandees, with their stolen wealth and estates to fall back on.' (More cries of 'Shame' from the back.) 'And the Diggers? Fisticuffs in their peace camps for planting crops on once common land. No protection from the law because Parliament stole common land by Acts of Enclosure, a guilty deed with an innocent name, enclosure; which is why Parliament has to be changed. We must recapture the dream, we must add to common land not enclose it. Remember when the Black Death ravaged the country? The 1340s. All right, you don't remember, but I'm telling you. A generation later, two, the peasants revolted. Their slogan from centuries ago still holds today: *when Adam delved and Eve span, who was then the gentleman?*'

They must make a collective effort, he would say, consciously, in pelotons and brigades, with arms and discipline and tactics, if they were to break the back of hierarchy.

Simon became a local celebrity for his speeches. The apprentices ate out of his hand. Strangers began hailing him in the street, waylaying him, repeating back to him his fiery ideas as if they were their own. One day, so would Kitty Jones.

Recumbent in his room, he gave a little squirm of delight at his own brilliance. Things were exceeding even his private hopes. But he checked himself. Credit for the initial opening was due to his older Speke cousin, Hugh. Spike's fellow devils at the King's Printing House may have done the typesetting and deliveries on the sly. They may have threaded the hook and cast the line. But the bait had been Cousin Hugh's.

And how the citizens had risen to it.

Hugh had a decade more than Simon of pent-up hatred for monarchy in general and for the House of Stuart in particular. His ancient family had been insulted; his older brother Charles had been judicially murdered by Judge Jeffreys after the Monmouth Rebellion; and he himself had spent three years in prison for sedition, unable to pay the same judge's extortionate fine. Now he had seen an opportunity to take revenge.

As soon as news of the Dutch landing reached town, Hugh had used his back-door contacts in Whitehall to insinuate himself into the King's presence. As Simon understood it, he had presented himself as the perfect royal spy. By chance the Dutch Prince had been flung by an easterly wind to the far southwest. By chance, Exeter had become William of Orange's base, where just months before Hugh Speke had been appointed counsel for the municipality. How many west countrymen in London could claim to know everyone who mattered among the Prince's latest recruits? Hugh had also offered to work for a performance fee: no information, no pay.

These arguments had won James over. Hugh had been given the job, received three blank passes from the Commander of the Royal Army, Lord Feversham, and ridden down to William's camp. There he had turned his coat, revealed his mission and offered his services to the Dutchman as a double agent. To prove his sincerity, Hugh had given two of the royal passes to Hans William Bentinck, Prince William's superintendent, while keeping the third for himself. He then began sending the King exaggerated reports of the numbers flocking to the Prince.

Seventeen days after landing, Prince William had begun his advance from Exeter. Godard van Ginkel's Dutch Foot had screened to the north. Henry Sidney, younger son of the Earl of Leicester, had led his English regiment to the south. Hugh had tagged along as William and his general staff took the high road up the middle, the Fosse Way, through Honiton, northeast towards distant Bath. Speke had dreaded seeing the tree in Ilminster market where brother Charles had been hanged in July 1685. But several miles short of that the invader had turned east toward Chard. Thereafter, Hugh could relax, idly mentioning his fraternal martyrdom for the cause to anyone who would listen.

It was while the Dutch were crossing from Somerset to Dorset that Hugh Speke had his stroke of genius: he would spread a lie. All it needed was some clever fakery. William had published moderate manifestoes before and after sailing from Holland, his *First* and *Second Declarations*. Speke would circulate a four-sided handbill modelled on these and call it *The Prince of Orange His Third Declaration*. Much shorter than the first, he would set it in slightly larger type and font but run it on the same sized paper. The difference would be in tone. It would aim to scare. It would talk of 'armed papists' in London and regional centres, looking 'to make some desperate Attempt on the said Cities, and the Inhabitants, by Fire, or sudden Massacre, or both'. It would warn of 'a Body of French troops' expected 'to land in England' at any moment. It would demand that the reader make a choice, popery or patriotism.

In Sherborne, Hugh had wangled an audience with the Prince and presented him with the idea. William had rejected it outright. He would not lend even tacit support to such a deceit. Who said papists could not be patriotic? Some of his best allies against Louis XIV were Catholics. But Hugh had resolved to prosecute the scheme anyway; had drafted it with the Prince's turn of phrase, even in the camp whence it purported to come, 'Our Headquarters at Sherborne Castle'. A 'Blessed and Glorious Design', he'd written. Catchy.

Nine evenings ago, he had slipped back into London.

Working late at the King's Printing House, under the nose of their employer, Henry Hills, Spike and the other apprentices had set the *Third Declaration*, tailed as his Highness would have signed himself for Englishmen, William Henry, a perfect forgery. Then, during the night of 3–4 December, they had slipped single sheets under the doors of booksellers around St Paul's. And the following day, once the news began to spread, they had handed out copies of this false proclamation in the coffee shops, dispatched a quire to Hills' clients in the provinces, and even sent one sheaf to Hugh's old friend, Benjamin Harris, now in Boston in the New England colony, in case a boat chose to risk the winter gales.

Hugh Speke had known his *Third Declaration* would catch like a spark in a tinderbox. However, the conflagration had proved bigger than even he had imagined – a spark in a keg in a gunpowder store.

The Prince's ostensible demand, that England choose popery or patriotism, had dropped perfectly into the political stand-off. Catholics trembled. The King believed it genuine. To even the most hardened sceptic it seemed plausible.

However, Spike's base wanted more. The lads had made that clear last night. They had swallowed his rhetoric even more than he had himself. They had been born for this hour, they said. The mob was ready to speak as one.

Where was Colonel Spike's grand plan? they demanded. The big one.

Kitty, 08:55

Pressed and dressed, Kitty stood by the window of her workroom on the second floor of the family home in the south-westerly corner of the old City. She was deep in a book on the lectern, breathing to herself the Latin names of hyacinths, waiting to be called down for their little ceremony.

It was a tall house, alone in its backwater of Blackfriars, between Ludgate and the river. Her father, Edward Jones was a printer. He had recently bought the *London Gazette*. Her mother, Mary, was the homemaker; and they lived with Edward's own mama, Johanna. Kitty had never known Edward's father, whose death had enabled Edward and Mary to buy the house, on the condition that Johanna could live with them if she wished. The arrangement had suited everyone. Her grandmother was playful, like an older sister to Kitty. The two were as thick as thieves.

The Jones home was often so quiet that the tick of the hall clock could be heard two floors up. However, this being a Sunday morning, the house was now filled with the sound of church bells as the ringers of St Bride's Fleet Street and of St Martin's by Ludgate competed over the rooftops to call the faithful to worship. The peals washed up the hill to the still incomplete cathedral of St Paul's, on the rumoured site of a Roman temple, and down to the equally unfinished St Andrew-by-the-Wardrobe, near the river.

As would any educated and inquisitive eighteen-year-old in such a home, Kitty Jones knew her way round her father's study. She often browsed the shelf reserved for marvels of print, Edward's professional collection. The book she had borrowed to examine today was volume II of Thomas Johnson's three-part 1633 edition of Gerard's *The herball, or, Generall historie of plantes*, prized for its typesetting and illustrations. Differing fonts marked departures from English into Latin, German, Dutch, French and Italian. Some 2,000 woodcuts added to the trilogy's prestige. However, to Kitty, the marvel was in the information, the meaning, the great puzzle of the floral kingdom laid out with method and good humour. Each plant received the same classification by form and root-type, systematic description and everything known besides: the places it grew; the time of year it flowered; its names in Latin, English and other European languages (though not, she noted with disapproval, the native name given by its indigenous people, if from far away); its properties; its virtues; and its uses.

Almost as wonderful was John Gerard's wit mixed into this orderliness. Kitty loved the anecdotes and adventures, the mention of gardens and gardeners known personally to the author. To cap it all, Johnson had added introductions and revisions in this expanded edition. For example, he traced the history of published studies of plants, from pre-Christian herbary to what the greatest expert in England, the late lamented Sir Thomas Browne, had recently christened Botany. Johnson had even concluded that John Gerard was sometimes guessing and sometimes plagiarising. In particular, Gerard's friend, Dr Priest, had translated Rembert Dodoens but died before he could publish. Gerard had used Priest's work but flatly denied it. Why would a man do that, wondered Kitty, and risk being found out in the end, and mocked down the generations?

In the 1633 edition, a single hand had drawn the illustrations from life. To achieve Johnson's consistent, simple style across so many images, without shading or hatching, took a confidence which denied any invented or imagined features. This was an achievement of great discipline and a labour of many years. Alongside dear Robert Hooke's *Micrographica*, with its drawings of observations made under a microscope, *The herball* was the pride of Edward Jones' bookcase.

Kitty had an idea how disciplined a botanical artist must be. She herself had sketched plants since she was a child. Her father had even shown some of her recent work to the neighbours, the Worshipful Society of Apothecaries. In reply, the Society's librarian, Nicholas Staphurst, had sent her a specimen cactus and asked for a drawing, to test her.

Last week she had returned the prickly and flowering plant to Apothecaries' Hall along with her submission. She had received back an invitation for tomorrow. Mr Staphurst wrote that he was going to the Society's physic garden in Chelsea, to inspect the seasonal pruning. Would Kitty be interested in joining him? If the weather cleared and her parents did not object, they would take a waterman from Blackfriars Steps, two bends and four miles upstream, and discuss his next publishing project on the way.

The opportunity to collaborate on a book was every young artist's dream. For this to come to a woman was rare indeed. And for it to focus on Kitty's personal area of interest, expertise even, must be unique, she thought. It could be the making of a whole career. She only needed to be herself to succeed. The hard part would be recovering if she was rejected.

Kitty's mother called up the stairwell that they were ready to start.

Jack, 08:25

Jack tramped across the yard. He tossed his jacket inside the windmill, grabbed a blanket from the stable, then went to the water butt, dunked his head, whooping at the cold. He threw the coverlet round his neck for common decency and knocked on the door of the mill house. The miller's wife gave him his clean smock, dried overnight high in the rafters above the fireplace and pleasantly smoky. At a penny a shirt it had been a profitable night's work for her, here on the level heath, in the fork of the roads leading west and southwest of London, that had been there for ever. Back in the windmill he finished dressing, pulled an oilskin pouch from his kitbag and put pen to paper.

Sunday, Hounslow Heath. Dear Kitty,

He closed his eyes, and her face swam into his mind, feature by feature: cherry lips; pale skin; straight nose; those astonishing, intelligent, violet eyes beneath angry eyebrows; white teeth and firm jaw; a wisp of malt-wheaten hair at her temple to hook over her delicate ear. His pulse beat fast and his breath came short. My God, to hold such a girl in his arms. But what to write? Dare he address her as My Dear Kitty? No she was not anybody's, let alone his. Dear Miss Jones? No. Faint heart never won fair maid. So Dear Kitty it was.

We have been on the road 30 days. Not one has passed without me thinking of you and how you came to wave us off. Hopefully you have received my last from Hartley Wintney. We are all safe and well. There has been neither fighting the invader, nor disease in the camp. Indeed nothing much has changed except we now do everything backwards. The mood of the people is also different, which makes me wonder how things are in Blackfriars. The train will be in London on Wednesday, home in the Tower by midday, I imagine. I hope we can meet soon after that.
Your friend, Jack Wilson.

He read it back over, saw that it struck the right balance, and folded, sealed and addressed it to the Jones home in Glass House Yard, Blackfriars.

Unlike Jack, his troopers were from the East End and beyond the City, Tower Hamlets, over the old Roman walls. It was a famously rough neighbourhood, nevertheless almost all gunners could read and write. He went over to their billet and called out, 'I've a letter for home to give to the adjutants when I make my report. Anyone want me to hand theirs in? Maybe we can catch the messenger.'

None of them had a girl like Kitty to dream of, but he still asked. A couple of others would increase the chances of his letter being accepted for the mails – not looking like favouritism. It being a Sunday helped too. As did his little deed earlier. A few of them said they did and asked for five minutes. So, he took out his oilskin pouch again and dashed off a second note, which came much easier.

Sunday, Hounslow Heath.

Dear Miss Forrester,

We have been on the road for 30 days, but are now almost back in London. Before midday on Wednesday, I imagine. Twice we saw His Majesty. Happily, there has been no fighting, at least not where we were. I hope to have a chance to call on you in due course and tell you of our adventures in person.

Your obedient servant, Jack Wilson.

He folded, sealed and addressed it to Ormonde House, St James' Square. Although Jack knew where his heart lay, he hated having all his eggs in one basket. Also, the girls' parents had once been neighbours in Blackfriars. Kitty admired Elizabeth. She might even feel a little jealous if he could make her see Elizabeth as a rival. To be frank, both were out of his league. Perhaps this made him calculating.

Finally, he scrawled a note to his mother. *All well. Home to barracks, Wednesday 11 a.m. J.*, and he added a motif of three flowers in a bunch.

Jack might be tall, and in better shape, but he was still the youngest at his rank. When Exe had been promoted Captain, on the back of his self-congratulatory dispatch after Sedgemoor, the Colonel had told Jack, then barely twenty, to prepare to move up to full lieutenant. 'I've had my eye on you,' Sir Henry had said, 'since I arrived. I was doing my first inspection, and Lieutenant Exe joked about how you had come before the recruiting sergeant with Roberts' *Compleat Cannoniere* under your arm.'

They had been standing in the hallway of the Commander's house in the Tower, the day the regiment had returned after Sedgemoor. 'That very edition I took with me as ordnance engineer to Tangier in sixty-nine. I've put mine on Lord Dartmouth's shelf in the archive.'

The gunnery manual was a family breadwinner for the Wilsons. Jack had known it since he was a lad. Back in the 1630s, his mother's father, John Okes, had been chosen by the author to print the first edition. After the Civil War, William Wilson junior, Jack's dad, had apprenticed at Okes' printing press in the Savoy. A bright, organised lad, Will had worked his way up from printer's devil, to marrying Ivy, the owner's younger daughter. Okes and Wilson junior thrived and, to stop any doubts among the customers about succession, Okes had passed the proprietorship to his son-in-law. The *Compleat Cannoniere* was reprinted with the same blocks under W Wilson's name in 1652 and 1663.

However, the plague had carried off Okes, Wilson and Jack's older brother, also called William, in the summer of 1665. Desperate, Ivy had taken a partner in the business, let the Savoy cottage for a peppercorn rent, keeping one room to store furniture and trunks, and fled with Jack to her older sister's in the country. The enterprise had failed, but years later, Ivy had returned with Jack to London and taken back the cottage in the Savoy. Jack, by then aged ten, had come by the gunnery manual when his remaining grandfather had picked it out for him from the effects of the deceased one. They might as well have chosen his profession then and there. Horses and guns – it was a career with both. At his interview with the Ordnance recruiting panel, Jack could name every type of cannon, from culverins to bases, and every part, from concave to cascabel.

Shere knew as much about founding, annealing and machining cannon as anyone in the King's service. He had continued Prince Rupert's ideas, so that now the best English cannon out-gunned anything the Dutch or French could field. Not that the artillery train had brought the high-accuracy Rupertinos with them. Secretary Pepys kept those for his precious ships. And, to be fair, Sir Henry had preferred shorter, eight-foot culverins and sakers, all of them lighter-weight drakes, for the soft roads. Otherwise, they would have made no progress at all.

Laying the elevation of a gun, weighing powder and shot, factoring in the wind, knowing the formulas, doing the maths in his head under pressure, that was Jack's edge. Others could back an ammunition limber, ram and swab a barrel, heft a ball, and put their thumb on the touchhole to smother the embers while reloading. But to learn the ballistic foibles of each cannon in your troop, now that was sport. That was what made a firemaster.

At the adjutant's desk, which was the miller's parlour table, Jack gave his report about the business with the baggage train. The staff officer wrote and asked occasional questions. The whole thing took fifteen minutes. Then a frown settled on Willoughby's face and he asked Jack to wait outside. When he called him back in, the frown had turned to a smile. 'Lieutenant, the Colonel agrees that this recent event will not yet be reported. These are strange times. It reflects well on you, which will be remembered, but not on us, the Royal Artillery. Thanks to your prompt action, the whole sordid affair was held within limits. In particular, no one was wounded, let alone killed. So, we will keep this report between ourselves for the time being. Until we admit otherwise, it didn't happen. Is that understood?'

'I quite agree, Sir. Leave it at that. By the way, I have some letters home from my troop. Friendly reassurances to loved ones, I have checked them all. Please, could they go to London with the next?'

'Certainly, Lieutenant, good for the general mood, the least we can do. They'll go with our dispatch to the Tower at lunchtime.'

Elizabeth, 09:10

Elizabeth was gathering news for Lady Emelia. She walked four doors down the north side of St James' Square, to Halifax House, the London home of the Marquess of that name.

She had visited a few times with Lady Emelia. To come alone was aiming slightly above her station. But Ormonde House was the largest in the square and she was on an errand for a nominal Duchess. Emelia was really a Dowager Countess, as her son had inherited the dukedom of Ormonde from his grandfather, but everyone had taken to addressing her as Duchess of Ormonde. It was a pretension Emelia had accepted with alacrity.

Elizabeth knocked. Would the Marquess' second son, William, be at home? He was, in her book, one that had got away. An Oxford man, Christ Church even. Two years her senior, he had returned last year from extensive travel in Europe on the untimely death of his older brother. However, he had been snapped up by Sir Samuel Grimston's daughter, also called Elizabeth, and hardly seen since.

Elizabeth Grimston had a mixed reputation. Some considered her to have floss for brains, while others who had experienced her sharp elbows thought her a scheming shrew. Her mother had died when she was an infant and her father was deeply out of favour at court. Whereas I am a Paget, thought Elizabeth, and the footman who answered the door caught the full force of her proud brown eyes.

'Hello, Spray,' said Elizabeth, who found names easy to remember. 'Is anyone at home?'

'Let me ask, Ma'am,' said the rattled man, and a moment later she heard, 'It's my Lady Ormonde's lady, M'Lady,' spoken from the hall into a room she could not see.

A short whisper ensued and out stepped William Savile himself, Lord Elland now, thin as a rake, looking down his long straight nose.

'Madam?' he said, with a flicker of disdain.

'Elizabeth Forrester,' she gave a little curtsy. 'The Dowager Countess asks if there is any news.'

The arrogance dropped away. 'Yes, yes. Jamie Butler's mama. He and I were at the House together. She came once. Well, you've got the right place. Wait here, please.' He stepped back into the shadows to her left. There was another conversation Elizabeth could not catch and a door closed deeper into the mansion.

'Come in, madam,' shouted her host. She entered a fine, panelled library. A highly polished floor reflected the glow from the fireplace.

'My father has this as his office,' said Elland. 'He calls it his Muniments Room, but really none of these papers are old or valuable. When he's away we sometimes sit here for a change of scene. My wife finds herself suddenly indisposed. But, please take a chair, Ma'am. What can I tell you?'

Elizabeth walked to the centre of the room and chose the wing chair facing across the fire towards the window. The mantle was in fine black marble and did justice to the generous space which, being in the corner of the square, was substantially bigger than she'd expected. Solid logs flickered in the hearth. Lord William settled into the chair at his father's desk, with his back to the window, facing her.

'Lady Ormonde decided to stay in London, My Lord,' said Elizabeth, 'rather than risk the roads at this season. And with so many soldiers about, who could be sure what passes she'd need? But now Town is empty, well at least this part of Town, and she wonders, perhaps that was a mistake?'

'For her personal safety, you mean?'

'Yes. She would look to her son, but we are not really sure where he is. Two weeks ago he was in Oxford with Prince George of Denmark. You heard the university made him Chancellor in his grandfather's stead. The youngest they've ever had.'

'I know, ridiculous. Jamie Butler, Chancellor. That's money talking.'

'Anyway, here in the square M'lady feels alone. She sees others have boarded up their houses. It is natural that she should be frightened. Tell me, Sir, what can I say to settle her nerves?'

Lord Elland paused a while. 'Oxford would be conveniently out of the way. But I heard that Jamie and Prince George of Denmark declared for the Dutchman a few days after Grafton and Churchill went over. So he won't be there. Her ladyship cannot try and reach Jamie now, as you say. And he won't be coming here. If she was going to run, she should have gone with Princess Anne, Sarah Churchill and the Bishop of London two weeks ago. To Nottingham, I hear.'

'But she didn't know they were leaving,' protested Elizabeth. 'No one imagined Sarah's, I should say Lady Churchill's, husband was going over. She will have run because he warned her. I don't believe in coincidence. And she went with Princess Anne to give Churchill cover, if the King wins.'

'True, true,' smoothed Elland.

Elizabeth smiled. It was like discussing a sunset with a handsome suitor, rather than a life-and-death decision. 'But what hope can I give her Ladyship?' she repeated, sensing that the attraction was returned. 'Since the day the King came back from Salisbury, we have had no comfort. Only that the invader is not yet in Berkshire.'

'You know my father is one of the King's three commissioners, sent to find out what terms his son-in-law proposes?'

'Yes.'

'They left here last Sunday. We got a letter yesterday. Father was at Collingbourne on Thursday night. They had still not even found the Prince. The fellow is playing cat and mouse with them, to wear down our nerves.'

Elizabeth nodded. This was the inside track Emelia wanted.

'And there's the thing,' continued Elland. 'William's hesitation also shows his weakness. You can tell your mistress that. While the King is on the throne he cannot be touched. But between you and me, His Majesty is not a well man. That business with the nosebleeds in Salisbury. And his run of bad luck would prey on the strongest mind. His two most loyal forces, the navy and artillery, Lord Dartmouth and Sir Henry Shere, both off the board at the crucial moment. The fleet hiding from the wind behind sandbars here in the estuary, and the cannon train bogged down on the way to Salisbury. His Majesty is, quite honestly, too merciful. Do we hear one word of criticism or complaint from him? Only on Thursday he issued passports for Anne's husband, George, to receive his servants and horses. It's this misguided respect of the King's for family. The man is too forgiving. Denmark and Princess Anne should be here in London by her father's side.'

Elizabeth wanted to defend the Princess and said, 'Since His Majesty's son was born, apparently he has eyes only for his infant heir.'

'Indeed, the Queen gets the last word on everything, as new mothers do, especially of heirs to the throne.'

'Poor Anne drops to third in line. And her older sister, the Princess Mary, may still have children.'

'Mary and Orange have been married for eleven years without even a pregnancy for the last eight,' said Lord Elland.

'She was wed at fifteen,' riposted Elizabeth. 'It could still happen.'

Elland shrugged. 'I still say the King is too merciful. And yes, now he weighs everything in terms of his little Prince. This softness may be our undoing. He sent the boy and his mother to Portsmouth last week to try and smuggle them away to France, but Lord Dartmouth wouldn't do it. They came back the other night. Dartmouth was right. The King saw sense. We can't give Frenchie a gift like that – the Prince of Wales in King Louis' clutches.'

'That question, offspring, family succession, hangs over a King. Colours his thinking,' mused Elizabeth.

'But your mistress knows that. She needs more substance. Tell her we have an army at Uxbridge covering the western approaches.'

'An Irish army,' added Elizabeth. 'Emelia is jumpy about them. The Dutch and the Irish are from different planets.'

'Well, tell her Lord Feversham won at Sedgemoor and he may again, if necessary. Or just say that my father is on it. If anyone can bring this to a peaceful settlement, he can.'

'Will you keep us advised?' asked Elizabeth, raising an eyebrow. 'We are only a few doors down.'

'Yes, of course. And you tell us if Jamie Ormonde is in touch. His influence on Oxford could tip the balance the Dutchman's way.'

With that, Elizabeth offered her greetings to her absent namesake, Lady Elland, curtsied again and departed. She had talked longer than she intended. Lady Emelia would be ready for church.

Simon, 11:45

Simon Speke swung his short legs off his cot in Clerkenwell. Today, tomorrow, something was going to give, he thought, and he needed to be ready. The smell of his landlady's Sunday lunch beckoned from the stairwell. Mrs Holmes must have grown up in kitchens. She was from the village of Highgate, a little to the north, a family of taverners, he believed. She knew how to beguile a young man with a mess of pottage.

Not needing to duck, Spike stood before the washstand under the dormer roof and poured in the jug of cold water. The window ledge was at chin level, low enough to empty the basin over afterwards. These ablutions were his Archimedes moments, when ideas came to him, and he badly needed one for the lads now. Meanwhile, he revelled in the sense of influence, of controlling his own destiny. Yes, the choices for the next seventy-two hours were his and his alone. Just knowing that made a young man feel alive. But choices meant choosing.

Should he press on, seeking the bubble reputation? Or lie low?

It was no contest. Forge on.

But how? He could urge the apprentices to attack the Catholic mass houses. These were magnets for every Anglican resentment. They had been springing up across the City and Westminster for the best part of four years now, since King James had succeeded his brother Charles to the throne and won at Sedgemoor. From Mr Stamford's in Lime Street to the Chapel Royal in St James' Palace, via the Franciscan Friars in Lincoln's Inn Fields, you could draw a line-of-march between these pimples of popery.

The next most likely targets were the Catholic ambassadors' homes – each with a chapel of its own. They were hot, of course, in the potato sense; but many wealthy and well-connected English papists were said to have deposited their valuables with foreign embassies, confident they were protected under the international code. In particular, the Spanish Ambassador's residence in Wild Street should have the petty criminals drooling. What drunken patriot, on the centenary of the defeat of the Armada, did not quiver at the thought of a return match with Spain? The Italians were in the Haymarket. And St James' Square had the Frenchman, Barillon. Louis XIV's embassy would go down well, too.

After that were the Catholic printers. The biggest prize was Spike's own employer. What would it require to best his own *baas*, Henry Hills, the King's Printer, in Blackfriars? It stuck in Simon's gullet, the amount of propaganda the lads were having to run off. To be serving the greatest spreader of papist falsehoods in English history did not sit comfortably, whatever the excuse about learning a trade. The apprentices had tried it in November, a mob in all but name, some said a thousand of them, but the Lord Mayor had posted guards in Printing House

Square, so only windows had been broken. While Simon thought of it, the King's Printing House was round the corner from Kitty's home, with her parents, Edward and Mary. Simon Speke could play the knight in shining armour. Kitty might be taller than him, but a hero gains stature during a rescue.

Last came the two palaces, each with a mass house. Loot beyond avarice.

So here was a scheme. The key would be speed and surprise.

Could the mob hold together long enough to negotiate terms? Could Prince William besiege a city the size of London? What about cannon? Dutch cannon against citizen barricades. How would Londoners behave under bombardment? Would England stand for it? What was needed was nationwide revulsion for both monarch and pretender. Panic. But how to engineer such a thing?

Speke looked into the mirror as he drew the razor across his face. He was so deep in thought that he nicked himself under the ear. He stood pondering, on the edge of revelation. Blood ran down his jawline and dripped into the basin. Muttering, he seized a cloth and dabbed at the spot. And then he had it. A phrase to whisper from door to door, to shout from horseback galloping through villages, a graphic image with a grain of possibility:

'The Dutch are coming, cutting throats.'

Speke dressed and descended for luncheon. He chewed on his capon stew, as his mother had taught him, thinking up a plan. He thanked Mrs Holmes absentmindedly, and popped his head out on to Clerkenwell Green. The churches had emptied, re-peopling the streets, an urban anonymity into which an atheist could vanish. He crossed the Green to Kingston's coffee shop on the south side, on the corner with Garden Alleys.

He banged on the door, stepped back and shouted up to the first-floor windows. 'Come on, Ike, it's Spike.'

Mrs Kingston threw open the light. 'Mr Speke, Don't you know it's Sunday?'

'Good afternoon, Mrs K, is Ichabod in?'

'Of course he's in, it's Sunday.'

'Would you permit a polite house call on the Sabbath?'

She grimaced, then nodded. 'Wait there.'

A minute later the smart red door swung inwards. Master Ichabod Kingston, also known as I.K., also known as Ike, and most recently, like Spike, a Colonel, second of three leaders chosen by the apprentices last month, greeted his friend. Ike was a year older and a foot taller than Spike. His mother, God-fearing Puritan that she was, had been close to death with the plague at the time of his birth. It had already killed her husband. She felt herself as doomed as Phineas' wife in the Book of Samuel, who, as she died, had named her new-born Ichabod, saying 'the glory is gone'. But Mrs Kingston had survived, and the experience lent her a no-nonsense mind for the management of her husband's assets. In time, Widow Kingston opened her own premises on Clerkenwell Green, serving coffee – it made for a more amenable clientele than alcohol – and the novel stimulant was catching on fast. However, to spread her risk she had arranged an apprenticeship for her son. Ike, like Spike a year later, was indentured to a printer.

Spike drew up a chair at a corner table. The place smelt of roasted grounds, mixed with sawdust resin from the floor and stale tobacco smoke. Ike came over with two empty beakers and, shortly afterwards, Mrs Kingston approached with a flat-bottomed coffee pot, before removing herself upstairs. Ike poured out the black liquid and waited for Spike to speak.

'You should have been there last night,' said Simon of his evening in Tower Hamlets. 'The lads were raving about the success of the *Third Declaration*. But they want more and they want it now.'

He confided his plan to attack Catholic chapels and destroy the King's Printing House. He did not yet mention the palaces.

'What about the sequence, timing?' said Ike. 'Riots burn themselves out. Rioters get exhausted, sated, weighed down with loot.'

'Really what we need are two mobs,' said Spike, 'one to set the tone, and the next to take over when the first one flags. It would become a rolling riot. The first could step in again where the second left off. If the lads could keep it up for two days and nights, it would be the militia who was run ragged. Better still, militiamen would join us.'

'Public order would collapse.'

'Exactly,' said Spike. 'Then we could go for the palaces.'

Ike pulled his dagger from under his coat and played with the blade's reflection around the room. 'But when would the King call out the army?' he asked. 'How long would troops take to arrive from Uxbridge?'

'That is the tricky part. We have to break the chain of command. Kidnap the royal family and seize the Tower of London.'

Ike blinked, frowned, pursed his lips, but heard him out.

'Imagine we have the Tower,' said Simon. 'Its arsenal is in our hands, the royal treasury. The King, Queen and little prince are our prisoners. James wouldn't be giving any orders. The army wouldn't come.'

Ike seemed to humour his friend. Conspiracy gaming was their strong suit. 'But you will need your own captains, lieutenants, runners, manpower, a plan for reinforcements.'

'You exaggerate again, Ike, but the point about a clear plan, delegation and discipline, is well made. I told them that last night. And you are my fellow Colonel. We have a week, two at most. William of Orange will want his troops in London by Christmas. That's sixteen days from now. If we can rush the Tower, sneak into the Palace and snatch the King and little prince and keep the Dutch out for a week, we can force our kind of settlement, the one our grandfathers threw away at Putney. But we have to put out the word today. Tomorrow is Monday. Everyone will be spread around their workplaces. We need to appoint our ringleaders this afternoon, tonight. Two riot teams and one to build a dozen barricades. The barricaders can spend the week organising squads, looking for carriages and carts to grab when the time comes, to block the bridge and cork the bottlenecks so we can face down the Prince of Orange.'

Ike backed off. This was going from game to real. 'Spike, you're mad. The Dutchman has regiments of foot, horse, cannon…'

'He wouldn't dare fire on the citizens of London. The whole country would turn against him. You and I weren't born, Ike, but anyone over twenty-five remembers the Dutch in the Medway. My God. Our own Royal Navy sank thirty of His Majesty's warships trying the block the Edam-eaters; to plug the route into the shipyard; to stop them capturing our flagship.'

'And still failed.'

'Up the tributary from the mouth of the Thames came de Ruyter on the flood tide, right into Chatham and towed away the Royal Charles on the ebb. Oh, the shame of it! The patriotic disgust is just beneath the surface. Who do these shits think they are?'

'Maybe,' said Ichabod, weighing the odds. 'William's whole rationale, his public face, is to unify, to show respect. With our blood on his hands, he could reap a furious backlash.'

'If the Orange turns autocrat, he will be dropped like a leprous lemon.'

Kingston pushed his chair away to pace the coffeehouse floor. 'With the King our prisoner it's a short step to the Leveller demands of forty-seven: the vote; land reform; church and university property; annual parliaments.'

'That's exactly what the lads say,' said Spike, and added. 'Also, William cannot pay his soldiers without London's coffers.'

'And what would happen to His Majesty?'

'We would hold him, Queen and Prince separately until we had our terms. Then exile. It worked for James Stuart the boy, sneaking over to France dressed as a woman. He could pick up with the frogs where he left off in his twenties. He would surely be able to cope with it again. He might even tell himself he could return.'

Ike looked serious and said, 'This is high treason. Riots are one thing, a few days in the stocks, but snatching the royal family would be a capital offence. Even to discuss it. This conversation leaks out, we die. So put nothing in writing about it. There are informers everywhere. From now, no more direct references to James. If we have to talk about him, we say You-Know-Who.'

They both laughed, unsure if the other was joking.

And then Simon Speke told Ichabod Kingston about how he'd nicked himself shaving and about the rumour he'd conceived – a maximum panic outcry to unite the capital.

'The country,' corrected Ike.

Kitty, 10:00

Living in a city still peppered with burnt out churches, the Jones family had a wide choice of Sunday congregations. This suited them well. They had learnt to exploit a loop-hole in the requirement for Anglican attendance. Their nearest place of worship, St Ann Blackfriars, was not to be rebuilt, while St Andrew-by-the-Wardrobe in one direction and St Paul's Cathedral in the other, were unfinished as yet. By attending occasionally across several venues (Sir Christopher Wren's new rotunda at St Stephen's Walbrook was Kitty's favourite), the family could give the impression of always being somewhere else, while in fact the Joneses worshipped at home. It was a breach of the Test Act and they could have been heavily fined. However, in that happy breathing space between births, deaths and marriages, they'd had no need for public ceremonies, and would not until Grandmother Johanna died or Kitty wed. This was a blessing because the Joneses were different; the most polite of the names Kitty had heard for their status was Roman Catholic.

Others were: papist, common enemy, idolater, heretic and Antichrist.

So the family worshipped at home, without communion for lack of a priest.

Kitty prayed for them all, for the King, and to land the publishing project with the Apothecaries. Afterwards, they sat down to eat lunch and conduct their regular meeting. It was a long-standing tradition for them to take stock once a week after they had prayed and sung together. The food was served by Edward and his mother received fond preference. His wife, Mary, came next. Kitty accepted her portion and her father, by convention, ate the rest. Edward, ever the fan of the written word, made an agenda, asking for suggested topics. Then they worked through it. Each family member spoke with unusual freedom, if not quite immunity. It had served them well over as many years as Kitty could remember. This morning she offered her coming visits, to Elizabeth Forrester at two o'clock and to the Physic Garden in Chelsea tomorrow, as worthy of discussion.

However, Edward opened with a more general point, that he and his wife were keen for Kitty to spread her wings. 'Your mother and I were your age when you were born, so we have no illusions about what's going through your head. But we want you to take things more carefully than we did. Enjoy life. If no one around here has caught your eye, then a change of scene would do you good. Ask your friend Elizabeth what she thinks, when you see her.'

'Papa, you know the Church guides my principles. I am more like Mama than you, in that regard. But how will we ever find a husband for me in England who joins us in worship, or can even live with a Mass? Yes, I feel friendships and suitors, but I am sure they are Protestants. Deuteronomy 22:10, "Thou shalt not plough with an ox and a donkey".'

'This is where your mother and I disagree,' said Edward, smiling and patting Mary's hand 'much as we love each other. No one person's faith is identical to the next's. People draw different lessons from the Bible. The Anglican and Catholic communions share much more than divides them. I feel, if you marry for love, it would in itself be a holy thing. After all, God is love. Surely a deep love would transcend religious sects. What would you do if I abjured the Pope and became an Anglican? Would you love me any the less?'

'That is a terrible thing to suggest, Edward,' said Mary.

'But he is right, Mama,' said Kitty, 'his soul would still be his soul, and we would love him no less. St Paul even speculates to the Corinthians that a married couple will not be divided in the afterlife, if only one of them believes. Even if the other is an atheist. However, for myself, I will try to keep things simple. A Catholic husband would not mind how I brought up our children.'

'It is necessary that you widen your circle,' said her mother. 'You may need to travel to France and bring a nice young man back. Which is why you had French governesses as soon as we could afford them. If the King prevails in imposing his toleration, such a man may even hold a military or government position.'

'If the King prevails, I will find him here,' said Kitty. 'Otherwise, I will have to take my chances in the world.'

'That's another terrible thing to hear, to be abandoned by an only child,' said Mary. 'Now, if I may change the subject, Edward, what about this trip to the Chelsea Physic Garden?'

'Nicholas Staplehurst is in his forties, thoroughly professional and probably married,' said Edward. 'There is no question of impropriety.'

'More's the pity,' said Kitty lightly, and the mood relaxed. 'And it's Staphurst, Papa, Staphurst. Seriously, though, he will be a perfect guide and an interesting friend to gain. He supplies botanists and is a mentor to adventurous young society doctors. And he is the apothecaries' chemist. Also, he is planning another book – he published the first list of the plants in their Chelsea Garden. It would be wonderful to become his illustrator.'

'But those young doctors are Protestants, you don't know their intentions,' spluttered her father, to which Kitty only shook her head and shrugged. All fathers are cautious for their daughters, she thought.

'High water is at half past noon, tomorrow,' warned Mary. 'You can be back well before dark. You know how I feel about the river at night.'

'I'll be back in time, mother.'

'She'll be back in time for tea and will invite the gentleman in,' said Edward, to Kitty's delight.

'Maybe a glass of Madeira, rather than tea,' she said.

'Well, you wrap up warm,' said her mother, who always had the last word.

Sundays after mass were Kitty's time for her reading project. Years ago, she had imagined being cast away (or was it marooned?) on a desert island with nothing to read but a King James Bible and a compilation of Shakespeare plays. She had asked for them as a fourteenth, and fifteenth, birthday present. Once a week her nursery became the island. It was an only child's fantasy. She had finished the Bible on her seventeenth birthday, and started on the plays. Quite how a 900-

page first folio could wash up undamaged on a deserted shore, let alone a 1,300-page Bible, she would not speculate. Nevertheless, at her current rate she should be ready for a new challenge by Easter. It rather helped that her home had a Shakespearean connection.

Elizabeth, 09:50

When Elizabeth returned from Lord Elland's to Ormonde House, Lady Emelia was booted and suited and ready for church. Elizabeth ran down to the kitchen and collected from the Dutch cook, Mrs Cross, a little pannier for her mother. This held the remaining cinnamon and almond *Janhagel Koekjes*, or Riffraff Cookies, as Emelia called them, left over from St Nicholas Eve a few days before.

The Countess and Elizabeth took their usual route to Westminster Abbey for sung Eucharist at eleven. It was a thirty-minute walk across the royal park and they set off in good time. Elizabeth related her visit to Halifax House and the Dowager Duchess was visibly calmed to have established such an inside line.

'You are a clever girl, Elizabeth. But vhat have you got up your sleeve now, I vonder?' looking at the basket.

'I was hoping to call on my mother in Covent Garden for an hour, after the service,' said Elizabeth, showing her the biscuits under the cloth.

But Emelia appeared not to hear. 'Tell me again, my dear. You say Lady Elland was too shy to see you. Qvite extraordinary.'

They had time for a detour round St Margaret's, the House of Commons' church, and up the footpath towards the Abbey's north door. Here were the galleried flying buttresses of Henry VII's chapel, with dozens of heraldic beasts leering down at them and each other, greyhounds, dragons, lions, interspersed with Tudor roses. Then came the bulging ribs of the north-side chapels, and finally the magnificent north entrance to the cathedral, with its rose window.

The Bishop of Rochester, Dr Thomas Sprat, was standing in the porch when they arrived. In his youth he had been an unprincipled charmer, managing to eulogise Oliver Cromwell one moment, yet become chaplain to his enemy, King Charles II, the next. That was when Emelia had first met him, over twenty years ago.

'Tom,' said the Duchess, 'vhat an unexpected pleasure.' Elizabeth was reminded by her tone that much water had flowed under this particular bridge. 'I take it you are here in your capacity as Dean of Westminster, my Lord Bishop?'

'Dear Emelia, the pleasure is all mine. And yes, I like to keep busy when I am in town, *in commendam*, as we say. These days even Rochester seems too far from the hub of activity.'

'Vhere vill ve all be, this time next veek?'

'One thing is certain, My Lady, I am going nowhere. Not for nothing do those naughty choristers chirp about the Vicar of Bray when I pass through the cloisters.'

'But my Lord Bishop, surely there is some point betveen popery and puritanism, vhich even you vould not cross?'

'Indeed, I may have such a point, My Lady. However, it has yet to be found by man, which reflects well on the glory of our Maker. Or by woman, I should add.'

'Vell, ve shall see vhich of us is here next Sunday.' And they each made a small bow. Throughout this exchange, Sprat had ignored Elizabeth.

Emelia took her usual easterly detour round the north ambulatory to the entrance to the Henry VII Lady Chapel. Many said this was the reason Henry VIII had given the Abbey the status of a cathedral at the time of the dissolution of the monasteries, to protect his father's tomb and this masterpiece. Tacked on to the nose of the old abbey, it was also where Emelia's departed menfolk and granddaughter lay below ground, in the generous Ormonde vault. She paused, but did not go up the steps. Elizabeth wondered yet again at the extraordinary pendant fan-vault ceiling, the apogee of English style, she thought.

'Oh, for kings alvays to die with a full treasury and an adoring grown-up son,' said the Dowager Duchess, poked her in the ribs and winked.

After the service, the usual friends and acquaintances in the congregation began to mingle and exchange news. Emelia said, 'Elizabeth, You really should go and see your mother for an hour or two,' as if it had been her own idea. 'I can make my vay home with the Pembrokes. Little Henri may expect you later,' and she turned away, leaving her helpmeet speechless.

From Westminster Abbey to Covent Garden was another comfortable half hour on foot. Shortly before Grannam died, Elizabeth's father had proposed a small step back to London. Suffolk winters were miserable and he had bought an unpretentious house to break the monotony. It was in Maiden Lane, Covent Garden, between St James' and the old City, on the corner of Half Moon Street. His Paget cousins-in-law were nearby in King Street, while William Paget, now the sixth Baron, was barely further away in the other direction, in Old Palace Yard, Westminster.

Patrick Forrester said he wanted to be nearer to the doctors for Isabelle. He also saw a need to improve Elizabeth's prospects. But his friends and family suspected a personal motive – he was the one who preferred the allure of Restoration London to the boredom of hunkering beneath the east wind off the Russian steppe. Elizabeth, after a seven-year absence, had a room in town again and spent the festive season rebuilding her store of cockney sights and smells, gossiping with her grander cousins and calibrating her tastes against those of Society. She was the quintessential fledgling, out to enjoy every moment. This extended to the usual fears – for example, friends could not be invited to meet her parents, they were too embarrassing, their house was too small and her mother so scatter-brained.

Her father was more presentable. Although lower-born, the dashing looks and rapier wit that had won Isabelle's heart in the joyless, puritanical 1650s, were still evident. Grannam once said that for the first ten years of parenthood he had been a loyal, amiable and well-meaning husband. However, after Elizabeth came along and Isabelle turned inwards, his charms sometimes led him astray. In the country this had not been noticed but, back in London, Elizabeth came to share her great-uncle's and grandmother's caution about him. Patrick wagered too much on whatever was in vogue – horses, dice and Basset, the bewitching card game from France – and he would never quit when he was ahead. Elizabeth doubted he had finished a day at the races or a night at the tables in profit. He attracted infallible schemes, each overtaken by the next before it could prove itself – some said, as soon as the hard work began.

Also, London renewed the risk of Isabelle wandering off. Elizabeth fixed little labels inside her mother's coats and bonnets lest the patient slip out unseen into Maiden Lane and become lost. So far, this precaution had worked, and Mrs Forrester had been returned by kindly strangers, found as far afield as London Bridge, looking down as the tide boiled upstream between the serried piers, and Marylebone Village, gazing at the duck pond. Yet Patrick made no suggestion of moving back to Suffolk after Grannam's death.

In particular, Elizabeth was disturbed by her mother's most recent perambulation, when she had been found halfway up the scaffolding of St Paul's. A passing apprentice from the Stationers' Company had spotted her, or was he from a bookshop in St Paul's Churchyard? He had scrambled up after her and talked her down. Elizabeth's name and address label inside her mother's hat had done its job. The boy had brought the confused old dear back to Maiden Lane, but left no contact details.

Bishop Compton of London had heard of it. He had dropped in to check on his friend, on his way from Fulham Palace. The two had chatted about their time in Oxford. It emerged that he, as the Hon. Henry, sixth son of a second Earl, had been an undergraduate at Queen's, and she, as Miss Isabelle, granddaughter of a fourth baron, had partnered him to a college ball. They took it in turns to recall the acts – a fire-breather, a palm-reader – so naughty in those puritanical days. What should have been the dim and distant past was clear and present to Isabelle. Such was the nature of her mother's illness. But it seemed to Elizabeth that Isabelle's recent wanderings now had a pattern. Without admitting it, perhaps without even knowing it, Mrs. Forrester was trying to kill herself.

Elizabeth reached home a while after noon. She had her key and entered quietly. Her mother's toy spaniel, Rogue, and her father's trusty batman since army days, Hurlstone, both spotted her, but she held her forefinger to her lips to ask for silence and they kept up the surprise. She shed her cloak, folded it over the hall chair and looked round the double doors of the main front room. As she had hoped, both parents were at home. Her father sprang up with delight. Her mother blinked and scowled as if trying to remember something.

'Precious one,' said Major Patrick. 'We've been expecting you. Isabelle, it's Elizabeth.'

After they had each embraced her and Elizabeth had ascertained their general health, father and daughter got down to the question of the hour.

'This business will not end in some small shift,' said Major Forrester. 'I have seen it before. Every so often comes along an earthquake in affairs of state. This is what revolutions look like. I saw it with the Civil War. It starts as a tremor, people expect a few pebbles on their heads, then the whole mountainside comes down. Do not wait too long to make your jump. Your mother and I are out of it. We had our chance of fun at the Restoration. But by then your elder sister had arrived and our hands were full. Later, Hurlstone was all we could afford. But for you, now is the time to strike. A great flux is coming, my angel, and in such moments the young can go anywhere, do anything. I don't want to hear from you again for a month. I don't want to see you at Christmas, or before Easter. When I do, God grant it, you will have done justice to us all. But you have to free yourself up.'

'Dearest Papa. Dearest Mama. That's what I'd hoped you'd say. And as for my freedom, I have a young friend coming to see me here at two who may be just the answer. Edward Jones' daughter, Kitty. She could have my job with the Countess.'

'Here? Oh dear, oh dear. And nothing ready,' said Isabelle.

'She will only come in this room, Mama. We will move you to the back parlour, or your bedroom. And I have time to straighten things up.'

'No, no. Nothing is ready.'

'Everything will be fine, Mama. Papa, what do you suggest? It's a Sunday, we cannot go out to a coffee shop, and I doubt that would be suitable anyway.'

'We thought, I thought, it would just be you, when we saw you this time, my dear. We have so much to catch up on, with all your news. But let me see. Kitty Jones, you say. Will the Dowager Duchess accept Miss Jones as companion? Is that not too much like trade?'

'Jones?' said her mother. 'Jones?' And scowled again.

'The Joneses in Blackfriars, Mother. Her Ladyship needs to meet her,' said Elizabeth. 'Kitty is such a cultured and beautiful creature. And I will describe her first as a cousin of Lord Ranelagh's, which is true. The Earl even has a daughter with the same name, Lady Catherine Jones, just a few years younger. And remember, Papa, how you painted me as Lord Paget's cousin, which tickled Emelia's fancy then. She is no blue-blood herself, either, a Dutch parvenu some people say, father was a bastard of the then Staatholder. But she knows the value at court of a pretty face and a slim waist, from long personal experience.'

'But,' protested Patrick, 'Edward Jones is much more distant from Lord Ranelagh than your mother is from Lord Paget.'

'The Joneses and Ranelaghs share a great-great-grandfather,' said Elizabeth. 'Mother and Lord William share a grandfather. So yes, it's a bigger jump. But Ranelagh's daughter has the same name. And Kitty has quality. She doesn't know it, but she lights up a room. She could do it anywhere, even a throne room. Lady Emelia will see the possibilities, even if Kitty herself doesn't. There is nothing like mentoring young talent when you are past it yourself. Kitty will do us proud. Also, I think Emelia would like to see me take to the air. She wants her chicks to fly, to dazzle, to show that her recipe still works, that she was right about them. Soon it will be Lady Henrietta's turn. It is a secret of womanhood, Papa, which men will never learn.'

'Well, you sell it prettily enough, my dear. But I fear it will not budge your mother.'

'A secret of womanhood,' said Isabelle, and began to rise from her chair.

Jack, 11:00

Breakheart Hill. To lug multi-hundredweight cannon over endless ridges on wintery roads, only to turn around and heave them home! Sisyphus came to mind – doomed to roll a boulder skyward for eternity. This was not what the lads had joined up for. Three and half years ago things had been better, out to the west, to the Somerset Levels, swinging along in the summer sun. The Thames and Kennet valleys had offered easier inclines and descents. The Battle of Sedgemoor they had called it. Only two artillery troops of the seven had seen action then. Ever since, the rest of the regiment had been spoiling for a fight. 'Why be a gunner?' the knuckleheads asked. They wanted action please, not sixty-one-gun salutes and royal firework displays. But battle had again eluded them.

By contrast, Jack was happy to keep it peaceful. His true love was horses. He disliked blazing away at his own countrymen. As firemaster, his gunnery was the bookish type. Big guns satisfied a cerebral curiosity in him – the chemistry of powder, the proportions of charge to weight of shot, rates of fire, barrel heat dissipation and the mathematics of trajectory. He also held well-developed views on the value of catching an enemy by surprise. But he knew first-hand that firing grapeshot in anger at serried ranks of clod plodders was no fun.

That night on Sedgemoor the King's commanders misjudged their upstart foe. Colonel Henry Shere's artillery had gone to bed with their cannon drawn up on the south side of camp, whence an attack was expected the next morning. Their horses had been stabled behind them in the village. However, the rebel Duke of Monmouth, with muffled hooves and ragged wheels, had circled around the main royal cavalry screen and assailed from the west, under cover of darkness and fog. Local knowledge had gained him the advantage of surprise. His invisible attack over supposedly boggy ground had given his motley army a real chance. If only they could have engaged hand-to hand, peasant scythe blades and artisan muscle would have prevailed over flintlock muskets and battle discipline.

As it was, double-blinded by gloom and brume in a bald landscape, the confusion had been complete. Opposing forces had passed each other with words of greeting. Friendly fire had wreaked havoc on both sides. Between the two armies was a shallow waterway, barely a ditch. If the rebel horsemen had found the fords across that first time and mixed among the King's fusils and cannon, Monmouth would have won. Likewise, a diversion from the expected direction, just a few muskets fired from the main road, might have sustained the surprise long enough for the Duke's column to cross the ditch at the second attempt.

However, a pistol shot out on the moor had betrayed the stealthy rebel advance. Whether it was accident or treachery had never been established, but the nearest watch, musketeers of the Royal Regiment of Foot under the Earl of Dumbarton, had heard it. Dumbarton had been told and sounded the alarm, his drummers beating merry Hell through his tents. The tough Scots were only recently back from a tour of duty in Holland, fighting for William of Orange, the King's nephew and son-in-law, against the French King Louis XIV. Within minutes their whole regiment was standing-to.

By contrast, only a pair of artillery batteries had managed to wheel across the camp and re-lay on the west side in the dark. One, led by the fighting Bishop of Winchester, 'Patch' Mews, had harnessed the prelate's own coach horses to pull its guns and ammunition into position. The other was Jack's. He had enlisted some of Dumbarton's musketeers to lend a hand, men who knew the value of cannon on a battlefield.

The gunners and the musketeers had become friends on the march out. The Royal Regiment of Foot had been the artillery train's escort. So, when Jack had called for help to manhandle his three guns and limbers into the front line, Sergeant Wems had leapt into action. In return, the battery had performed like clockwork – as if at training camp on Hounslow Heath just months before. Jack and his own Sergeant Bull had drilled the men blindfold in broad daylight, to relieve the boredom. Anything was better than the endless waiting for a drawn-out parade of the whole army in front of their new Catholic monarch.

That murky night on Sedgemoor, the flash of rebel cannon and the glow of fuses as their infantry blew on antiquated matchlocks before firing had shown the gunners where to aim. The Duke of Monmouth's few ordnance had been on higher ground to the royal army's right, above the fog. Jack had spotted their lanterns and tapers. They were well-managed, Dutch mercenaries, he had guessed, dealing steady blows to Dumbarton's Foot. But Jack's troop forewent their lanterns and kept their own tapers well covered, ramming and sponging by the blaze of others' powder. Accordingly, enemy shots flew low, wide or high, while Jack's went home. Lit sometimes from in front by their own infantry fire, and sometimes from behind by the Dutch cannon, the battlefield was a theatre of silhouettes until Jack's own battery had fired and, briefly, night became day.

Jack had started on the enemy guns, beginning a brief artillery duel. The observer from the naval shipyards, Edmund Dummer, had suggested they block their eyes as well as their ears as they fired, man-o'-war style, the quicker to regain night vision after the flash. That meant they saw where their glowing shot flew and, combined with the recent blindfold drill, it gave Jack's battery the higher work rate. Soon the three insurgent guns fell silent, which brought a gratifying cheer from the Scots. Then Lieutenant Exe had joined them and aimed on a flatter line – more depression than elevation. The fog blew away. At each barrage, black stripes would show through the rubied field, where unseen rebel cadavers now lay on tamped-out wicks. Canister deals more than scratches at that range.

'Making lanes,' Dummer had quipped.

'Shakespeare?' asked Jack.

'*Two Noble Kinsmen*,' said the seaman with a smile. He had come up with the bye-train from Portsmouth, and proved better-read than any of them.

Exe in his boorishness had adopted the phrase, and 'making lanes' had been in regimental parlance for a few days. The pink-faced, blond-haired Exe was more of a swine than ever that night – were such a thing possible – Jack had thought.

But Dummer was good company, a source of salacious yarns from his travels as a spy in the Mediterranean.

The two gunnery troops had ceased fire at first light to let the cavalry mop up. Then the Royal Horse had forded the eastern and western plungeons and swept in from both flanks, capturing the rebel artillery in the process. A duke's grandson, the eighteen year-old Earl of Ossary, had led the charge. Strange, noiseless murder, it had seemed to Jack – his ears still ringing from four hours of handiwork. Royal wraiths. Even the warrior Bishop, over to the left with the second battery, had said a word of prayer at the sight when dawn broke. A thousand countrymen lay before them. Artisans, weavers, carpenters, young and old, lay ripped and strewn together as thick as straw, some still moving, calling out, left to die. Their scythe poles and perfidious matchlocks were already being gathered into piles by the victors. Behind them, abandoned pikes, pruning hooks and pitchforks marked the path of the rout, scattered across the moor like gleanings.

Of the King's army, some claimed only eighty dead – a victory with no infantry hand-to-hand engagement – although Jack alone saw more bodies than that. Ed Dummer, who always spoke his mind, reckoned on 300. He praised the gunners' performance, but criticised the army leadership. However, 'You can paint it whichever way you want. Winning is wonderful.'

'Well, we gave you the exhibition you came for, fishhead,' Lieutenant Exe had replied.

Dummer could not ignore the barb. 'You should see a real broadside, Lieutenant. We work better than most in the dark, too. We can't have much light near all that powder.' Jack chuckled now at the memory of Exe's face.

The battle won, others had gravitated to Jack's battery, with its central view over the field of glory. He had shared flasks and swapped flashbacks with Colonel Shere, with Bishop Mews, with the young Ossary, and even with Lords Churchill and Feversham, the two commanders on the day. The Duke of Albermarle had appeared with a small staff of gentlemen-in-waiting. Albermarle, Jack heard, was Chancellor of Cambridge University, while Ossary had ambitions to follow his grandfather as Chancellor of Oxford. The two had chatted like old friends. For an hour, the gunners' grassy sward had become the centre of the universe. In that brief brotherhood of victors, the only criterion for membership was being there – Jack had praised Wems to Lord Dumbarton, which later earned the sergeant a £40 reward for his gallant help. One of Albermarle's beardless companions, James Something-or-other, too young to enlist, was carrying a gunnery textbook, so Jack had given him the tour. Not that age had stopped Lord Monty Norreys, the twelve-year-old son of the Earl of Abingdon, from joining in.

At last the matrosses had harnessed the artillery horses to the guns and limbers and the party had broken up. Shere had raised a final toast, 'Still alive and still together.' As a motto, it was more palatable than 'making lanes'.

Many surviving rebels had fled to the coasts – the Channel Ports for Protestant Holland, Bristol for America. New England was a particular destination. In the months afterwards, the harbours and creeks of Maine and Massachusetts were said to be awash with a steady flotsam of Sedgemoor fugitives. But most had not made it – chased down and captured. Summary justice had awaited: death by hanging, with added drawing and quartering if the bench was in a bad mood; deportation to the sickly West Indies for the lucky ones. Judge George Jeffreys' conduct of the Bloody Assizes gained him the Lord Chancellorship of England and the title of Most Hated Man in the Country. His brutality lost much sympathy for the King.

However, the real point went beyond that, Jack reflected, as he saw his scruffy crew back to their quarters. Since Sedgemoor, the monarch had begun to implement his plan to legalise Catholicism. The French ambassador, Monsieur Paul Barillon, had been shown particular favour. Worse still, a Nuncio from the Holy See was received, nay installed, on English soil, the first diplomat from Rome to London for nearly 150 years, when Bloody Mary had welcomed Cardinal Pole. Not since then had the papacy enjoyed such influence. One or the other, Paris or Rome, were now within reach of controlling England, at least so the pamphleteers blew.

Simon, 11:40

Simon, also known as Spike, had tracked down his cousin Hugh. He was at Old Man Chiffinch's private house in a corner of Whitehall. William Chiffinch, now in his eighties, had been Charles II's and James II's backstairs gatekeeper. As Page to the Bedchamber, his official apartment in the palace still adjoined the King's, with a connecting door. More royal mistresses had passed through his quarters, and more hush money through his hands, than any palace amanuensis in English history. Many owed him favours and none had him in their debt. It was Chiffinch who had helped Hugh Speke to meet the King after William of Orange had landed, and Chiffinch who had persuaded Feversham to sign Hugh's free passes.

Spike waited alone in the hall of the unassuming town house. Hugh was apparently trying to extract payment for the risks he had undertaken spying for the King. Spike heard him say something about 'invaluable information provided'.

Chiffinch was having none of it. 'Invaluable as without value,' he roared. 'Had you been of any use, we would not be in this mess. If I had my way, you would be hanged this afternoon for treason. But His Majesty is too merciful. Count yourself lucky that you leave here a free man. Now go. And let's hear no more of money.'

Hugh stormed out. 'Too merciful, indeed,' he spat as he passed Spike. 'That man is the one who should have been hanged, long ago, the harm he has done this country.'

Spike caught his cousin's sleeve. 'Cousin, cousin, calm yourself. There is much to discuss. This is no time for blind rage.'

'By God, I will avenge myself on this nest of vipers.'

Back in the street Spike said, 'Yes, maybe, but listen, I have an idea. Where can we talk and not be disturbed?'

Hugh blinked and looked at his scrawny kinsman.

'All right. I'm all right now, Coz. Which way will we need to head afterwards?'

'The City. Tower Hamlets.'

'Then the river is our best bet. The tide will be turning about now. Let's see if there's a boatman on a Sunday on Whitehall Steps. We can talk out of earshot.'

And indeed the water was high and, despite the Sabbath, a solitary rowboat was moored to the chain, tugging as the tide picked up the direction of the river. Hugh settled them on the hard plank across the stern. The waterman grumbled, loosed the painter, and moved himself to the bow-ward rowlocks to balance the boat. It meant the pair could no longer be overheard.

'The lads are aching for another scheme,' said Spike. 'And, honestly, after your *Third Declaration*, the country is ready for one. Couldn't we cause a panic? Terrorise everyone so that they see through this whole stinking hierarchy, turn on their masters, to build a world for the people.'

Hugh looked thoughtful. 'A panic you say?'

'Word of mouth.'

'And the word is?'

Spike paused for dramatic effect, 'The Dutch are coming, cutting throats.'

'Not bad, not bad,' said his cousin. 'But shouldn't it be the French who are coming, cutting throats? I can see it now. Night time. Families trembling in doorways. Neighbour against neighbour. Every man for himself.'

'But the French are not even in the country,' said Spike.

'That's a point. Something's still not quite right. This is not what the *Third Declaration* warned of.' Then Hugh's face jutted into a grim, bitter smile. 'My boy, I have it. It's perfect. It's in the *Declaration*. It touches every nerve. And it could even be true.'

It was his turn to pause for effect. 'The *Irish* are coming, cutting throats.'

Spike looked at him in horror. 'Can we really do that?'

'Oh yes, and I know just how. The only question is when.'

'Cousin, it needs to be soon,' said Spike. 'Before Prince William reaches London. He must not get his hands on the palaces, the treasury, the mint to pay his troops. Or the Tower. We need a riot; the mobile to make such a diversion that we can capture You-Know-Who. By the way that's,' and he whispered, 'the King,' before talking normally again, 'and storm the Tower.'

Now it was Hugh's turn to look in horror. 'Can we really do that?'

'Oh yes, and I know just how. Then we barricade the city gates, block the bridge and hold out until our demands are met. But it has to be this week. The

Prince is at Hungerford.' And he counted on his fingers, 'Newbury, Reading, Windsor, Chiswick, London, he could be on us in five days.'

'The old snowball effect. Big, bigger, biggest. A big action, a bigger lie, the biggest prize. It could just work,' said Hugh.

'Surprise and timing. Both will be crucial.'

'Then we have to start tonight,' said the older man. 'I worked this out as a little amusement for myself a year ago. It's not much, a few letters in the post every day. York, Leeds, Liverpool and Chester are three days away. Norwich, Nottingham, Worcester two. Cambridge, Oxford, Ipswich, Canterbury, Southampton, Portsmouth one day away. So, if we want a panic in York and Chester on Wednesday night, we have to catch the post tonight. Norwich etcetera tomorrow. Cambridge and co. on Tuesday. The Irish are coming, cutting throats.'

'But who do we write to? Who will believe us? And who would be believed?'

'It sounds crazy, Simon, but after prison I spent months on the road. It was freedom, working as a chapman for the book trade. But in all those towns I kept notes. Who was listened to and who believed what. Ha! And now I know why. Revenge. As for who writes, the letters will be anonymous. To the Whigs we just say, as a good Whig, you are privately warned; and to the Tories we say the same, as a good Tory. They both hate the Catholics, and the Irish Catholic army James Stuart has marshalled on their soil, doubly so.'

'Do the London apprentices need to know about this?' asked Spike.

'No. When it comes to the panic, they must believe it. If it is to work, I don't want anyone sniggering. They only need to know that Wednesday is the big night.'

Simon was struggling to keep up. 'So, when do we grab the, I mean, You-Know-Who, take the Tower, seize the City gates and put up the barricades?'

'Wednesday night,' said Hugh. 'The tide runs for the Tower from two.'

'And the story for the apprentices, this evening?'

'Is that rioting starts the day after tomorrow and barricades go up on Wednesday night,' said Hugh.

The boat approached London Bridge. Spike looked to the left bank, to Blackfriars Stairs, where Kitty Jones lived. He wondered what she was up to. He even imagined for a moment that he saw her on the footbridge over the River Fleet to the Bridewell. Then the waterman was lining them up to shoot the piers. The natural flow of the river and the ebb of the tide had combined into a modest pressure. The waterman stowed his oars and the passengers braced themselves. The little vessel was gripped by the current, sped up and under this wonder of medieval construction. Immediately the stream widened and the pace stalled. The boatman remounted his oars and leant to his task – this was where he would earn his hire.

'You will need to share the plan with someone,' said Cousin Hugh. 'You cannot do it on your own. I'm too old to be storming fortresses while you go kidnapping You-Know-Whos.'

'Ike,' said Spike. 'Ichabod Kingston from Clerkenwell Green. You know, elected with Nat Brazier from Tower Hamlets, and me as Colonels by the apprentices last month. Ike has a lady friend in Southwark who can help too – and Rosa is even madder than him. Between us we have the East End, northern suburbs and south of the river well covered. Anything Ike and I decide, Nat will go along with. He's the methodical one. Recorder's assistant at Stationers' Hall.'

'Yes, yes, but have I met these reprobates?' asked Hugh.

'Ike helped with the typesetting last Sunday. He's in as deep as us. A real rotten apple. Cold heart. Itching to kill a Tory prig. Maybe that is what IK stands for. Itching to Kill. Anyway, he's meeting us at two, before the main group, with an hour to work out the details.'

'Well, he'll have to do,' said Hugh. ' *Il meglio è nemico del bene.* Perfection is the enemy of good.' And he spat over the side.

Kitty, 13:00

Kitty set off from Blackfriars in plenty of time for her call on Elizabeth Forrester. She had no need to lengthen her stride. It would be a comfortable stroll to Covent Garden. She took the footbridge over the Fleet, went past the rebuilt Bridewell Prison and turned north to Fleet Street, which she followed as far as St Clement Danes, where she dawdled and admired. This church, which almost blocked the road, had been pulled down after the Plague and Fire in the general passion to build back better, even though the flames had not reached it. Wren had imposed his preferred Mediterranean style. In the Ald Wych, the Sunday lull was pervasive. To Kitty it felt like the calm before the storm. She was early. She made a small detour to her father's print shop in the Savoy. This allowed her to see what was happening at Somerset House, the residence of Catherine of Braganza, Charles II's widow and the senior Catholic woman in the country. Kitty considered the dowager queen a model of how to carry the faith gracefully.

The clocks struck two, and she turned back into Covent Garden. At the corner of Maiden Lane and Half Moon Street she saw Elizabeth waiting on the doorstep to greet her.

'Come in, come in,' said Elizabeth, and kissed her cheek. 'Punctual as ever. Here, give me your cloak and gloves. Down, Rogue.'

But Kitty greeted the little dog, picked him up and carried him into the empty parlour. 'Town's deserted,' she said. 'Even more than a normal Sunday.'

'My parents are sorry to have missed you but send their love. Please sit with me by the fire. I'm dying to catch up. Dear Kitty, what have you been doing? How's business? Tell me all.'

'And I want to hear the same about you. But first let me get something off my chest. I need advice. I was discussing it with my parents at luncheon. Papa says I should go to Paris, but am I ready for that? I will be better company once I know your view. You are, well… I am already eighteen and, to be honest, no one in my circle catches my eye. There's a young soldier, I think you know him; and a printer's apprentice makes advances; and of course the apothecaries. But I need a change of scene. Tell me, dear Elizabeth, what would you do, if you were me?'

'Oh Kitty, would that I was you! Young and wise and beautiful. But yes, you need a change of scene, you are too cloistered as things are. And no, you do not need to go to Paris to achieve that. French women may have charm, but French men, ugh! And look at their government. One Sun King and a vegetable patch. Or is it one cockerel and a giant dung heap? Versailles – could you bear the awful pecking order, the constant invitations you didn't get, the extravagance and superficiality?'

'But if it meant I found love?'

'Take your time, Kitty. That was my grandmother's dying advice to me: choose your man at leisure; we are quicker and brighter than them.'

'So you think I should stay in London?'

'I do, I do. Why leave at such an exciting time?'

'Well, I have my reasons.'

'Look, Kitty, here's an idea. Come to St James' Square on Tuesday and I will introduce you to my mistress.'

'Lady Emelia?'

'Yes. She has been very kind to me, more than I deserve, and she will have some helpful advice for you.'

'Heavens, Elizabeth, I didn't mean that. The Duchess! This is Kitty Jones you are talking to. Let's be realistic.'

'Well, if you said no, I would quite understand.'

Kitty's true feelings shrieked. 'On the other hand, what harm could it do? You and she are friends enough to survive an embarrassing house call from me.'

'Oh, Kitty, you have no idea how much fun we could have. I will ask Lady Emelia this evening. To be honest, she needs the distraction. Our end of town is dead. The silence is deafening. It even woke me up this morning. And her headaches are getting worse. If I suggest ten o'clock on Tuesday, would that fit with your plans?'

'For Lady Emelia, I think I could make time,' laughed Kitty. 'If you invite me, I will come. But I quite understand if you don't. Also, I will be out from mid-morning until dusk tomorrow. A trip to the Physic Garden at Chelsea. But I will reply by return if your message comes when I'm in.'

'You'll have our invitation first thing, and twenty-four hours to prepare. Now, tell me, how are your dear parents? And what is this adventure you have planned?'

Elizabeth, 15:00

After Kitty had left, Elizabeth sat alone for a while. Hurlstone came down from his kingdom on the top floor and together they put the family parlour back as her parents liked it. Elizabeth set a kettle on the stove and with some difficulty coaxed her mother from her bedroom. She put on a display of love, fussed over the fire, brewed the tea and produced the Dutch biscuits. Her father lit a pipe, her mother stroked her lapdog. Elizabeth told them how the Dowager Countess and the Dean of Westminster had sparred that morning; and caught up with their Covent Garden gossip. Once she was sure they were settled, she stooped to kiss each on the forehead, and bid them farewell for the next few weeks. 'At least a month,' added her father, his confidence in his daughter and her social trajectory restored.

Setting off for St James', Elizabeth took the Shandois Street route. She walked past Long Court and looked in on Orion, her father's horse, at Mr Jorrock's livery stable. When they'd first come to Covent Garden, Elizabeth went there daily to give carrots to the chestnut hunter and check his feet. Sometimes she would help out with the steeds of the smart set who rode in Hyde Park on sunny days. That had been when she'd first noticed the boy from the Savoy.

Jack Wilson had been a part-time stable lad, three years older than her, who came and went as he pleased, for pocket money. He had an air of the country about him, which the animals also recognised. When Orion fell, cast against his stable wall, the livery had called Jack to calm him while they tried to stand up the big animal. This had been easier said than done. Orion was not a gelding you'd completely trust. Even a fit horse after four hours 'down' is unlikely to survive the exhaustion, injuries and risk of a twisted gut. It had taken all that time to lift Orion up. Jack had climbed in between his belly and the wall to straighten his neck so he could breathe. One kick could have maimed the boy permanently, or worse, but he had saved the horse's life. Afterwards, Jack was the first to notice that Orion was off his food and had hand-fed him grasses to tempt his appetite, and bound his raw flesh to keep the flies off.

As for Elizabeth, she was smitten. For two happy days, she had taken it in turns with Jack to keep watch, nor just for the horse's sake. And in Orion Jack had made a friend for life. The big chestnut would lean his head on Jack's shoulder when he was tired and put his head down for Jack when being dosed, which otherwise he would have outright rejected. And so, despite the social divide, Elizabeth had drawn the stable lad into conversation. The young pair had grown close over the following months. Jack had told her about his dream of joining the Royal Ordnance. She had disclosed her concern about her mother's condition. Elizabeth had been proud as punch when Jack was accepted by the gunners, but it had pained her to see him go. She had written to him when she'd gained the position with the Dowager Duchess of Ormonde. But he had not replied. It seemed that he had the sense to let things be – with her beyond his reach. However, his name still cropped up in conversations with Kitty, who sometimes saw him when he was on leave and looked in at her father's print shop while visiting his mother.

Mulling over these memories, Elizabeth turned into St Martin's Lane. Candles were already lit in the west windows of the newly lengthened nave of St Martin-in-the-Fields – a name that would have to change she thought, given the construction spree around it. Many still remembered those meadows. The church should really have become St Martin-Charing-Cross. However, Parliament had ordered the medieval high cross to Queen Eleanor's memory demolished during the Civil War, as a symbol of popery and monarchy. Elizabeth wondered what could have made it so potent. Did people kneel in the street before it? Or cross themselves as they passed? She had never even seen a picture of it.

The road intersection was dead. No one was about. Elizabeth gained the same impression Kitty had reported earlier, a town of ghosts.

She was welcomed back to Ormonde House by Lady Henrietta, Emelia's fourteen-year-old. The porter, Drizzle, had just brought the girl home from a young people's party held by the Dowager Duchess of Richmond. Lady Richmond, one of the richest women in England, was childless, having been widowed young, shortly before Henrietta had been born, and she compensated by throwing impromptu parties for friends' children of the age and rank hers would have been. Today's tea party had been to mark the birthday of the poet John Milton, even though few of her young guests had heard of him. Milton had been dead as long as they had been alive. In a way, that was the point. Lady Richmond had read aloud verses from *Paradise Lost* in which Satan, in the form of the serpent, successfully beguiles Eve – strong stuff for fourteen-year-old aristocrats.

Henrietta, or Henri, as Emelia and Elizabeth called her, was the baby of the family and had a youngest child's preciousness. Today she was bubbling with joy, 'I just love Louis. You know, Lady Richmond's parrot. It has such a cheeky look. Have you seen it?'

Elizabeth admitted she hadn't. 'I only heard that its beak exactly matches its mistress' nose. Personally, I never understood royalty's penchant for big noses.'

'It has grey plumage with orange feathers under its tail,' continued Henri. 'Lady Richmond said she has a pleated dress in the same colours. Grey silk with orange under the pleats, which flash when she twirls. I told her that sounded rather incorrect, politically, at the moment. But you know Lady Richmond, she doesn't care about things like that.'

They spent an hour reading to each other and sketching parrots and ball gowns, until Henri's bedtime. The Countess came in to kiss her daughter goodnight and then settled down at the Ruckers harpsicord. Emelia's late husband, Thomas the vice-admiral, had found it in Antwerp and given it to her as a fortieth birthday present. Emelia and Elizabeth would normally take turns to play music they knew. Had it been earlier in the day, Henrietta might have squeezed on the end of the stool to make a trio, taking the high notes. But this evening Emelia had an innovation.

'Ambassador Barillon has lent me zis music by a young Parisienne,' she said, turning back the front cover to show Elizabeth. 'Your namesake. Élisabeth Jacquet de la Guerre. Imagine, a voman publishing vorks for ze harpsichord, and only twenty-two. Barillon says he heard her play for King Louis at ze age of five. She deserves our support in London, vhatever else we say about ze French. She has four svites here, but I like ze look of zis in D Minor – ze *Allemande* – only tree minutes or so, and not too fast for beginners. Indeed it looks suitably dignified and rather feminine.'

Emelia made a start. Then Elizabeth had a stab at it. And so they progressed, egging each other on. Elizabeth hoped that the melody, laughter and candlelight were projecting into the Square, bringing the first smiles to the neighbours in days. Maybe even to the Frenchman whose sheet music it was. Would he have a window ajar in his study to hear their sweet strains?

'My parents send thanks for the cinnamon biscuits,' said Elizabeth, during a pause. 'I saw a young lady at home. A cousin or something of Lord Ranelagh, our neighbour over there.' Emelia turned to her with interest. 'Kitty Jones. Our parents are old friends. She is an only child, eighteen now, and the apple of her father's eye, but full of life and well-tutored. Her mother mothers her too much, and of course my poor mama is in no position to guide.'

'You must bring her to see me,' said Emelia.

'Oh would you? She is at that stage where a girl needs advice from a woman.'

'Vell, ve can certainly do zat.'

'She's out tomorrow on an adventure, to the Apothecaries' Garden at Chelsea Manor.'

'Ah, Chelsea. I remember Lady Hamilton selling it. Did you know, Anne of Cleves died zere? She outlived Henry VIII and all his uzzer vives. Zere is somezing to be said for outliving husbands and rivals, you know,' and she gave Elizabeth a friendly wink and another poke in the ribs.

'The Flanders Mare?'

'Zat vas unfair on many counts. First, she vasn't from Flanders, but east of Dusseldorf. Zat's as far from Bruges as Exeter is from London. Second, zere is nuzzing wrong wiz Flanders. I'm from Flanders if you take it vide. It just means flood land, vitch means miles and miles of fertile plain. Vhy do you zink it has been so fought over? And vill be again, mark my vords. Third, she didn't look like a horse, just a straw-haired German. *Blont* as ve say in Holland, cooler and taller zan average, and Henry liked his vomen varm and small. Fourth, zere is nuzzing wrong with Flanders mares, ze finest varhorses in the vorld. And last and most important, Anne outlived zem all and died vealthy and loved by ze people. So she vasn't stupid either.' With her usual flair the Dowager Countess finished, 'Now, let us have one more assault on ze *Allemande*, in honour of all Flanders mares.'

Later, Emelia's headache returned and she decided to make it an early night. As they were bidding each other *bonne nuit*, Elizabeth asked, 'What day and time shall I ask Kitty Jones to come?'

'Vell, we must see her vhile her garden adventure is still fresh. Vhat about ten o'clock on Tuesday?'

'I shall ask Hendriksen to send that message first thing.'

'I hope she's even half as naughty as zat Ranelagh. He vas a thorn in my father-in-law's side in Ireland and zen suddenly his most ardent supporter. And he alvays had an eye for a pretty boy.'

Jack, 16:00

The Colonel's inspection parade on Hounslow Heath passed with the usual fuss. For hours before the physical count came the shining of buttons and cap badges, the polishing of weapons and boots, the fettling of felt and fluffing of facial hair. Then a seemingly endless period of shuffling troops, cannons, limbers and horses, forming up in loose squares, which tightened on commands such as 'right dress' and 'front dress'. At least they were not being drenched with rain or frying in a summer heatwave. Finally, when all were present and correct, the Colonel and his aides de camp went up and down the rows, looking each man in the eye, the lines stiffening visibly at their approach and relaxing after they had passed.

A watery sun came out in time to set. Shere mounted his grey and raised his voice, 'Tomorrow we march for Chiswick. On Tuesday we camp in Hyde Park. On Wednesday we will be back in barracks. You are a fine group of men. We are still alive, and still in fighting trim.' A murmur of approval rippled round the ranks. 'We have been through a strange test this past month, but the next three days will be stranger still. What we saw this morning, the insolence of the people, will get worse. It was a warning. We were caught napping and we got off lightly. Bloodshed was avoided. But now we know. And make no mistake, England will be watching. For her sake, for your fellow soldiers and for yourselves, we must stick together. None of us wants civilian blood on our hands. I will do my damnedest to avoid that, I promise you. But in return, I want you to hold steady and obey strange orders like never before. For now, the orders are simple enough. We move off at sunrise tomorrow, so make ready this evening. Get an early night. If you are on sentry duty, the change of watch is on the hour, and I expect you all to be fresh at first light. We have a straight and level run. Let's make the most of it. Colour Sergeant, dismiss the parade. Commissioned officers, to a council of war at my billet in five minutes.'

Corporal Terry ran to Jack and pressed a drawing into his hand. He had been out earlier, sketching the pioneer corps as they sorted out dropped booty in the field where the looting had been. 'For the miller and his wife. To say thanks for letting us sleep in the windmill. It's called *Retrieving the Baggage at Heath Mill.*'

Jack entered the miller's house where the Colonel was billeted and found the owner in the kitchen. The miller called his wife, who was delighted. Holding the sketch in both hands at arm's length because of her long-sightedness, she asked that Corporal Jones be thanked. 'How much baggage did they lose? I've been so worried.'

But the Colonel's meeting was starting. Jack shrugged politely and shut the door on her.

'As I told the troops just now,' began Sir Henry, 'the people are close to a state of panic. The rabble in town will be up. It calls for fresh thinking. For the next few days appearances will matter more than usual. This may be the only time that our parading and drill pays measurable dividends. We must strike awe like never before. If we find crowds, I want no waving to sweethearts, no idle chatter in the ranks. To the populace, we must be a creature from another world. Something to admire if they are loyal, or from their worst nightmares if they are not. I need suggestions. Questions? What do we do if we hit trouble?'

'Fix bayonets and charge through?' said an older officer. 'To strike awe?

'I see several problems with that,' said Shere. 'Our priority must be the guns, and guns cannot charge. If we charge, we leave the cannon unprotected. So, we must all move at the speed of the guns. Second, whatever its speed, an artillery train cannot fight and move at the same time. When cannon are moving they point the wrong way. A big gun that can advance facing forward is not a new idea. An Italian called da Vinci did some designs. It was even discussed at the Royal Society. The issue is where to put the poor horse. Unless you want the gunner to push it himself.' He smiled and his officers laughed.

This humour is what builds *esprit*, thought Jack.

'Only in extremis, for the last stretch, can the guns and baggage be separated,' continued Shere. 'A rabble can easily outnumber us, but if we close up we will reduce our vulnerable flanks. We have only flat, wide roads ahead. Tell your men to expect a new configuration for the column. It may take the whole width of the highway, up to five abreast. I will give you a new order of march tomorrow night – a new close formation. We will try ideas out between Chiswick and Hyde Park, through Hammersmith and Kensington, and put our findings to good effect on Wednesday.'

'Would it help if the pioneers went ahead and cleared obstructions?' asked the Commissary of the Draught Horses. 'I mean, bottlenecks like gates and trees.'

'Good suggestion Mr Hardyman. Pioneers? Mr. Blood, where are you?

'Here, Colonel,' called their captain.

'Scout a day ahead of us again. Get your men up to Chiswick this evening. If you leave now, you should be there by ten. Tomorrow, start clearing our route to Hyde Park. I want no obstacles that would prevent us riding abreast. But consult back before you knock down whole buildings,' he smiled, and again there was general laughter. 'And Mr Blood, send a sergeant now to give your men fair warning of departure, but please stay for the rest of this council. We may need your further good advice.'

The Pioneers' captain briefly left the room.

'Colonel, what about breakdowns of carts and horses when marching abreast?' asked Jack. 'How can they pull out of a column without stopping it?'

'Yes, Lieutenant Wilson. We must be ready for every eventuality, hence my plan to practise. The problem will be with the centremost column. Please discuss that with your fellow officers and give us your proposal in Chiswick tomorrow evening.'

Now that Jack had spoken, Captain Exe was quick to pipe up. 'What happens at the front of the column, Sir?' he asked. 'Blunt or pointed? Mounted or on foot? Would you be at our head?'

'I'll consider that, Captain. On Tuesday we will pause the column every two hours for an hour. That will give us a chance to rearrange the van a few times and find out what works. The attraction of putting the horses in front is that people see them coming and fear to be trampled. The problem is that our horses are not trained for it. They may go too fast. And if one shies or is spooked, the whole thing could be in jeopardy.'

Captain Blood returned.

'How much provocation should we tolerate from the rabble, Sir?' said a voice from the back.

'Excellent question, thank you. The answer is, a lot. But this is where the element of surprise will help us. Bridging Master?'

'Here, Sir.'

'Go ahead with Blood to give him an excuse for what you are doing. When people ask, do not say that the artillery train is coming. Think up something credible, highway maintenance, public safety, long-term plan, I leave that to you. But I want the populace unaware of our approach. And that goes for all of us. No letters to loved ones giving our movements. But back to the question of provocation. If we can survive the next few days without a mention in the history books, we will have succeeded. That means we must show restraint, the denial of self. I know that goes against the honour of the regiment. But I want no bloodshed between here and the Tower. After that, we can await new orders. Any other questions?'

There were none.

'Then, captains and below, brief your non-commissioned officers first. After that, call your men together and tell them the plan. In these next few days, we must ask every private to think like a corporal. I want no one in the dark any more than they need to be. But also, no loose talk. In fact, no more letters home. Council dismissed.'

Jack avoided the adjutant's eye.

Kitty, 15:00

Kitty set off from Covent Garden back to Glass House Yard. Before the Commonwealth it had been Playhouse Yard, and before that the entrance to the refectory of the old Dominican priory, and those worthy, black-robed friars. Their hall had become Shakespeare's Blackfriars Theatre, the winter venue for The King's Men, when the Globe was most at the mercy of the elements. The Bard's penultimate play, *Henry VIII*, had opened here, under the very roof where some of its real-life proceedings had occurred. Shortly afterwards, the puritans had banned theatres, and all references to them. The new name, Glass House Yard, was the thespians' parting joke at hypocrites who throw stones. Then all had been lost in the Great Fire, before Kitty was even born. But she knew and would not forget. She had a dream that one day the name Playhouse Yard would be restored.

She tripped along home on winged feet. Elizabeth had lifted her burden, at least for now. The idea of France was not abandoned, but her relief that friendly circles might yet open in London, and wider ones among the aristocracy and gentry, was delicious. She also believed that nice Catholic families were still holding out in the English heartlands, willing to marry down if the right girl should appear. And she would not be sacrificing her own career by doing so. She could combine partying with drawing flowers for the Apothecaries.

Her parents and grandmother also liked the news. Her grandmother pointed out that the Dowager Duchess was famously tolerant on religion. 'Not that I would breathe a word to her, or anyone, but she *was* a lady-in-waiting to dear Queen Catherine.'

Edward Jones took up the theme. 'Indeed, as Countess of Ossary, she worked long and happily at the heart of the establishment with someone openly Catholic, who was the focus of impudent and outlandish rumours. So, I think you can take her advice more seriously than most. She would be a wonderful person to befriend, if she offers you a chance to see her more regularly.'

'Let's not get ahead of ourselves here,' warned her mother. 'The girl hasn't even had the invitation, or an interview, let alone got the job.'

'Knowing Elizabeth, there'll be a footman round first thing,' said Edward Jones.

'It's going to be quite an interesting week,' said Johanna. 'Life is so entirely unpredictable. All you know is that caterpillars become chrysalises and hatch into butterflies. When you get to my age, the vicarious pleasure of watching the young unfurl their wings is pretty much all that's left. But that doesn't make it any less pleasurable.' She reached over to Kitty and gave her a hug.

Kitty reciprocated. It was strange, she thought, how time seemed to pass for Johanna. Her grandmother viewed a week as a blink of an eye, while for her an hour could be agonising. How alone she would feel if Grandmother died before she could found a family. And what a joy if she could present her with a great-grandchild. But that was all speculation. She must be down to earth or her romantic side would fly away with her.

'Mama,' said Kitty, 'I was wondering whether I could borrow your orange cloak to go to Chelsea tomorrow. You know how it suits my hair and I want to make an impression.'

'Yes, of course. And the weather should have cleared, but don't raise your hopes. The Apothecaries' Garden in midwinter is hardly a masked ball at court.'

Kitty tried to hide her irritation. Her mother seemed to be a fount of negativity. 'Come on, Mama. I'm eighteen. Can't I live a little?'

'Better lamb dressed as lamb,' chuckled her father, cutting it fine.

His wife glared at him and concluded with, 'Well, she's not wearing it on Tuesday.'

Simon, 15:30

In the Tower Hamlets barn, the third people's Colonel, Nathaniel Brazier, had also arrived early. Simon Speke, Cousin Hugh and Ichabod Kingston had been able to brief him. They had gained his approval for the part of their plan involving rioting and barricades, and mentioned that they had two raids in development, without giving details. Now, all four mounted the platform and gazed out at a crowded room. Three dozen eager faces looked back from the floor. It being a Sunday evening, only the keenest apprentices had gathered, and they were in high excitement, matching the uniqueness of the summons.

Nat opened the meeting. 'Lads, thank you for coming.' The chatter stilled. 'I see most of you from Tower Hamlets got the message. You won't be disappointed. You all know Colonels Spike and Ike, and some of you met Hugh last weekend. For those who haven't, his *Third Declaration* had the Spartans up late, typesetting and proofing last Saturday. If you thought that was a triumph, wait until you hear what they have cooked up now.'

The hubbub bubbled. Spartans, Simon thought. That sounds like Ike's invention. Sometimes he comes up with a cracker. He stepped forward and waited for silence. 'We know what we want. One man, one vote. Regular elections. Frequent parliaments. Universities that teach practical subjects. Churches that serve the poor. The return of common land. An end to hierarchy based on wealth or birth. These were the dreams of our forefathers. We are close. As close as Englishmen have ever been. The old system needs just one kick to collapse. The King is weak, while the role of William of Orange is yet to be established. If we can seize this moment, we can hold them both to ransom. But it will take discipline, and secrecy, and sacrifice. So, before I set out our plan, I have to ask you: are you with us? Because if you are not, please leave now.'

Briefly, the apprentices looked at each other, stunned, but no one made a move.

Spike was having none of it, and rammed the question home. 'There is no shame in backing out at this stage. Really, you *are* free to go and there will be no hard feelings. But if you stay, you are willing to be our captains, to keep our secrets and to pay the ultimate price for our dreams, if it comes to it.'

This time there was a shuffling. At the back of the room, the door opened and several friends left, with murmurs of assent and pats on the back.

One voice shouted out, 'I can't do it, Spike. It's built on lies.'

Spike called after him, 'That's fine, no hard feelings mate.' He had always known who the weak reeds were and it was good to see the back of them.

After the door had shut, he said to the remaining majority, 'Yes, we are using false news. As if the hierarchy doesn't lie to us! We are going to give them a taste of their own medicine. Once the system falls, the lies can stop. But for now, the bigger the lie, the quicker we win.' He dropped his voice, 'Are we brothers?'

'Yes,' they said.

'Will we brothers keep our plans secret?' more quietly now.

'Yes,' they said, louder.

'If necessary, brothers,' he almost whispered, 'will we pay the price to buy our dreams?'

'Yes,' they almost shouted.

'So here's the plan. We act this week. We seize our city before the Dutchman gets here. And we hold it, just for a few days.' The silence was total. 'We are going to need barricades and weapons, but most of all we need the street on our side. That means our fellow citizens must despair of the authorities. We must plan for days and nights of rioting, a rolling riot to bring on a panic. We kick off on Tuesday. Between now and then, what we are going to need?'

'Organisation,' shouted one of the older printers.

'Exactly, Len,' said Spike. 'For speed and secrecy, we will share out who does what. Some steps, only small groups of us will know about, because the ideas are too explosive and must not leak, even between ourselves. Are you still with me for this? A rolling two-day riot to peak on Wednesday night?'

'Yes,' came the chorus.

'I can't hear you,' said Simon, putting a hand to an ear.

'Yes, Wednesday night, let's do it,' they shouted in a tumult.

'Thank you, thank you lads. Now, we are going to need four groups. The biggest will be the riot ringleaders, because we need two riots. That is where Nat comes in. He will need to pace you, with half resting at any one time. Twelve-hour shifts. Have a plan of attack: Popish chapels,' a small cheer, 'escalating to Mr Hills, our very own papist printer,' a louder cheer, 'and then spreading out to the Jesuit school in the Savoy; the Catholic ambassadors' chapels; Weld Street,' an even louder cheer, 'The Haymarket; St James' Square; and finally, St James' Palace and Whitehall Palace itself.'

The lads were beside themselves, hollering at each other and blaspheming at the scale of the thing. Ike had to call for order by banging the table with the heel of his Moorish koummya, as Rosa called it, too curved for a stiletto.

'The riot group must develop its own tactics and timing,' continued Spike. 'Nat will need runners to co-ordinate things. The riots start in less than two days, on Tuesday morning. So Nat has his work cut out. The second group will be responsible for our defences – barricades and traps. Let's see who wants to be in that, and who they'll put in charge. He'll need a ringleader at each city gate to make a stand on Wednesday night and be ready to retreat behind the walls if the King's troops or the Dutch attack at the end of the week. That means local knowledge. Where can we get wagons? What about London Bridge? Should we make an outer perimeter ring at Temple Bar? Holborn? And what about diversions? Snares? With a few marksmen and explosions, we could make the invaders go house to house through the West End. That could be a laugh. But, to be honest, I doubt either side will fight us. It would lose them too much support in the country. They are more likely to fight each other, if there is to be any bloodshed. But right now, even that seems unlikely. Try to imagine a revolution they will call glorious. Anyway, this second group will also need its runners and scouts to give warning of where troops are advancing. We will keep a generous pot of loot for you.

'The third group will be led by Ike, and the fourth group by me. They are still in development for Wednesday night. Both will be small, to do crucial jobs that are extremely dangerous, and will rely on surprise and absolute commitment. They are too secret to discuss, or to be speculated on among yourselves. Members will be picked later from the best of us. We will brief them only just before they go in.

'Now I want everyone here to take a side, group one or group two, riot leaders or barricaders. Once you know who you are, choose your tactics and decide your roles. On Tuesday, when we can see numbers and who is doing what, Ike and I will come in and pick our squads. We will try to balance things out and not upset your teams unduly. So: rioters over here,' he stuck out his right hand, 'and barricades and traps here,' indicating his left.

The apprentices chose their sides of the room, with much pushing and joshing, and worked out who would lead the barricade group. Nat, overseeing rioters, assigned two captains and a riot group to each, which he called 'Bands of brothers'. The lads generally stuck together. One band came from the western part of the City and its northern suburbs – Moorgate, Clerkenwell, over to Bloomsbury; the other from across the bridge, the borough of Southwark, with its prison and bear-pit on the Bankside, the low-life around St Saviours Dock and the apple orchards to the south. Nat had overall command, and divided his men from Tower Hamlets and the east end of the City between the two, to achieve depth of control. They then appointed scouts to be ready to blaze trails when the time came, to daub the lesser-known houses of Catholics with a large C, for later destruction. This mostly applied to Bloomsbury.

A carter, Blackie Lockyer, was chosen by the barricaders as their leader. He was a generation older and respected as a witness to the execution of Charles I, albeit as a six-year-old, and as the son of the Leveller martyr, Robert Lockyer, shot by firing squad in front of St Paul's Cathedral that same spring of forty-nine. The whole City had seen Blackie walk behind the coffin at the funeral. He had taken up shining shoes in the early days of the Restoration. Long since, he had moved into carting, but his nickname had stuck. He had never lost his loathing of the monarchist braggarts at whose feet he had knelt as a young man, blacking their boots. And, of course, he knew where all the wagons were.

Spike asked Blackie to join the four of them on stage and called for silence again.

'Now let's hear what Hugh here has to say about why we are going for Wednesday night.'

A respectful silence fell.

'Fellow Londoners,' said Speke Senior. 'If we are to pull this off, we need to lock down the city with time to regain our breath before we start negotiations. If Prince William marches his army from Hungerford tomorrow morning, he could be here on Friday: Newbury Monday night, Reading Tuesday night, Windsor Wednesday night, Chiswick Thursday night. So you see, Wednesday night is the latest that we can wait to seize control. We need riots on Tuesday and Wednesday and action on Wednesday night. On Thursday we will rest. That night we will meet and take stock. On Friday we'll be ready to face the Dutchman on the barricades.'

'What about the King's army at Uxbridge?' came the question.'

'We have a way to counter them. But so that it is effective, I will not divulge details. Likewise we plan to panic the waverers into supporting us. And, with your approval brothers, this panic will happen on Wednesday night.'

Spike was concerned that Hugh was saying too much. He stepped forward and turned to Ichabod. 'Colonel Ike, would you like to add a word?'

'Brothers,' said Ichabod. 'I said you would not be disappointed. If this plan surprises you, imagine what it will do to the hierarchy. The advantage of it being so short notice is that their spies are less likely to get wind of it. It won't leak out. Nevertheless, I ask you all to keep it among just us. You are the first and only people to hear of it. If we are betrayed, we know it was one of us in this room.' Spike nodded. He was glad that Ike shared his unspoken concern. Ichabod continued, 'Whoever breaks this brotherhood of trust will be risking all our lives. We will know who it was and will have our revenge.' He made a sudden movement and drew his blade, brandished it at them and gave a malevolent leer. 'Understood?'

'Easy, Ike,' they muttered, frowning, cowed.

He smiled and put away the knife. 'Do not speculate about Spike's and my jobs for Wednesday night, even among each other, let alone with people not here. You are none of you stupid, and can probably guess some of it. That should be a consolation. But whatever, keep it to yourself until Thursday. Even Nat is largely in the dark. Nat, do you want to add anything?'

Nat took up his organiser role, 'You will report in sick for work tomorrow. My groups, use the day to refine targets and timetables. Talk to your networks during the day. Call together likely helpers tomorrow evening. Know who will be in the first wave of rioters, to go in around nine o'clock on Tuesday morning. We meet up at the Crown on Leadenhall Street at eight. Tuesday and Wednesday will not be normal workdays for anyone in London.'

He turned to Blackie, who took up the theme. 'Barricaders will need something similar for Wednesday night. This has all come a bit sudden so I suggest we meet at the Boar's Head tomorrow morning, nine o'clock. I will bring a plan.' He raised a fist.

Spike added, 'If you are picked for one of the jobs for Wednesday night, you few will need to get some rest during the day on Wednesday. So, we will tell you on Tuesday. Wednesday will be a busy night.' He raised his voice to dismiss them. 'Great meeting, comrades. Thanks for coming. See you at the Crown on Leadenhall Street, eight o'clock on Tuesday morning.'

Jack, 21:40

Settling to his second night in the windmill, after so many weeks under canvas, Jack still followed his private ritual. He sorted out his boots, scraped off the mud, stuffed straw inside, and greased the uppers, soles and seams. Then he washed today's socks, wrung them out and hung them up to dry, and put out yesterday's pair near the stove to warm in the morning. Next, he laid out his bed roll, putting his head where the moonlight fell on the wooden floor. At ten o'clock, the Moon was precisely in the east. He put the lamp and the little New Testament volume where he could reach them when he woke, before he got up to light the fire. Finally, he put his backpack to his right, so that he could swing it onto his chest to prop the book on. Reading the Bible was the core of his sanity, his refuge when past shame overwhelmed him. A chapter at the start of the day, except Sundays, when the Army held a communion service. With this approach, he managed the whole volume about every eight months – at which point he would write the date on the front flyleaf and start again. One day, when army life permitted, he would return to the Old Testament.

He said his evening prayer for peace, that peace which the world cannot give. Normally it would put him out like a light, but tonight he couldn't sleep. He was thinking of his letters, which had betrayed the cannon train's movements. He would confess first thing in the morning.

Lying back, he looked at the waning Moon. When it was new, sometimes one could see the whole disc, very dimly. Moonlight was just sunlight reflected to the earth. It followed that, on the Moon, earthlight would just be sunlight reflected off the Earth. And seen from the Moon, how much brighter it would be, given that the Earth's diameter is several times the Moon's, yet it is the same distance away. Moonlight on the Earth is white. But what colour would earthlight be on the Moon? If the globe is mostly water, then from the Moon the Earth would be blue. And so, in a new Moon, the shadow part seen from Earth would be lit with blue earthlight, some of which we would see back – hence the idea of a blue moon. Once in a blue moon, people said, but that was as often as once a month.

The white Moon crept across the aperture with subtle persistence, higher and towards the south, on its way to setting in the west around daybreak. Whether this progress was due to the Earth's rotation, or the Moon's own trajectory, or both, he was unsure. Anyway, he did not need to move his head to be soon out of its light, which tracked across the floor, glowing up into the gear loft.

He wondered at the effort which goes into buildings. A tent is easy to pitch and strike, and gives something of the shelter of a windmill, which is such a different degree of difficulty to erect. All the drystone walls, all the earth banks he had seen on this march, not to mention all the houses, all the roofs, someone had cut and lifted and placed them, each piece by hand. The shelter gained by brickwork and roof only gradually repays the effort of building it, not in the first weekend, nor fortnight, that you occupy it, nor even the first season. But it continues to exist for years, decades, lifetimes, generations. It becomes an investment in the tribe, the race, the kingdom.

He thought of the nomadic life before settlements, in tents made of cloth, and before that from leaves and animal skins. Then he thought of caves, and sheltered overhangs gouged out by rivers, and the rivers themselves, and herds coming down to the water to drink, in their own skins, and then he fell asleep.

Simon, 21:40

Simon and Hugh Speke were burning the candle late in the first-floor room of the Boar's Head Tavern in East Cheape, just north of London Bridge. Ike had slunk off to cross over before they raised the central drawbridge, to see his girl in Southwark, leaving them to their prose. They had nearly finished their ten letters - one each to a Whig and a Tory in York, Leeds, Manchester, Liverpool and Chester – but still needed to catch the last dispatch from the postmaster's office. Spike had the fairer hand, which was not difficult, and Hugh held a pocketbook of names and addresses and varied each message slightly to personalise it. But the theme was always the same. As a good citizen, the recipient was urged, by 'A Well-wisher' for the Whigs and 'A Patriot' for the Tories, to call out the watch and raise the trained bands, as the Irish were coming, cutting throats.

'This fuse, once lit, cannot be put out,' said Hugh. 'Also, it cannot be repeated. These gentlemen will not be duped of their reputations twice. Nor do I think another chance like this will come along to dupe the country for many a generation. Even if one of the apprentices from tonight blabs and we are betrayed, word cannot get to Hungerford in time for the Dutchman to stop it. Likewise, if Whitehall is tipped off, they will scorn it, stupefied as they are by events out west. The King would take days to call a council to discuss a rumour about us, let alone to decide what to do, or to put it into action.'

In this fashion, they sealed the last letter and hurried to catch the post at its headquarters in Lombard Street, making it with minutes to spare.

Afterwards they walked west and parted at St Paul's Churchyard. Hugh went on to Whitehall. Spike made the detour into Blackfriars, to his master's mighty workshop in Printing House Square, to drop off his sick note. He spent many minutes afterwards watching the candlelight in Kitty's window, high above Glass House Yard, hoping to glimpse her undressing, without any luck. He then sauntered back to Clerkenwell Green, floating on the heady fumes of ambition and love.

Ike's group, capturing the Tower, is where the fame will be won, he reflected. We will bury the dead with full honours and strike medals for the living. But for me, the real trophy will be her.

Day 2. Monday 10 December 1688

Elizabeth, 07:00

In St James' Square, Elizabeth Forrester was awake early. She hopped out of bed with her shawl around her, raked the hearth, laid and lit it, folded back the internal shutters and retreated to her blankets. From there she watched the flames take as the dawn rose. Propped up on pillows, she penned two letters. One to Obadiah Faken in Suffolk, chasing him for the report on how the harvest had gone. He had promised it by the end of November, to cover the quarter from the summer solstice to St Michael's mass at the end of September. It was now ten days late. She also composed a brief invitation to Kitty. At eight o'clock, shortly after sunrise, the butler knocked.

'Breakfast in half an hour, Miss.'

'Has the postman come, Hendriksen?' she asked.

'Not yet, Miss.'

'If he does, and he has nothing from Suffolk, please could someone give him this for my steward.' She handed him the first of two letters. 'And tomorrow we can expect a young lady at ten o'clock. Miss Kitty Jones to meet the Countess. She has already accepted but here is the formal invitation. Please ask Torrance, if he is free, to take it straight away to Glass House Yard, Blackfriars.'

Thirty minutes later, Lady Emelia, Lady Henrietta and Elizabeth were at the breakfast table when Hendriksen brought in the mail. There was only one letter. It was for Elizabeth, but not from Suffolk. The other two looked on with interest as she opened it.

'Vell?' said Emelia, in a teasing voice, noticing how Elizabeth had read it and placed it coolly aside.

Elizabeth felt she had little to hide. 'It's from Jack Wilson, the young lieutenant in the Royal Ordnance. They are nearly back in London.'

'I do like a man in uniform,' said Emelia.

'What else does he say?' asked Lady Henrietta. 'Will he come and see us?'

'I expect so, dear,' said her mother. 'Vhy else would he write?'

'They were at Hounslow Heath yesterday,' answered Elizabeth. 'He says that since they went away, they twice saw the King.'

'Our dear King James,' said the Countess. 'He is a better man zan people credit. Ven zey realise vhat a heartless *varken* my cousin Vilhelm is, zey will come back to our side qvickly enough.'

'I'll be relieved to have the artillery train and fusiliers in the Tower again,' said Elizabeth.

'Zat's ze truth. And so vill ze King.'

'I mean because of the mob. It calms them. They think twenty cannon can raze a city to the ground in a morning.'

'Long may zey believe zat,' agreed Emelia.

'Has it ever been done?' asked Henrietta.

'Oh, yes, even here in England,' said her mother, 'but not flattened in a morning. If you vant to capture a town you can hit ze private houses. Most citizens qvickly capitulate. People still talked about it vhen I came here in sixty. Even now ze old ones remember zese zings. It was said ze Royalists started zat kind of fighting in forty-tree at Rozerham and Gainsborough, shooting red hot cannonballs into ze town to start fires. Ze burghers quickly forced ze garrison to surrender. Of course, sometimes zey hold out. Taunton was almost burnt to ze ground by ze Royalists in forty-five, before ze New Model relief force came. Zen ze Parliamentarians took it up. General Fairfax did it at Bridgevorter and with much show. A veek later ze City of Bart surrendered to him vizout a fight.'

'I thought cannon were to break town walls' said Henrietta.

Lady Emelia turned out to be quite the military tactician. She pointed to the chief advantage of capturing a town intact, for its taxes. So, a crafty trick was to smoke out the defenders, burning some buildings upwind, outside the town. The English called destroying a town as a punishment, to set an example to others, Continental Practices. They had a point. In her homeland, during their war of independence, a century ago, the Spanish general in Antwerp had let his soldiers go mad, The Spanish Fury. The same in the French Wars of Religion, the Massacre of St Bartholomew's Day in Paris. In England, in living memory, the Royalists had sacked towns, Liverpool was one; and on the Parliamentary side, the Scots burned and looted Newcastle. If you were about to retreat, you might slow down your pursuers with some house fires, or conduct a scorched earth policy. But again, not cannon, but torches, or gunpowder placed in the cellars.

'You see, Henrietta,' said Elizabeth, hoping to end the subject. 'This is why no one so wants another Civil War.'

Emelia took the hint. 'Darling, your father adored such stuff. Until King Charles broke his heart vith zat absurd Tangier command, designed to fail, such a dishonour it killed him… and me avay at your sister's. Ask Jamie when you see him.'

'Is Brother coming home, too?' asked Henrietta.

'No, dear. But I wish he vould. He's in Oxford suffering all sorts of temptations.'

'What sorts of temptations, Mama?'

Emelia sighed. 'Some of Jamie's friends have become traitors, dear. If ve are to avoid another civil var, men like him must stand up for ze King. Like he did at Sedgemoor. Jamie vill remember his duty to ze Stuarts. You can rely on zat. But dear King Charles, God rest his soul, vould never have got us into zis mess.'

This last part of the conversation was nonsense, her son had already gone over, but Elizabeth let it go. She was looking down at the letter from Jack, with temptations of her own. The man was unsuitable, her mother's word, of course. Printer stock. Almost a nobody. However, he had been her first crush, his tall lean body, his intelligent eyes, his ease with horses, and every rank of human too, free of that foppishness she despised in her own suitors. Yes, she was flattered.

And there was something else. Surprise. Long ago, Jack had ignored her letter. She had thought he had dropped her, that he was interested in Kitty. So what was going on? If she was being played, she would know it quickly enough. On the other hand, if he just wanted friendship, what harm was that? *On se comprend.* They understood each other. He saw a future for her, as she did for him.

Simon, 07:00

Simon Speke had had a bad night in Clerkenwell. The fear had come over him. A black dread. He had woken in the dark from a dream that his father was beating him. What had he done this time? Then he remembered. His little plot. The insurrection of the people against the hierarchy. Another catastrophe in the making. Who was he fooling? So much depended on others. What if, of a sudden, they all felt as lonely as he did at that moment, and just forgot the whole thing? Whom could he trust? Who could trust him?

Eventually daybreak filtered in. It promised a crisp morning.

Where did these mood swings come from, this burning resentment, this need to prove himself? His childhood had started smoothly. His parents, William and Barbara, had turned their back on the viper's nest of Somerset Spekes, and cohabited with a young widow and her little boy near Tavistock in Devon, to start their family. His father, also not a tall man, was now making a success there, as a land agent for the fifth Earl of Bedford, who owned many square miles of tenanted farms between Dartmoor and Cornwall. Simon had had a twin brother, Peter, built like him but not identical. His mother had adored them both.

Their commune occupied a loop of the River Tamar, the ancient frontier between the kingdoms of Wessex and Cornwall. The homestead was on the Wessex side, the eastern bank, a forty-acre toe of Devon projecting into Cornwall, almost surrounded by flowing water.

Beside his job as land agent, William Speke bred horses. He had a favourite, a liver chestnut stallion, and three brood mares. All four were working animals, they were ridden or put in harness almost daily to draw a cart, except a mare when her foal was due. The stallion, Story, became well-known around the district and admired for his temperament. Neighbours paid to have their mares covered.

The Speke horses and foals thrived on the well-drained land, living off the meadow and watering down at the river. They had nothing to frighten them and did not stray up or down stream. The far bank, the Cornish side, where the river was deep, was also too steep to tempt escape that way. William kept a few sheep among the horses, for their wool and to maintain the health of the soil. These too only needed a fence across the neck of the peninsula.

Country life brought early responsibility. Young Simon helped herd the white geese when they were still larger than him, which anyone who knew geese would respect. Aged four he had been let loose to coppice willows down by the river with his own little hand-axe. He could tickle trout under the far bank almost as soon as he learnt to swim across to it. The labourers took him seriously, although he was small. Everyone knew that, outside the classroom, Simon Speke would be making a contribution. The farm became Simon's moated kingdom. Even Peter, his twin, looked up to him.

When he was fifteen, Peter had been thrown from the stallion and had broken his neck. They'd been daring each other to ride bareback. Simon was blamed for Peter's death. His claims to have been against the idea, and to have helped only under protest, were dismissed as self-preservation. His father had taken out his own pain on Simon with a severe beating. Simon was barred from his twin's funeral and told never to visit his grave. He was called a devil, a murderer, by his father, and his mother withdrew into herself, unable to help. It was the end of an idyllic childhood, a trauma no else one understood. The loneliness was complete. He often thought of running away.

Almost a year later, a mysterious fire had broken out at the old watermill, a few hundred yards up the stream which fed the Tamar opposite the Speke's place, on the Cornish side of the river. It had happened at night and, although no one was hurt, the damage to the mill had been extensive. Simon had recently been rejected by the miller's daughter, and she now turned the finger of blame on the demon neighbours from across the county border. The dead Speke boy was said to have appeared, whooping and gesticulating from the shadows. Everyone assumed this must have been Simon pretending to be his non-identical twin. The sad fact was that Simon had indeed been out, but peeping in at another girl's dim-lit bedroom window a mile away, in the village of Horsebridge, where he'd previously had more luck with 'titillation', as he put it to himself. His father had looked for him when the call for help went up, to stand in the bucket chain with all hands, including guests from London. But Simon had not been in his room, as he later claimed. His flawed alibi led to another fearsome thrashing, beyond rational excuse. Simon still had night sweats about it.

He and his father had never spoken again. Rather than bend the knee, Simon left home as soon as he could walk straight. He called at his dead brother's plot on the way, partly for love and partly out of spite for the ban. His howl at the graveside expressed many emotions; fury at his father, grief for the deceased and pity for himself at having to leave home. But also anger at the injustice of the world, a rage which stayed with him.

Secrecy had made it impossible to say goodbye to his dear mother. Soon after, he'd heard that she had died, broken-hearted they said at losing both her children in a year. Simon's sense of shame was mellowed by a whiff of vengeful joy, knowing that his father was now a widower, working his land with no heir, facing a sad and lonely old age.

Simon took his bruised body to his Somerset cousins at West Lackington, where his uncle George Speke welcomed him like the prodigal returned. Simon adopted some of his views. In particular, the Spekes had been parliamentarians in the Civil War, and were angry about the subsequent Restoration.

However, without their patronage to enter national politics, Simon developed a more extreme view, that all Parliament, not just the Monarchy and the House of

Lords, was the problem. The House of Commons must reform too. The franchise must be widened, elections must be held with a steady frequency, and parliaments must sit regularly.

His new life gave Simon prolonged access to several country house libraries. The owners collected volumes for prestige, but rarely opened them. The explosive growth of the secular printed word since the 1640s had unleashed a wider dogfight between faith and rationalism, between authority and freedom. Dusty corners presented the book-starved boy with tracts from the radicals of the mid-century, Levellers, Diggers and Fifth Monarchists. Most owners didn't even know they had them. For a year he took the Speke family hatred of Stuart absolutism to its logical conclusion; this battle had barely begun. For him, political philosophy offered a rationality which religion lacked. So, aged seventeen, he had abandoned Somerset and walked and hitched to London.

He had travelled via another Speke manor house, at Hazelbury, near Bath. It was occupied by Lady Anna, the elderly widow of a distant cousin, Sir Hugh Speke. Their only son, another George, had died recently. Simon had imagined for a moment that Anna might be looking for an heir. However, she was suspicious, having beaten a claim to the estate by cousin Hugh in the Court of Chancery. The tough old bird had caught Simon red-handed pocketing some silver teaspoons and had whipped him from the premises, telling him never to return.

London had offered a fresh start. He determined to dive into the print revolution and see where it took him. To learn the power of the new media he'd signed his next five years away, devilling as an apprentice to Henry Hills at The King's Printing House. Then some older hands found out his politics, adopted him and introduced him to the streetwise circle which led the urban mobile.

In 1685, Simon's father, William Speke, had been visiting the Rector of Ilminster in Somerset, when anonymous letters began arriving from London inciting rebellion. They predicted that, 'a certain person will forthwith appear in the West'. The tail-end of this mass-mailing had been intercepted at the Ilminster post office. The postmaster had shown one to the rector, who had discussed it with his guest. This was shortly after Simon had arrived in the metropolis. William had been sufficiently concerned to ride on Story to the capital with this sample of the missive, dated 28th May, to warn Whitehall. He had not been taken seriously. Indeed, King James had called the letter 'enigmatical' and slighted the bearer for wasting court time. William had gone home with his tail between his legs. Then, on 11 June the bastard son of Charles II, the Duke of Monmouth, had landed a small invasion force in Dorset.

Simon had heard all this from Hugh. Being his cousin on the West Lackington side, uncle George Speke's third son, (Spekes seemed to be called George or Hugh), he was a rare source of family gossip. Hugh had recently served a prison sentence for sedition and knew all about May's multiple mailing. He and Simon had become comrades. The two had agreed on their approach – to move quickly and break the mould, to upset the Whig country gentry as well as the Tory royalists. Hugh viewed Simon's apprenticeship at Henry Hills' as an opportunity. Simon could spy out the wellspring of Stuart propaganda, while learning the ropes in the new communication age. Best of all, as a printer's apprentice, Simon could gain the trust of the City's angry mass of literate but unrepresented workers.

Spike had discovered a reason to live. He had come down in life, but at last he was his own man. Recent events might have conspired against him, but he had survived. He discovered he could speak on his feet without notes, and that he had read more revolutionary tracts than anyone except Ichabod Kingston. This new confidence turned his head. As the years ticked by, it became obvious to him that he had been born to be different. In the summer of 1688, after the birth of a Prince of Wales, he went on the offensive. In the alehouses and coffeeshops he floated the idea of a Roman-style triumvirate of colonels to give the mobile a voice. To his surprise, the apprentices accepted it. He put himself and Ike forward as two of those three. Again, he was successful.

Spike's streak of ruthlessness was as much a part of him as his diminutive height. Looking back, even in those happy days in Devon he had done mean things for a laugh: kittens drowned; a neighbour's vegetable garden uprooted; shops pilfered when money was in his pocket; ants fried in the sun under a magnifying lens; the dog locked up with only scrumpy cider to drink; self-strangulation contests with his sibling. His warped side had just been waiting to hatch. He even suspected the bareback stallion ride had been his idea.

Spike roused himself from these ruminations, washed, dressed and crossed the Green to call on the Kingstons. However, Ike was not at home. His co-conspirator was probably still with Rosa in Southwark. It didn't matter. Simon headed back to the City to help Hugh with the next mailing. He would catch up with Ike later, at the Boar's Head.

The people's colonel now faced what he considered his biggest waste of time, the walk into town. Life was too short to live in the suburbs. After this week, he would have his own suite in St James' Palace. Or in Whitehall. Who knew? He had never set foot in either. He would serve Mrs Holmes his notice. She was a nice old dear and he hoped to stay in touch. She would be welcome to enjoy the clip-clop of his personal four-in-hand carriage, bringing her to the hum of bees in the palace garden from time to time. He imagined searching the neat beds for Kitty on a summer's day, finding her painting flowers by a south-facing wall, honeysuckle perhaps, turning to him, a smile of delight, a little toss of her head, beckoning him with her brush and her violet eyes.

How similar, and yet how different, his Kitty and Ike's Rosa. Both bright and well-educated. Yet Rosa was more dangerous, much more, more than Ike. Ike had a side job at the Smithfield slaughterhouse and his trademark punishment was slicing a person's face next to the eye with his beloved koummya. But Rosa was into meat cleavers and went for the top finger joints. Yes, Ike and his girlfriend were well matched. Rosa was the only woman of roughly Ike's age who wasn't frightened of him. Sometimes she said she was drawn to him for his physical height. Or she would admire his book-learning on peasant and slave revolts. But what really made Rosa tick was anyone's guess.

Her story was complicated, and she was reticent about it. The more Simon learnt, the more intrigued he was, but he had still not fathomed everything. Somehow, Rosa's adolescence had left her more angry about the injustice of the world even than him.

A yell from a rider brought Spike back to his senses. In his waking daydream, he had stepped into the path of a mounted Royal Mail messenger. The close call reminded him of his own mission for the morning. Today he and Hugh would send letters to Norwich, Nottingham, Wolverhampton and Worcester. Spike thought it a delicious irony: the Stuarts would be brought low by their own most successful innovation – opening up Henry VIII's Royal Mail to the public.

It had been the same with printing. James I had authorised a translation of the Bible into English some eighty years before. The copyright to this vast money-spinner went with the patent of the King's Printer, excepting the two university presses. The pod at the King's Printing House, and the seeding of its alumni across the city, had helped spread the print industry in London. Now the free press was running wild and the public appetite for canard and fakery knew no bounds.

Anonymous tattle-sheets, many bearing false witness in breach of the ninth commandment, blew like autumn leaves through town. The younger generation was being debauched. Coffee houses addicted their patrons to alternative news as well as the roasted bean. The previous generation had been lost to tobacco, now it was information overload. Printers were as common as barbers, and publishing houses popped up and rotted down faster than mushrooms.

Thinking of printers reminded Simon to warn Kitty before the King's Printing House was attacked. He had asked Nat to bring a giant map tomorrow morning. Everyone must know the sequence culminating in Wednesday night – who was to be where, and when. Only then could he identify the moment of greatest danger to Kitty. It was just stupid that he did not already know.

He needed a staff of his own. Personal assistants. Secretarial support. Twenty-four hours a day, seven days a week. Delegation was all very well – good for speed and secrecy. But how could he have let himself be so clueless about what was happening? Charisma and oratory were never enough. He would have to learn to monitor and guide, not just delegate. Who was bending the rules? Who was breaking them? Were rival masterminds plotting to remove him? And where were his enforcers? In this frame of mind, he reached Cousin Hugh's lodgings, stomped up to the first floor and knocked. How far Hugh had advanced with the letters, would decide the outcome of the day.

'Come in Coz, come in,' called the older man. 'I have eight here for you.'

'But your handwriting,' protested Spike.

Hugh ignored him. 'Every one to an influential citizen, signed, sealed and addressed. Norfolk and the Midlands won't know what's hit 'em.'

The auguries were good. Spike's day was going to go well.

'Hugh?' he asked. 'I don't suppose you could get hold of plans of Whitehall Palace and St James' Palace by this afternoon?'

'Certainly, my boy.'

Simon took the letters to the post office, then tracked down Ike at the Boar's Head. The place had been rebuilt in brick following the Great Fire, but retained its leading role in the City's underworld, dating back to the Ark.

Ike was listening to Bishopsgate Blackie expound their planned barricade of the Bridge, a stone's throw to the southeast.

'And why are we letting those scum from Southwark in on this?' said a Billingsgate lad.

Spike saw Ike's eyes roll, then spot him and his face lit up, 'Colonel Speke, just the man.'

'What's up, Colonel Kingston?'

'Welcome to my headquarters for Wednesday night,' said Ike, taking him aside. 'These blokes think I'm here because of them. You know, checking that they remember to raise the draw on London Bridge. But we are a few minutes' boat ride from you-know-where. I've been down there for a wander twice this morning. Time spent in reconnaissance is seldom wasted. And look, I also pulled a map from the library at the Stationers' Company first thing this morning.' He opened his jacket to show a scroll of paper.

'What do you mean, you pulled it?' asked Spike.

'Lifted while they were opening. It's a floorplan of the Tower from their archive. *Haiward and Gascoyne, 1597*. Come upstairs and we'll have a gander.'

Nodding to the barricaders, Simon followed Ichabod up to the smoking room, empty at that hour. Ike had to stoop under the nicotine-stained ceiling. He pulled out the document, unrolled it and spread it wide on the table. It was a detailed map of the Tower of London, nearly two-foot square, complete with scorch marks from the Great Fire.

Spike gave a low whistle and said, 'The keys to the kingdom.'

'There are three ways in,' said Ike. 'The one on this side, the west, via Tower Street. Well defended – five gates to pass through, three of which have big watchtowers; not to mention the inner ring after that. Ridiculous. Second, here on the river, Traitors' Gate. The watergate. Apart from itself and St Thomas' Tower on the outer ring, it has towers watching it from the inner ring. Add in the hazard of the river at night – I can't swim – and we can forget that way too.'

Spike pointed to an afterthought of an entrance at the downstream corner of the fortress, two skinny little posterns built above a short footbridge over the moat. 'And this one?'

'Precisely.'

'O and P on the map,' said Spike. 'Do they have names?'

'Well, they do, of course, O is the Iron Gate, and P is officially just the Tower over the Iron Gate. But known locally as Robin's Tower, or the Devil's Tower. The Iron Gate is how the Tower Hamlets people get in, the cooks, repair men, cleaners. Otherwise, the place would grind to a halt. No one walks a mile round the outside of that moat to Lion's Gate in the dark, just to empty latrines. By the way, did I say, the servants usually go in and out at night?'

'The Tower must be deserted at the moment,' said Spike. 'Most troops left with the cannon train. On riot night, anyone still in there will be either in bed or on the walls on the west side looking at our fires.'

'Exactly,' agreed Ike. 'We go in with the cleaners. Dot's lot won't ask questions. When they call for the Iron Gate to be opened, we'll bind and gag the guards, and bring in the boys. Let's hope there's still someone left on the east side to let us in.'

'And what then?'

'We're here,' said Ike, pointing to the southwest corner of the bastion, 'in the Privy Garden. The alarm hasn't been raised. I assemble our company. The idea is to take the Lanthorn Tower, R, from the inside, overpower the guard, cross at ground level to the Hall Tower, S, and the Bloody Tower, T, still without being spotted, and bar the gate…'

Spike was examining the map closely and broke in, 'Which is the only other way through the inner ring to the keep. Shut that and any guards on the outer towers are as locked out as if they were attackers. But what about those asleep on the inside?'

'We could creep round, from building to building, tying them up. Or we could create a diversion on the outer ring, for example frighten Byward Tower into sounding the alarm. Perhaps the troops still inside the inner ring could be fooled into running out before we shut the gate.'

Spike smiled at the thought. 'Probably decide that at the time. But whatever you do, keep the Iron Gate open. Partly for messages and reinforcements. But mainly because I will come in by boat with You-Know-Who and his family. Traitors' Gate will remain closed, so I'll land here at St Katherine's, The Stairs Without. I'll bring them through the Iron Gate two hours before first light, blindfolded and hooded. Which means you need to seize and hold this tower, M, Salt Tower, early.'

'Good point,' said Ike.

'You decide where we can put them.'

'When they arrive, they must also be gagged,' said Ike. 'No one must know who they are, at least not until the garrison has surrendered. Troops locked out of the bailey may fight harder if they think they are rescuing You-Know-Who.'

'What do we do with the skeleton crew we capture inside the Tower? Our prisoners of war.'

'You talk to them, Spike. Tell 'em it's been done with no troops killed – not that I'm averse to a little of that,' and he patted his dagger. 'They'll have wounded pride, yes, but no blood feud. Yet.'

'Yes, I'll speak to them. After nights of rioting and a mass panic about the Irish, the rank and file may even feel like joining us. Otherwise, disarm, pay and disband them. Again, if they are correctly paid, no personal animosity. So, when you find the army paymaster and the money, no looting. Be nice about it. But lock up the officers.'

'We have another day to think about this,' said Ike. 'Let's not rule out some bloodshed.'

'How is the riot group coming along?'

'No idea,' said Ike, cheering up. 'I have only heard these barricaders. We'll find out tomorrow morning at eight. But you can trust Nat to organise a riot. They've had enough practice. He's going to paint their plan on a bedsheet to show us.'

Spike looked back at the plan of the Tower. 'Great map, Ike. I hope theirs is a good as yours.'

'Just as long as yours of Whitehall and St James' are too,' said Ike.

Kitty, 08:00

Kitty was hovering by the door when the footman from Ormonde House arrived. Elizabeth had been as good as her word. Ten o'clock tomorrow, proposed the card. A clear day's notice. Kitty asked him to wait while she penned her acceptance.

The post came later than usual. She took it. Her parents barely noticed, still remarking on the ducal messenger and Kitty's imminent trip to the apothecaries' garden. One letter was for her, which she put in her skirt pocket. The others she placed as usual on the hall table by the clock.

Edward left for the Privy Council office in Whitehall, on *Gazette* business. Mary and Johanna went in the opposite direction to Leadenhall Market. Only after Kitty settled at her lectern in her workroom did the little missive rustle in her dress to remind her of its presence.

She had to sit down and read it twice. Jack Wilson. She was at a loss. When had she misled the dear man? It might have been years ago. He and his mother lived in the Savoy. Her father had known his before the latter died, and members of the Worshipful Company of Stationers looked after their widows, young or old. A May Morning celebration came to mind, fancy dress stuff for young'uns. Jack had worn his west country buckskin pants and white wool stockings. That had certainly caught her eye. Prior to that, his gang had spent a month of evenings and weekends planing and painting the Savoy's maypole. Later, she had been impressed that he had joined the Royal Artillery and his gallant action at Sedgemoor had piqued everyone's imagination. But to be honest, she saw Jack as an older cousin not as a prospective match. She had not thought of him since waving him off a month ago, and here he was thinking of her every day.

As a Protestant from Roundhead stock, Jack had no chance with Catholic Kitty, but she could not tell him that. She pondered her options and none of them appealed. Maybe if he knew her secret. If he loved her – rather than some fantasy of her – he would understand.

Her mother and grandmother returned. They remarked that Kitty was quieter than usual.

Nicholas Staphurst called at the Jones' punctually at half past nine. Kitty was ready in her mother's orange cloak and they walked the short distance down to Blackfriars Stairs in silence. Nicholas chose a boatman and settled them towards the bow, so that the rower was facing the other way, and they could look upstream unimpeded. Staphurst opened the conversation. 'Do you remember the frost fair on the ice, Miss Jones, after Christmas in eighty-three?'

'Oh yes, Mr Staphurst. I was thirteen. I remember coming down those steps and walking out on the river exactly here.'

'Who could forget it?' said Nicholas. 'A street of booths down the middle of the Thames, all the way from the Inns of Court to Southwark. The bargemen used sledges to bring our fuel.'

'I also remember the travelling animals. Performing lions and horses and monkeys. And the elephant. When it stood on its hind legs I thought it would fall through the ice, Mr. Staphurst.'

'May I suggest we call each other Nicholas and Kitty, Miss Jones? I hardly recognise myself when you say Mr. Staphurst like that.'

'I agree, please do call me Kitty. Although it should really be Catherine. I won't be Kitty much longer. But anyway, it was the elephant I was most frightened for. Although I suppose they all got cold feet.'

'Chipperfield had the sense to put down boards I remember, inside the enclosed ring. Probably to spread the weight, but it must also have been warmer for the animals than the ice. And their cages had bases and straw in them, I saw.'

'People claimed it was the first time performing animals ever came to England, which I didn't believe.'

'No,' said Nicholas, 'The Romans would certainly have had something in that regard, and surely the Normans too, it just wasn't recorded.'

'Dio says that the Emperor Claudius crossed the Thames with elephants. Of course, war elephants are not performing ones. That was at the start of Claudius' reign, in the forty-third year of our Lord.'

Nicholas looked suitably impressed. 'A friend of mine found an elephant tusk and some bones in Gray's Inn Lane, in a gravel bed opposite the Black Mary inn. Eight or ten years ago, now. John Conyers. He thinks it was left from Noah's Flood.'

'Maybe it was one of Claudius' elephants,' said Kitty.

'Maybe. But so much about ancient times is unexplained. Another friend in Essex, John Ray, has seen seashells in the sides of mountains. How do we explain that? Who is to say elephants didn't once live in England?'

They fell into a silence while the oars dipped and the incoming tide swept them towards Westminster. As they passed Lambeth Palace, Kitty added, 'This is where Claudius crossed, the first fording point at low tide, coming from Kent. In those times the bridge was a day's march further upstream, at Staines. That's why the Romans built Londinium, they could span from Cornhill to Southwark.'

Again there was a silence and Kitty began to fear she had been showing off. So she asked about Nicholas' next book. What would be his approach to the classification of plants?

'Ah, now there's a question. You can classify plants in many ways, Kitty: by how long they live; by their size at maturity; by their medicinal effects. The Moors of Andalusia categorised plants by their shapes and by their behaviour in seasons, climates and locations – direct light or shade and so on. My friend in Essex…'

'John Ray, he's a hero of mine,'

'Yes, well, as you know, John claims that all plants put out either one leaf or two from the seed. For him, that is the starting point. He also groups by common ancestor, what he calls species. He has travelled widely, not only in the British Isles but Europe, and has quite a collection. He's a walking encyclopaedia, but getting him to put it all down on paper is the challenge. The second, thousand-page volume of his *Historia Generalis Plantarum* is just published. But you know all that. One more still to come, God willing. Henry Faithorne sells them at the Sign of the Rose in St Paul's Churchyard.'

'I've seen it. Printed by Mary Clark,' said Kitty, 'She's one of my heroines.'

'A woman printer, Kitty? I don't know. I mean I didn't know.' He paused. 'Personally, I would group plants by reproductive process, but it would be a heap of work to prove. The problem for us all is the sheer amount of knowledge to be mastered. Take John's book. Three plants per page, a thousand pages per volume, two volumes, probably six thousand plants so far. He's getting there, but still not a single drawing. Yes, it would make it much more expensive, but we have to ask, how useful is a plant book without pictures? What does it mean, when we cannot compare what we have in our hand with something on the page? It forces us to learn the author's language, to think the way the author thinks, which makes a certain expertise prerequisite. That's where skilled illustrators like you might be able to help popularise botany.'

'I supposed it is better that he publishes what he knows, than waits for the right patron and artist to come along,' said Kitty.

'True; it would be a tragedy if he died without conveying what he knows. Anything is better than nothing. And John makes nothing up. He is meticulous in testing and proving.'

'Another discouragement is that it's all in Latin. I suppose he does that for the international readers.'

'Yes, foreign botanists like their science done in Latin. The Germans, in particular. So we correspond in it. There is something logical about Latin which appeals to the method of the modern age. But I fear it has become a pretension.'

This seemed to Kitty to be a more personal view, which she wished to encourage. However, before she could pick it up, Nicholas took a personal line himself. 'If you don't mind me asking, Kitty, why the orange cloak? Is it a political statement?'

'A political statement, Nicholas? Heavens no! It's my mother's, I just borrowed it. But I see what you mean. No. Orange just suits redheads in the autumn.'

'I would call you amber blonde.'

'But what if it was political?' she said, dodging the compliment.

'Ah, now there's a real question,' but he didn't follow it up, and Kitty felt the distance between them widen.

They had turned the second bend of the Thames and the river now ran west. On the north bank stood the Earl of Ranelagh's Chelsea Hospital for injured servicemen. This was Charles II's smaller imitation of Les Invalides in Paris, still incomplete three years after his death, a Ranelagh project. The Earl had apparently fixed up a grand apartment for himself in one portion, while he tried to buy the neighbouring fields. Candles glowed in the downstairs rooms and Nicholas expressed the opinion that his lordship was at home. Finally, they saw the butter-coloured garden wall which enclosed their destination.

To reach land, the boatman let the tide carry them upstream a few yards. Then he rowed the craft back into a little creek, and bumped the landing stage. Nicholas paid him to wait before climbing ashore and giving Kitty his hand to follow.

The Apothecaries' Garden had a door through the wall on the jetty side. Nicholas unlocked it with a large key, but left it shut for her to open. Kitty stood before the heavy panel and held her breath for a moment, enjoying the sense of anticipation. She slipped off her hood and her hair lifted in the breeze. The low sun had warmed the dark oak and when she pushed the portal, it streamed through, casting her shadow up a stone path directly ahead.

She stepped into an ordered, winter world of bare, pruned branches and naked beds. Side footpaths followed the shade of the pale clay wall to left and right, buffered from the brickwork by loamy borders no wider than the paths themselves. Trim vegetal cores stood around the bases of umbra-loving climbers trained in skeletal fans against the yellow flanks.

Nicholas remained on the riverbank to give Kitty a chance to absorb this first vista alone and undistracted. Ahead to the right she saw trim rows of herbs, each tracking its own little ridge and divided from the next by weed-free runnels. To the left was an area of evergreen bushes, possibly bays, along with fruit trees, damsons or perhaps quinces – undressed of leaves it was hard to tell.

While she was still in the doorway, she noticed two men a stone's throw ahead. One, in his mid-forties, was looking away, gesturing with downward cuts of his arm. The second, younger, perhaps his apprentice, stood upright and stock still. He lifted his right hand, trying to shade his eyes from the sun and stared straight at her. He was her own age and build, but taller, with a particular poise and aura. Kitty and he were far enough apart to gaze upon the other without offence, yet close enough for every detail to be clear. The men were gardeners, or maybe apothecaries, and in those interminable instants it came upon Kitty like a wave that the young man was attractive, magnetic, beyond beautiful, so that her stomach knotted and she wanted to look away, but was too proud to break the stare first. Each held the other's gaze, and when they both smiled, angels sang.

The older of the two men tapped his lanky companion on the arm, as if to regain his attention. At the same time, Nicholas spoke from behind, 'What do you think?'

Kitty swept back the tail of her cloak with her right hand and half-turned towards him, relieved to have been forced to sever the connection. She took some more steps into the garden, moved aside, and watched her companion come in and lock the door. When she looked back, the two men were gone.

'Gardens,' Nicholas was saying, 'are the first mark of civilisation.'

Kitty was still unsteady from the effect of the young man. She drew her cloak back around her, smoothed down its front and composed her face to show she was listening.

'Of course the greatest was the first, Our Lord's own Garden of Eden. But, to me that was unrepeatable, an extraordinary coalescence of glades and woods, sunlight and shade, colours, scents, streams, rockeries, waterfalls hung with rainbows and many days' walk across.'

It seemed to Kitty that Nicholas voice had softened. Not that he was whispering in a churchy way, but he was in a place that made him happy, merry even. Or perhaps it was just she who was happy, she thought, but no, she was also frightened and disappointed – to have loved for the first time and lost in the blink of an eye.

'After that,' continued her guide, 'we read of gardens in the courts of the ancients, the Hanging Gardens of Babylon, Luxor on the banks of the Nile, the Palace of Augustus and Tiberius on Capri.'

'Or the garden in Jerusalem where the stone had been rolled away on Easter morning,' said Kitty.

'Yes, yes. Gethsemane. God mistaken for a gardener.' He paused for thought. 'Is Heaven a garden? Our word paradise comes from the old Persian for walled garden, *pairi* for around and *daeza* for wall.'

Kitty saw that he was oblivious to what just had happened. Or perhaps it had not happened, perhaps she had imagined it.

'But what we have here is something different,' he continued, and his gentle mood grew more delighted, so that it began to recapture Kitty's focus and to carry her along. 'You and I are tiny footprints at the forefront of a winding trail of botanical enquiry which, we now discover, goes back to the distant Hindus of India and the remote Chinese. What we understand from the Greeks…'

'Theophratus of Eressus,' nodded Kitty, 'who taught Alexander the Great, and made the gardens of the Lyceum in Athens the finest ever physic collection in Europe.'

'Well, at least until recent times,' smiled Nicholas, further impressed. 'Leiden University's trove is good – not that I've seen it. Paul Hermann, their Professor of Botany, was here. It was Leiden's collection of tulips from Turkey that started the mania back in the thirties. The East Indies in the last century and the New World in this have challenged natural historians like nothing since plants were sent home from Alexander's conquests. We are standing on their shoulders, just as Theophratus must have stood on the shoulders of Aristotle. But his moments of epiphany on germination and climate, such flashes we understand all too well.'

'The Greek climate must have helped,' said Kitty. 'I don't suppose Athens sees winters like ours.'

'But our northern weather can be an advantage,' protested Nicholas. 'Many plants from New England would not survive a Mediterranean summer.'

They continued like this until they reached a boxy lean-to in the northeast corner, catching the sun. It had a door on one side and a low brick skirt around the front. Beams sloped forward from the high back wall to rest on the low frontage. The roof and sides were tiled in overlapping panes of glass. Kitty was delighted. Having lived so long in Glass House Yard she had always wanted to see one.

'This is what we call the Stove House. Back in eighty-one we started heating it, to coax the tender biennials through the winter, two of each, and it works.'

'Like a Noah's Ark,' said Kitty.

'In the Great Frost, thanks to this glasshouse, we saved more than we could ever have hoped. But replacement of stock is a constant battle. And heat loss through the glass is much more than, say, a thatched roof. King Louis' new orangery at Versailles has a double layer of glass, one behind the other. It works so well that they have not needed artificial heat yet. But the initial cost would make your eyes water. Also, the result at Versailles is summer overheating. So, it's a balance. I wrote to their gardener, Monsieur Lopin, to suggest that next spring he try moving the trees out once the frosts are past. They will need some sort of wheeled crane. And they have over a thousand trees. Wouldn't it be marvellous to see the Orangery at Versailles?' Nicholas finished.

But Kitty's thoughts were closer to home. She said, as if it was of little consequence, 'The gardens here are already wonderful. Who does the gardening?'

'Yes, yes, the pruning. I'd say it's gone rather well.'

'And the gardener?'

Jack, 07:00

The second morning on Hounslow Heath proved cold and dry. It would be a fine day. Jack had been up to light the stove and was looking down from his windmill window, when the cornets sounded. Out in the gloom, the baggage train stood close-drawn and closer guarded. Lights moved reassuringly among the cannons in the artillery park, glinting off frosty barrels, iron wheel rims and brass axle hubs.

By sunrise the whole caravan had broken camp and they moved off punctually on the easy march towards Chiswick. The roads were empty for a Monday and the going flat. The horses seemed to sense that at last they were headed home, and showed a pace which might have changed the outcome of the campaign, if it had happened a month ago. The dogs sensed it too but began playing up, hanging back to worry anything at home by the wayside.

The fusiliers produced a piper and, as they swung along, Jack's thoughts turned to the question the Colonel had left with him. How do you extract a broken-down wagon from the middle of five moving columns, without stopping the entire train? If the road was not six lanes wide, the whole train would have to halt while the offending object was pulled out of the line.

Jack puzzled over the signal to alert the troops to danger. The obvious one would be a pistol shot into the air, which would tell those ahead as well as behind to watch out for a problem. Jack reckoned that the compressed column would still be 200 yards long. Although a fraction of its usual length of a nearly a mile, four groups of signalmen would be needed, at fifty-yard intervals, a quarter, halfway and three-quarters and at the back of the train to repeat any warning shot they heard, to bring a message from the back to the front, and vice versa.

If the whole train was required to stop, this too would need a signal. Three shots, thought Jack, in case the first was muffled by something, more than one would still be heard. So, at any time, three loaded pistols must be present at fifty-yard intervals down the train, to stop the whole column as one. Even then, it would be a mess, because not everything could stop at the same speed, and even breakdowns may roll on for a while.

Perhaps these manoeuvres should be practised tomorrow, one each, a single-shot swerve and a triple-shot emergency stop. He also thought the musicians should go at the front of the column on the last morning, so as not to drown out the shots. That would cause by-standers greater bafflement than advancing with fixed bayonets. Humour is more powerful than threats.

The artillery train and its accompanying soldiers and supplies made such good time that the Colonel granted a longer pause for lunch. The field kitchens were given fair warning. So, the Royal Artillery Train dropped in to eat at Syon House, the west London home of the twenty-two-year-old Charles Seymour, sixth Duke of Somerset, who had gone over to William of Orange some weeks before.

The big house was on an island, broad and flat, tucked in against their bank of the Thames. Captain Exe, as Comptroller to the Train, did not miss the opportunity to water the horses from the Duke's channel and to let them graze his lawns. A little thing like that would not bother a man who had made such an advantageous marriage, he bragged. The cooks arranged the field canteens along the Tudor south terrace, overlooking the Isleworth reach, and the troops spread themselves around, lay down for a smoke or to play cards. The quartermaster and farriers found some stores to commandeer, partly replacing those that had been stolen yesterday morning.

The officers dined in the monks' refectory (a Tudor copy) to put their feet up and consult on progress. Jack was asked to outline his plans to some of his more interested fellows. Gradually, as men finished eating, they coalesced around Jack's table, until even the Colonel was part of the conversation.

The general consensus was that 200 yards was still inordinately long for a road convoy liable to attack from a mob. Likewise, five columns in one caravan was too wide for the streets of London, where the danger would be greatest. Working backwards from what was practical, and assuming the baggage train could be left to fend for itself on the final leg, a 165-yard, four-column wide force drew widespread support. Two columns of cannon flanked by 160 fusiliers on each side. That would leave fifteen soldiers to escort the bandsmen and fifteen to bring up the rear. If each combination of cannon, limber and gun team took up nearly fourteen yards, then twenty-two teams in two columns would take up the best part of 150 yards, leaving ten or so yards for the vanguard and five for the tail.

That left fifty soldiers to guard the baggage train, which must remain in Hyde Park during Wednesday morning until the cannon were safely back in the Tower. The fusiliers could return at noon and escort it in as a second caravan.

After the scandal of being looted on Hounslow Heath, the officer corps seemed more willing, among themselves, to speak up, chip in and ask the stupid questions;

and more able to take the side of common sense.

Other parts of Jack's plan went down well: bandsmen to the front; putting the heavier gun carriages in column two; and his proposed arrangements for signalling a problem up and down the line.

'One pistol shot for steer over to the right but keep moving, two or more for stop the convoy,' said Colonel Shere. 'Repeaters spaced at one-third and two-thirds and at the back. It could catch on, Lieutenant Wilson. And four columns, not five. Questions?'

'Without the baggage train, Sir, the risk of a breakdown in the first caravan will be minimal,' said Jack. 'Which could be a good thing, because shots fired in a breakdown could be mistaken as fired in anger.'

'Yes, let's think about that. If we start firing, the mob may turn it into a battle. But the more important point is that, without the baggage train and the risk of a breakdown, we can come on fast. The Ordnance, on its own, can sustain a quick march, so more like four miles an hour, rather than one,' said Shere. 'The surprise will be greater. Seventy-five minutes from Hyde Park Corner to the Tower. Any more questions?'

'What will we practise tomorrow? The fast version or the slow one?' asked Major St Clair of the Fusiliers.

'This afternoon, we march in two columns and then three, at the slow pace. Tomorrow we will be in the four-column formation, still at the slow pace, all together, no band, no vanguard or tail escort, but we can practise the pistol signalling. The high-speed run is only for Wednesday, without the baggage.

'Well, if that's all gentlemen, let me repeat. Go out and tell the men what we have been discussing. Adjutant, get a message up the road to the pioneers that it is only a four-column path they need to clear. And Mr Willoughby, bring me a report of what they have done so far. Major St. Clair, can you rustle up your musicians, agree what they will play us into town with on Wednesday morning, and have a practice? And I want another inspection parade in daylight, when we get to Chiswick. So, we should be moving by half past one, that gives us an hour to regroup. Get your rations and then it's skates on. Dismissed.'

After the council of war broke up, Jack found one of the Duke's staff waiting at the door.

'Lieutenant,' the man said. 'Please could you introduce me to your Colonel?'

'And who are you?' asked Jack.

'RH Dew, estate manager for His Grace here at Syon House. And who are you?'

'Wait here, Mr Dew,' said Jack. He went back into the refectory and stood by Colonel Shere until he had finished his conversation.

'What is it, Lieutenant Wilson?' asked Shere.

'The estate manager for the Park here would like a word with you, Sir.'

'Name?'

'Dew.'

'Excellent, bring him in and introduce us.'

Jack went back to the door. 'Mr Dew,' he said. 'I am Lieutenant Wilson, Firemaster, Royal Artillery Regiment. Colonel Sir Henry Shere over there has agreed to see you. Can I just check you for weapons?'

'Good gracious man, of course,' said the manager. He raised his hands and Jack patted him down.

'Clear,' said Jack. 'Follow me.'

Shere had seen them approach. 'Mr Dew, thank you for coming forward. Is there anything I can do?'

'Colonel Shere,' said Dew. 'His Grace will want a report from me about your visit. To whom should I refer him regarding compensation for losses, damage, etcetera?'

'Good question. Captain Exe has been a bit flip about taking what we needed. I don't like looters. But I also dislike bureaucracy. There will be no referrals and claims. Lieutenant Wilson here will take you to our quartermaster. He has money for things like this. The three of you assess your losses, agree what you think is fair and settle up before we leave this afternoon. I am sure that will be preferable for you too, Mr Dew, and by association His Grace.'

Dew went away content and Jack's respect for his Colonel rose even higher.

By the time he got back to his troop, the field kitchens on the parterre had already packed up, but the lads had saved him a ration.

Simon, 11:20

Spike was in Whitehall at his cousin's lodgings. Hugh handed him a last bundle of addressed envelopes.

'Here, Coz,' said Hugh. 'My best handwriting. Post them first thing in the morning. Cambridge, Oxford, Ipswich, Canterbury, Southampton and

Portsmouth. Get them out of the way early. Tomorrow will be a busy day.'

Spike looked at his cousin with gratitude, 'You know I couldn't do this without you?'

'I don't know that. Whereas I do know that I didn't do this without you. I have wanted to bring this hierarchical scum down for years and now we have a real shot at it. Look, here are the maps you wanted.'

'The plan of Whitehall?'

'And St James' Palace, I filched them from Chiffinch's place. Waited 'til he went out. He thinks he's so clever, but I've known his housekeeper in ways he hasn't. Half-a-crown in the right palm. They are all as corrupt as each other. Anyway, here's Whitehall Palace, the exact layout, only for pages of the bedchamber, keepers of the private closet and kidnappers of royalty.'

Speke looked at the ground plan. The detail was extraordinary. The palace compound had two dozen inner streets and yards, each named, and around these perhaps a thousand rooms, the main ones allotted an alphabetical or numerical mark. These were interpreted in the keys – two lists of over a hundred occupants each, which took up both margins. A state secret, reproduced for a very limited circulation.

His printer's eye went to the small wording round the edges, which he read out, 'Brayleys – Londinium. Penner on Paternoster Row. I have never heard of either this printer or this bookseller. Either I'm stupid, or someone is doing this under false names. Nevertheless, I have to say I'm grateful. How do we get in?'

'As you see, Whitehall Palace on the landward side is a maze. Fortunately, the royal apartments overlook the river, here, either side of this watermen's jetty, the Privy Stairs. Look, Chiffinch has a room between You-Know-Who and the Queen, like a watchtower, right by their private landing, with a bay window too, to see up and down Westminster Reach and over to the market gardens around St George's Fields. His room is three times the size of the Queen's – in Good Queen Bess' day, that would have been an anteroom for her. What a cheek.

'You'll go in by boat to the Privy Stairs. High tide is a quarter to two a.m. To reach the… You-Know-Who, you cross Chiffinch's apartment, in the footsteps of dozens of mistresses, priests and plotters, from Nell Gwyn on. Don't take risks with that man. If he's there, kill him. No one will mourn the loss. It won't even be noticed.'

'I was thinking I'd leave the killing to Ike,' said Spike. 'But this will involve less than expected.'

'You'll need a diversion nearby to draw the guards off the stairs. And there's the, er, wife and the little one to find.'

Spike looked worried. 'Where will they be?'

'Probably here,' said Hugh, pointing to a smaller room immediately downstream of the stairs. 'We don't know. But someone will. If I can't divine it in the next twenty-four hours, you will have to coax a flunky into telling you on the night.'

'What if mother and child are in St James' Palace, not Whitehall?'

'You-Know-Who likes to keep them close. Or out of the country – he tried shipping them off to France from Portsmouth last week, but Lord Dartmouth wouldn't do it. You-Know-Who will have learnt his lesson. But if he has split them up for safety, you decide whether to extend the operation. Here's the plan of St James' Palace.' He unrolled the second scroll on top of the first and pointed to the bottom left-hand corner. 'I doubt you'll need it, but if you must, go in from the Park, through this stable courtyard. Here's the staircase you'd want, up to the Royal Apartments, into the Boudoir, through the Council Chamber, Throne Room and Drawing Room and this is the wife's bedroom. See the Guard Rooms, here in Engine Court on the ground floor, and here on the first floor, diagonally across the yard from the Boudoir. So you should have a clear run. Anyway, the whole palace will be looking the other way, towards the rioting in St James' Square.'

'We'll check the riot group has got that: St James' Square, Wednesday evening,' said Spike. 'But you say the family is not in St James'. All three are at Whitehall?'

'Someone reported sixteen carriages on the Dover Road last night. That might have been the wife and little one. But then there are always rumours. Personally, I don't credit it. You-Know-Who was there all day today. He's ordered a Privy Council meeting for ten o'clock tomorrow, after which he goes to Uxbridge to inspect his troops.'

Spike wanted to think more closely about the Whitehall operation. 'What about the diversion nearby, on the river, to draw the guards off the stairs?'

'Something minor, like some fireworks downstream, at the Whitehall Stairs, the next along. I can arrange that from a second boat just ahead of you. How is Colonel Ike shaping up?' asked Hugh, changing the subject.

'Well, he has a great plan. You must take my word for it. The main point for him is that I arrive with You-Know-Who on the ebb tide in the first hours of

Thursday, during the panic.'

'Ha, so you will escape by river. The captives must be gagged and hooded.'

'That's what Ike said.'

'To anyone who asks, they were behaving suspiciously around the palace and are being taken to the Tower for questioning. You don't want watermen raising the alarm. Where should I arrange a boat to wait for you, when you bring out your captives? You can't use the Privy Stairs again, too watched for the boatman to wait at. What about by Westminster Hall? Or further up at Horseferry?'

'Or at Old Palace Yard, in between,' said Spike, pointing to the map. 'Least busy, if anything is, at that time of night. Upstream won't matter, with that tide.'

'Yes, cut the walking distance, with half the party blindfolded. Leave down the Garden Stairs, by the Bowling Green. Close enough to walk in the dark, but not central to Whitehall.'

In this way, the mid-operation rendezvous was agreed: the jetty called Whitehall Garden Stairs, by the bowling green.

'What else will you need?' asked Spike.

'Hoods, gags, bonds. And somewhere to meet you tomorrow evening. Around nine o'clock? What about here? I'll have chosen my team by then and can bring them along.'

Hugh looked horrified. 'Not here. I'm in the background now. I'll be going to the country first thing on Thursday. And I certainly don't want your henchmen knowing where I live. Choose a public place that's busy. Let's say, the Red Lion Inn at Charing Cross, eleven o'clock on Wednesday night. I can tell you the password for the boatman then.'

'So you won't be there tomorrow morning at the Crown?'

'You don't need me. My work for now is done: the *Third Declaration*; Irish Night – footnotes in a bigger story. I just ask that you and Ike remember me when this is over. There will still be things to draft, election warrants, constitutions, laws, speeches to delegations, warm words to foreign missions. If you don't give me a peerage, I may even stand for parliament.'

They both laughed.

Spike said, 'We are going to build the fairest, most inclusive political system in the world. And the name of Hugh Speke will honoured down the generations.'

Elizabeth, 13:45

In Ormonde House, Elizabeth and Henrietta withdrew for their Dutch lesson with Hendriksen. This was a part of the week they looked forward to. For the last month, since news had reached London that William of Orange had landed in Devon, they had sat down together after Monday luncheon to learn Emelia's and the butler's mother tongue by singing nursery rhymes. Emelia had joined them for a laugh, but this afternoon her headache was coming back so she excused herself.

Hendriksen had been firm on how to begin. 'Ze best vay is to learn it like a native. And natives learn viz cradle songs at zeir muzzer's knee.'

So it was that the north side of St James' Square, at quarter-to-two on the last three Mondays, had hummed to unaccompanied performances of, for example, the one about a sheep with white feet which drinks its milk so sweetly.

'What's a *varken*?' asked Elizabeth, thinking of Emelia's earlier remark.

'A porker, a pig,' said Hendriksen.

'And windmills?' said Henrietta.

'I'm sorry?'

'Lullabies about windmills?'

'Oh no, vindmill songs are to vake up to. Ve have one vere you vave your arms like a vindmill, slowly for ze millstone and zen fast for ze sails:

Zo gaat de molen
de molen, de molen
zo gaat de molen
de molen.
Zo gaan de wieken
de wieken, de wieken
zo gaan de wieken
de wieken!

'Other *kinderliedjes* test your memory, or twist your tongue, or simply go faster and faster, so zat your fear of speech is pulled out of you.'

'Yes, but how do you, Hendriksen, *you*, know so many?' persisted Elizabeth.

'I see you are not going to let me escape. Ze truth is, I learnt from many aunts. I don't remember parents, but both had sisters, and my aunts took me in, in turns. Zey vere all good singers.'

'And did your own brothers and sisters sing along?' asked Henrietta.

'No, no. I was ze youngest, by just ze wrong age. I vas too boring to zem.'

'I know what *that* feels like!' said Henrietta.

'But zey sang to zeir own children,' said Hendriksen in their defence.

Elizabeth ran through her vocabulary list. 'Good morning, *goedemorgen* and good night, *goedenacht*. Thank you is *bedankt*, and thank you very much is like hearty thanks, *hartelijk dank*. But we must practise phrases that might be useful immediately, for example: Welcome to London, the palace is that way.'

'That's easy – *welkom in Londen, het paleis is die kant op*.'

'Please leave me alone, my husband is coming.'

'Please is *alsjeblieft*, husband is *man*, so: *laat me alsjeblieft met rust, mijn man komt eraan*.'

'I like that there is no word for husband, only man,' said Henrietta. 'I mean, that's all they are, right?'

'No, no,' responded Hendriksen, 've have many vords for zis. *Echtgenoot*, is about vedlock, so vedded husband, vereas *wederhelft* is also about vedlock but more like my uzzer half. *Eega* is formal, more formal zan spouse, and zen zere is *gade*, vhich is perhaps master of ze house, and finally *gemaal*, vhich is very grand.'

'Like consort?' suggested Elizabeth.

'Perhaps,' said the butler. 'Her Ladyship would speak of her Lord Ossary as her *gemaal*, in the old days.'

'What will you call your husband, Elizabeth, when you marry?' asked Henrietta.

'I hope that sometimes he will be a *man*, and sometimes a *wederhelft* and sometimes a *gade*. I don't think I will ever be grand enough to have a *gemaal*.'

'Miss Forrester,' said Hendriksen. 'Do not underserve yourself. *A virtuous voman is vorth far more than rubies*, Proverbs 30 verse 19. Every man knows that, even the Prince of Orange himself. *Een deugdzame vrouw is veel meer waard dan robijnen*.'

'As a Dutchman, Hendriksen, what do you think of him?' asked Elizabeth.

'Ah, zat's a qvestion,' said the butler.

'And what is a virtuous man worth?' asked Henrietta.

'Prinz Wilhelm vould say many virtuous vomen.'

Kitty, 13:45

In the Chelsea Physic Garden, Nicholas was answering Kitty's question. 'Our head gardener is an apothecary, John Watts. He planted these cedars on the four corners of the pond, and set up our seed exchange with Leiden. But the upkeep recently has fallen to his apprentices. Watts sometimes disappears for weeks at a time. The worst part is when this becomes known. Thieves come over the wall at the slightest hint of neglect.'

'It is hard to believe people steal plants, looking at this tranquillity. I saw two gardeners when we came in. Maybe he was one of them.'

'Quite possibly. He's in his late sixties now, very stooped. I saw nobody. Now, come and look at our winter beds.' As they walked past he listed them, 'Yarrow, hyssop, tarragon, oregano, basil, winter savory, the sorrel family, and of course our old friends, parsley, sage, rosemary and thyme. Mint is at its best around now – opportune for decongestant steam inhalation. We plant it only in pots because it spreads and then you can never get rid of it. And on the other side we have our quinces.'

'And I thought maybe damsons.'

'We don't have damsons, plums or apples, they are just too common for the space they take up. Mulberry is here, for a master who tried farming silk. Some people prize the bark, as with cedar, so that was the excuse...,' and he chatted on while Kitty enjoyed the simple pleasure of being somewhere she had often imagined and, moreover, where reality exceeded expectation.

Nicholas fielded Kitty's questions about availability, seasonality and the market price of rarer herbs; about transplanting between countries, for example whether coffee could grow in Java, or tea in India; and if so, how the local farmers might benefit, because otherwise it would be a crime; and why was this called a physic garden when they were apothecaries, not physicians?

This last enquiry seemed to prompt Nicholas. 'Kitty, the Royal College of Physicians always jostles us apothecaries about our relative places in the world – they want to stop us playing doctor, and we want to stop them making medicines. The Society is keen to gain Lord Ranelagh's support in this dispute. As army paymaster, he regularly sees the King, and the court is all back in London now. Do we have time to call on him, if he's at home? He has a natural interest, being our neighbour. The current Master even gave him a key.'

Kitty imagined her mother's delight, 'I think that would be a marvellous idea, if he has time. Such issues are best resolved in person.'

'But we need to be gone by half three. Low tide is six thirty. Perhaps Ranelagh has a library you can dip into while I talk politics, to fill in more of the history. His hospital project and our garden take up just part of Old Chelsea Manor, both this side and north of the King's Road. He may have the deeds from Tudor times. Bess of Hardwick. Let me go and warn the boatman.'

When Nicholas was back from the riverbank, he and Kitty left the garden by the northeast gate, walked along Paradise Row and up to the facade of the overdue Royal Hospital.

'Lord Ranelagh is an efficient administrator,' he said, 'which is why the late King had him run the treasury in Ireland. And why James keeps him as paymaster of his standing army. But he creams off almost as much as his efficiencies save. Hence this lavish personal lifestyle.'

They reached the latest stepping stone in the Ranleagh ascent. Windows still glowed in one part, and they could see a carriage waiting in front of the building site.

'We seem to be in luck,' said Nicholas.

Kitty thought it looked as if Lord Ranelagh had visitors, but held her peace.

A footman opened the door. Nicholas boldly introduced himself as a fellow member with his Lordship of the Royal Society, and as Chemyst to the Worshipful Society of Apothecaries, with Mr Edward Jones' daughter, Catherine. They were asked to step inside and wait while they were announced.

Two voices were heard through the doorway of the south salon.

'James, my dear boy, I insist you stay over.'

'Dickie, you are a bad man. You know I have my orders. I wouldn't have dropped in at all had not that horse gone lame on the King's Road.'

'Fie! You'd not have been that rude, to pass me by without a word of gossip.'

The newcomers heard the footman cough and announce them.

Kitty was looking around the remarkably complete interior when the man she had taken to be the head gardener in the physic plot an hour before sprang out into the hall. 'Another Catherine Jones? My daughter has the same name. But what a remarkable coincidence. And Mr Staphurst, RS. The honour is all mine. Let me take that lovely cloak, Miss Jones.' He passed it to a second footman.

Kitty smiled, curtsying nicely, puzzled.

'Please come through.' Lord Ranelagh ushered them into the room he had just left, with its fine view over the Thames and told the footman, 'Thomas, tea for four please.'

The fourth tea-drinker-to-be was the young man from the garden. He was just as lovely close up. Long, well-knit, playful without superciliousness, smooth beyond his years. Kitty heard her own name as her stomach tightened, but did not catch a word of his. Fortunately, Nicholas was doing the talking. To cover her blushes, she walked over to a window and admired a row of nine elms bordering the country road on the far bank of the river.

But then Lord Ranelagh said, 'Thomas, please serve two of the teas in the library and light some candles. James, this is local politics, dopers versus bleeders, it won't interest Miss Jones. But you can't possibly let her drink my tea alone. Now Miss Jones, please come with us. Staphurst, I will be back in a trice.'

He took Kitty's arm, proceeded down the salon and into a room that made the east corner of the ground floor. The tall stranger, James, she now knew, followed as commanded. Seconds later they were alone.

Kitty again turned her back and walked to a window.

'Dickie's a frightful bully,' said James.

'Well, if Mr Staphurst can win his support, that will be an advantage,' said Kitty.

An awkward pause developed while a third footman came in and began lighting candles. Kitty turned into the room, crossed to the inner wall and walked down the bookshelves trying to understand the cataloguing. She felt the young man's eyes on her. In the end she said, 'So clever of Lord Ranelagh to have this part of the hospital done and furnished, before the rest is even finished.'

'Yes, Dickie's problem is that he never stops building. If he waited until he had finished anything, he would have nowhere to live.'

Tea arrived and now it was Kitty's turn to look at her companion. She had the feeling of having seen this face before, in a much older man. Perhaps she had met his father. Somehow it made the attraction even stronger.

'What did you think of the Apothecaries' garden?' asked James.

'Well, to be honest, the best bit was at the beginning,' said Kitty, lifting her chin. 'What about you?'

'Well, to be honest, the best bit was at the end.'

Now they looked at each other square on, and the feeling was strong between them.

'Catherine. May I call you Catherine?'

'It's Kitty, really.'

'Kitty. And please call me James. Kitty, look, I thought I had lost you this afternoon. I don't want that again. It's a miracle to have this second chance. But I have urgent orders to Reading and then down to Portsmouth. Will you let me write to you?'

Kitty paused. This was going fast. A military man, perhaps. How she loved his directness. 'Of course. But I must tell you something, because we need to be very quick now, and I don't want either of us misled.'

'You are engaged to be married.'

'No, no, James, worse than that.'

'You are dying.'

Kitty laughed and then James laughed, and the books and candles laughed and the silver teapot, the matched porcelain cups and saucers, and the sugar bowl, the tea-strainer and the teaspoons. The sense of relief in the room was endless.

'Before you tell me,' he said, 'let me say one thing. I have never seen anything to match your entrance through that gate this afternoon. The sun behind your glorious hair, the winter light on the shoulders of your cape, the way you turned and caught the edge of it, flowing like a single tongue of fire, so that I saw your own shape underneath. Unannounced, radiant, shining out of a dull prospect, the surprise was complete. I will never, ever forget that, whatever your something is. There, that had to be said first.'

Kitty considered. But she could not wait, 'James, I'm Catholic.'

James looked at the teapot. He took the tea-strainer, placed it over her cup and refilled the delicate porcelain bowl, then did the same to his own. With gentleness and accuracy he put everything down, leant forward, placed his hands either side of hers and whispered, 'So am I.'

Kitty was electrified. She withdrew her hands and smoothed down her dress. Her body tingled under her own touch. She said, 'Not to be outdone, and not wanting to make you big-headed or anything, James, I too quite liked the look of you this afternoon. And I too thought I had lost you. And I too am glad to have a second chance. So please do write. Glass House Yard, Blackfriars. Write when the mood takes you. Not out of duty, but if you feel like it, whenever you feel like it, to let me know that you are alive and, oh dear, you're not engaged to be married are you?'

'No,' said James with a wistful tilt of the head. 'There was a suggestion, but she rejected me. Or maybe her family did.' He chuckled. 'Fortunately.'

Kitty laughed at that and they both laughed long again. Then James' face went serious and he said softly, 'But I am a soldier, on the King's side, although we don't seem to be doing much fighting, let alone dying.'

'So I guessed,' said Kitty, but she now knew what they all felt, the mothers who waved sons away to war, the maids who saw off sweethearts. This was not how she had felt bidding farewell to Jack. 'You will take care,' she said, knowing how idiotic that was. 'Portsmouth?'

'Yes, the Navy is loyal and my dragoons are posting there, from this side of Reading. It's the second biggest ordnance *depôt, après Londres.*'

'Mais vous parlez Français.'

'Bien sûr. J'ai été huit ans à l'école en France.'

'Alors, écrivez-moi en Français si vous voulez.'

'On peut se tutoyer?'

'Avec plaisir, puisque tu es le gardien de mon plus grand secret,' said Kitty with a toss of her hair.

'You are killing me, Kitty,' said James.

Lord Ranelagh and Nicholas opened the door from the salon and broke the spell.

James stood up and asked, 'Satisfactory council, Dickie? Sadly, I really must be off. Mr Staphurst, Catherine, it has been an unexpected pleasure.' He bowed to each as he said their names, turned on his heel and marched out into the hall. His footsteps could be heard ringing over the marble floor, a door opened and closed, and he was gone.

'Who says they have no Tudor in them?' said Lord Ranelagh. 'Pity he couldn't stay. Such a good-looking boy.'

'And we must catch our boatman,' said Nicholas, glancing at his pocket watch. 'Lord Ranelagh, that was most helpful.'

'Yes, you can count on me.' Turning to Kitty he added, 'Miss Jones, I would so like my daughter, Lady Catherine, to meet you. Will you give your address to Thomas on the way out, and we will see what we can organise when this Dutch kerfuffle is over.'

Jack, 14:30

The cannon train was halfway from Syon House to Chiswick. The two-column formation had gone without a hitch. Cutting the length of the caravan to barely half a mile had benefits. The jostles at crossroads were fewer – side street traffic feared to barge through. The travelling public was less likely to meet a shortened column, and more willing to wait to an end which was often in sight. Several officers commented that they should have done this from the start.

Now they would test the three-column formation. The prospect scared some drivers in the baggage train, while the fusiliers found it hard to keep step either side of the cannon, so just walked. But the mood in the main was positive. The horses were heading home and the men had eaten well.

During the afternoon stop, a royal express messenger cantered in from the west, heading for London. He asked for a change of steed. The rider told Captain Exe that the Commissioners negotiating with the Prince of Orange had been well received and the terms he was conveying meant a satisfactory settlement looked possible. He carried a sealed report from the Marquess of Halifax for the Earl of Middleton, King James' Secretary of State for the Southern Department since September. The messenger was given a fresh horse and had gone before Colonel Shere heard of it, which caused some recriminations. Shere would have added a reassuring note to the King from himself, he said, giving his position. He regretted not doing so yesterday, but such trivial news did not justify a special delivery. Anyway, the man might report it verbally.

Back on the move, the flaws in the new tripled-up formation were fewer than anticipated, while the benefits were greater. The drivers chatted to each other and the fusiliers relaxed, no longer on the slowest of slow marches. There was no question of side trouble from local traffic. The caravan had become a battering ram. They were swinging along at two miles an hour and you could see how the Ordnance on its own might hit four miles an hour for a short period on Wednesday, even perhaps tomorrow.

In almost no time, the train reached Chiswick. The pioneers had marked out a parade ground and two campsites on the adjoining commons, with lines for tents, horses and guns. Prudent local herdsmen and poulterers had cleared their livestock and the whole neighbourhood had locked up its daughters. However, when the residents saw the discipline and professionalism with which the troops pitched camp and paraded, how there was no foraging, let alone rape and pillage, they came out to watch – man, woman and child. The Colonel and Mr. Willoughby moved along the tidy ranks, congratulating, thanking, commiserating even, and the mood of self-assurance and pride spread to the spectators. There would be no raid on the baggage train here. The people were grateful that someone was in charge.

As evening fell and the guard was mounted, well-wishers with baked gifts moved between the campfires. Pipes were smoked and flutes and fiddles fetched.

Henry Shere called a final meeting of his officers once they'd been joined from Salisbury by His Majesty's Engineer, Sir Martin Beckmann, and Blood and the Bridging Master had returned from Hyde Park.

'Gentlemen, we have learnt a lot today and tomorrow we will learn more. But just as important as our order of march, which will henceforth forever be double or triple column, we have discovered what I might call a softer power. We see how the troops step up to the mark when we explain why are asking what we ask. And how villagers respond when we show that we are here for them, not for ourselves. This is what I want remembered in the years ahead, whatever happens in the coming months.

'Tomorrow we move to our quadruple column formation. We will still march as one van, rather than two; and we will hold off the musicians until Wednesday. But everything else will be as we will do it going through London. This is the dress rehearsal. I want it taken seriously. Captain Blood, is the way clear for four columns all the way through?'

'Yes, Sir.'

'I liked how things worked at Syon Park at lunchtime. Adjutant, do we have anything similar planned for tomorrow?'

'Brook Green for the midday halt, Sir. There's water for the horses in the creek at this time of year. And we'll have the Westbourne once we get to Hyde Park.'

'Enjoy it while you can, gentlemen. Let's stay alert. I want no mistakes, no more Hounslow Heaths. Not tonight, not tomorrow, not even after we are in the apparent safety of the Tower.'

Shortly after, a second messenger approached the sentries at the edge of the Royal Ordnance camp, asking for a change of horse. This was the Royal Mail postman, who protested vehemently when the fusiliers broke the seal and opened his pouch. They found various missives to recipients in town. In light of the earlier episode with the King's messenger, the captain of the guard left the letters unopened but had the postmarks and addressees of the packages listed. This list was brought with the horseman to Shere. It included one letter franked in Reading to the Countess of Ossary in St James' Square; one from Windsor to the Earl of Elland, also in St James' Square; and one with a light green seal from Hampton Court for an address in Blackfriars.

However, the Colonel again expressed irritation. He said the Royal Mails were not to be thus intercepted, let alone inspected. They were inviolable in law and if the King's Fusiliers could not protect them, then he didn't know who could. So the officer of the watch sent the postman on his way with an apology and a decent courser.

Jack heard the details of all this from Captain Exe. He might be a blond moustachioed bully with a narcissistic streak, but Jack sometimes found himself playing along, for the information it yielded. Exe was still smarting from the Colonel's reprimand for his own mistake with the messenger from Lord Halifax. 'Too hard on the officers, damn him, and too soft on the ranks. And don't think I haven't noticed you worming your way into the Colonel's affections, pretty boy.'

Later, after Jack had greased his boots and said his evening prayer, he realised that he had forgotten to confess to the Colonel about his own letters home. He lay for a long time musing on Elizabeth, wondering how well she had taken hers.

Elizabeth, 20:20

The daily domestic duties at Ormonde House had nearly finished. Elizabeth said bedtime prayers with Lady Henrietta, recalling the girl's relatives, dead and alive, including her barely remembered father, the vice-admiral; her much older sister Elizabeth, now Countess of Derby; her brother Jamie, now the Duke, rumoured to be with the Dutchman; her other brother Charles, somewhere in Italy on his grand tour; and, of course, her mother Emelia, with her recent aches and pains.

When it came to the Lord's Prayer's *lead us not into temptation*, Henri added her usual joke, but with a twist, 'Elizabeth is in tempertation', to which Elizabeth said coolly, 'We are all in danger of that, keep going. *And deliver us from evil…*'

Afterwards Elizabeth went to her room and looked again at Jack's letter. He would be back in town on Wednesday. The artillery train must come this way – the road from Hounslow Heath to the Tower led from Hyde Park Corner, either via Piccadilly or the open green to the west of the Palace of St James. If they passed along the palace's north front and entered Pall Mall, they would be within yards of St James' Square. She resolved to find out what time, or post a lookout, and be sure to take Lady Henrietta to see the spectacle.

It occurred to Elizabeth that the imminent return of dozens of cannon and hundreds of fusiliers to the Tower was so interesting that she should have told Lord Elland. She would go round to Halifax House after the post was delivered tomorrow morning, before Kitty arrived, and pretend Jack's letter had just come.

After Pall Mall and Charing Cross, the big guns would pass her parents in Covent Garden and Jack's mother in the Savoy – once the finest palace in London, demolished in the Peasants' Revolt. On that occasion, the mob had really gone to town, using gunpowder to finish the job. It was good to remember what Londoners were capable of.

At ten o'clock at night, Lady Emelia called her into her bedroom. The dowager was propped up on her pillows with her hand on her head.

'Elizabeth dear. Vhat is the plan for tomorrow? I don't know how long I can keep up zis, pretending zat all is normal.'

'Emelia, Emelia,' cooed Elizabeth. 'Everything will be fine. Have a sip of water. There. In the morning I will go to Halifax House for the latest news. And Kitty Jones is coming to amuse us at ten o'clock. Then I suggest we take some air with Lady Henrietta and, after lunch, a little nap. I can send a note to Margaret Pembroke to ask if she is at home for cards in the evening.'

'I have been feeling so out of sorts today I'm not sure I could face a card game vith anyvone tomorrow, even dear Margaret.'

'You get some sleep now and see how you feel in the morning,' said Elizabeth. 'You know how you bounce back from these moods. We are going to be alright.' Then she checked the windows, shutters and curtains against the winter night, blew out the candles, and withdrew to her own room above.

Simon, 17:00

Simon Speke let himself out from Hugh's apartment in Whitehall and took what he reckoned would be his penultimate walk home to Clerkenwell. He might do it again tomorrow night, but after that he would be riding at the nation's expense. Tomorrow would be a long day and he needed a proper meal and a night's rest. He had no money, neither in his pocket nor under the mattress. He thought himself possibly the poorest man ever to lead a revolution. At least the prudent Mrs Holmes had always required rent and board in advance, and he was up-to-date with his payments.

He might flatter Cousin Hugh but he, Simon, was the real hero. What a contrast between this lowly start and the end he imagined for himself. His coffin draped with the cross of St George, would be borne on a simple cart drawn by a pair of donkeys, no just one, through the crowded, silent streets. Hundreds of thousands would turn out to pay their respects, flowers would be thrown from the hushed crowd, white lilies and red stem roses, lying askew on the flag. Old men would lift grandchildren onto their shoulders, so that they one day could tell theirs what they had witnessed. In the mausoleum, his and Kitty's own would join delegations of simple people from towns and cities up and down the land. That would require a few days' warning, after months, years, of preparation in advance of the tragic day. It would have a codeword, to go out by post, triggering simultaneous mourning across the nation.

Long before then, he would have left politics. He would retire at the top, of his own free will, despite the protests. His parting speech would ring down the ages, about the importance of moving on, handing over to the next generation, of learning to say goodbye. They would choose a successor who would be a compromise, a disappointment, which would only serve to highlight what a golden age his own decades of leadership had been.

The mausoleum would be a national monument for the remains of distinguished citizens – he had heard that the Pantheon in Rome was impressive. It would be paid for from the confiscated wealth of the former hierarchy, of course. What would they call it? He had no idea. Names were not his thing. Ideas, language, truth, these were important. Thinking up names exhausted him.

Mrs Holmes welcomed him back, fed him another of her excellent stews, took a long, hard look at his eyes and tongue, shook her head and packed him off to bed as if she had been his mother.

Women. He didn't understand them. Take Ike's Rosa. He only knew the start of her story. She had been born in the seaport of Trinkimali, Ceylon, and named Roshna, meaning bright or shining, or pure of heart, something like that, by her doting Tamil father. But he had died and her mother had quickly remarried. Aged six, Roshna and her four-year-old brother had fled their tyrannical new stepfather. Finding themselves in the Trinkimali docks on the first night, they had hidden on a merchant ship, which had promptly sailed. When the little Tamil stowaways emerged from hiding they were nearly thrown overboard as bewitchments. Females at sea were almost as much bad luck as cadavers. The only thing worse was a dead one.

However, once fed and watered, Roshna had made herself useful, running errands for the captain, Henry 'Lucky' Luxmoore, and had shown a quick facility for foreign languages. The siblings were not put ashore at the next port. A year later, Luxmoore had ended a profitable voyage in London and adopted them both. He had christened them Rosa and Carl, given them his own surname, and presented them as a crowning, exotic present to his childless wife. Spike reflected that nothing in that background explained the courtly polish yet driving sense of injustice that had emerged in Rosa.

Sometime he must ask Ike why his girl was quite so classy, yet so crazy.

Kitty, 17:45

Kitty and Nicholas returned to Blackfriars Stairs in the dark, an hour after nightfall. The boatman was paid handsomely on the Society's shilling.

At home, Mary Jones had grown frantic with worry. By daylight tomorrow, the tides could have her daughter's drowned or murdered body anywhere from Teddington upstream to Gravesend on the estuary. More likely it would never be found.

But her daughter was unrepentant. It had been the best trip, Kitty declared. Nicholas had been a knowledgeable guide and a complete gentleman, upon which confirmation Edward happily offered him the promised Madeira.

The two men stood by Edward's roaring fireplace speculating over the rumour that the Queen and infant Prince of Wales had been smuggled away to France by boat that very day, having left in a convoy of coaches during the night. Edward, whose reliable sources at Whitehall had been adamant, believed it to be true. Nicholas felt it too nonsensical to credit. Who would put the heir to the throne in the hands of England's most dangerous rival?

Kitty waited until after their guest had left to mention the visit to Ranelagh House, and His Lordship's invitation. As expected, her mother could not contain herself. Recriminations about the late hour and the dark river melted into a fountain of gratitude.

'Quite apart from the honour you have done our family by re-establishing a long-lost connection, you will certainly have something to drop into your conversation at Ormonde House in the morning,' Mary said.

Day 3. Tuesday 11 December 1688

Jack, 03:30

The darkness of the Turnham Green camp crushed down on Jack. He was doomed to eternal hellfire. The anxiety was more sickening than the prospect of military surrender to Prince William; worse than the fear of battle; or of maltreatment at the hands of brutal victors. This was the misery of having thrown away both his life and his soul.

Who was he kidding, playing at soldiers? Marching back and forth, hither and thither, dragging cannon around, what was there to be proud of? Action for its own sake. It built nothing, produced nothing. Nothing useful, artistic or even Godly. In fact, it was infantile.

As for the next life, he was equally ashamed. He often abused the credulity of others. Only on Sunday he had coaxed letters from his comrades to add weight to his own. It was all manipulation. What would Kitty think of him writing to Elizabeth? He'd sought to whip up rivalry between the two women, callous about which accepted him. He should hold fast to his hopes of Kitty, but last night he had spent long musing on Elizabeth.

He had neglected his mother. He was also lazy. He had only joined the professional, peacetime, standing army to earn steady money for doing nothing. Worse still, he had betrayed his regiment by leaking sensitive information, and the date of its arrival into London.

And then there had been that awful night seven years ago at the mill. Don't even think of that, he told himself.

Lastly, he was disloyal. The Crown's brutality after the Monmouth Rebellion had shaken his faith in this king. Since then, he had been offended by the infiltration of Catholics into court – His Majesty's Jesuit confessor, Father Peters, promoted to the Privy Council last November – and the indulgence of Catholicism preached from Anglican pulpits. He was chilled by the birth of a Prince of Wales to be brought up papist; and scandalised by the replacement of good Protestant army officers with inexperienced Catholics. The ousting of the Earl of Oxford as colonel of his own Blues cavalry regiment this summer, replaced by the King's bastard son, the Duke of Berwick, had particularly stuck in Jack's throat.

However, that was no excuse for treason during an invasion. If the King could hold out against outrageous ill-fortune, so could the kingdom, and so must he.

Jack told himself he had time to mend his ways. He would report himself this morning to the Colonel. He could pray more earnestly for his mother and all the friends he could think of.

He said his prayer for peace of mind. Amazingly, it still worked. He didn't deserve it, but a calm came over the tent, his mind settled, he recalled that Christ died to save those who truly repent. And repent he did. He slept at last.

Jack presented himself at the Colonel's tent at first light and asked for an interview when convenient. The camp was packing up all around him. The tentmaker, tent-keeper and his assistant had it down to a fine art. Jack was allowed to wait in the porch. He stood back as boxes passed out of the entrance and the quartermaster's team began to dismantle the structure around him. A few minutes later he was called through.

'Lieutenant Wilson,' said the Colonel. 'An unexpected pleasure. What's on your mind?'

'I sent three letters with the pouch on Sunday, before communication to family was withheld.'

'So did several others.'

'Yes, but theirs did not say we would be arriving back at the Tower tomorrow. I should have told you then and there, on Sunday evening.'

'And what do you conclude from this?'

'That I am a self-centred, disloyal fool and not worthy to be an officer of His Majesty's, let alone a gunner in the Royal Ordnance.'

'Hmm,' said Shere. 'Let us walk together, Mr. Wilson, and see how the camp is coming down. Otherwise they will strike this tent about our ears.'

Jack followed his commander out into the early daylight. They strolled in silence down a row of hitching wagons and out among the lines of cannon.

'First,' said Shere, 'this matter of the information leak. You are right to confess. I hope you will do so sooner in future. But it is not severe, indeed, it changes little. We should have come to this question anyway, eventually. By speaking up now, you make our rehearsal today all the more important.'

'I'm afraid I've betrayed your confidence, Sir.'

'Wilson, you have not betrayed my confidence. You have had some of our best ideas about how to handle a mob. In all likelihood, you will come up with more today. Your job this morning is to think what, if anything, we should change if we do prove to have lost the element of surprise.

'Second, and more serious, is your wider claim that you are a self-centred, disloyal fool and not worthy to be an officer. Put that out of your mind. Every sentient man has such thoughts from time to time. And we need thinking men in this regiment. Do you imagine that I never have doubts? Did I accuse myself of foolishness in my career? Of course, many times. Can you imagine the feelings of absurdity, of waste, of disloyalty, to spend thirteen years of your life building a naval base in Tangier, thirteen years, only to spend the fourteenth destroying it? The strategists who ordered that it be demolished could not even remember why it had been wanted in the first place. Queen Catherine's wedding gift to Charles II? Poisoned chalice, more like! None of us is perfect, from the King down to that cart boy. Wherever we are in life, we will see our superiors do stupid things. If less than half of what the men and women around you are saying is self-centred, disloyal foolery, you are already in good company.'

He paused, and Jack realised he was expected to speak.

'But I have begun to doubt the justice of our cause. I am corrupted. I am only interested in me.'

'These are confusing times,' said the Colonel. 'Not one of the choices we are offered is optimal. We cannot know the consequences of any, what they may lead to or which is the lesser evil. Yet we must keep our self-respect and integrity. But 'twas ever thus. As Socrates says in Plato's *Dialogues*, only the soul can be beautiful. And we each are responsible for our own soul. Therefore, we turn to God and to each other. We surround ourselves with men and women of sound judgement. A man who can come to me of a morning and say what you have said *is* of sound judgement. I want that man in my regiment.'

The Colonel stopped walking and turned to face the young lieutenant. 'You are not corrupted. You are not only interested in yourself. And as to whether our cause is just, that is not for you or me or any of us to know for sure. What we do know is that we have sensible orders, from the highest authority. We are to herd this colossus of killing back into its pen. And that is what we will do. You and me and a few other leaders of men.'

Jack was moved. They looked each other in the eye and Jack felt tears in his.

'Thank you, Sir,' he said. 'Yes, that's what we will do.'

Simon, 06:30

Simon Speke stepped out of Mrs Holmes' lodgings and crossed Clerkenwell Green. He collected Ichabod Kingston from the coffee shop and together they strode into the capital which they planned to have in flames by nightfall. They were making history. It was a great time to be alive, better to be young, and best of all to be them. Artists in future years would compete to recreate images of today hung in national galleries with names like *The Speke* and *The Kingston*, adding noble poses, wide gestures and beetled brows, unfurling flags painted in gorgeous colours across huge canvases. Travellers from distant lands would marvel at the accolades showered upon the two of them by a grateful nation and return home to name seas, archipelagos and mountain ranges in their honour. There would be Simon stars, and Ichabod craters on the Moon.

They walked fast because they were due with the print apprentices in The Crown at eight, and Spike wanted to be early to catch the postbags leaving Lombard Street for country destinations. These last twelve letters would set on course tomorrow night's nationwide orgy of destruction with a last, loving touch. It would be the biggest spontaneous panic in English history – a surprise to all but Hugh Speke, Ike and Spike himself. Once mailed, forever nailed. Unstoppable. This postal shot would be the high point of modern rabble-rousing, the coming of age of the new communications medium.

He would also advance his suit with Kitty Jones. She didn't know it, but she would be seeing more of him after today. Even Elizabeth Forrester would come, craving audience, if not quite on bended knee. That would do him good, to see the snooty bitch apologise, after how ungrateful she had been about her mother.

Some of this he said to Ike, but most he kept to himself. Ike was good for a conversation about consequences, pushing a scenario to its logical conclusion, but he was also a little too elemental. You would want him on your side in a knife fight, but not for choosing women. There would be no Uncle Ike, or Godfather Ike, after he and Kitty were married. In fact, Ike would have to be kept away, also from the levers of power – he might go for years without a bad day, or he could just flip, never to recover.

Side by side they walked to the Lombard Street post office. They were the first in the queue as the postmaster himself was opening up.

From behind them, they overheard a rumour that the Queen and her baby Prince of Wales had fled the capital two nights before and were thought to be in France by now. Spike's heart sank. As soon as they were back in the open, he turned to Ike, 'What do you make of that?'

'Relax, dear boy,' said Ike. 'In a way it would be easier. A six-month-old infant screaming in the night was never going to make your job of smuggling You-Know-Who down river any easier. I'd rather have just him to kidnap – if the story is true. But it won't be. You-Know-Who would be mad to put a trump card like that into Louis' hands. I doubt it's even legal, constitutionally. And his lackies would hate him for it. We must still assume we are grabbing all three. Keep them separate and the King will sign anything we ask.'

A man in the street looked round at Ike.

'You mean You-Know-Who,' said Spike, through gritted teeth.

In silence, they cut up Lime Street past the rebuilt Pewterers' to the Aldgate ward of the City. In Leadenhall Street, they turned down a short passage off the south side, behind number forty-six, to the Crown Tavern. The courtyard was a perfect assembly point for a crowd, as the owner had transferred its coaching function to much larger stables outside the city wall.

About a hundred printers' apprentices had squeezed on to the open apron. Spike and Ike were fifteen minutes early but already Nat's plan of attack, painted on a large sheet, had been pinned up on the handrail of the first-floor balcony by the riot group. Ike pushed through the throng towards the outside stairs, and Spike followed tight in his wake. This was one remaining humiliation for being so short, to be elbowed, blocked and starved of air by youngsters who didn't know who he was.

Simon looked up at the plan for the rioting. The leaders had done a nice job. The first target, just round the corner, would be a joint effort to stiffen the sinews. The well-fortified mass house in Lime Street was the scene of recent preaching against that cornerstone of Anglicanism, the English language King James I Bible. The chapel claimed immunity as the official residence of the Elector Palatine, although that august personage had never been seen there. The mob, suitably fired up, would go on to the Carmelite house at Bucklersbury. The northern mob would then take out the Catholic stall holders at Newgate Market, while the southern division would attack Spike's own place of work, the King's Printing House in Blackfriars. Spike thought he would look by once the staff had fled.

The two mobs would continue to move west, converging on the house of the Franciscan monks in Lincoln's Inn Fields. That would bring the operation into the night, when the second wave of rioters would take over, hopping west to the Spanish ambassador's house in Wild Street while the first wave rested.

Dawn of day two would bring the West End into their sights with Somerset House, the Savoy, Haymarket and St James'. By then every bad boy and girl in the underworld would join in, many as first-time opportunists, rather than true believers. The French Embassy in St James' Square was a natural flashpoint, leading up to the royal chapels in the St James' and Whitehall Palaces. Then the big prizes, the palaces themselves, would be looted. Resistance from the King's side would have been run ragged, overwhelmed by fatigue and the sheer numbers of swarming looters. The militias would join the mob.

The plan had a subtle beauty, starting with attacks on preachers, printers and friars who had taken vows of poverty, which would yield little loot; proceeding to Catholic embassies, which had their own chapels, and where wealthy papists had deposited their plate and jewels for safekeeping; and finally the two Royal palaces – with pickings beyond their wildest dreams.

What the map did not show, but which made it so radical, was that on the evening of the second day he and Ike would emerge under cover of London's own 'Irish Night' panic to sneak their respective squads, each by the back door, into Whitehall and the Tower. By Thursday morning the deed would have been done. The panic would be over, the barricades up and the capital secure. Peace would be restored. The populace would be resigned, united, even grateful. It would only remain for James II from his cell in the Tower, and William of Orange from the suburbs, to concede to the people's demands. What other option would they have?

As eight o'clock struck, Ike led Spike to the staircase and onto the balcony. All faces turned upwards and silence fell, without a need to be hushed.

'Friends,' said Spike. 'The day of destiny has dawned. You need no lecture from me on how important this is. Yes, by tomorrow night most of us will be rich and avenged. But we do not do this for loot or vengeance. We are here for freedom – to reject popery and slavery, to honour our brave forebears and to liberate future generations. From this yard you go forth to light a beacon of liberty that will be seen across Europe and project out to the New World. You have the plan in front of you on the map. By tomorrow night when the barricades go up, we will have the capital in our hands.'

The crowded courtyard cheered. Ike drew his dagger and brandished it. Those who had brought clubs and jemmies waved them too.

Spike continued, 'Now, I ask you to divide into your groups. The first wave for today and tomorrow morning, the second wave for tonight and tomorrow afternoon. Second wavers, feel free to join in with destroying Stamford's Chapel now, to get it out of your system. But after that I want you resting and recruiting. So, let's see who you are. The first wave over to this side and the others over here. Come on guys. This is what is going to beat the militia. We must do the thinking. Discipline will win this.'

The crowd began to move and, in short order, a narrow gap ran down its middle.

'The other thing is this,' said Simon. 'You are not here just for fun. You are the leaders. For every one of you, we need fifty more. By the time the first wave hands over to the second in Lincoln's Inn Fields tonight, we will not be the one hundred of us here, but five thousand. I don't want to see groups of you having fun among yourselves. Spread out as you move. Recruit in the shops and houses along your route. Call down the people who open their windows to watch. This is an easy sell. Our city is a tinderbox. Word of something like this has been on the street for weeks. People just need to know it has started and they will join in. But you must tell them. Is that understood, lads?'

Various shouts came back of, 'Yes, Spike, we get it.'

'No one knows what resistance we will face in the next thirty-six hours. We must assume that some of us will receive wounds, and that a few won't make it, like last month at St John's Clerkenwell. But those who are to die will have done it for a winning cause and their names will be venerated down the years by a grateful nation. Because we are going to win. We have right on our side, and numbers, and surprise, and good tactics. The citizens will rise up with us. At ten o'clock tonight our second wave takes over. The militia will drop from exhaustion, or stand aside, or even join us. And tomorrow, all the major towns of England will follow. Tomorrow night, when the barricades go up, will be our finest hour, England's greatest moment. We will be free of absolute monarchy, free of foreign meddlers, free of popery! Now look lively, fill your pockets and God go with you.'

Throughout this last part, members of the crowd had been whooping and yelping their individual support but now they became a thinking mob, as Spike had imagined it. Streaming out of the courtyard, baying and howling, they stripped battens and bars off the buildings they passed along Leadenhall Street, round into Lime Street and towards the Palatine chapel.

Spike and Ike were left alone as the sound of the pack died away. It had begun. The talk had turned to action. Spike clutched the balcony rail and began to shake. Ike was panting, red-faced and eyes bulging, but he sheathed his dagger and put his arm around him. 'Come on old man, I am due at the Boar's Head to conclude things with the barricade group.'

Elizabeth, 08:00

Over breakfast young Lady Henrietta asked Elizabeth if the two of them would sneak out tomorrow morning to watch the cannon train pass. Her mother was taking her tray in bed and Elizabeth agreed, seeing no harm in it.

Emilia had slept badly. Her heart palpitations, she said. However, she conveyed via Hendriksen that she would be down in time to meet Kitty at ten. Elizabeth waited for the post to come, so that she could go round to Halifax House with her Royal Ordnance news. She asked Hendriksen to tell her, but by eight-thirty the delivery was an hour overdue and they both declared that nothing would arrive today.

So, at a quarter to nine she presented herself at Lord Elland's door. Her predicament was resolved by the postman almost following her through, with apologies for being late. She was shown into the muniments room by Spray while William Elland intercepted the delivery in the hall.

The young lord marched in, gestured Elizabeth to her previous wing chair and himself dropped into the Savonarola behind his father's desk.

One letter was from his father. 'As I expected,' he said, scanning the open sheet in his hand. 'The deal is firm but fair – dismissal of papist officials and withdrawal of any case against those who have gone over to the Prince's camp; both sides' troops to stay forty miles from London – that will mean moving the royal army from Uxbridge, north I imagine; calling a parliament; London to be garrisoned by the City militia; Portsmouth to be under a neutral person, to be jointly agreed (not that French-taught bastard Berwick, if you'll forgive the technical term); and the exchequer to help pay for the Dutchman's army. Papa adds that he will be home tomorrow, in other words this afternoon.'

He paused for a moment. 'Of course, he doesn't know about the Queen and Prince of Wales having gone to France.'

'They haven't!' exclaimed Elizabeth, to whom this was news. 'But that would be insane.'

'Yes,' said Lord Elland. 'Meanwhile, how are you, Miss Forrester? What developments on your side?' And his tone was soft, genuinely interested.

Elizabeth decided to come clean. 'I've not seen this morning's post, but yesterday I had word from Sir Henry Shere's artillery column. I should have told you before. They will come through here about ten o'clock tomorrow morning.'

'Well, that's the best thing I've heard for ages. Two dozen or so cannon and several hundred fusiliers will at last give the King some firepower to back up his position in town. And they won't be forty miles away. He must know that better than anyone. I might have got the message to him if you had told me about it yesterday, but no doubt Shere keeps him informed.' William had stood up and come round the desk and was now leaning against its front with his legs out towards her. 'No news from Jamie?'

'Maybe. I left the house before the postman came.'

A door slammed upstairs and Elland stiffened.

'Well, let's stay in touch,' he said. 'I would offer you breakfast but you have probably eaten. Also, my wife has headaches and… well, she will be disappointed to have missed you.'

Elizabeth rose to leave. 'You have been too kind, Lord Elland.'

'No, no, you must call me William.'

'And please call me Elizabeth,' she said with a little curtsy. 'So, William, I will return if I have further news of interest. Perhaps Lady Elizabeth would like to join Lady Henrietta and me in the crowd when the troops pass tomorrow morning? Lady Emelia may well feel up to it too, by then.'

'That's a kind invitation, I will pass it on to my wife. We will be at home today, at least until my father arrives. And give my greetings to Jamie's mother.'

Back at Ormonde House, Elizabeth found chaos.

The post had indeed arrived, bringing a letter from Emelia's son dated Friday the 7th in Hungerford confirming the rumour. He and Prince George, the King's other son-in-law beside the Dutchman, had defected to Prince William, and were hoping to divert him up to Oxford, where they could offer a warm welcome. But she should write to him in Reading, in case that plan came to nothing.

'He can't, he mustn't have,' pleaded Emelia to Elizabeth, batting the letter with the back of her hand. 'Ze Stuarts vill never forgive us. Ve vill be ruined. Everyzing gone. Elizabeth, vhat can ve do? My whole life has been serving ze King and his older brother.'

'Emelia dear, there will be a settlement. Lord Elland had word this morning from his father. One of the conditions of the settlement will be an amnesty for all who have gone over.'

'No, no. The Stuarts will never forgive us.'

'Dearest Emelia, this is not like you. Calm yourself. Think of the ups and downs of exile and at court. You always bounce back. That's because you are you. Everyone loves you. And the Duke is a chip off the old block. Who knows what opportunities he envisages? The House of Ormonde will be wooed by both sides. What gains it will make! Look, here, he mentions the Duke of Somerset, Charles Seymour, has already gone over, and "I am offered my same position as Gentleman of the Bedchamber if it works out".'

'Vell, *my* heart is viz ze King. Anyzing else is treason. Zese young fools have opened Pandora's Box. Ze only zing holding back ze rabble is ze steadiness of ze King and ze loyalty of ze Tover.' Then she seemed to breathe more easily and said, 'But zose are still solid. Let us put a brave face on matters. Vhat else can ve do?'

'And we have Catherine Jones coming shortly, who can tell us about the Apothecaries' Garden.'

'Yes, ve have Caterine coming, I vas forgetting zat. Let me know vhen she is here.' And the Dowager Countess swayed back upstairs to gather her wits.

Elizabeth was burning to tell Lord Elland that his friend had at last written. His defection was no longer a rumour. Elland must join their side. This seemed almost more important than honouring her commitment to Kitty.

So she was greatly relieved when Kitty arrived on time. She had suggested Lady Henrietta join the three of them in the salon. As soon as mother, daughter and visitor were comfortable, she would seize on an excuse and slip back to Halifax House.

Kitty and Simon, 08:00

Blackfriars being close to the main post office in Lombard Street, the Jones household received their post earlier than most. Kitty came down to breakfast with her head full of possible conversations with a dowager countess, and found a letter waiting. Her father had already left for the print shop, but her mother and grandmother were both hovering. They had read the Hampton Court postmark but been unable to interpret the green wax seal closing the back of the envelope.

Kitty slipped the missive into the pocket of her skirt.

'But… but…,' said Mary.

'But nothing. We have an important conversation to plan, Mama. Now, what will the Countess want to know, and what do I need to say?'

Kitty stepped out of the door of Glass House Yard an hour later, well-rehearsed and planning to read her mysterious letter on her fifty-minute walk. Instead, she found little Simon Speke pacing up and down across the street.

'Hello, Simon. Who are you looking for? Have you been waiting long?'

'I just got here. Been in the City in meetings. I am looking for you. Are you going out?'

'Yes, I am walking over to St James'. I have an appointment at ten.'

'Then I will walk with you, if I may. I too have business in the west end of town.'

'If you can keep up,' she said, setting off at a brisk pace.

'Kitty,' said Spike, trotting along beside her.

'What is on your mind, Simon?' She lengthened her stride further.

Spike saw that pleasantries would be useless. 'I need to warn you. The King's Printing House, my own employer, just there round the corner, is going to be attacked later today.'

'Attacked? Attacked by whom?'

'Rioters.'

'What rioters?'

'The Protestant apprentices.'

'What Protestant apprentices?'

'The apprentice printers.'

'How do you know this?'

'I'm an apprentice printer.'

'I know that, Simon. What I mean is, where did you get this information?'

'It doesn't matter where I got it. What matters is that your family home, your home, is just yards from the target of a riot.'

'We've survived angry crowds outside Henry Hills' place before. A mobile of a thousand was there last month, on the night of the twelfth, coming and going, chanting, breaking the windows, trying their luck. But the Lord Mayor posted a guard and eventually they went away.'

'It will be different this time,' said Spike.

'How different?'

'Because today there are going to be several riots in the City and outside, more than the Lord Mayor can handle. No guard will come. And the rioters will not be a mere thousand, but more, maybe three thousand.'

'How do you know this?'

'It doesn't matter how I know. The question is, if Henry Hills' goes up in flames, the fire may spread. Or a mob that big could go mad and loot the neighbourhood as well. The Apothecaries, the whole street.'

'If you know so much, why don't you stop it?'

'I can't stop it. I tried. That's why I'm telling you. You need to go home, get your mother and grandmother out of there, and your valuables.'

'What do you mean, you tried?'

'There was a meeting. Of printers' devils. About a hundred. A firebrand whipped up the lads. I tried to speak.'

'Simon Speke tried to speak?' asked Kitty, as if talking to a small child.

'Yes, dammit. It's the Prince of Orange's *Third Declaration* that's done this. It says we are threatened by Catholics. People must make their choice. The apprentices are coming through the City today and into the west end tomorrow, pulling down anything remotely Catholic, and Henry Hills is on the list for today.'

'They won't be doing anything tomorrow,' said Kitty.

'The ball is rolling. It can't be stopped.'

'Ha!' said Kitty.

By now they were approaching St Clement Danes and it was Spike's turn to ask the questions.

'Why Kitty? What's happening tomorrow morning?'

'The Royal Ordnance is due home tomorrow morning. Twenty-six cannon, a hundred and seventy gunners, guarded by four hundred fusiliers.'

'What!'

Kitty saw that he was shocked. 'The artillery train will be back in the Tower by lunchtime, if they haven't been delayed massacring printers' devils.'

'How do you know this?'

'I saw them go. I counted.'

'What I mean is, where did you get this information about tomorrow?

'It doesn't matter how I know.'

'They must be stopped.'

'The ball is rolling, they can't be stopped,' Kitty was enjoying this.

The pair walked on in silence past Somerset House.

'It's Jack Wilson, isn't it. He wrote to you.'

Kitty did not rise to the bait but asked, 'Why do Protestant printers' apprentices hate the Catholics?'

'We must regain our sovereignty,' said Spike.

'Has it got anything to do with God?' asked Kitty.

'God?' said Spike.

'The God of love? Do Protestant printers' apprentices know anything about love?'

Spike looked up at Kitty, striding along, so intelligent and straight and sure. She was beautiful all the way through, he thought. He loved her. He had loved her since he had first seen her three years ago helping out with the *Gazette* at the print shop of Thomas Newcombe Junior in the Savoy. That was before Edward Jones had bought it, when he'd still been only the manager. On almost Spike's first day as an apprentice, he had been sent on an errand to borrow some typeface. There she was, standing among the presses, counting the next batch to be carried to the collating room. Focused, unselfconscious, perfect. And here she was, asking him about love. With no idea that she was asking a man of destiny. Unless this business with the artillery train was true.

'Kitty. Stop,' he said outside the precinct of the Savoy.

She stopped. He placed himself in front of her. He was going to tell her he loved her.

Kitty was gazing past him, 'What is going on down there?'

His words stuck in his throat. He looked at her and his inadequacy overwhelmed him.

'Look,' she gestured through the Middle Savoy Gate. 'Is that part of your riot?'

'No,' said Spike, still facing her. 'They're not due here until tomorrow. Tonight at the earliest.'

'Well, what is that?'

Through the gateway, the Jesuit School and Seminary, which had closed in October, was being set upon. In broad daylight. By maybe twenty people Kitty did not recognise. At the military prison beyond, the Dutch and English rebel officers were being released. Rioting had started spontaneously in the West End.

'Let's ask,' said Spike.

Kitty was already heading down to the group and he hurried to catch up. A crowd was gathering in the first courtyard. She knew this school building, just across from her father's business. She used to play with the younger pupils. The Jesuit teachers had been kind to her. One of them, Father Stupfer, she had even had a crush on for a while.

'What do you think you are doing?' she asked the strapping young ringleader.

The boy looked at her. 'Who are you, sister?'

At that moment an ornamental chair came crashing out through a ground floor window of the seminary, showering the forecourt with colourful shards.

'What right have you to invade private property?' Kitty asked.

'Every right, Miss Busybody. We are all free now. There are no laws. There is no *private* anything.'

'What are you talking about?' asked Spike.

Still addressing Kitty, the boy said, 'In case you and your dwarf friend haven't heard, the King made off last night to France. His Catholic bitch and spawn went two nights ago. There is no law, the rules from now on are the ones we make.'

'How do you know the King has gone?' asked Kitty.

'Go and look for yourself, if you don't believe me. Whitehall Gate is unguarded. The soldiers are standing around with their hands in their pockets. The flunkies are thieving whatever they can carry.'

The crowd of spectators was growing, some were joining in. Word was spreading like wildfire. Kitty looked at Spike.

'Not one of yours?' she said, gesturing to the gathering mob.

'I must return to the Boar's Head. Will you come with me?'

'Why would I do that?'

'Because I love you, Kitty Jones,' said Spike.

A second ceremonial chair crashed out through another window.

'You don't know the first thing about me,' said Kitty.

'Kitty, you are flesh and blood like the rest of us. You must love someone one day.'

'Well, it's not you, birdbrain,' said the large boy. 'Buzz off.'

A few spectators laughed.

'I'll be late,' said Kitty. 'Simon, you need help, but not from me. Go back and try fixing what you have broken.'

Then everyone ducked as a long bench flew out of an upstairs window, landing on the second chair with a crash. She turned on her heel and marched back towards the Strand.

'Come on, we're missing out,' she heard the big lad shout to the crowd.

Kitty did not care what Simon Speke did. She was furious, insulted. What did he mean, flesh and blood? Well, yes, if he had been James from Ranelagh House. But him? That creep? Mechanically, she continued towards St James' Square. She needed to talk to Elizabeth. Elizabeth would know what to do.

Only as she entered the square did she think of her father, who had been so close, immersed in producing the Monday issue of the *London Gazette* next door to a riot. And what was that about a similar riot in Blackfriars? How could a man so aware of what was happening in the world be so oblivious of the immediate risk to their home? She almost turned back, but it now seemed too far, and Ormonde House so near.

Stepping up to the Ormonde's imposing front door, Kitty promised herself she would stay for just ten minutes. After the pleasantries she would explain the position on the streets outside, the threat to her family, living close to the King's Printer, and her hope to come back another day. She rang the bell. It was precisely ten o'clock.

The porter opened. She was expected.

The household put on a good display. Elizabeth welcomed her warmly and introduced the fourteen-year-old Henrietta. The butler passed her coat to the first footman and led the way up the grand staircase to the salon, which ran across the front of the first floor. Emelia, graciously arranged on a chaise longue that matched the room's Parisan carpet, did not get up when the girls entered, but smiled warmly and indicated for her daughter to sit beside her.

'Lady Ossary,' said Elizabeth, 'I would like you to meet my friend Catherine Jones; Catherine, the Dowager Countess of Ossary.'

'Now my dear,' said Emelia to Kitty. 'Please sit here in ze light and, before you say anyzzing, can we offer you a cup of tea? Yes? Excellent.' She rang a little silver bell on the table beside her. 'Elizabeth tells me you have been looking to branch out.'

'Emelia, Ma'am,' said Elizabeth, 'let me arrange for the tea. And while I am out of the room, I will just pop over to Halifax House with this morning's news.'

'Ah, yes dear, you must. Villiam Savile should be told,' said Emelia.

Kitty looked wistfully after Elizabeth as the latter left the room. However, she thought, the news of the King was indeed serious and Elizabeth would be back forthwith.

'That's a lovely harpsichord,' said Kitty to make conversation.

'From ze Low Countries, like me. Do you play?'

'The violin a little, but such a fine instrument must be irresistible.'

'Last night ve tried some new music from Paris. Composed and published by a young lady of tventy-two. Yes, I see your surprise. Élisabeth Jacquet de la Guerre. Ve should have another foray vhen Elizabeth is back from delivering our news.'

'Is that the news about the soldiers and the cannons marching past tomorrow?' Henrietta asked her mother.

'I don't know about zat, dearest,' said Emelia. 'Or do I?' She touched her temple.

'Oh yes,' said Kitty. 'The cannon train is coming home tomorrow morning. How well informed you are, Lady Henrietta.'

'I remember. Elizabeth had a letter from one of zem,' said Emelia, frowning.

'Well, I will be glad to see them,' said Kitty, surprised at the coincidence. 'We need the forces of law and order now that the King and Queen have fled to France. They are already rioting in the Strand, and I have it on good authority that my home is next on the list, as the mob will sack the King's Printing House round the corner from us.'

'Ze King has fledge?' said Emelia, blinking, and her face began to twitch. 'Flegged? Vedged?'

'Oh, didn't you know? I thought that was what Elizabeth went next door to say.'

'Ze kungf...' But Emelia never finished the sentence. The left side of her face twisted, her eyes rolled, she gave a slurred groan and her hand clutched her head. She tried to stand but fell forward, hard onto her nose and lay still.

Henrietta looked at Kitty.

Kitty looked at Emelia.

Kitty said, 'Henrietta, come with me, we must get your mother some water.'

Trying not to shake, she stepped round the prone figure, took Henrietta's hand, picked up Emelia's little service bell, led the girl out of the room and closed the door. Standing on the landing she rang the bell. Servants appeared above and below.

'Who is in charge?' asked Kitty.

'I am Ma'am,' said the butler. 'Hendriksen.'

'Your mistress has had a fit,' said Kitty. 'Please could Lady Henrietta be taken to her room and be comforted? Someone stay with her. We need three strong men to carry Lady Emelia to her bed. Someone should fetch the doctor. Tell them it's apoplexy. And someone else, if anyone is left, should fetch back Miss Forrester.'

Hendriksen went pale and hurried past them into the salon. He came out white. But he did what Kitty had suggested, quickly allocating the roles. Few doctors would be available at such short notice, he said, so three were sent for, one being Dr James Chase, a name Kitty had heard at the Apothecaries. Other members of staff appeared. The body was moved, carried by three footmen upstairs. It looked to all as if their mistress was dead. Several began to weep.

Kitty tried to soften the blow. 'Until Elizabeth returns, I will sit by your mistress' bedside to see if anything can be done before the doctor gets here.'

Henrietta, on the landing above and looking down the stairwell, let out an awful howl of 'Mama', and the tragedy of the newly orphaned hit home. Everyone felt the paralysis, the stupor, of shock. If they could move at all, a quarter-speed was the most they could force from themselves.

Hendriksen himself went to find Elizabeth at Halifax House.

Elizabeth, 10:20

When Elizabeth left Ormonde House for Halifax House the second time, she took with her the letter from the Duke, Jamie Ormonde, to his mother. Spray showed her to her usual chair and William came down from the floor above.

'Elizabeth. Back so soon,' said Elland, with a mischievous smile. He had a feline quality, like a panther-man one might read about in a forbidden book.

'His Grace has written from Hungerford,' she said. 'It is probably better you see this rather than I try to explain. Lady Emelia will want it back.' She passed him the letter. 'She was horrified.'

William reclined against the desk and read the letter twice. He shook his head and sighed. 'All gone over. Denmark, the second princess and Ormonde. And Somerset too. Interesting times for a beautiful girl like you. Of course, it makes Emelia's situation almost impossible. But the King will have spies. He will know this.'

The front door bell rang. Spray entered and passed William a note. 'Please wait one more second,' he said to Elizabeth, giving her back her letter as he slipped out of the room. Elizabeth could hear birdsong from the square and a girl wailing inconsolably in the distance. Returning he said, 'Your mistresses' position has just got a good deal easier. The King fled last night to France. Apparently he sent the Queen and Prince of Wales two nights before.'

Elizabeth jumped up, 'I must get back to Emelia before she hears of this. The shock could kill her.'

Immediately the bell rang again. Elizabeth, running out, almost crashed into Hendriksen running in.

'Ah! Miss Elizabeth. Exactly. You must come.'

William and Elizabeth exchanged a look.

'I am here if you need me, Elizabeth,' said William. 'We, if you need us.' He squeezed her hand, but she knew what he meant, and liked it.

In the street, Hendriksen just ran. He said nothing. Drizzle, the porter, was holding the door open. Up the stairs they leapt, and now it was clear that the wailing was Henrietta on the top floor. In Emelia's room they found the Countess laid out on her bed, eyes closed, hands crossed across her chest, a weal down the front of her face. Kitty was seated on a dressing stool beside her, tears drying on her cheeks.

'Doctor?' asked Elizabeth.

'Sent for,' said Hendriksen.

'Too late,' said Kitty. 'An apoplectic fit. Could have happened any time. Henrietta saw it too. It was the news about the King that did it. But how can so few words do so much?'

'No, no. Not too late,' cried Elizabeth as she reached over and put her hand under Emelia's her wrist, then on her still-warm forehead and sighed. 'Yes, too late.'

She was transported back five years, to her grandmother's room. Once again, this mystery called death. Once again, she knew what to do.

'It was the last straw,' she remembered. Then she looked at Hendriksen, 'Please could you gather all the staff in the Servants' Hall. I will speak to them. We will need all hands to secure the house, this afternoon. No one is to leave until that is achieved to your satisfaction.'

'Yes, Ma'am,' said Hendriksen, and went out of the room.

'The last straw?' said Kitty.

'His Grace has gone over to the Dutchman.'

'Ah.'

They looked at each other. Elizabeth showed Kitty the letter.

After a pause Kitty said, 'And you should know that there will be rioting and looting across town tonight. The apprentices have hatched something, to start in the City, due in the Savoy tonight or tomorrow morning. One of them told me. But they hadn't reckoned on the King leaving, so there's already a riot in the Savoy and pilfering in Whitehall. And they didn't foresee the train of artillery, which Henrietta says you know about.'

'Yes, Jack wrote. I expect he also wrote to you.'

Again they looked at each other. Something sad passed between them, sad for Jack, he was a nice boy, but their faces showed that neither of them aspired to be Mrs Wilson.

'Kitty, I would be grateful for your assistance. Could you help me write some letters? We must tell the Duke, he needs to be here. And break the bad news to many other people. Can you spare me two hours?'

'Of course, Elizabeth dear. Maybe you should bring Henrietta down. She can sit with me here while you talk to the staff. She needs to come to terms with what has happened.'

'That's wise advice,' said Elizabeth. She went up to Henrietta and spoke gently to her about how her mother had been strong and would want her to be strong now. She also reassured Henrietta's lady's maid, Modesty. She placed Henrietta in Kitty's care, saying that if a doctor came in the next ten minutes Kitty should deal with him. She went on with Modesty to the Servants' Hall.

Nine members of the household were seated at the scrubbed refectory table, Hendriksen at the head and Mrs Cross at the foot. They stood up when Elizabeth walked in. She gestured to the maid to take the tenth chair and asked them all to sit.

'Last night Lady Emelia was uncomfortable. Her nerves were tight. This morning she received two pieces of bad news, more terrible to her than to you or me, and something snapped. I will not hide that news from you, you will know it soon enough anyway, but I want you to take it calmly. It will not affect your positions here, nor how you will be treated in future. However, it does mean that we must all show the highest standards of conduct towards each other and the outside world for the next few days, if we are to hold together.'

There were murmurs of approval around the table.

'The first news was a letter from His Grace. He was writing on Friday evening from Hungerford. He confirmed to his mother that he went over to the Prince of Orange two weeks ago. George of Denmark and the Duke of Somerset too.'

She paused but they appeared to know it already. There were appreciative grunts for having it out in the open.

'Zis vas exactly vhat M'lady feared,' said Hendriksen.

'The second news was that King James and his family have fled to France.'

Sharp intakes of breath were heard from several servants.

Hendriksen spoke again. 'Zis is vhat M'lady feared most. She said it vould kill support for His Majesty more zan anyzing.'

'Perhaps the first news triggered the second,' suggested Drizzle.

Elizabeth bowed her head. 'I'm sure His Grace would have considered the consequences when he made his decision. As I say, he was in excellent company. And he has been promised he will keep his previous rank in any new arrangement.'

'When will the funeral be?' asked Modesty.

'We cannot wait for the Duke, or for his sister. They may be a week away, counting the delay with messages. The Duke is probably at Reading now. We can get the sad news to him. But he is not necessarily free to come immediately. And should Lady Derby trust the roads from west Lancashire just now? And Lord Charles, in Italy, is even less likely to get here. I propose we do it as quickly and quietly as possible. Maybe even tomorrow, if the Abbey will help out. All of you who wish can come, leaving a minimal staff.'

'Of course we will,' came from various parts of the table.

'Meanwhile, we must expect widespread rioting in the City and the West End. I don't think it will reach us here, but just in case, all valuables need to be inventoried and locked away today. If we are attacked, it was not us who took things. We are like a big family, and we trust each other. Nevertheless, at a moment like this, control is better. We must not be suspected of having stolen anything if His Grace arrives too late.'

The Servants' Hall was filled with appreciative murmurs.

'The point is, in case the house is looted by the mob we should be able to prove that nothing was missing beforehand. That no one took advantage of Lady Emelia's death. And the front of the house must be shuttered, fortified and drabbed-down as best we can. We will need boards, nails and dirt. Hendriksen will be in charge of this. These are extraordinary times and it is simple self-protection.'

'What will you do Ma'am?' asked Mrs Cross.

'I will be here tonight to help make arrangements. And I will attend the funeral tomorrow if it can be then. But I must also see that my own parents are safe. Covent Garden is in the direct line of the riots.'

'God bless you, Ma'am,' said Hendriksen. 'Vith His mercy, ve vill manage until His Grace comes.'

'We have a busy afternoon ahead. I suggest we go up together to Lady Emelia's chamber now and individually pay our last respects. Then Hendriksen can sort you out while Henri, Kitty Jones and I sit in the salon and write letters.'

Jack, 09:00

The artillery train left Turnham Green down the Brentford Road. Shere wanted to see how the four-across formation worked. The fusiliers flanked the front half of the caravan and the baggage followed in two lines, unprotected for now. In the wider half, signallers were posted down the line of cannons after one-third, two-thirds and at the back. The cannon pairs were matched by size, so that the horse teams were side by side and the internal columns were the same length. This gave a parade-ground effect and seemed easier on the animals. Perhaps they were better distanced from the heels of those diagonally across and suffered less from flicked-up mud and stones as they went along. It wasn't an issue for Jack and Terry, who had been put in the leading pair.

Jack recalled the Colonel's 'big gun that can advance facing forward', for which some Italian had once shown designs. But without such a wonder of weapon-making, the outcome of an artillery charge was easily imagined. Harnesses would break, horses would panic, the formation would be lost, with those on foot left behind. Anyone who had seen cavalry in action knew that. An image came to Jack of ancient Egyptian chariots, lightweight, two-horse affairs, with wide axles and low centres of balance and a swordsman or archer beside the driver. Useless against the Red Sea but possibly rather good at dealing with mobs.

The Brentford Road led towards Hammersmith, wide and straight, being directly along the old Roman highway. Blood's Pioneers had done a good job of dumping local stone into the worst of the ruts and potholes. In one section they had taken down a fence, gate and gateposts where an innkeeper had encroached on public space to make a waiting area for coaches. But no trees had been felled and the cavalcade passed easily wherever brick buildings stood facing each other.

After Chiswick, Colonel Shere asked that three pistol shots be fired from the back of the artillery column, to test the arrangement for stopping the convoy. It worked rather well. Then he split the whole caravan into two, with the cannons and fusiliers going ahead at a quick march, to see if they could rate four miles an hour without the baggage train. They could. Finally, he tried an emergency stop with the cannons going at four miles an hour. He, the adjutant and the major fired the pistols themselves. Although everyone was braced for the test, it still took forty yards to come to a standstill and several teams wound up in neighbouring fields. The problem would be solved if the front echelon counted forty paces from the pistol shots, before they expected those behind to be able to stop.

The guns re-formed and tried again. As they approached Hammersmith, Shere sounded the emergency halts to let the baggage train catch up. The solution worked perfectly.

It was at that moment that an express messenger from the King's main army at Uxbridge rode down the line, calling for Colonel Shere. He handed him a sealed order and waited for a reply. The Colonel appeared to read the message several times. Then he told the messenger to wait. He trotted his grey out into a stubble field, evidently deep in thought, and dismounted. The baggage train approached and halted after its own three-shot signal repeated down its line. Shere still did not return or even move. Finally, he slapped his hat on his head, led his horse to a low wall and remounted. Then he trotted briskly back and said, 'Gentlemen, we shall go through Hammersmith to Brook Green with the musicians playing at the front after all. Give us what you plan for the morning. Let's cheer ourselves up. Normal march for the cannons, so the baggage train keeps up and we all stick together. Quartermaster, at Brook Green I will want a tent pitched and guarded and all officers to meet me there for a council of war at a quarter past noon.'

To the messenger he added, 'You have done your duty. You are dismissed.'

'Do you have any orders for me, Sir?'

'No, Ensign. But I suggest you return to Uxbridge.'

The convoy passed Hammersmith village green to the strains of *Sir Edward Nowell's Delight*, an unsuitable quick march. Jack was wondering what his Colonel had up his sleeve. He was again struck with foreboding.

It was the same dread that had swamped him earlier. Someone was in trouble, perhaps himself, perhaps his mother, perhaps Kitty. He felt it across his chest and as a queasiness in his stomach. It was the fear a small child has when it loses its parent at the market. Or the scalp-crawling nightmare of a traumatised veteran. The Colonel's news was bad. Perhaps someone close to him had died. The tune's quick tempo clashed with the slow marching speed of the wagon train, mocking Jack's show of confidence, pitted against his misery within.

Simon, 09:20

Spike was running down the Strand. What a moment, to have no money for a cab. He felt his plan wobble a second time. The King gone? This was much worse than just the Queen and Prince of Wales. The news, along with his information about the artillery train and the fusiliers, could change everything. On the other hand, the Royal Army was leaderless, which was close to his and Ichabod's intention.

He had to find Ike before the latter left the Boar's Head. If the barricade group had prolonged their briefing, his partner in crime might still be there. Otherwise, it was anyone's guess which way he would be headed – to Blackfriars, or on some mission of his own.

At Temple Bar Spike was overtaken by a trumpet outrider preceding three Privy Council carriages speeding east. As these slowed to pass under Wren's new Portland stone gateway, Spike jumped up unnoticed on the backplate of the rearmost coach and hitched a ride down Fleet Street. At last, some luck, he thought. In no time he was up Ludgate Hill and through the old City postern at the top. He guessed correctly that the coaches would turn left at St Paul's Churchyard, heading for Guildhall, slightly north of his destination. He held on to find out what was happening. It would cost him only a minute and he had saved fifteen.

The carriages bowled up New King Street, slowed to cross Cat Eaton Street, then clattered into Guildhall, the City mayoralty. Some aldermen were gathered in the wide yard. The convoy stopped at the grand entrance. Spike hopped off the rear carriage as three elegant Privy Councillors disembarked. He heard one say, 'I agree, Rochester, the Archbishop will have to take the chair,' which made him think that nothing too violent would be decided at that meeting.

He ran back down to Bucklersbury, with the intention of following Walbrook and Cannon Street to the Boar's Head. However, the mob was still busy with the Carmelite house and the rioters spotted him. Pausing in their demolition work, they raised a cheer.

Then Ichabod Kingston came out of the doorless frontage in high spirits, carrying an icon of Elijah and Elisha. 'This is it, Spike. Look at us. The fuse is lit. The revolution has started. Scant pickings here, though – these Carmelites are more cheapskate than the Puritans. But what do I care? Loot is not the point, is it? What am I doing with this thing? Look, I can just smash it. No one cares.' He swung the ancient wood against a corner of the building so that it broke in two.

Spike was horrified. He addressed Ichabod as he would a drunk. 'Ike, listen to me. Simmer down, man. I need your head clear. We have a problem.'

'No, no. They have a problem.' Ike's arm flailed up, past the mass house to Heaven itself.

'Actually, it is two problems. Firstly, You-Know-Who has gone. He can't be kidnapped.'

Ichabod stopped.

'Evidence?'

'Rioting has broken out in the West End. I've spoken with them. It's spontaneous, nothing to do with us, our lot haven't got there. Whitehall knows the King has gone. Also, the Privy Council and other grandees are meeting at Guildhall. I followed them in. The Archbishop of Canterbury is going to chair it.'

'Well, no archbishop's going to stop us. What's the other problem?'

'The artillery train with twenty-six cannon and four hundred fusiliers is coming through to the Tower tomorrow morning.'

Ike looked like he did not want to know. 'Evidence?'

'Kitty says. She has a swain in the gunners. Jack Wilson. I think he wrote so she'd come out and wave.'

'Did she say he'd written?'

'She didn't deny it.'

Ike looked longingly at the mob. He wanted to go back to the fun. 'That's not evidence Spike, and you know it.'

'Ike. You have got to bring forward the attack on the Tower to tonight.'

'Can't be done. They only clean the latrines on Mondays, Wednesdays and Fridays. Tonight, we wouldn't even get through the Iron Gate. Can't you find a way to stop the gunners?'

'I would rather risk it at the Iron Gate than take on an elite regiment like that.'

Ike said, 'Well, I won't. Not on the say-so of some girl you are moping over.'

'Then the Tower won't happen.'

'It will if it can. You have got to stop that cannon train. If it exists.'

'Let's imagine I can find a way. Without capturing You-Know-Who, could we still make the whole plan work?'

'Without You-Know-Who, the rioting will be greater. The panic tomorrow night will be massive in the towns that hear about it, within one day's journey.'

'On the other hand,' worried Spike,' now we have this upstart Council; and the Dutch can walk straight into London.'

'We always assumed the Dutch would come fast. So our timetable still works.'

'I doubt I can organise a battle against twenty-six cannon and four hundred fusiliers by tomorrow morning, when I have no weapons and my prospective helpers are already up to their elbows in loot, on the biggest treasure hunt of their lives.'

'Well, we have surprise on our side. Where would we stop them?' asked Ike.

'It should be within reach of our full mob. But far enough from the Tower that the train can't get covering fire or make a run for it.'

'What route will they come?'

'Knightsbridge, the corner of Hyde Park, over to St James' Palace, down Pall Mall, Charing Cross, Fleet Street and home.'

'St James' Palace fits the bill,' said Ike.

'Yes, St James' is the first bottleneck,' mused Spike.

'Gather your ambush in St James' Square and jump them going down Pall Mall. We can still do it. If you can hold the cannon train, I can still take the Tower tomorrow night.'

'And still divide our forces? I don't want to fight at half strength.'

'Recruit the Savoy rabble. They will have plenty of energy left. We reckoned five thousand. It could easily be ten with this news about You-Know-Who. I will still pick my team at Lincoln's Inn Fields tonight.'

'The lads expect me to pick one too.'

'But they don't know what your target is,' said Ike. 'Tell the wider mob that the objective is the Chapel Royal at St James' Palace, ten o'clock tomorrow with rich pickings for all in the vicinity afterwards. That will bring every last urchin out. Say to your Spartans that the mission is to take and hold St James' Square from the militia tomorrow afternoon. But don't breathe a word of this artillery train nonsense or you'll scare them off.'

'Our teams were supposed to rest tomorrow for operations tomorrow night.'

'Well, yours won't,' said Ike.

Spike's mood lightened and he joked, 'I'd print a newssheet inciting this, if I knew a printer who was open today. I'm going up to Newgate to see how the north group is doing. By the way, don't let this lot beat up Edward Jones' home when they do Henry Hills' place.'

Ike was puzzled. 'Of the *Gazette*? They won't do that. If I don't see you at Lincoln's Inn Fields, wish me luck at the Iron Gate tomorrow night.'

'Good luck!' said Spike.

He could not help but smile as he and his fellow conspirator parted, happy they had done what they did best, conspire.

Elizabeth and Kitty, 11:15

They were in the French salon in Ormonde House. Elizabeth wrote letters to the Duke of Ormonde, the Countess of Derby and their brother, Lord Charles Butler, about their mother's death, checking each text with Henrietta. She offered the only consolation, that the end had been mercifully quick. To His Grace, she added that the King had withdrawn from the country the previous night, following the Queen and Prince of Wales who had gone the night before. To Lady Elizabeth and Charles, she suggested coming to London for a memorial service and asked for their thoughts on dates. She would do her best to hold the funeral tomorrow, hopefully in the afternoon, saying that the Ormonde crypt stood ready for just this occasion. She had a footman send the letters immediately by express.

She also wrote to Emelia's former employer, the old queen, Charles II's widow, Catherine, whom she had met at Somerset House; and to Emelia's sister, Dowager Countess of Arlington, care of her daughter, Duchess of Grafton, at Euston House in Suffolk. The Dowager Countess had told Emelia she was going there when her son-in-law joined the Prince of Orange. These letters were both carefully personalised.

Meanwhile, Kitty started on Emelia's friends, a list which Elizabeth had accumulated over the past three years. These received a standard letter informing them of the sad news; that a private interment had taken place in Westminster Abbey; and that a date for a memorial service would be announced once the wide-flung family had been consulted. Once Elizabeth was done she joined Kitty in this laborious task, and they roped in Henrietta as a third copyist. By a quarter to one, the pile of letters was sealed and ready for dispatch.

The only friends not written to were the neighbours in St James' Square who might attend the service tomorrow, including the Pembrokes, the Halifaxes, Lord Ranelagh and Sir Robert Southwell. These Elizabeth would visit in person during the afternoon, once she knew a time for the service from the Dean of Westminster.

After an hour, Doctor Chase called. 'The King's apothecary,' whispered Elizabeth to Kitty. Hendriksen showed him to Emelia's bedroom but only to confirm death. He did not stay.

'Kitty, I'm so grateful,' said Elizabeth, after he had gone. 'This has not been what either of us hoped for. When will I see you next?'

'What are your movements?'

'Tomorrow, after Emelia's service, if it can be arranged that quickly, I'll go to my parents. I'm worried about them in this rioting. Let me send you a message when I know. Perhaps we can meet at Maiden Lane tomorrow evening.'

'I would love that,' said Kitty. 'Your own plans will now change. But an hour together would certainly ease my mind.'

So they left Hendriksen to arrange postage of the remaining letters and parted on the doorstep.

Elizabeth, 13:00

Elizabeth continued alone to Westminster Abbey. She took with her a small purse of gold sovereigns from the housekeeping. Funerals in national cathedral-mausoleums at short notice cost money, she imagined, even small ones.

At the Abbey the Bishop-Dean's chaplain was disdainful. The King's departure had caused the Council meeting to be moved from Whitehall to Guildhall in the City. The Lord Bishop was an exceptionally busy man. Who did she think she was? Elizabeth explained. At the Duke of Ormonde's name the chaplain recanted. Indeed, he was late taking the Bishop his afternoon repast. Would Elizabeth accompany him into the City in the episcopal coach? He might even direct her through to the right rooms. The Mayor and Aldermen were using the newly built Mayor's Court, so the Council of Lords Spiritual and Temporal had taken the Council Chamber.

The coach was full with the chaplain, Elizabeth and two servants to carry the large luncheon hamper. It swayed up Whitehall through the open and unguarded gates, past scenes of petty thievery, up to Charing Cross. The Strand around the Savoy was crowded with rioters, but after that they had a clear run to Guildhall.

In no time Elizabeth was in the Council Chamber lobby. Dr Thomas Sprat appeared torn between an aversion to female minions and a thirst for palace intrigue. Curiosity won. He asked Elizabeth to accompany him while he ate his lunch in the anteroom, off the top of the wicker crate.

'Miss Forrester, *such* an unexpected pleasure. Will you eat something yourself?'

'Thank you, My Lord Bishop. I have no appetite. I'm afraid it's bad news.'

'The King fleeing to France? Quite, quite. High tide was one a.m. Perfect for a covert flit over to Vauxhall. Are you sure you won't have some chicken? Or a spot of this German wine? From Alsace, Riquewihr, so floral, so delicate. They go well together.' And he took a generous swig from his *façon venise* goblet.

'No, Bishop. It's about the Countess. She died this morning.'

The Right Reverend Dr Thomas Sprat spluttered and choked.

'I am arranging her funeral for the family,' continued Elizabeth. 'It must be tomorrow. There will be a small contribution, if you can make it happen.' Elizabeth hefted her purse just enough to make it chink, but kept it close.

'But how did this tragedy come about?' He was still clearing his windpipe.

'The news of the King's departure. Apoplexy. But everything is under control. We just need to set a time when she can be laid to rest with her husband in the crypt. Tomorrow afternoon at, say, three o'clock?'

'Oh heavens. Dear Emelia. I knew her in her heyday. Nothing stopped her. No one could resist. Of course I would be honoured and delighted to officiate.'

'She spoke fondly of you, too, My Lord. But what time can we bring her for burial?'

'Tomorrow, fortunately, we are moving this Council back to Whitehall. Privy Council Chambers. Proper facilities. More convenient for everyone. So I will be nearby. Not too early in the day, or late in the afternoon. We have a convention of Rural Deans in the Abbey from three, up from Rochester.' Sprat was eyeing Elizabeth's purse. 'What about half past eleven? I'll give the eulogy, the least I could offer. She deserves much more. And we'd be done and dusted in time for luncheon. No, make that eleven o'clock.'

'Can you recommend someone to arrange the coffin and a black carriage at such short notice?'

'A Mr William Russell set up nearby this year, offering such a service, calling himself an under-taker.'

'How can I contact him?'

'My chaplain will know. And we have a man who can go round.'

'Could he ask Mr Russell to meet me at Ormonde House for four o'clock today?'

'Yes.'

'Then we are agreed,' said Elizabeth and pushed the purse across, which clinked over the uneven wickerwork. 'May I humbly suggest that the crypt be opened and swept this afternoon? We don't want any last-minute hitches.'

'Of course,' said the Bishop, taking the money, acknowledging its weight with a nod. 'Tell my chaplain to come in for my instructions.'

Elizabeth felt a little giddy as she rode back with the priest, the servants and the wicker basket. She sensed the respect her fellow passengers now showed her. She had glimpsed a male world of power and government that few women beyond the King's close circle had ever witnessed. It was as unprepossessing and venal as she had supposed. She needed some air. Reminding the chaplain to send round Mr Russell, she had the coachman drop her off on the corner of Charing Cross and walked down Pall Mall back to St James' Square.

Now for her verbal invitations. She called first at Ranelagh House, but the Earl was away, expected later in the week. She left a note, more in hope than expectation. Sir Robert Southwell was in town, but out, and there she left the same. The French Ambassador, Barillon, gave his apologies, due to the current flux in state affairs. At Pembroke House, the pregnant young Countess Margaret was at home, but Thomas, the thirty-two-year-old eighth Earl, had gone to the same meeting as Bishop Sprat.

'The King called a Privy Council for this morning in Whitehall,' said Margaret.

'Guildhall,' said Elizabeth. 'I just came from there.'

Lady Margaret frowned. 'No. The King said Whitehall. But with this mysterious Withdrawal of His Majesty, as they call it, the Archbishop wanted to reassure the Lord Mayor and Aldermen. And now Thomas writes asking for a bag as he is likely to be sent to the Prince with the Council's Declaration. I don't know when the dear man will leave, tonight or first thing tomorrow. It may take him days. Certainly not available before Friday. But he was delighted to see the back of

King James. Of course, Emelia felt differently, but I am still surprised such news could kill her.'

Elizabeth then felt obliged to explain the earlier letter from the Duke of Ormonde, about his going over to the Dutchman.

'Such timing, that Jamie Butler,' said Margaret. 'Luck of the Irish. You will have written, of course, and he will hurry in. Let me see. Tuesday today, Wednesday, Thursday, Friday. So, Friday afternoon too. Please ask Hendriksen to let us know the moment he's in town.'

Countess Margaret was so encouraged that the Ormondes and Pembrokes would be on the winning side that she agreed to come to tomorrow's funeral, despite her husband's unavailability. 'At least someone of rank should be there to see her off.' Adding, rather too late, 'And to support the good work you have been doing, dear Miss Forrester.'

Elizabeth then crossed the square to Halifax House. Spray opened the door and let her into the hall with an unaccustomed solemnity. 'The Marquess returned an hour ago,' he confided, and disappeared into the library to announce her. Elizabeth sensed the household was on its best behaviour.

A rustle of skirts came from the stairwell and a figure, presumably Elland's wife, appeared round a curve, looked at her, pressed her handkerchief to her mouth and retreated. Seconds later a door on the first floor slammed.

Spray shimmied back into the hall and bade Elizabeth 'step into the muniments room'. He followed her and placed a matching wing chair from near the door next to one in the centre of the library, from which rose George Savile, first Marquess of Halifax. William stood up from leaning on the desk. It was three o'clock by the mantel timepiece.

'Miss Forrester,' said Lord Halifax. 'My son has vouched for you. I have been away ten days. Please take a seat and tell us the local news.'

Jack, 12:00

The Artillery train halted at Brook Green for its lunch break. The horses needed water and the sergeants a chance to chew over their new formation. Orders were issued forbidding any fraternisation with the locals and guards were posted. Once the canteens had a stew going, the Colonel quietly collected his officers and withdrew into the tent the quartermaster had conjured up.

'Gentlemen, an hour ago I received news that will spread through the country like a furze fire, and I want us to be the ones to tell the men, before anyone else does. It included an instruction from our Commander-in-Chief, Lord Feversham, which I may decide to ignore. I can do this because, fifteen days ago, His Majesty himself, face to face, gave me a direct order to the contrary, which in my eyes still takes precedence. I will now lay the facts before you and ask your views, before making my decision. That decision will be final, and I will expect you to obey it.

'This is the dispatch you saw me receive, verbatim:

To Sir Henry Shere, Colonel, Royal Traine of Artillery.

Order to disbande ye Traine and Regiment of Fusiliers.

Sir, His Majesty the King last night privately withdrew Himself to France, whither He sent His young ffamily on Sunday. This morning I received His Order in His owne Hand from Whitehall not to resist ye fforeign Army.

You are to disbande ye Ordnance Traine and its escort of ffusiliers. Do not return to Barracks. Do not surrender to ye Enemy. Each must slip away to their own Home. I now retire to a private Liffe in attendance on her Majesty, Dowager Queen Consort Catherine, currently at Somerset House.

Written at Uxbridge Camp, ye 11th day of December 1688.

At 8 of the clock.

Feversham, Commander-In-Chief.

He sniffed and let the text sink in.

'So gentlemen, your thoughts?' He sniffed again. 'Questions?' Another pause. 'While we remain in this tent you may speak freely. However, I will then make my decision and, once we leave, I want no quibbles.'

The consternation was total. For a full minute no one spoke.

Eventually, Shere broke the silence himself. 'All right, since the cat seems to have got your tongues, let me ask you a question. Starting with you, Major. How do you feel about being disbanded without pay or notice?'

'Terrible, Sir.'

'What about you, Captain Exe?'

'The same, Sir.'

'And what will the men think?'

'Nasty thoughts, Sir,' said Major St Clair, and several officers chuckled.

'Correct. Now, what will the people of London think if we abandon our cannon and ammunition to any Tom, Dick or Harry who wants them, and disband our men without pay?'

'Worse thoughts, Sir?' came a different voice at the back, but this time no one laughed.

'Correct. And what will the people of London think when they hear that thousands of soldiers have just been disbanded in Uxbridge, a few miles from their capital, without pay and without disarming them first, and the King has washed his hands of them?'

Jack's blood ran cold. 'The mob will rise, Sir,' he said. 'The people will panic. It will be that state of nature speculated about by the ancients.'

'Correct, Lieutenant. Not to mention Hobbes and Locke.'

The silence in the tent belied the images flashing through each man's mind. Pillage, revenge, petty scores settled. Families caught up in an orgy of looting and destruction. Jack noticed several others pass a surreptitious hand over their faces. Why didn't someone say it? It was so obvious.

'We cannot disband, Sir,' said Jack. 'We cannot do it.'

'Correct, Lieutenant. Does anyone disagree?'

There was another long pause.

The Colonel continued, 'So, you are thinking, what is our justification? How can we disobey an order from our Commander-in-Chief? It is simple. My last, as I say, direct, face-to-face order from His Majesty was to take this fighting unit back to the Tower of London. Until he comes and tells me otherwise, that is what I propose to do.'

Murmurs of assent rippled around.

'Last chance to object.'

Silence.

'Then we agree. I now order you to disobey the order of the so-called Commander-in-Chief. I take full responsibility. Any questions before we go out and tell the men?'

'What does that make us, Sir?' asked Captain Exe.

'As of now, we are the only thing standing between London and what Mr. Wilson eloquently calls that state of nature speculated about by the ancients. So, back to your troops. Tell them everything. They will pick it all up by nightfall, if not along the way, then from the flames on the eastern horizon. We start for Hyde Park in thirty minutes. Adjutant, Major, Mr. Wilson, I'll see you back here in ten minutes for the Lieutenant's thoughts on a question I posed to him this morning.'

Exe made a lewd licking gesture at Jack with his tongue as they left.

When Jack returned to the tent after briefing his troop, a coach had pulled up beside it. He drew the canvas aside and the Colonel called him in. Three men he did not recognise stood with the three officers he did.

Colonel Shere said, 'Your Lordships, this is Lieutenant Jack Wilson. Lieutenant Wilson: the King's Commissioners, milords Halifax, Nottingham and Godolphin, returning to Whitehall from Prince William of Orange in Hungerford.'

Jack gave his best salute and the three Commissioners bowed slightly.

'Mr. Wilson,' said the Marquess, 'the Colonel has told us of your role on Hounslow Heath. Nice work, though unlikely to be recognised.'

'Well, My Lords,' said Shere, closing his conference. 'I had hoped you would overtake us like this, on the road. Thank you most sincerely for stopping by. I must not detain you further.'

Jack held the tent flap aside, then sprang to the carriage. He had the step lowered before the footmen realised what was happening.

After the coach had pulled away, Shere said, 'They didn't know the King had fled. They were thunderstruck. If I hadn't had this order from Feversham to show them, they would not have believed me. Anyway, they confirm the terms I heard from their dispatch rider, sent on Sunday afternoon.

'So, His Majesty saw His Highness' offer before he fled. The compromise they struck was good. Of course, they feel betrayed. Dishonoured. As for Lord Feversham's order to disband, well, the less said the better. At least they are no longer in the dark. Imagine what awaits them. But enough of that. Lieutenant Wilson, your analysis of the question I left you with, please. What do we do if we have lost the advantage of surprise?'

Jack told the other two officers how he had caused a potential security leak. He listed the options if the artillery train faced a proper ambush: continue as planned – parade-style; change route; change timetable; plough through in some defensive formation under locked shields like the Roman tortoise; pick a defensible spot and dig in; or prime muskets, fix bayonets and charge; perhaps bribery; conceivably surrender.

The three listened intently.

'The key point is that these are civilians and our fellow countrymen,' said Jack. 'They are patriots at heart, they love a display, and their mood can turn on a sixpence.'

He concluded that there was no alternative to continuing as planned. 'Whether or not the rabble knows we are coming, the best way is to push through as if nothing is wrong. Not to fight back, not to stop for the wounded. Because to stop would be fatal. I feel that the crowd will stand aside if the column comes on at a decent pace, four abreast, playing music. We will pass like a hot knife through butter. But I cannot be sure.

'Looking at the route, our biggest risk is after the Strand, at Temple Bar, where the road narrows after St Clement Danes. If the flanks take the pedestrian side gates, a four-column train would fit through. But if the mob should catch us there, we could never hold formation. So we should probably stop in the Strand and scout ahead.'

'Thank you, Lieutenant. Security leak or no, we would have needed to think this through. We three will ponder it further. You are dismissed. On your way, please find the quartermaster and tell him he can strike this tent.'

Jack passed on the instruction, then rejoined his troop. They were in the line, ready to move off. 'Everything sorted?' asked Terry Jones.

'What is this, the Spanish Inquisition?' asked Jack with a smile.

'Not now the King has gone. But who were the three gentlemen in the coach?'

'The Marquess of Halifax and two other lords. His Majesty's commissioners heading back to London to propose terms. They were due at court this afternoon. Their express reached the King yesterday evening. It was meant to sound hopeful but maybe came across wrong. Well, that's my guess.'

'I know the feeling,' said Jones with heart. 'Misinterpretation. If you think you have a problem with English, don't even try it in Welsh.'

'I hear it is a great language for poets and lovers,' said Jack.

The horses were in their traces, the axles had been greased and the mud chopped off the big wheels on the guns. From old familiarity, each team of animals took the strain and together gave a small jerk to break the friction. With a creak of leather and jangle of brass the convoy moved off again.

Jack mused aloud on how the movement from standstill to half a mile an hour is the hardest. Once you have momentum, things seem to roll along.

'We have a Welsh proverb for that,' said Terry, '*Dye-parth gooeyth ew eye thechrye* – starting is two-thirds of the work.'

'I never got to Wales, yet,' said Jack.

'It's a land of contrasts. Giants and fairy-folk. Dragons and flower-maidens.

Obdurate mountains around green valleys. When you see a drystone wall running across a barren hill, think of the men and women who built it. A hard-scrabble life, clearing pastures, walls made of necessity from the rocks lying within. When you see a Welsh shepherd, think of his tough wife and his children, dragons all of them. We have another proverb, *Oorth gick-yor ah bra-thee my car-yad un mag-ee* – while kicking and biting, love develops. That's the story of the Joneses.'

'I have a particular interest in Joneses, Terry. A girl in London. Who are the Joneses?'

'It's a simple thing, Jack. Before you English came, our father's given name was our surname. Jones means son of John. And we had a lot of Johns, seeing as he was the disciple whom Jesus loved. Ieuans and Iowans and Ioans and Iwans, or even Siôns. Then this business with a family surname caught on, or maybe you forced it on us. All these Sons of John drew together into Joneses. There's poor ones and rich ones – even an English Earl, I believe.'

Jack marched on in a daydream of Kitty. He dared to imagine Edward Jones as a father-in-law. Jack was not so proud as to expect Kitty would take him without her father's approval. She had that Welsh stubbornness, he had seen it from the start. But her father had given her the love and attention he might otherwise have reserved for a son. An only son. Jack knew what that felt like. With a father and older brother whom he could barely remember, dead in the plague, mother-love propelled him. It was a terrible, two-edged blessing but had trained him to decide things for himself. Such self-confidence meant that Kitty, too, would ultimately decide for herself. She could be wooed away, if necessary.

However, Jack would not want to split her from her family. Just as he would not be split from his own mother to take Kitty to wife. He had seen old people rock babies in their arms. The smile of a grandparent cradling a tiny, first-born grandchild was wonderful to behold. Amazement and happiness uncontrolled. Joy welling in the eyes, mixed with surprise at their own surprise. Such a sight he would not want any wife of his to miss.

Some things we cannot know about ourselves until they happen to us, he thought. We do not know how we will feel when a child is born or a mother dies. We have no foretaste of the emotions by the first cot or graveside. It is this thing called love.

Kitty, 13:00

Kitty turned east out of St James' Square when Elizabeth went south. A sense of desperate urgency overtook her. What had she been thinking, indulging in sad announcements? She had to fetch her father from his print shop in the Savoy and bring him home to Blackfriars to defend Mary and Johanna, before the rioters arrived. Running in the street was not her style, but she fully strode out. She blazed through Charing Cross, weaving among the assorted carts, barrows and beasts of burden bringing loot out of Whitehall Palace. Turning into the Savoy precinct, she found the former school for Jesuits was now just a smoking gap. It had been demolished brick and rafter, down to its foundations, in barely three hours. A taxi cab stood outside the print shop.

She intercepted her father putting on his cloak.

'Thank goodness I have found you, Papa. You know about the King?'

'Yes, Kitty my dear, big news. And we will have it in print, despite the apprentices not showing up to work. How was Ormonde House?'

'The apprentices plan to sack Hills' place this very hour. They reckon on a mobile of five thousand. It may spill up the street to us. We need to go home.'

'You saw my Hackney waiting outside. I'll drop you off.'

'You'll drop me off? What about you? What could be more important than protecting our home at a time like this?'

Kitty and her father bundled into the little coach.

'Blackfriars then Guildhall,' shouted Edward to the driver. To Kitty he continued, 'I'm going on to Guildhall. And if Henry Hills is out of the running, all the more reason for me to be with their Lordships. You warn your mother and grandmother, and fend the mob off.'

Relieved as she was to have found her father, Kitty was appalled. 'You'd fend them off better than me Papa. You should be at home to protect us.'

'No, my dear. You will learn that a flair for business, for networking, for being in the right place at the right time, is the most precious asset a family can have. The freedom to manoeuvre which we enjoy today, as a family, is not down to whether we save our trinkets in a riot, but because the *Gazette* is flourishing. The necklaces hang on that. And this newspaper should be a goldmine.'

'Sometimes I think I am losing you, Papa. How can your business affairs take priority over protecting those you love?'

'How can I explain? Imagine the *London Gazette* as one of your plants, say an iris hybrid. Someone took two bulbs, cut each in half and joined them to make something new. Beautiful and unique on God's Earth. That is also something to protect.'

'But the *Gazette* won't be killed if you stay at home.'

'And neither will you, if I don't. Someone is baiting you.'

Kitty thought of Simon. 'In this instance, the question is not death but fear.'

'And I fear for our *Gazette*. We need it to serve the government during this crisis, or the government will kill it off. At the moment, it is Middleton, as minister responsible for law and order in England, who is melded with a private newspaper proprietor, me, to produce the twice-weekly *Gazette*. As Secretary of State he takes half the profits to pay his costs, and the other half goes to us. But who will be the next Middleton? And what will the Prince of Orange have to say about it?'

The cab bounced and twisted through the traffic. Kitty was so angry, she would have stopped the cab and got out, if it would not have delayed her reaching home.

'Or, imagine the *Gazette* as an egg. For three years I warmed it, as Thomas Newcombe's manager. In July I bought him out. Now I can hatch it and feed the chick. And I am doing that. A wholesome broth – first claim on government news, to which I add my own.'

'But Papa, the Newcombes and the Joneses are just printers. Nothing changes.'

'No, no. Newcombe and his father were print shop owners. He's still around, elsewhere, in partnership with Henry Hills. I'm a newspaper man. Kitty, imagine our circulation figures in a few years' time. Our readership will be ten times what it is today. We will translate every issue into French and be read across the courts of Europe. The *London Gazette* will be the staple source of news about these three kingdoms, and about what matters to us abroad. As this country and its colonies grow, so will we. Anyone who is anyone will have to read us. Other papers will come and go at the margin, adding, embellishing. Just today we saw a new one. The *Universal Intelligence*. John Wallis in Whitefriars trying his luck. Tomorrow it will be Dicky Baldwin with some new *Courant* or *Currant*. If they can't try it now, then when? But we will be the indispensable core. Reputations like ours are forged at times like this.'

'Papa, dearest, you know I will help you all I can.' Then Kitty lowered her voice and leant close to his ear. 'But have a heart. Have a heart for me. And a sense of proportion. With the King gone, there is no future for us Catholics.'

'Ludgate for Blackfriars,' shouted the cabbie, and the coach drew to a halt at the top of the hill.

Kitty jumped out and looked back through the window.

'We must continue this conversation,' said her father. 'I love you all the more. I will be home this evening. Make sure our house is still standing.' With a chuckle he banged the underside of the roof with the knob of his stick to signal the driver to move off.

Kitty watched him go, smoothed down her dress and turned towards home. Her father was being ridiculous. The priority must be the safety of her mother, her grandmother and their home. As soon as she was behind the London Wall, out of sight of the main thoroughfare and into Blackfriars, she ran to the entrance of Glass House Yard and stopped.

Silence.

She heard no sound of riot. What if Simon Speke had been ribbing her, as her father had said? No, he had been truthful, she knew genuine emotion when she saw it, however warped. What if he was wrong? Or deceived? What if he had mended what he had broken, as she had challenged him to? No, the King had gone, the apprentices were coming. She had simply beaten them to it.

Whom to warn first? Joneses or Hills? Kitty found her mother and grandmother by the fire in the parlour, knitting. 'Mama, Grandmother, it's bad news. I need you to be calm. Papa and I are both safe and he will be home this evening. But for now, you must drop what you are doing and help me protect the house.'

'Good heavens child. What has happened?'

'The print apprentices have raised a riot against the Catholics and are coming to sack the King's Printing House round the corner.'

'But that has never spilled over to us in the past, dearest. Eventually the Lord Mayor sends the militia,' said Mary.

'This time it will be much bigger. And the militia will have other fish to fry because the King fled to France. Last night.'

'Oh dear Lord,' said Johanna.

'It's a coincidence,' said Kitty. 'Speke was planning this attack anyway. But now the Mayor and militia will be paralysed, and the mob will know it, and everything will be five times worse than before.'

'What should we do?' asked Mary.

'We need to prepare for a siege. No one suspects us. Anyway, we have nowhere to run. I suggest that we gather our most valuable things at the top of the house, close the shutters, barricade the front door from behind and move all the furniture into the stairwell so that the stairs can't be easily climbed. We must work out our escape route in case they get in or set us on fire, from the attic on to the roof and down the back with ropes.'

'But you are talking nonsense,' said her mother. 'Your grandmother can't possibly go climbing around with ropes.'

'Well, if you can think of a better plan, you do it. I must go to Henry Hills to warn him. I will return in five minutes. Don't bolt the door until I'm back inside.'

'What about your father?'

'He will come when it is all over. His parting words were "Make sure our house is still standing". He has gone to be part of history up at Guildhall.'

Mary was incensed. 'He's really done it this time.'

'Edward, Edward. Silly boy, always news, news, news,' said Johanna. 'So, where do we start?'

'Jewellery, family portraits, irreplaceable bits and bobs to the top floor. All shutters closed and barred. Then move anything heavy that can brace the front door into the hall, ready for me to return from Hills.'

'I'm too old for this,' said her grandmother.

'No you aren't Grandmother. This is an exciting day to be alive, and you will talk about it for years to come. Now shake a leg and I will see you in five minutes.'

Kitty lifted her skirts and ran back out into Glass House Yard. She felt the envelope in her pocket, but now was still not the moment. Round into Printing House Lane and she was in the treeless square in front of the King's propaganda hub. All spick and span. No weeds. The building had an imposing facade, re-erected in the modern idiom after the Great Fire, with tall windows and stone facings. For a moment she was unsure. Then she went for the central entrance, under the triangular pediment. Inside the porch, a doorman came out of a little bedroom on the left and sat behind a wooden counter.

'I'm here to see Mr. Hills,' said Kitty.

'Do you have an appointment?' The man looked down at a visitors' book in front of him.

'No, but it's vitally important I see him immediately.'

'He has given instructions not to be disturbed.'

'He is about to be more disturbed than he can imagine.'

'And who shall I say is calling?'

'Kitty Jones, Just take me to him.'

'Edward Jones' daughter?'

'Let's go.'

The man led the way upstairs to the office over the front door and knocked. Kitty pushed past him, turned the door handle and walked in.

At first, she thought the room was empty. At one end was a six-legged *bureau-plat*, the most fashionable and expensive available from Paris, an ebony desk inlaid with tortoiseshell, brass, pewter and marquetry, in the style made famous by Boulle. Papers lay strewn across the surface, but the high back, dark tan, leather chair behind was unoccupied. At the other end of the room was a fireplace with two equally empty tapestry chairs with walnut arms. Kitty looked at the porter, mystified. He gestured to the banquette under the window. Between the scrolled ends, facing the wall with his head on a cylindrical red velvet cushion, a man was sleeping off his lunch.

Kitty realised this was not a sight for the staff. She thanked the employee and signalled him to leave. Once the door was shut, she hurried over and shook the King's Printer's shoulder. 'Mr Hills, wake up, you are in great danger.'

Hills turned with a start. Hearing a woman's voice he moderated his language, but he was clearly furious at being disturbed.

'What is this? Who the devil are you? Why on earth are you here?'

'I am your neighbour, Edward Jones' daughter, Catherine. I have information that may save your life. The King has fled with his family to France. A mobile of Protestant apprentices is at this moment on its way here to destroy your business. The authorities will not be able to save you, or even to help. You must alert your people, gather your most precious things and decide whether to fight, fly or hide.'

'Is this some kind of nightmare? Am I dreaming?'

'Yes, this is a nightmare, the end of days for some. No, you are not dreaming.'

As if to confirm her point, a distant baying drifted into the courtyard from the direction of St Paul's. As they listened it grew louder, more chilling than a pack of hounds in full cry – the howl of a mob whose blood is up.

'And why are you here?'

'Because I have the information. I have it because my father is a printer and I know some apprentices.'

'Yes, but why are *you* here, rather than someone else, someone who also knows print apprentices.'

'Because you and I are both C… C… C, kind.'

'Catherine, you said?'

'Yes, kind Catherine Jones.'

'I choose to hide. At your house.'

'That is impossible. My mother and grandmother are there. I cannot risk them.' Immediately she regretted having let that slip.

'If you don't help me, I will tell the mobile you betrayed them to me. They won't like that.'

'Goodbye, Mr Hills. And good riddance,' said Kitty. She walked smartly out of the office, down the stairs and through the central door into Printing House Square. She was not going down that road with a blackmailer.

The mob was beginning to pour in from the lane on her right. She just had time to sprint across to Printing House Street, straight ahead. However, at the first junction a new mob appeared, or rather the flood tide of fury found a second way in, running at her down Duke Humphrey's from Puddle Dock on her left. She dodged into an alley on her right.

Both sets of rioters saw Kitty escape but found her of no consequence.

Panting for breath, more from shock than effort, she looped round the back alley and came out behind the original van, now packing into Printing House Square. She would have waited to see what happened, but had told her mother five minutes. She pressed to the wall and worked her way against the flow of tailenders, the few yards up to Glass House Yard.

'Thank heavens it's you,' said Mary, letting her in and bolting the door top and bottom behind her. 'We heard them coming and started to do what you said. But we haven't got very far.'

'Where's Grandmother?' asked Kitty.

'Upstairs, moving her favourite stuff to the top of the house.'

'Then it's you and me, Mama. You bar the shutters and I'll work out how to brace this front door. Maybe I can wedge some of this shelving back to the dining room door frame.'

In ten minutes, Kitty and her mother had fortified the ground floor frontage from the inside to their satisfaction. All the while the noise from the mob in the surroundings grew.

As they worked their way up the house, obstructing each staircase with mattresses and bedsteads, an almighty crashing rumble came from the next street.

By the time they reached the attic room, where a window opened to the roof parapet, smoke was rising from the King's Printing House. They had with them under the rafters a table and three chairs, bedding, food and water, the Tompion from the hall, Mr Jones' collection of print marvels, including the *Micrographia* and three volumes of *Herball,* three chamber pots, and sufficient knitting wool and rainy-day entertainments for a short siege. Then they locked and braced the door behind them and settled down to wait.

Kitty had not seen Simon Speke in the mob. She said nothing to her companions about Henry Hills' threat to betray them. Nevertheless, her mind was busy weighing up the likelihood of being discovered.

The two older ladies took a while to settle. When the quarter-repeating clock, which was her father's pride and joy, struck three, her mother quickly turned its chime dial to silent, 'lest it betray us up here' as she put it.

Kitty settled into a corner by the window and reached into her pocket for the mysterious envelope with the green wax seal.

Simon, 11:30

The destruction at Bucklersbury was complete, but Spike was no longer convinced of victory. As the leader, he must show outward confidence. However, inside he struggled to fit narrow events to his vision for a happier, fairer England. He had thought that he, Simon Speke, was being thrust forward by fate as the people's hero, riding to the rescue of ordinary folk caught between two grasping aristocrats. But with the King gone, so had the tension. His Majesty had become the underdog. Instead of clinging to power, he had put the peace of the nation before his own ambitions. Previous sceptics would now beg William of Orange to fill the vacuum. Meanwhile, Spike's rioters risked being cast as the villains.

He had to work out a way of ambushing the cannon train and its guard of fusiliers – by tomorrow morning. However, quite apart from the practicalities, or perhaps he meant impracticalities, of such a proposal, the optics were grim: a mob of ruffians, unprovoked, attacking the one land force of which the English could still feel proud. People would ask why, what had the dear old Royal Ordnance done to deserve it? Eyewitnesses would paint it as a black deed, and the average listener at several removes, or reader of the elites' political news sheets, would condemn it. It would be iconoclasm – not as bad as Oliver Cromwell melting down the historic, irreplaceable crowns of King Arthur, King Alfred and King Edward the Confessor, but almost.

Nevertheless, thought Spike, James II's departure had given him an alibi. If the people's revolution failed, it could be brushed under the carpet. Both victors and culprits could claim it had never been attempted. A spontaneous mob had been whipped up by irresponsible, absolutist James, out of stupidity or spite. Not by the people. Not by Simon Speke. The worst outcome now was an oppressive Protestant monarchy under William of Orange, but better than a Catholic one. While the best outcome would be a negotiated blend, perhaps with a figurehead Queen Mary II, heading a Protestant parliamentary democracy.

The future of his revolution hung in the balance.

He told himself that every cause ever worth fighting for had moments that felt like this. Every successful general had been here. He steadied his breathing. He was up to this. Wednesday night was still more than 24 hours away. He could still roll the dice and meanwhile fill his pockets when they reached the juicier targets.

Spike put the word out to down tools for a briefing before they set off for Newgate Market.

'Lads,' he said. 'We don't want this next lot escaping with their moneybags. There are six ways into that market, and I want a team of you to come in from each. So, work out who you are, north, south, east or west, plus northeast and northwest. The northeast team will need a little time to get in place, so they will give the signal to attack. A whistle will do.'

The mob was pacing itself now, but they marched with pride and, as they went, fresh faces swelled their number. Once he was convinced that the momentum had returned, Spike peeled off into the meat market at Smith Field. Several smithies had gravitated to the enclave, attracted not so much by the word Smith in the name as the constant coming and going of horses, carts, barrels and blades, all of which consumed iron and steel in one way or another.

'I need something to stop cavalry, mounted patrols,' he said to the first blacksmith he came to. 'A cluster-ball of spikes that can be dropped in the road to lame a horse or a man if they tread on it. Lots of them. Any ideas?'

'You mean a caltrop, or cheval trap, I haven't seen one of those in forty years,' said a brawny old smith, perhaps a former foot soldier. 'Some called 'em crow's feet. About the size of a fist. Four iron spikes pointing away from each other. Whichever way it lands, one spike sticks up straight and the other three act as a base. Horses won't cross 'em and riders are terrified of being thrown and landing badly on one.'

'Yes, caltrops. Where do I get some? I mean sackfuls of 'em?'

'No, no, that's a military job. We're all horse and cart lads here. Maybe a knife or two, but no one makes battlefield weapons. Although Freddy over there does arrow tips, mind, ask him.'

Freddy said, 'I'm the last resting-place for arrowheads. They went out of fashion. Blacksmiths' widows give 'em to me.'

'Could you make a caltrop?' asked Spike.

'I could. Two bent bars, welded in the middle and then tipped at each end, that's possible. But it will cost you. Show me the money. If you can't pay for things, don't waste my time discussing them.'

'I'll be back,' said Spike, and moments later he was hurrying after the rioters. He caught up with the northwest team outside the Bell Inn just as a whistle sliced the air from the opposite entrance. A cry rose from all six passageways. Spike saw rioters streaming in from Rose Street on his left, and White Hart Street on his right.

His own target now was to steal some money to pay for caltrops. He watched the stallholders to see who grabbed pouches and purses without trying to save their stock. A pewter seller did just that, despite the value of the wares on display. Spike was the first to reach him, distracted him by kicking over his table, grabbed two ten-pound bags out of his hands and ran weaving back through the throng towards the Bell Inn alley. This was the moment to be short of stature, he said to himself. He could hear the market trader close behind in hot pursuit, until the man was taken down by a couple of printers' devils.

Once in Warwick Lane, Spike moderated his pace so as not to draw attention to himself. He walked out through Newgate exuding innocence, and was soon counting out silver crowns and half-crowns with Freddy the blacksmith.

'Discount for a half-payment up front?' asked Spike.

'No, but some payment now would be nice, in the circumstances.'

'Discount for a bulk order?'

'Hold hard, we still have to make each one, you know. Anyway, I'll be sharing it round the fellow liverymen. An arrowhead is tuppence at the bulk rate, and there's four per caltrop, then the labour is another four pence, and sixpence for the trouble, makes one shilling and sixpence for one. No discount.'

'Thanks. How many can you and your friends make by eight o'clock tomorrow morning?'

'If it works, each would take only a few minutes, as the furnaces are going. For the right money, a smith could do fifty and still get some kip, so with five blacksmiths, two hundred and fifty.'

'Yes, that'll do, I'll want five sacks of fifty. That's three pounds fifteen shillings per sack, so nine pounds seven shillings and sixpence down now and the same tomorrow on collection.'

'Sounds like a good night's work. A thousand arrowheads sold and couple of guineas profit for each of us in the pocket, out of the blue. Sir, you're a gent.'

'No, don't call me that,' said Spike with a smile. 'Neighbour will do.' And he handed over the first moneybag. 'Simon Speke is my name, Freddy. I am relying on your discretion.'

So now he would have the means to stop the cannon train. As he trotted off back towards Newgate to find his mob, he imagined the Royal Ordnance and their escort heading straight into his trap. It would be a city street. Buildings on both sides, the only way forward. Foot-speared fusiliers and grievously lamed horses prancing around in agony, gun carriages and limbers overturning. Pall Mall was perfect, flat, after a gentle downhill slope so that the tail end of the train would come rumbling on, oblivious, then unable to stop, while his 'prentice boys slid in from the side streets to finish the job with open blades. The Tower would be Ike's after all.

The remaining question was what to do with the second bag of money until he paid it over tomorrow morning? He couldn't carry it around all afternoon, and he was too far from home to garner it in his garret. As he turned back down Warwick Lane he noticed the grand, rebuilt Physicians' Hall in a courtyard off to his right. 'I'll leave it for safekeeping with the doctors,' he said out loud to himself, quelling a vague sense of madness.

Spike bounded up the four wide steps and through the double-height Ionic portico into the main hall, unsure what to expect. On his lips was a cock-and-bull story about quartering a few quid with a quack. However, he met nobody. To the left was an oak-lined cloakroom, with pegs for gowns and wigs, a shelf for hats running round above head height, and a similar bench below to sit upon while pulling at boots, beneath which items could be stored. Unable to reach the upper shelf, Simon pushed the moneybag under the boot bench in the darkest corner and was out again before anyone saw him. No one would notice the dark pouch before he returned in the morning.

He hurried back to Newgate Market to retrieve his rabble for their next adventure. The stallholders were running a gauntlet of beatings from exit to exit, unable to escape, having all been deemed Catholics, although most were not. Once again, the red mist of riot had descended and it took Spike many minutes to bring his followers back to earth with the promise of far greater treasures awaiting them in the west.

It was three o'clock when his northern group set off for the Franciscan House in Lincoln's Inn Fields. Once he was sure they were back on track, Spike headed across St Paul's Churchyard to Blackfriars to see what was happening there.

Elizabeth, 15:15

Elizabeth was pleased with her update to the Marquess of Halifax. She had covered: the Duke's desertion; the King's departure; Emelia's death; what little she knew from Kitty of the Spekes' plot, leading to the likely sacking of the King's Printing House; the unconnected looting at Whitehall; and the Earl of Pembroke attending a meeting at Guildhall, which had originally been called for Whitehall.

The Saviles listened with seeming astonishment at such knowledge in a woman.

'But you must be tired after your journey, Sir,' she finished. 'I really only came to explain about poor Lady Emelia and to say that the funeral will be tomorrow morning at the Abbey at eleven o'clock. Lady Pembroke is kindly coming, and our household, of course. But it would be an honour if someone from Halifax House also wished to be there. And Sir, as I mentioned to William this morning, Colonel Shere's Ordnance and Fusiliers will be home tomorrow morning, to the Tower.'

Lord Halifax chipped in, 'Ah, Lieutenant Jack Wilson.'

It was Elizabeth's turn to stare. 'You know him?'

'We met on the road just now. A young man with a future.'

Lord Halifax was famous for his balanced impartiality, notorious even. Perhaps she had been hasty about Jack. He seemed to be moving up as fast as she was.

Lord Elland filled the pause.

'Elizabeth, I had guessed about Jamie's mother. Her butler, calling you away like that. I am truly sorry. Is there anything I can do to help?'

'Thank you, William, I appreciate your offer. Yes, a little later, once the inventory work is finished, I would very much appreciate your advice.'

'Later this year, or later today?'

'Oh, today, most assuredly, if you are free,' said Elizabeth, now recovered.

'For you, I am free. Shall we say eight o'clock?'

'That would be perfect. And what news, My Lord, from the cannon train?'

Lord Halifax said, 'The bad news is that the King ordered Lord Feversham to disband the army, without paying or disarming them; and he has done so. The good news is that the Royal Ordnance has held together. Colonel Shere ignored the order, based on what he considered an overriding command from His Majesty to return to the Tower. Nevertheless, Feversham's action has gravely imperilled us all. Between him and the King, the last twenty-four hours have plumbed new depths of royal recklessness, not to mention moral cowardice. I have rarely been so unimpressed.'

After a pause, he added, 'I will be in Whitehall and St James' Palace this evening and tomorrow will formally advise the Council of Lady Ossary's death. It will be a day of days for us all. Sadly, I will be unable to attend her funeral, and William must stand by me to help with matters. But please convey our condolences. As for the republican plot, tomorrow's Council will quell the mobile, I promise. And now, we must let you go back to your sad duties, Miss Forrester.' He rose from his chair.

Elizabeth glanced at the clock. 'Yes indeed. The man who will manage the funeral is due at Ormonde House.'

She and William stood, and Elizabeth curtsied to William's father.

'This has been most illuminating,' said the Marquess. 'I seem to be meeting remarkable young people this afternoon. I hope to see you again soon, in happier circumstances.'

Elizabeth returned to Ormonde House. She told Hendriksen what time the Dean had set for the funeral and prepared Drizzle for the arrival of a Mr William Russell. Then she went up to see Lady Henrietta. The girl was in her mother's wardrobe room, trying on her clothes. Elizabeth recalled her own fascination with her grandmother's gowns immediately after she had died, and thought the dressing-up healthy. The blow Henrietta had suffered could hardly be overstated. She would need encouragement for many months to come. Either of her two married siblings could take her into their homes. However, Elizabeth knew that

Henrietta would be best-served making friends of her own age, to draw her out of herself. Meanwhile, the wardrobe was one amusement and the service tomorrow would give some comfort.

The under-taker rapped on the door of Ormonde House like a man possessed. His enthusiasm suggested that the Countess would be his grandest corpse in six months of business, and his most profitable. It seemed his assiduous cultivation of the Abbey was paying off.

Elizabeth hurried down to the hall to greet him.

'Welcome, Mr Russell. Elizabeth Forrester. I was the Countess' companion and am assisting the family. Thank you for coming at such short notice. Before we get down to business, are you and your team available this evening and tomorrow morning until midday?'

'We most certainly are, Ma'am.'

'Then let's go up to the salon. The Countess' butler, Hendriksen, will join us.' She was concerned to have another pair of eyes on the arrangements, and to approve the expense.

Once the three of them were settled, Elizabeth continued.

'What can you provide by way of coffin, pallbearers, carriage, flowers for the coffin, decoration in the Abbey, ushers and service sheets at such short notice? What do you suggest for transport for the mourners? What will you charge and how will you expect to be paid?'

Russell recommended simplicity. Time was too short, for example to decorate the Abbey, and no one would be there to appreciate a lavish display anyway. Also, the mood of the times was hardly appropriate for attracting attention, with rioters in the street not so far away. He proposed an ebonised coffin from his stock, with brass handles and screws provided. It could be delivered within an hour of Elizabeth agreeing terms. Tomorrow he would come with a cortège – a hearse and three black carriages, drawn by matching black horses with black feather plumes on their heads. He and the pallbearers would ride with the hearse. Since there would be very few guests, they would not need ushers. This would leave the three carriages for family, friends and staff.

'Lady Pembroke, Lady Emelia's daughter Lady Henrietta, and I will be in the first carriage; Hendriksen and senior staff in the second, and remaining staff who wish to attend in the third. How many places in a coach?'

'Six.'

'Plenty,' said Hendriksen.

Elizabeth said, 'I would like the coffin brought here tonight, for the Countess' maid to dress the body and for the staff to place M'Lady in and close the lid. We will bring the coffin down to the hall ready for your bearers to collect in the morning.' She looked over to Hendriksen, who nodded.

'What about timing?' asked Elizabeth. 'There is no need for you to walk in front of the cortège until we are nearly there.'

'So, ten-fifteen departure?' asked Russell. 'Carriages here at nine forty-five.'

'And the price?' asked Elizabeth.

William Russell took out a small pocketbook and licked the tip of a pencil. 'Coffin, five guineas; flowers, five shillings; six pallbearers, a shilling each; one funeral director, two shillings; hearse, three carriages, horses, drivers, two pounds per team; so thirteen pounds eighteen shillings.'

Elizabeth looked at Hendriksen and countered with, 'Eleven pounds.'

'Eleven guineas,' said William Russell.

Hendriksen nodded.

'We have a bargain,' said Elizabeth as she stood up and they shook hands.

Russell measured the body and left, with promises that he had the perfect coffin in stock. Elizabeth said to Hendriksen, 'Thank you for sitting in with me, my friend.'

Hendriksen gave a small bow. 'It is me who should zank you, Ma'am.'

'Do you think you can organise this end for half past nine tomorrow? And send to Lady Pembroke to be here for then as well? Also, I am expecting Lord Elland at eight this evening. I will need someone to stay up until he has gone home.'

'Yes, Ma'am. Very good, Ma'am.'

'Meanwhile, I will help with the inventory. Three more hours should do it.'

Jack, 14:30

The artillery train marched through the afternoon in its four-column formation without incident. Jack, in the second column, was still on edge, expecting trouble, but found nothing suspicious as they went through Kensington, past Holland House, set back in its own land sloping up to a wooded crest on the left; and past the road leading away to the right to Earl's Court farm. After that came a couple of fields and then Nottingham House on the left.

'Lord Nottingham's wife is young enough to be his daughter,' tutted Terry Jones.

Finally they reached Hyde Park, with its deer harking back to Henry VIII's royal hunting ground, more than 600 acres divided by the river Westbourne. It had been given to the citizens for public recreation by Charles I, in other words, within living memory. Although briefly sold into private hands by Cromwell, Charles II had reclaimed it for the people. So, it was a popular bounty of the Restoration.

Dusk was falling by the time the cannon train had dispersed into its gridiron layout in this large public space. Colonel Shere had debated on which side of the stream to pitch camp. Were the Dutch to his rear more of a danger than the mob to the front? He plumped for the east bank, hoping to keep out any Dutch scouts, but tight to the serpentine bend in the water, between the ancient abbey fishponds, to have some protection from the south as well. Before the light faded, he posted a double screen of fusiliers and had these pickets practice their musketry on targets hung on branches at different ranges and in different directions. The field of fire was excellent if trouble came from town. He would avoid using canister if he could.

Yet, for all the slick professionalism, Jack felt tired and disillusioned. He knew he was missing something. It did not help that the night sky over London was red with the fire of riot. Summoned to the Commander's tent, he found the Colonel, Adjutant Willoughby, Major St Clair of the Fusiliers and Captain Exe all there, along with the Chief Engineer, Sir Martin Beckmann, whose clerk had brought back first-hand reports of the mob's rampage.

'Ah, Lieutenant Wilson,' said Henry Shere. 'We have been discussing your question about losing the advantage of surprise. You said you sent letters to two lady friends in London on Sunday?'

'Yes, Sir. One in St James' Square and one in Blackfriars.' Perhaps this was why he felt so bad.

'I want you to find those two girls and question them. If they have spread the news, they must tell you to whom. It may be harmless or it may be fatal to us. I suggest you go with one trooper you can trust. Does anyone spring to mind?'

Jack had thought a weight would lift from his shoulders. It didn't. Buildings aflame at night brought back ugly memories, too. 'I'll take Corporal Jones, if he'll come. He has a nose for trouble and a sense of humour, and I'd trust him with my life.'

'Captain Exe, can you spare Corporal Jones?'

'A little insolent, Sir,' protested the blond braggart.

'All the better to blend in with the rabble,' commented Shere. 'If something is amiss Wilson, use your initiative. Any problems, you or Jones must get word back. If we hear nothing, we march at half past nine tomorrow morning. If there's an ambush planned, disrupt it. Otherwise, I will need your warning at least half an hour before we go. Understood? We are trusting you with our lives.'

'Understood, Sir.'

'Now, get some civilian clothes from the baggage train. Take one of the Hounslow wagons and a docile horse. You won't be stopped going in – the Bridging Master says that all the King's troops have stood down since Feversham's order, and the militia has stayed at home.'

'We'll need to show something to our own guards to report back, Sir.'

'If you are caught by the rebels, passes would be incriminating. I will have the morning watch informed. Fear the republican ringleaders more than our guards. Any other questions?'

'Money, Sir?'

'Draw ten pounds from the paymaster, I'll send him word. He will need an account of how you spend it. You can do that when we all get to the Tower, if time is tight. Anything else?'

'No, Sir. I'm glad to go. But I still feel bad. My suggestion regarding the musical march should be checked. It feels weak, like some angle I have missed.'

'We will look at it again. Many heads are better than one, Lieutenant. Meanwhile, if you're to catch those girls, you must leave now. It is going to be a long night. Dismissed.'

They saluted each other and Jack bounded out of the tent. He was at least on the front foot again.

He sought out Terry. 'Mate, how do you fancy a night on the town?'

'That sounds like a terrible idea. When do we start?'

'Now. We must change, pick up a civvy horse and cart, and drop by the paymaster. I'll tell you about it on the way.'

'Weapons?'

'No weapons. We are just carters, on the empty leg back into town.'

'Troop,' said Jack to his men. 'Corporal Jones and I have a little errand to run for the Colonel. The Captain has given it his blessing. We should be back before we march tomorrow. I leave you in the capable hands of Sergeant Bull.'

They found an anonymous, ramshackle cart and a sturdy old mare in her full winter coat to pull it. Civilian clothes and a couple of bedrolls came from baggage train drivers, among whom Jack was now something of a legend. The paymaster was expecting Jack, and gave them a heavy purse of coins – crowns, half-crowns, nothing in too high or too low a denomination.

As they were about to set off, Captain Exe walked up. 'Don't go getting ideas above your station, pretty boy. And you, Corporal, keep your hands off him.'

Terry flushed red with anger, but Jack laughed it off, 'We're saving ourselves for you Captain. So, wish us luck.'

'Off you trot, then.'

Terry shook the reins and shortly afterward the cart passed through the two cordons of fusiliers, out over the dark, frost-nipped turf and down towards the oil lamps on a post at the southeast corner of Hyde Park. The trees and rooftops were silhouetted against the bonfire cloud-base. It was going to be a mild, wet night.

'Where to?' asked Terry.

'I'll explain as we go along. It serves me right for trying to be clever,' said Jack. 'First stop, Ormonde House, St James' Square.'

It began to rain.

Kitty, 15:00

Seated in the attic at Glass House Yard, waiting for the mob to turn on them, Kitty broke the green seal on the letter she had been carrying with her since breakfast.

> *Hampton Court Palace, Mon., 10th Decr. 1688*
>
> *My Dear Heart,*
>
> *In this sea of troubles, I have at last found an island of consolation. Was it not sweet desire, when we first gazed upon each other in the garden? Was it not a miracle that we found each other again? Was it not trust and clarity and purity when we confessed our faith?*
>
> *I think of our eternal moment, holding hands so briefly. Yes, that was bliss. That was a love beyond.*
>
> *Whatever my tribulations on the road, I will write to you nightly until I see you again, so help me God, for the good it does my soul, for the purpose it gives my life. Your man, James*

A wave of hot emotion crashed over Kitty. It was all she could do to stay on her chair. She would either faint to the floor or float away. The seed her beautiful gardener had planted in her heart germinated, rooted, sprouted and burst forth in one single, easy, flowing caress. She threw back her head and bathed in an explosion of happiness.

When she opened her eyes again, the letter was still in her hand, she was still in the attic room at Glass House Yard, and her mother was looking at her curiously.

'Are you quite all right, Kitty?'

From outside the building, borne on the smoky breeze, came a distant chant of 'Heave, heave,' and then a second almighty and prolonged crash. They were reminded of their predicament, of being barricaded in a house next to a rioting mob who would tear it down if their Catholicism were revealed.

Kitty took a deep breath, 'Never better, Mother.'

'I'm sure your optimism defeats me,' said her grandmother. 'I have rarely seen a worse day than this.'

Johanna had given Kitty the excuse she needed to turn the conversation away from herself, 'Tell me your happiest memory, Grandmother.'

Old Mrs Jones took the bait with alacrity and claimed several competitors for that title. For the next twenty minutes she reminisced, and Kitty heard barely a word. The girl was chasing down the many thoughts which James' letter had set running. Every word he had written was true. Yet how could he know? How could he be so bold? Was this the letter of a man or a demon lover? If a man, how could he make himself so vulnerable? Was it all in her mind? If any other suitor had written those words, she would have laughed and tossed them aside.

But no other man was placed to write like this. With everyone else she knew there were screens of privacy, veils of dissemblance. Her feelings for her parents, friends and neighbours, even the print employees, were encrusted with a history of petty slights and vanities, shyness and selfishness, and little white lies, often in layers, excused by forgetfulness, soothed by forgiveness, or at least tolerance, a need to live and let live.

Here was an untarnished relationship, as yet free of even a single mistake. A love at first sight. A complete stranger. Kitty barely knew his name. James. James who? No, she told herself. It was madness. It may have happened, but it could not last. Kitty reread the letter and shook her head. Her mother had just taken up the theme of happy moments, and her gesture was misread.

'No need to be high and mighty about it, Catherine Jones,' said Mary.

But Kitty wasn't listening. She was resolving to seek out Nicholas Staphurst at the Apothecaries. Nicholas knew who James was. She would visit as soon as the mob left. But maybe Nicholas had fled town. He was only the part-time librarian. He must live somewhere. She would track him down. A caretaker was always at Apothecaries' Hall, even if council, staff and members couldn't travel in because of foul weather. He was bound to have an address, or know someone who knew it.

But then, what matter who James was? He loved her and she loved him. Surely that should be enough. They had met under respectable circumstances. He was a friend or protégé of Lord Ranelagh's, a well-educated, well-travelled young man, a budding cavalry officer. What was it he had said? 'I have urgent orders to fly down to Portsmouth… my cavalry regiment'? Nevertheless, a girl needs something to tell those who live outside her screens and veils – neighbours, friends, even parents who had not yet met James, who would wish to prepare for conversation with him, or with each other about him. No, she could say nothing until she knew who he was. But the temptation was there, to run shouting his name in the street.

'So sorry, Grandmother, I was listening to the riot,' she said after a while. 'Do you think it is getting quieter?'

They all leant forward, attuning, and at exactly that moment a furious banging on the front door made them jump with fright. All three put their right forefingers against their lips, with eyebrows raised, so that Kitty almost laughed at the comical sight. But then she heard a voice below shout, 'This house is locked up, nothing here lads. On to the rendezvous at Lincoln's Inn Fields.' It sounded like Simon Speke.

A pang of gratitude twitched in Kitty. She had not believed Simon when he had claimed to have spoken against such violence in front of the mob. She had doubted his claim to be an organiser, but now she had heard the voice of a leader. It was too late for him to earn her affection, but she felt a grudging respect.

The women remained silent for several minutes. The hue and cry eventually died away and Mrs Jones senior asked, 'Who do you think that was?'

'Simon Speke, the print apprentice,' said Kitty.

'Sounded a nice boy,' said her mother.

'No nice boys in a mobile like that,' said Grandmother.

Through the window the smoke from the Printing House was thinning. The building had been designed to resist conflagration and was not ablaze. 'I'm going over,' she said. 'They won't be back. Then let's get the house ship-shape for Papa.'

Heedless of her mother's protests, she worked her way down the blockaded stairs, unbarred the front door and stepped into the street. Blank and printed sheets of paper had been caught by the updraught of smaller fires and were feathering down like the aftermath of a pillow fight. She walked round to Printing House Square where the transformation was complete. The whole front of the building had been pulled out into the quadrangle, so that bricks and masonry were splashed across the expanse of cobbles. It was a doll's house with the front open, exposing Mr Hill's first-floor office. The banquette was in the street, crushed under the shattered pediment, while the Boulle desk, with its drawers pulled out, and the tapestry-backed walnut chairs, now upturned, still clung to the room.

As she watched, the door to Hills' first floor office swung open and a figure stepped towards the void. It was the porter. She yelled a warning, 'Get back, it will fall.' The man's weight tipped the unsupported floor further. Just in time, he grabbed the door frame while the massive desk slid away, launched into the air and landed with a sickening crunch beside the pediment. The porter and Kitty looked at each other in horror.

She called up. 'Are you all right? Can you get down?'

He shouted back, 'The stairs are still here. I thought I might do something to help.'

'If you want help, we can ask at the Apothecaries. I'm going there now.'

'I'll come with you.' A minute later he had picked his path through the rubble to Kitty. 'I will need somewhere to doss down tonight.'

'Did Mr Hills get away?' she asked.

'Yes, Miss,' said the porter. 'Thanks to you. He owes that to you. The back exit. He took his son and was leaving for France. St Omer he said, if friends asked.'

'He's no friend of mine. But this destruction is outrageous. Did you recognise any of them?'

'Only that Speke boy. Our lot must be rioting elsewhere, they didn't show up for work. But many of their mates were in this mob. They knew how to break a press, good and proper. Frames bent, platens kicked off, tacks poured down the screw and wound in. A dozen good presses that will never work again. The Gaffer is ruined. Some of us old 'uns won't work no more neither.'

As they set off, a second figure came running out of the ruins. It was Simon. The porter spat.

'Hello, Mr Speke,' said Kitty. 'What are you doing here?' She smelt alcohol on his breath. 'Looking round the place for old times' sake?'

'Waiting for you, Kitty. I knew your curiosity would get the better of you. Mine too. Neither of us could resist, could we? But you must listen to me. The hierarchy is finished. You need to join us. Your like will be swept away.'

'This is madness, Simon,' Kitty said, waving an arm at the shambles. She began to walk off, but Speke tagged along. 'We're going over to the Apothecaries' Hall, perhaps we can get you something for your brain. Anyway, I thought you were headed for a rendezvous in Lincoln's Inn Fields.'

'Ah, so you heard me outside your house just now.'

'Yes, and I should say thank you. Thank you. There, I did. Acts of good can evidently come in evil packages. I'm sure my father will show his gratitude.'

They turned into Water Street.

'I don't want your father's favours,' snapped Spike. 'By this time on Thursday, he will be seeking mine.'

'You are forgetting the cannon train, Simon.'

'The cannon train will be stopped, scattered, panicked. Without a shot being fired.'

'Ha! Are you some kind of magician?'

'Yes, I will cast my magic in front of them. All those fusiliers and gentlemen and horses will be plunging in agony. Then we will fall on them and they will be swept away, winnowed, chaff in the wind.' It sounded like the alcohol talking.

They were almost at the entrance to Apothecaries' Hall and Kitty stopped. 'Simon, listen, you are sick. You need help.'

The printer's apprentice grew furious at her tone. 'Speke's Spikes. Just remember, when your father comes crawling for favours. Caltrop. That is his password to tell me you have unlocked your heart to me.'

'Goodbye, Simon.' Kitty turned away, muttering under her breath, 'Crawling. Heart. How dare he talk to me like that!' She wished him dead.

She and the old Printing House porter walked through the Apothecaries' Hall, calling out 'Hello'. They found a warder, but he seemed to have difficulty understanding them.

As Kitty had guessed, Nicholas was not there. Nor was the Master. However, once the functionary had gathered his wits he told them that the Society's library opened to liverymen on Wednesday mornings and, accordingly, Mr Staphurst could be expected to appear at nine o'clock tomorrow.

'Do you know where he lives?' asked Kitty.

'Sister,' said the warder airily. 'Even if I did, I would not be at liberty, scribberty, bibberty, to disclose that without his permission.' And he gave a high-pitched laugh, as if he had been funny.

'Of course,' said Kitty, meaning rather the opposite. 'I can wait until the morning. Meanwhile, I wonder if you have any charity in you to help this friend. The King's Printing House has been demolished by the mobile, and I think he lives there.'

'Man, that sounds awful,' said the dopey concierge to his fellow. Focusing again on Kitty, he replied, 'Yes Sister, he can stay with us while he sorts himself out. Just the job. Come with me, man, you probably need to relax. You're just in time for a new smoke we're trying, a virile little hemp from Ceylon, previously unknown. Yes, yes, they will have a name for it in India. Captain Knox brought it in this week. He calls it bangue. You know Knox? Knocks you out!' and he dissolved into giggles as he floated away. But she had done her best for the old man's shelter.

She returned to Glass House Yard. She and her mother set about straightening the Jones nest and when Edward came home to the hall clock chiming half past five, everything was back in its place. They all repaired to the candlelit parlour. Edward sat next to his elderly mother to hear her story first.

Johanna was full of life. 'Kitty said to choose what mementoes to rescue. So, there was I, up in the attic with the wrong ones, thinking of all I had left behind. Then came the bang on the door. How we sprang out of our skins! Really, I have never been so grateful to be alive as this evening, with my things around me. Imagine, Edward, I was resolved to climb out on the parapet, to escape over the roofs. I rediscovered the ten-year-old in me.'

Next came Mary, who protested his absence. 'Really, dearest, to leave my virtue to the mercy of a mobile, with no man in the house to protect us, what were you thinking?'

Edward brushed this aside. 'I knew Kitty would cope, otherwise of course I would have come. But what a clever daughter we have. And look how bravely you yourself rose to the challenge, Mae. Here we are together, still alive, some of us more than before, eh Mother?'

They all hugged and laughed and felt like the family they'd been a long time ago.

'Now, Kitty,' said Edward, 'you show me what has happened to our friendly competitor and I will tell you what I found at Guildhall.'

They lit two storm lanterns and made the short walk to Printing House Square. In the dark, the site looked even more desolate. Where lights would have been burning at windows, only room-sized coal-black sockets stared back at them. What had been the kingdom's greatest hive of information activity was now a drained honeycomb.

'Shed no tears for Mr Hills, Papa,' said Kitty. 'He tried to blackmail me into us hiding him at home.'

'Well, he misjudged you there. But I weep for any man whose legitimate business is literally pulled down around his ears, and all for prejudice and lies. The *Gazette's* own apprentices are out with the rioters tonight, and I wouldn't want them turning on me.'

It began to rain.

'He did heed my warning. That's how he got away. The caretaker said so.'

'You were right to do that. There, but for the grace of God, go we.'

'What will happen to his contract with the Crown?'

'That's what I wanted to tell you. The Council of Peers and Bishops have drafted a proclamation. It's to go in tomorrow night's *Gazette*. It is big news, mass news, so they want leaflets and posters too. Look at this,' he gestured to the wreckage in front of them, 'they can't use the normal channel. It's a simple question of what's possible. They'd probably prefer a different printer anyway, to distance themselves from the King. But now there's no embarrassment in switching.'

'That would be such a coup, other Crown contracts beside the *Gazette*.'

'We are not there yet. Landing the royal patent has always been a murky business – fought behind the scenes by the most ruthless printers of each generation. In my grandfather's day, John Bill, the Nortons and the Barkers were always taking each other to court. Then came the Newcombes. Thomas Junior may have sold us the *Gazette*, but he is still a sleeping partner to Henry Hills. And Henry will be back – the patent is just too lucrative to ignore. Imagine. Exclusivity on all Bibles, Testaments, psalters, books of common prayer, including translations. And on all government statutes, with notes or without, abridgements of statutes, proclamations and injunctions. It's a franchise to make your eyes pop.'

'Let's look around,' said Kitty.

They took their lanterns and ventured in. Shadows twisted and leapt away, then crept back up behind. The blackness tried to envelop them. The building creaked and the smell of burnt paper became almost overpowering. Edward pointed out the organised flow of production through the large site. They found the proofreaders' rooms on the north side of an inner courtyard, where the natural light had to be good; windowless storerooms full of ash and collapsed shelves, where religious texts had been stacked to the ceiling; and on the first floor, a directors' dining room where a clean, third-full port decanter stood on the dust-strewn table, mute witness to the restraint of a passing looter. The fires had burnt themselves out, but raindrops still hissed on charred timbers. Quantities of fine paper had been scorched, while some reserves of blank stock appeared undamaged, although more rain would change that.

'This is someone else's problem,' sighed Edward, as they left the building. 'I have heard one can insure against fire, but probably not for anything like this.'

'Insure against fire?' asked Kitty. 'How does that work?'

'You join a club, pay them a bit each year, most of which they save for a disaster. They send firefighting tenders if a member's place is alight. If it does burn down, the club funds the rebuild. London has a couple of schemes like that, although they took a while to set up after sixty-six.' They continued to pick their way across the dark square. 'As for the State contract, we can only wait and see. You and I will go back to Guildhall tomorrow and secure the bills for that first proclamation. Even if we must set it with our own hands and print them on the old spare press. Then we will see which side comes out on top, Jacobites or Williamites, but it sounds like we will be cultivating the damnable Edam-eaters.'

'Papa, when we get in, I need to talk to you. Without Mama or Grandmother.'

'Oh yes? About our being Catholic?'

'No, silly. There's a man.'

Simon, 15:00

After the northern mob's synchronised attack on Newgate Market, Spike had detached himself and headed south to Printing House Square. The sight which greeted him exceeded his hopes. Five times more rioters, fifty times more destruction.

This mob had brought its grappling hooks and was pulling out the face of the Printing House. 'Heave, heave', they chanted in unison, and Spike watched the front of a building he knew crash into the square. A human wave of those too near stampeded to safety. Hotheads then dashed forward, keen for first pickings. Fires were lit among the stores of top-class materials and stationery, but the building was brick and stone, standard practice following the Great Fire, and did not all ignite.

Cooler types retrieved the hooks and slung them through the remaining windows. Soon, the whole facade was down, with most of the interior still standing. The temptation to join the pillage returned. Simon's feelings were mixed. The main print room held fond memories. He looked away as skilled hands permanently incapacitated the twelve iron printing presses. Beautiful, helpless innocents that he had greased and oiled as he worked through nights and even weekends to keep the river of public and religious documents flowing.

On the other hand, he enjoyed poking about in offices and corridors that had been off limits to a mere apprentice. The foremen's common room, named in envy as 'The Fannery', the bookkeepers' 'Boudoir', both exotic spaces in his imagination, now shown to be mediocre and grim, even before they had been filled with smuts. One pleasant surprise was upstairs at the back, the directors' dining room. He liberated a decanter of port wine and left it on the boardroom table emptier, for others to polish off. He was likewise cautious about entering the first-floor rooms facing the square, for fear of their collapse, although others did. He needed to be alive, and compos mentis, if this plan was to work.

Back outside, the mob was beginning to disperse. The word went around, as planned, that the next target was a joint one with the northern lads – the Franciscan House in Lincoln's Inn Fields. As they re-passed the end of Glass House Yard, Spike made a little detour and banged heavily on the Jones' front door. None of the rioters followed him. He then stood back and shouted to the shuttered windows, 'This house is locked up, nothing here, boys. Let's head on to the rendezvous at Lincoln's Inn Fields.' A few looked across to him from Water Street, puzzled, but he smiled back, shrugged and beckoned as if to others further down the cul-de-sac, round the corner, to follow him back to the main throng.

But Spike was unable to tear himself away. It was what he had warned of in Tower Hamlets, 'love and all that idiocy.' Kitty would grow curious once the mob had gone. She would dart out to see for herself the damage she had been unable to prevent.

So, he crept back into the ruins of the King's Printing House to lie in wait. He was dragging a comfortable chair from the Fannery to the porch when he heard her call. She had spotted someone, up on the floor above. He watched from inside the building as the ceiling under the front first-floor office sank sickeningly and Mr. Hills' large Boulle desk crashed into the square in front of him. Whomever Kitty had been talking to did not fall with it. Rather, he ran down the stairs, and out into the square. It was the watchman who seemed to live in the porter's lodge.

The two were talking, Kitty so slim and four-square and guileless, and the porter gesticulating up at the ruins of Henry Hills' office. Spike had to try again to win her. He ran out. My God, he thought, she makes even this rubble-heap look regal.

Her tone with him was gentler than before. His ruse of banging on her front door had worked. He begged her to join the cause, for her own good.

But she insulted him. 'I'm sure my father will show his gratitude.' As if he, Spike, was a beggar. She mocked him for daydreaming, sneered at him as pitiful.

He lost his temper. She stalked off into the Apothecaries' Hall.

Spike trudged on to Lincoln's Inn Fields. Success with Kitty was now inextricably linked with the success of the action. What had he said? When your father comes crawling… and a password? Crawling. That had been too strong. But from her reaction, it had gone over her head, as it was supposed to. But she would remember his offer later, when she heard how he had stopped the cannon train, when she needed him.

He must clear his head. The next twenty-four hours were crucial. Collect the caltrops, transport them to St James' Square and orchestrate a successful ambush. If he could do that, they would be back on track. And he would have to invent a new task for his snatch squadron, without You-Know-Who in town. They would be disappointed if he neglected to put together a team, if Ike was leading one. What had Ike suggested? Making St James' Square the lynchpin of the battlefield. He began to see the logic. Yes, he would cook up something there.

Facing onto Lincoln's Inn Fields stood a large house with a community of Franciscan monks. No one could miss where the action was. A spectacular bonfire blazed on the open grass opposite the friary, lighting a crowd of some six or seven thousand. Willing hands were taking it in turns to demolish the building. Everything popish and flammable was hauled out, crucifixes, hangings, vestments, hymnals, missals and mass books were tossed into the flames. As for the floorboards, joists, rafters, doors and window frames, the mob stole them all, down to the very stones. People were carrying off bricks in handcarts.

Spike pressed to the front of the crowd to see, hailing acquaintances and gathering news. Evidently this morning's Whitehall mob had come up from the Savoy, much expanded, having chosen this target of its own accord. They'd been looting for an hour before the Blackfriars and Newgate rioters arrived, so the best pickings were gone. The militia still made no appearance. Last month's cavalry incident at St John's was beginning to look like an aberration. No further attempt was being made by the authorities to stop the rampage. The streets were Spike's.

He asked if anyone had heard from the Guildhall meeting. 'The Archbishop and Privy Councillors? The Mayor and Aldermen?'

He was told, 'They called it a day at four o'clock and all sat down together at the Mayor's invitation for a noble dinner.'

A woman spoke up. 'I work in the Guildhall kitchens. The Mayor and Aldermen were all for grovelling to the Prince, inviting him to come to London. But at least they got their letter sent. The Lords spent hours on a cooler version, and then couldn't even decide who should deliver it.'

'The Mayor's lot have an idea what we are capable of,' said Spike, 'even if they don't know the extent.'

Others chipped in. 'They can see that the militia won't be enough this time.' And, 'That's right, Spike, with the King gone, the militia won't know who they're keeping order for.' And, 'I heard the roads in from the west are terrible. The Dutchman won't be here for days.' And, 'It's working out like you said, Spike.'

'I didn't anticipate the King running off,' said Spike.

'What about this special assignment, Spike? Can I be on your crew?' said another.

'Look, Spike, here comes the night mob to take over. What are we doing tomorrow?' asked a third.

Simon Speke felt his hopes rise. The sight of the second shift trickling in over the Fields from the north and southeast, brought his strategy back into focus.

'Fair enough, guys. You remember the plan – next is Wild Street, the Spanish Ambassador's. That will keep the night shift busy. They'll have more plunder there than everything we've seen so far, put together. But the real fun starts tomorrow in St James'. We are going for the French Embassy in the morning. And you know what that means: gold coin, silverware, jewels. Then the Chapel in the Palace, the royal apartments, everything. And last stop, Whitehall. But for an attack on the palaces we are going to need to be fresh. Which is why the Newgate and

Blackfriars lads need to turn in now and get some sleep. Leave the next eight hours to the night boys. They deserve it. They are the ones who'll be missing out tomorrow. This story has hardly begun.'

'What about the special mission, Spike, the crack squad?'

'Yes,' said Simon, 'I was coming to that. Colonel Ichabod and I both have our missions tomorrow. Has anyone seen Ike?'

'He left ten minutes ago. He's picked his men, about fifty I would say. Said he would only tell them the target when they meet tomorrow. They're even keeping the rendezvous and the time secret. He really wound us up. Made it sound like a suicide mission. He's a bit scary, your friend, when he gets going. Some hard cases volunteered, gang enforcer types. He swore them all in, went off into the Fields in a huddle and then sent them to bed. He wouldn't tell them the mission for anything. And God help you if you try to pump one of them for details of the meeting place.'

Good old Ike, thought Spike. He grabbed a passing looted chair, said, 'Thanks mate, just for a moment,' and stood on it.

He shouted, 'What *I* need is not so secret. Comrades, we are here because we are patriots fighting for our rights and freedoms, which means wresting power from the papists and froggies. Bedlam is part of our strategy. But only for the next thirty-six hours. By tomorrow night the politically blind of this great city, which is most of them, will be so tired of mayhem and rumour that they will welcome the stability we can bring by calling off the riots and hunkering behind our barricades to negotiate. So, here's my objective. To take and hold St James' Square against all comers tomorrow. So, we need to be several hundred, even better, a thousand. We will be armed, we will kill and even be killed. The militia will rally at some stage and the cavalry may even produce a have-a-go hero, like we saw in Clerkenwell last month. But remember, they are few and we are many. They are slow and we are quick. They are fighting for a lost cause, for a papist king who has run away, while we have right on our side. Who's with me?' he yelled, punching the air.

A forest of hands went up and Spike had his team to take and hold St James' Square against the militia.

'Swear that you are with me.'

A hundred voices swore.

'You are my Spartans,' said Spike.

'Spikes Spartans,' they cheered.

Simon continued, 'St James' Square at ten in the morning. If you know others of like mind, urge them to come too. The fewer we are, the greater the glory. But we are not proud. The more we are, the bigger the victory. Now all of you get some sleep and bring knives in the morning.'

All this while, the destruction of the friars' house continued. After Spike had finished, most listeners dispersed home but some went back to the demolition. A few still followed him around, asking questions, which irritated him. He needed a plan and these disciples got in the way of thinking. How to transport five sacks of fifty caltrops each across the West End? It would take a horse and cart.

'Spartans,' he said to his most tenacious acolytes. 'I'm going to need a small wagon and a driver first thing tomorrow for a couple of hours, in this neck of the woods, west side of the City. Could you look around for one and bring them to me now, to make the arrangements? It's important.'

It started raining and Spike pointed towards a house with a porch. 'I'll wait in there.'

Jack, 18:20

Jack and Terry pulled up in St James' Square in the dark. Ormonde House was looking strangely drab and the ground floor windows had been boarded up. However, lights burnt at almost every upper aperture.

Terry stayed with the horse and cart while Jack knocked, suddenly conscious that he no longer wore an artillery officer's uniform to do the talking for him.

The porter opened the front door and said, 'Have you brought the coffin?'

'Coffin?'

'It's a box you put a dead body in. Who are you?'

'Who's died?'

'Who's asking?'

'I'm Lieutenant Jack Wilson of the Royal Ordnance, here to see Miss Elizabeth Forrester.'

'Not the under-takers?'

'Has Miss Forrester died?'

'The Dowager Countess. Is Miss Forrester expecting you?'

'No. Please tell her Lieutenant Wilson, in civilian disguise, urgently requests an audience.'

'This is a bad time. Her Ladyship died this morning. We are expecting the coffin any minute. Perhaps you can come back after the funeral.'

Jack drew himself up to his full height, took a step forward and said in a low voice, 'I am here to avoid many more deaths. I need to speak to Miss Forrester. Please tell her Jack Wilson is here.'

'Is there a problem, Drizzle?' a woman asked from the hallway.

'Yes, Miss. This gentleman says he is from the Royal Ordnance, looks like a country tramp to me.'

Elizabeth stepped forward. 'Jack Wilson! Well, come in out of the rain, Lieutenant. What a surprise.'

Jack looked at Elizabeth and was again struck by the aura of intelligence, energy and looks which had first caught his eye in the stable off Covent Garden.

'Did you get my letter?' he asked.

'Jack, give Drizzle your coat and come into the library and dry off.'

'My Corporal is waiting with the horse outside. I must be quick.'

'I insist we discuss this in the library, Jack,' said Elizabeth, stepping across to it. She held the door until Jack had followed her and closed it behind them both.

'Yes, I got your letter. What is this all about? Why are you not in uniform?'

'The cannon train is at Hyde Park. We will come through in the morning. We need to know if we have the element of surprise, or will be ambushed. I should not have told you our movements when I wrote. Since then, all letters home have been stopped. You are pretty much the only person in London who knows exactly when we are coming. Did you tell anyone else?'

'Heavens, Jack! Do you think I am a republican?'

'No, no. I hold you in the highest esteem. But think, did you mention our coming to anyone else?'

'Oh my goodness. The funeral cortège. You will clash with Emelia's funeral procession.'

'Elizabeth, there are other lives at stake here. Maybe even cities and governments and kingdoms. Think, did you tell others we were coming tomorrow morning?'

'No. Well. Yes. The Pembrokes here in the Square, and the Halifaxes. But Lord Halifax already knew – he even mentioned you. How do you do it, Jack?'

'Who else?'

'Lady Emelia, before she died. We are burying her at 11:00 in the Ormonde crypt in Westminster Abbey. We will try to leave earlier to stay out of your way.'

'Who else?'

'Emelia's daughter, Lady Henrietta. But she is only fourteen and has seen no one. But Jack,' she said archly, 'your Kitty Jones knows. Who else did you write to, you big flirt?'

'You have seen Kitty?'

'Yes, she was here this morning when Emelia died,' said Elizabeth. 'Such a pretty girl, quite the brightest, took it very well, a real help. I know what you see in her, Jack Wilson.'

They were standing in front of the fireplace and she moved closer.

'This isn't to do with me,' said Jack, trying to stay official. 'This is about the security of the regiment. Orders from my colonel.'

Elizabeth gave a little shrug. 'Well, I appreciate the visit. I am in the clear. But you need to go and find Kitty. I think she has told others. Come back when you can. I want to hear all about it.'

She led the way back into the hall. Drizzle stood up from his usual chair and went to open the front door. Raising her voice, Elizabeth said. 'We are expecting the Duke on Friday afternoon. I would appreciate an update before then, Lieutenant. But please come in uniform next time, so that Drizzle has a chance to greet you properly.'

Spotting the butler, Jack played along. 'At your service, Ma'am,' he said and gave his smartest salute.

At that moment there was a knock. The empty coffin had arrived. 'Wait a second, gents,' Drizzle said to the bearers.

Jack slipped out past a fine black box with brass handles. The rain had stopped. He looked up and down the square in the dark, but Corporal Jones and the cart were gone. Then he spotted them in a corner and ran over.

'Sorry, mate, had to move for the hearse,' explained Terry from under his oilskin. 'Any joy? Who's died?'

'Blackfriars,' said Jack.

'Who?

'We need to get to Blackfriars.'

'Where's that?'

'Ludgate. Here, let me drive for a bit. I'll explain on the way.'

Down Pall Mall they trotted, their big cartwheels rattling over the surface of random-laid stones, following the route they hoped to march the next morning.

Past the Savoy, where Jack kept half an eye out for his mother. Two sentries stood at the gates of Somerset House. General Lord Feversham must now be hiding in there with his former employer.

'I see he didn't disband the Dowager Queen's guard,' mocked Terry under his breath.

Many pubs and a few houses had bonfires outside. The glow in the sky was strongest around Holborn. 'Probably Lincoln's Inn Fields,' said Jack, but that soon disappeared as they entered Fleet Street. No one gave them a second glance.

After crossing the River Fleet, they slowed the mare and jumped off to walk either side of her head, up Ludgate Hill. She might have a long night of it and they did not want her worn out. Also, Jack was suddenly nervous. Elizabeth Forrester brought out his cool side, but Kitty Jones could render him tongue-tied, if she wished. He led the horse and cart into Glass House Yard in a silence Terry respected.

The Jones' windows were lit up and when Jack knocked on the door, a woman's voice called, 'Who is it?'

'Lieutenant Jack Wilson of the Royal Ordnance, calling for Miss Catherine Jones.'

'Wait there, please, Lieutenant. Kitty, it's a soldier for you.'

A brightness flared in the transom fanlight and a man's voice called, 'Jack Wilson, is that you?'

'Hello, Mr Jones, Sir. Good evening. Yes, it's me, Jack. Can I come in?' There was a pause. Jack added, 'Corporal Jones, no relation, is also here. He will stay outside with the horse.'

Bolts rattled and Edward opened up, 'Good God man, where's your uniform? Have you deserted?'

'No, Sir. Jones and I are here in disguise on instructions from our Colonel, Sir Henry Shere.'

'Well, what can we do for you?' said Edward, happy to leave him on the doorstep.

'I have orders to…'

'Arrest us? What on earth for?'

Jack was astonished that the man could jump to such a conclusion. 'No, good heavens no! I wrote to Kitty last week and gave information which I shouldn't have. I have been ordered to confirm that this will not lead to any unpleasantness when we march into town in the morning.'

'So, you are dressed like that to do some spying?'

Why so aggressive? Jack wondered. 'Investigation, Sir, if you'll permit.'

Edward snorted, which might have been a laugh. But he had only been teasing. 'And you are Corporal Jones, I presume. Printer Jones at your service. If you need to feed or water your horse, we have an empty stable round the back. We Joneses must stick together.'

'That'd be much appreciated, Sir,' said Terry.

'Just follow the wall round. Meanwhile Lieutenant Wilson, you had better come in and explain yourself.'

He showed Jack into the parlour, where he and Kitty had been sitting alone.

'Is this the man?' Her father asked Kitty. Jack wondered whom they had been discussing.

'No, Papa. This is William Wilson's son. They used to live at the Savoy. His mother is still there.'

'I know that. Jack Wilson, who didn't follow in the family footsteps, with father and both grandfathers printers and publishers.' He looked a Jack with affection, visibly resisting the comment that he had grown into a fine man.

Under hooded eyelids, Kitty saw the respect in her father and Jack rose in her estimation.

'Can I speak to Kitty alone, Sir?' asked Jack.

'Kitty?' said her father turning to her and leaving the decision open.

'No, Father, I would rather you stayed. We may need your advice.'

Jack gave a grimace, aware that this was a gentle rejection. However, he pressed on. 'May I sit down, Sir?'

'Of course, man, sit, sit.'

'Kitty, did you get my letter?'

'Yes.' And she blushed.

Jack thought, good, she hasn't mentioned it to her family.

'In it I confided that the cannon train would be coming through to the Tower tomorrow. Did you discuss that with anyone?'

'Yes, absolutely. And now I think of it, you are in great danger. Thank goodness you came.'

Edward and Jack both leant forward.

Kitty evidently decided to tell them all she knew; that the apprentices were hatching something big, an uprising, revolution even; that one of the ringleaders carried a foolish romantic flame for her, an apprentice at the King's Printing House, Simon Speke – at this point Jack could not help but frown, and she noticed it; that Speke had tried to warn her; that she had said the arrival of the cannon train would stop their little game, which had worried Speke. She repeated his idea that the King's flight to France had played into his hands, because the forces of law and order had abandoned the field – witness a mob at the Jesuit school in the Savoy this morning, and at least one huge mob prowling town this afternoon unchecked, which had destroyed the King's Printing Press, as Speke had predicted. Speke had been here to gloat over his old employer's destruction and had hung back after the mobile left, anticipating her appearance. And he seemed confident now that he could stop the artillery train.

'He is drunk on his own quick-wittedness, Papa. He thinks you will be begging favours of him by Thursday night. If I change my mind about him, you will be rewarded. The code word to tell you is caltrop. Do you think it means something? Who or where is caltrop, Jack?'

'I have no idea,' said Jack.

'A caltrop,' said Edward, 'is a fist-sized clump of four steel spikes, pointing away from each other so that however they land on the ground, one spike always sticks up. You throw a few dozen caltrops across a road surface to slow down infantry and stop cavalry. Three prongs will act like a tripod and the fourth slices into your foot. Some say they came from ancient China. The Romans used them against chariots. We did it in Tangier against the Moorish cavalry. The whole purpose is to maim. Awful against horses – stabbing the soft frog under the hoof. Caltrops can lie rusting for decades, the longer they rust the more deadly the wound. So many unintended victims. Soft-shoed old people, barefoot children, livestock. They ought to be banned. Even military boots will be pierced if the point is sharp and enough weight is applied, and the ground underneath is hard.'

Jack exhaled. 'That is horrible.' His unease was justified. 'Yet it would work. Simon Speke, eh?'

'He gives me goose bumps,' said Kitty.

'Horses look where they are putting their feet,' said Edward. 'They bolt at the sight.'

'Fiendish,' said Jack. 'Stopping tomorrow's cannon train will not be like stopping one horse. We plan to march in at twice our normal speed. If the front hits trouble, the back end ploughs into it. If the street is narrow, or there's a crowd of spectators, the results… well, you can imagine.'

Edward had been thinking. 'If you come via St James' Palace, the first bottleneck after Hyde Park is Pall Mall. For best effect, he would let the whole train into the street, then they couldn't break out sideways.'

'We have practised a stop signal,' said Jack. 'But even with everyone ready, and no lags, a train of two-ton cannons at quick-march on paving stones takes forty yards to halt.'

'Meanwhile, the mob is on you, cutting throats,' said Edward.

'You have to find Simon Speke and foil him, Jack,' said Kitty.

'Once he has the caltrops,' said Edward, 'it doesn't matter which way you come, Piccadilly, even Oxford Street, he can keep them bagged and move them faster than you can switch routes. He only has to see you in a bottleneck and he can throw them down.'

'What if you don't march at all?' asked Kitty.

'No,' said Edward, 'that is what he wants. You must get the guns to the Tower.'

'How many of these caltrops are we talking about?' asked Jack. 'How much do they weigh? Will he need a cart to transport them?'

Kitty did the numbers out loud. 'To seed a square yard, with each spike spaced six inches apart. That's six deep and six wide. Thirty-six for a square yard. Three hundred and sixty for ten. But it depends on the shape, if it's not rectilinear it could be less. Two hundred and fifty would probably do it, at a pinch.'

'We are coming in four columns, the train will be more than ten yards wide,' said Jack.

'He would scatter them thinner than six inches,' said Edward. 'What she is saying is that he might not close a road with a hundred, but two hundred and fifty would do it.'

Jack nodded, and Kitty shook her head, as if to say how it was sad that even Jack took advice like this better from a man.

'Each of these things must weigh, what, two pounds?' said Jack. 'You are talking about a quarter of a ton of metal. That's not so easy to hide, or transport.'

Kitty said, 'They went to Lincoln's Inn Fields. I know what he looks like, you don't. I will come with you on the cart and point him out and you can take it from there.'

Jack kept silent while Edward considered. He did know Simon Speke. But it was not a happy memory. Also, he had not appreciated that Speke aspired to

Kitty's hand. If he kept quiet, he might keep his secret. Kitty would come along to make the identification, a rare pleasure and opportunity, and he would have the satisfaction of watching his rival dispatched.

'I see the point,' said Edward to Jack. 'You and Jones must promise to bring her back home by midnight. Her mother will have, er, reservations, about this. But Catherine is old enough to make up her own mind. And the cause is certainly just. Only, I want no mention of her involvement to anyone. You can boast of your achievements all you want afterwards, Lieutenant, but we are publishers of the *London Gazette*, and that means strict neutrality.'

'Always one eye on the business, Papa. But thank you. I will go and tell Mama and Grandmother.'

'You and I will have our little chat tomorrow, Kitty,' her father called after her, as she flew up the stairs.

Turning to Jack he said, 'So, you have been writing to my daughter, eh lad? Well, don't raise your hopes about that.'

Jack was unmoved. 'Let's just get through the next twenty-four hours, Sir.'

A yelp of protest came from the room above and Kitty scampered back down with her mother's orange cloak around her, calling back up, 'Thanks, Mother. Well, that's sorted out,' she said to her father. 'Probably rather good politics right now. And it may help Jack spot me in a crowd.'

Jack thought to himself that he had never seen anything so lovely. The idea of someone failing to spot Kitty in a crowd was as absurd as mistaking the sun for a cloud at noon on a fine day.

Edward opened the front door for his daughter, but then held Jack back to say, 'Another thing you need to know. Tell your Colonel that an expanded Privy Council met today in Guildhall to try and run things. I was there all afternoon. They are drafting a Declaration commending the actions of the Prince of Orange. The *Gazette* will run it tomorrow night. Also, the Mayor has invited the Prince to come into the City. The Council will meet daily until the Prince gets here. London is a powder keg, as Kitty just said. If Colonel Shere has thoughts for the Council on maintaining order, get word to Guildhall in the morning. They will meet at ten.'

Terry had fed and watered the mare and found some straw to rub her down. He had turned the wagon round, picked up a bag of oats for the mare's breakfast, put her back in the traces and was standing ready for action. At the sight of Kitty, he flashed Jack a questioning look.

'I'll explain on the way, mate,' said Jack.

'That seems to be tonight's dance tune.'

'Kitty Jones, this is Terry Jones. Terry, Kitty.'

They climbed up to the driver's bench, with Kitty squeezed in the middle.

'Lincoln's Inn Fields, for a start,' said Jack to Terry. 'You drive.'

'See you back here by midnight,' said Edward as he slapped the horse's rump.

Off they trotted. No one spoke. Jack was conscious of mixing a military mission with unsoldierly feelings of affection.

He imagined that Kitty was wondering how she would spot Spike without him seeing her, and thinking the orange cape might have been a mistake. She seemed happy with Jack but unsure of Terry. Evidently Terry had his doubts about her, for it was he who broke the silence.

'So, Kitty Jones, explain to Terry Jones what we are doing, because Jack Wilson seems unaccustomedly mute.'

'As Jack feared, I let slip to the ringleader of the riots that your cannon train is coming home tomorrow morning. The rascal later told me that he has a way to cause mayhem when you reach town. Father thinks in Pall Mall in St James'. We are going to find him. I am here because I know what he looks like. You will drop me home afterwards and take it from there.'

'Fireworks?' asked Terry.

'Road spikes,' said Kitty. 'They have a name, caltrops. Four sharp points and whichever way they land, one sticks up to go into a hoof or foot. Particularly effective scattered in front of horses.'

'So, we find this guy, drop you home, nick his caltrops and run for Hyde Park?'

Jack snapped out of his reverie. 'He would need quite a load. They are probably bagged up on a cart. Kitty reckoned two hundred and fifty to block a street.'

'Or we could kill him,' said Terry.

'And risk someone else doing the job?' said Kitty. 'No, he is our only lead, we need him alive. By the way, his nickname funnily enough is Spike. Simon Speke, Spikey Speke. Pesky Speke if you ask me. He said something about the Boar's Head Inn. I think that has been their headquarters.'

'In East Cheape. Almost on London Bridge,' said Jack. 'A long way east from the rioting. I wonder why there?'

'Jack,' said Kitty. 'Why are you holding out on us about Simon Speke? He knows you. When I told him about the artillery train returning, I never said the information came from you. Simon guessed it. He said, '*It's Jack Wilson, isn't it. He's written to you,*' and I didn't reply. How did he guess that?'

'You know the riot ringleader?' Terry said to Jack. He indicated Kitty with his head. 'So why is she coming along?'

'Four eyes are better than two,' said Jack. 'She can look one way while I look the other. It will be like finding a needle in a haystack. We have to improve our chances.'

'Also,' Kitty said to Terry, 'I want to come. I want to stop this anarchy. But that doesn't answer my question, Jack.'

'I told you in my letter Kitty that I think about you a lot. Why would I say something to your father that would stop us having this adventure together? This is probably the most fun I've ever had, sitting next to you in these dark streets on an assignment that could change history. Maybe it is the most fun I will ever have. Even if Terry is here to play chaperone.'

'Jack, you still haven't answered my question. How did Spike guess?'

'I don't know. He's not stupid. We must have all crossed paths, the three of us, one of those Stationers' Hall evenings for apprentices and liverymen's children. Maybe he saw how I look at you. Maybe he noticed me get tongue-tied around you. But when Terry and I went to Elizabeth Forrester's this afternoon she also said, your Kitty, and teased me about you. So maybe Simon asked about you and someone mentioned me. I suppose it is general knowledge how I feel.'

'And nevertheless you wrote to Elizabeth, like you wrote to me.'

'Yes. A different letter. Much easier to write.'

'To make me jealous. Pride comes before a fall, Jack Wilson,' said Kitty.

Jack had no answer. It started to rain.

'But,' said Terry, 'Simon Speke would only notice these things if he was feeling the same. He was the jealous one. Otherwise, he wouldn't care who Jack was, would not have put two and two together about the letter so fast, that Jack was out west with the artillery train.'

'It's as old as time itself,' said Jack. 'You get a free spirit like Kitty and the hare-brains of the world dance attendance. I'll bet you've a few more up your sleeve, eh?'

Kitty did not answer.

'Well, there's a silence,' said Terry. 'Plenty of awkward pauses tonight. You two realise that if this Spike guy sees either of you, our caltrops are lost?'

The sky was redder now. The bonfire ahead of them was burning brighter. They were approaching the southeast corner of Lincoln's Inn Fields.

'Stop,' said Jack. 'You are right, Terry.'

Terry called 'Whoa' and stopped the cart.

A man carrying a lantern came down the street towards them.

'Evening neighbours,' said the stranger, raising the lantern to his face so that he could be seen. 'We are looking for a cart for a job tomorrow morning. First thing, for a couple of hours. Would you be able to help?'

'For loot?' asked Kitty.

'No, Ma'am. Sorry, Ma'am, I didn't see you there. No, this is a job for Simon Speke. Somewhere on the west side of the City. He'd pay. Just needs the cart in the morning, not now.'

Jack said, 'Hop up, neighbour. Of course, Terry can help you. Terry, drop us on the corner. Neighbour here will take you to this Simon. Find out his terms and where you need to be in the morning. Then come and fetch us lovers at the west entrance to St Clement Danes church in half an hour.'

'St Clement Danes?' asked Terry as the man with the lantern climbed on the back.

'Fancy new church,' said Jack. 'East end of the Strand. We passed it earlier. Before the Temple Bar. You remember it. Trot on!' He reached over and gave the reins a shake.

'Have you heard anything about the cannon train coming back to the Tower?' he called over his shoulder to the stranger.

'What?'

'The Royal Ordnance regiment that went out west in November. Any idea when they are due back, neighbour?'

'Search me,' came the reply.

At the bend in the street, Jack called 'Whoa', dismounted and caught Kitty by the waist inside her cloak when she jumped. 'Chuck me down the money bag, Terry,' he said, and took it almost as neatly, despite the poor light. 'Now don't let this Simon fellow rip you off. Carts are gold-dust just now.'

The man with the lantern climbed over to the front seat, and the dray set off into the square.

Elizabeth, 18:40

At Ormonde House, the empty black coffin was carried into the hall. With it came a gust of winter air. It was a grim moment, as if death had finally come to call. Elizabeth and Hendriksen took six chairs from the dining room and lined them up, three on each side so the bearers could lay down the heavy box in front of the grand staircase.

Under-taker William said, 'We have brought a stretcher for bringing the body down and can do that now if you like.'

'Please leave it with us, Mr Russell,' said Hendriksen.

Russell bowed. 'As you wish. And a turnscrew for the lid.'

'You think of everything,' said Elizabeth.

Russell took a black cloth and wiped the mirror-smooth ebonised lid as he said, 'Let's hope the weather clears up for tomorrow. Carriages here at nine forty-five. Ten-fifteen departure.'

'Ah yes,' said Elizabeth. 'There's a problem. An important convoy is coming down Pall Mall from Hyde Park at ten o'clock. I doubt they will stop for anything. Please could we bring the timing forward half an hour?'

'As you wish. Nine forty-five departure, carriages here at nine-fifteen.'

'Ve will be ready,' said Hendriksen.

'Goodnight then,' said Russell. He gave a signal and led his colleagues out. Drizzle closed the door.

'Little steps, Hendriksen' sighed Elizabeth.

'Indeed Ma'am, one step at a time and ve vill get through this.'

'Inventory or body next?'

'Inventory, Ma'am. Or ve vill be at it all night.'

The staff had started before midday. Lady Henrietta wanted to join in and was made scribe for the team with the grandest rooms. Elizabeth added her impetus after the second break. She spent time with each team, jollying them along, finding words for objects, speeding them up, for example, 'Salon, floor, rug, seven foot seven by ten foot three, French Aubusson, that's A-U-B-U-S-S-O-N, yellow with floral design'; or 'Dining room, wall, painting, Holbein the Younger, oil on wood, Garden of Gethsemane – G-E-T-H-S-E-M-A-N-E', and, 'The second half always goes quicker than the first. Think of holidays.' And indeed it did. The teams hit a rhythm, the process, vocabulary and spelling became more familiar, and the rooms became simpler as they worked their way to the top of the house.

Elizabeth warmed to the task. She felt at home leading from the front. Were it not for the sad circumstances, she would even say she had seldom been so happy. She was using her brain, her energy and her charm as never before, and it felt good. She had responsibility, authority and her plan was working. She liked her colleagues and they looked up to her. This was all so different from the farm, where things moved at a snail's pace, with huge manual effort and for little if any profit. Yet the big questions of politics and family were still on her mind.

The unexpected appearance of Jack Wilson had fired her up as a woman. Such a tall, handsome young fellow. Clearly going places, now with this mission from the Colonel. She had enjoyed teasing him about Kitty. In fact, those two were probably cuddled together right now. She felt almost jealous. She hadn't spent seven years on a farm for nothing. She had seen all that and yet still it wasn't the same. She wanted to know. Oh, how she ached to know.

Sooner than she expected, Hendriksen announced that the inventory was complete. He had checked the lists, signed them off and would keep them under lock and key until the Duke arrived. Meanwhile, he had marked the chattels, the *eigenaardigheden*, he judged most valuable to be secured in strong boxes and moved to one room in the cellar. The paintings were also to be moved from the front of the house to the back, propped up face to the wall, but not to change floors for fear of damaging them – and the hand-painted stairwell wallpaper.

Once done, he asked for volunteers to move Lady Emelia's body down to the coffin. The heavy lid was removed. Elizabeth suggested they did a trial run with a bolt of curtain material on the stretcher, to understand the mechanics, wallpaper in mind. This led to the twin bank of dining chairs holding the coffin being reduced to one to give access from the side. It was suggested that Emelia's corpse should be carried face down on the stretcher, so that it could be rolled into the coffin to land face up. However, this was rejected as disrespectful.

Emelia's maid had done her proud. The body wore the garb Emelia had ordered for her husband's funeral eight years before, then worn at her mother-in-law's interment four years later, and her father-in-law's and granddaughter's this summer. With pale faces and trembling hands, the volunteers lifted and turned the stiffening corpse. The staff lined one branch of the stairs while the stretcher was brought down the other.

It was at this moment that a firm knock came on the front door.

'No, Drizzle, let them wait,' ordered Elizabeth.

The stretcher was aligned beside the coffin. The knock came again. Lady Henrietta began to cry. Gentle hands from both sides lifted Emelia's body, carrying the grey-faced head in line with the spine, transferred and lowered it.

Elizabeth gave Drizzle a nod and he opened the front door.

'Lord Elland, Ma'am,' announced Drizzle.

The sight of a candlelit hall, with the whole household present and looking at him, gathered around a black coffin with no lid and a dead dowager duchess on show, would have taken most men aback. And yet in all that scene, the tearful orphan, the cool butler, the colourless corpse, the visitor seemed to have eyes for only one figure.

'Elizabeth,' he purred. 'Is this a bad time?'

'Not at all, William, you are expected. Everyone, this is our neighbour from Halifax House, Lord Elland, whom I asked to come round and give us his advice. William, I believe you met Lady Emelia up at Oxford.'

'Goodness yes. She was visiting her son at The House. I never imagined seeing her the next time like this. It is an awful day for us all. When do you expect Jamie to arrive?'

Hendriksen took it upon himself to reply. 'Ve reckon His Grace cannot arrive before Friday, My Lord. Ve have sent him a message but as yet he still cannot know vhat has happened.'

Elizabeth wished everyone to see her visitor as a figure of authority. 'William. Do you think we should close the coffin now or in the morning?'

'I would do it now,' he said.

Hendriksen gave a nod and stepped forward with the turnscrew, while two footmen replaced the lid.

'No, vait!' said the butler. 'I have forgotten the jewellery she is vearing. It is not in the inventory.'

Elizabeth came to his rescue. 'It's all right, Hendriksen, I made a separate list. Drizzle, please take Lord Elland's coat. Who will stay on duty to attend to us? Thank you Drizzle. Everyone else, it has been a long day and we have another big one tomorrow. You have all been wonderful. We must hold together to be ready for Friday so you need your sleep. From Hendriksen and myself, thank you all from the bottom of our hearts. Please get what rest you can.'

The staff began to disperse.

'Come with me, Henrietta,' said Elizabeth. 'Let's tuck you up for the night. William, come too. You have been here many times before, I presume. We are denuded of pictures in the front rooms just now. Security, you know. Oh, Drizzle, while we are upstairs please pop over to Pembroke House and tell her Ladyship's butler that Lady Emelia's cortège will be leaving at nine thirty to avoid an important convoy.'

'I think we said nine forty-five, Ma'am,' said Hendriksen.

'Yes, we did, Hendriksen,' said Elizabeth with a smile, 'but if she's late, we may still make it.'

She took Henrietta by the hand and they led Lord Elland up towards the salon, while Hendriksen screwed down the coffin lid on his much-loved mistress, weeping but clearly happy that he was the last to look on that still-striking face.

Elizabeth left Henrietta in the hands of Modesty and returned to the salon. William was looking particularly lithe, she thought. She asked him about his recent grand tour and their conversation was transported to sunny climes and steamy cities, places she had never seen, and never would. She complained about the difference between the sexes, how young gentlemen got to learn things, particularly when it came to carnal knowledge before matrimony. He understood her. And so, with the correct precautions, deliberately and most satisfactorily, not too quickly or even too quietly, on the Aubusson rug, she caught up on that.

Jack and Kitty, 21:30

Jack and Kitty dodged through the rain, south towards the Strand in the dark.

'That was lucky,' said Kitty. 'I wasn't sure how we were going to get out of our little fix.'

'Double lucky for me, to have you all to myself for half an hour in the dark. I just hope we don't spoil your mother's cloak.'

Kitty wanted to slide her hand round his waist as they walked, but feared it would be misunderstood.

'It is lovely isn't it – and still dry under here.'

'I won't touch you if you don't want me to.'

'It's not that. I'm flesh and blood too, you know.'

'Then what? Are you worried about my other women? You would be my first, Kitty darling. You know that.'

'No, something else.'

'There's someone else?'

'Jack, you would make any girl proud. But no, it's not that.'

'You're dying?'

'Ha. No, that would be all the more reason to do it.'

'Then I give up.'

'I'm Catholic.'

They had crossed Clare Market and were in New Inn Yard.

Jack turned to look at her. The rain had stopped.

'And I'm Protestant,' he said.

'I know,' said Kitty, and the pain was on her face. 'I know. And you won't change.'

'Does that make me so awful?'

'No, just ineligible.'

'But I love you.'

'You don't even know me.'

'Is that what you said to Simon Speke?'

'Yes, but I didn't tell him why.'

Jack took her hand. They came out into Wich Street and turned right. A few more yards and St Clement Danes stood in front of them, with its symmetrical western frontage, triple doors and stumpy tower. The eerie light of bonfires, reflected off the clouds, gave it a wedding cake silhouette.

'No, I can't do it. I can't change faith,' said Jack. 'But equally, I can't stop loving you.'

'I think I have found someone who loves me, who doesn't need to change,' said Kitty.

'But does he even know you?' asked Jack.

'Ah, there you have me. No.'

'What a mess.'

'Yes.'

Jack pushed on the church's central door, the one under the tower. It opened.

'The churchwardens forgot to lock up,' he said.

'I'm not going in, Jack.'

'Why not? It will be warmer inside. We can dry off.'

'Exactly. If we go inside, I won't be able to resist you. We will wind up making love.'

'Well, it would be love on my part.'

'And lust on mine,' said Kitty.

'Do you even believe in love?'

'Oh yes. I even believe in love at first sight,' said Kitty.

'At least let me kiss you. Terry will be along in a minute and he will give me Hell if we haven't even kissed.'

Kitty laughed, so they did.

Terry, 21:30

When Terry and the neighbour approached the huge bonfire in Lincoln's Inn Fields, Simon Speke saw them and came out into the rain.

'One cart and driver as requested, Spike,' said the neighbour.

'Good work, good work,' said Spike, patting the horse's neck. Turning to Terry he asked, 'What's your name, friend?'

'Terry Jones,' said Terry, climbing down,

'Where are you from, Terry?'

'Wales.'

'You brought this cart all the way from Wales?'

'No, no, the cart is from Hounslow Heath.'

'Never mind. What are you doing tomorrow morning?'

'I live in hope of catching some sleep. Been a long day.'

'Well, I need your help. You know Smith Field, this side of Newgate?'

'What of it?

'I want to hire you and your horse and cart for a couple of hours. I'll meet you there at eight tomorrow morning. Simple carting job. What would you charge?'

'Eight o'clock? I could do that. What are you offering?'

'Ten shillings.'

'Two pounds.'

'Two pounds! Man, do you think I am made of money?'

Terry shrugged and looked around, 'Something fishy going on here, if you aren't.'

'All right, two pounds.'

'With half up front.'

It was Spike's turn to look around. 'Is anyone here carrying a pound in money?' he shouted. No one answered. He looked desperately at Terry. The rain ceased.

'All right,' said Terry. 'Two pounds, at Smith Field, at eight in the morning. Before we start the job.'

'It's a deal, Terry Jones.'

They shook hands, looked each other in the eye, and found an understanding of sorts.

'Now, can someone point me in the direction of St Clement Danes?' asked Terry.

Five minutes later he trotted the horse and cart out of Wich Street to the sight of Jack and Kitty kissing in the central doorway of what he considered a rather tasteless new church, oblivious to the ash which had replaced the rain.

'Smith Field,' he said, as the couple climbed back up to their places beside him. 'Wherever that is. Eight o'clock tomorrow morning.'

'So, he's still having them made,' said Kitty.

'How do you work that out?' Terry was less than pleased.

'Smith. Field. Terry. Jones. What do you think they do? Make pots?' asked Kitty.

'I thought it was just the main meat market.'

'The smiths followed the meat. All those knives and horseshoes, flanges, rims and hubs for the carts. After Guildhall had the butchers moved out to the old jousting ground – the smooth field – the aldermen went for the smiths. Noisy business. All that hammering and smoke suddenly wasn't genteel. Too crowded inside the city walls so they put up the rents. You are right. I was being unfair. The smiths moved to what had already become Smith Field.'

They rode on in silence, variously grappling with what had just happened.

Jack brought them back on track. 'Presumably, Spike would collect now if he could.'

'So, it was a late order,' agreed Kitty. 'And the bellows will be working all night. Well-paid work, that. Have you got money?'

'Ten pounds,' said Terry.

'Might do it,' said Kitty. 'Depends on how well he bargained. What did he offer you?'

'Ten shillings, but we settled on two pounds.'

'So, he has cash and is not bargaining,' said Kitty.

'I was rather tickled,' said Terry.

'Except you won't see it.'

'I won't?'

'Because you are going to pick up the caltrops before he gets there, and save me, my city and our country from that madman. Not to mention your comrades in arms,' finished Kitty.

The silence fell again, all the way to Blackfriars. In Glass House Yard, Jack jumped down and gave Kitty a hand. She knocked at the door and her father opened.

'Job done?' asked Edward. 'Ten o'clock. Two hours early. Mrs Jones will be most grateful. You lads like to come in?'

'No, Father, it's down to them now,' said Kitty. 'Terry, Jack, I wish I could come with you, but Blackfriars will not be on your route home from Smith Field to Hyde Park, and you will need every minute to get there in time. Jack, thank you for a great adventure. Adieu.'

With that she was gone.

'Goodnight, Sir,' said Jack. 'If we don't meet again.'

As they trotted off, Terry said to Jack, 'But she kissed you.'

'Consolation prize,' said Jack. 'Mercy kiss. She's found someone else.'

'I don't believe it.'

'She was out of my league.'

'That's women, mate. These things are bound to happen. Take my word for it – men friends are more reliable. Now where is this Smith Field?'

Simon, 22:00

Spike was walking back to Clerkenwell, planning the capture of the artillery train. How do you spread caltrops on the ground? Off the back of the cart, perhaps. Would two hundred and fifty be enough? It would have to be. When to do it? If he moved too early, the column might take another route. Too late and some troops and guns might slip through. And how to disarm the fusiliers, to capture professional soldiers, take them out of contention? What if they surrendered? Prisoners of war – now there was a problem.

And the militia? They were still nowhere to be seen. He had expected them to shoot their officers and join the mob. But they had not even appeared. Something funny was going on. It was more than just the King running away. What had happened to the chain of command? Why had the professional soldiers not reacted? The organs of oppression had ceased to co-ordinate. Was it because the Archbishop had taken the chair? No. That would not account for it.

He began to ponder all the things that could go wrong. What if the money bag had gone from the College of Physicians? What if the smiths had taken the down-payment, laughed and gone to bed? What if that carter, Terry Jones, received a better offer between now and eight o'clock tomorrow morning? But who'd offer more than two pounds? He was glad he hadn't paid half up front. And yet. What was it Kitty had said? 'You need help.'

What is it with us Spekes, he wondered. There had been Spekes at West Lackington, overlooking the Somerset Levels, at least since the reign of Henry VII. The parish register recorded the birth of George Speke in 1507, who later became Gentleman of the Privy Chamber. Over the generations, in their entitlement, they had become a rogue breed, always thinking they knew best, and usually on the losing side.

The current Speke of West Lackington, George, Simon's uncle, had been a parliamentarian in the Civil War and had lived in and out of the courts ever since the Restoration. In the general pardon issued by King James to his subjects this September, George Speke of West Lackington had been among those specifically excluded.

Then there was Uncle John Speke, Member of Parliament, who had sought to exclude the then Duke of York and heir apparent from the succession. He was another denied a pardon in September. And Cousin Charles, hung for treason after Sedgemoor. Not to mention Cousin Hugh, a proper jailbird with his seditious pamphlets.

Well, thought Simon Speke, as he reached his lodgings and tumbled into his cot, no longer rogues after tomorrow.

Day 4. Wednesday 12 December 1688

When Jack woke, the smiths had fallen silent. It was still dark. For a moment he hovered between dream and reality, clinging to the memory of that sweet embrace with Kitty. A hot, voluptuous drowning in another's soul, which he had not known before, nor could have imagined. Then he recalled what she had said. The black cloud re-descended. He had loved Kitty from afar, for longer than he could remember. It was agony to have lost her and he expected that pain to last for many years. The only question was, for how much of each day would he hurt? Today, surely it would be every waking hour. But tomorrow, perhaps a little less.

He and Terry had reached Smith Field around ten thirty last night. They had found all five forges aflame, hammers ringing. A lucrative rush job. Kitty had read it right.

Jack had unharnessed the mare and walked her to a water trough, where she had drunk, and then had tethered her on a long rein to a tree out on the mead, where she had shown an appetite for dead nettles.

'Good to like something no one else eats,' Terry had said.

They had bunked down in the centre of the plateau. The pair had lain under the cart on their rugs and ground sheets, protected from wet earth, dew, frost and possibly more rain. Better to be cold and dry than less cold and wet in the cart.

'Shall we snuggle tight to stay warm?' Terry had asked.

'Don't be ridiculous,' Jack had replied. 'You snore.'

Which indeed Terry had done soon afterwards.

Jack's thoughts returned to the immediate pain. Why had he lost Kitty? Protestants, Catholics. Was the difference so great? Same Bible. Same Christ. Same Beatitudes. Well, he would have time enough to think it over. Better to have known love and lost it, than not even to have tried. Last night, he had said his prayer for peace of mind, for *that peace which the world cannot give*, adding, *and thank you for giving me Kitty, if only for a minute*, and the spell had worked again.

What time was it? Sunrise was eight, and by then he must have done the deal with the smiths and be gone. Twilight would start at about half past six. Was that it in the east? Then he should start moving. The horse had lain down to sleep. He would wake her gently. She would be glad of her oats.

He had always been good with horses. He had lived with them until he was six. He had been a toddler when his mother, Ivy Wilson, took him to her sister's farm in Devon to escape the plague, after it had killed his grandfather, father and older brother (known in the family as William III). Jack had loved the horses there. He had sometimes even slept in their stables. He knew their skittishness, and how much horses appreciate – how well they remember – being woken gently.

Local people said the Wilsons had brought the plague to Devon. If so, how come he and Ivy had never caught it? But then again, neither had the west country generally. Jack's mother always told him the sickness had crept in through Plymouth and up the river to the farm. Anyway, once again, she and he were the only two to survive. First his Auntie Holly's unmarried younger brothers-in-law and then her husband had succumbed. Holly herself was dead before the year was out.

Jack recalled the aftermath – his mother struggling to work the land, which had devolved to her. A couple had moved in to help, a godfather of Jack's, another William, and his new wife, Barbara. They had lived like that, a family and a half, for four years, during which time the couple's twins, Simon and Peter, came along. But Jack's mother was not cut out for the country. She missed London. Twice she took Jack on the long trip to the capital to visit her father in the City. In the end, elderly John Okes took ill, and sent the message she needed. She sold up to Jack's godfather and moved back to nurse her father. He had been so happy to have them home.

Such a lovely man, John Okes, whose name was written JOkes, with daughters Holly Okes and Ivy Okes, who would sing the Christmas carol 'The holly and the ivy, when they are both full grown'. Such a fund of stories…

Enough reminiscing, Jack thought, What about breakfast? Terry and I will be starting on empty stomachs, unlike this horse. And Terry is never great first thing anyway.

He took a half-crown from the £10 money bag and nipped across to the meat market. Some stalls had bread ovens and griddles well aglow, providing oversized portions for the beefy Smith Field porters. He found a likely baker-cum-griddler and came away with a couple of steaks and sausages, each wrapped with fried onions in a pancake. Mouth-watering.

On the return route, he scouted the blacksmiths from a distance. All but one were closed, but the fellow who was reopening, under the sign of 'Freddy's', had five likely sacks at the front of his forge.

Back at the cart, Jack had the idea to heap oats on the back deck and see if the mare noticed. She did. Having stood up and worked out where she was, she ambled over and began to lick and munch them up. This woke Terry, who briefly thought he was being trampled. But he took it well and was pleased to have five minutes to doze, for once. Then he fell upon breakfast with an appetite. At half past seven they led the mare back to the water trough, and each took a long drink from the fountain which fed it. Ten minutes later the cart was hitched and they presented themselves at the forge.

'Morning, Blacksmith Freddy,' said Jack. 'Busy night?'

'None of your business.'

'Simon Speke sends his apologies.'

'Ah, that's who you are. How was I to know? Have you got the money?'

'Remind me how much is owed.'

'Nine pounds seven shillings and sixpence.'

'Nine pounds seven shillings and sixpence,' said Jack, picking two more half-crowns from the moneybag, handing one of them to Terry and pocketing the other. He jumped down, walked over to the front slab and dropped the purse on it with a satisfying chink. 'Would you like to count it?'

'Would you like to count the caltrops?' riposted the smith.

'Not at this time in the morning,' said Jack.

'We'll trust each other then.'

'Are they safe to pick up, these sacks?'

'Hold them by the neck. I'll give you a hand. That's a hundredweight of iron in each, and you don't want to drop one on your foot. What's it for anyway?'

'Neighbour,' sighed Jack. 'Simon thought you'd ask. Said it was none of your business, quite bluntly. If he comes this way you can ask him yourself.'

'Fair enough, mate, it's just that the lads were wondering,' said Freddy, helping to load the sacks.

'Hop up, Jack,' said Terry, 'We haven't got all day.'

'Well, I suppose he's right,' said Jack and, putting his foot on a wheel hub, swung up onto the front board. 'Thanks for everything,' he called down to the smith, who was already dividing his pay, and the cart set off.

'Head for the southwest exit,' hissed Jack, 'and make it snappy. Speke will be here any minute. As I remember, he lives in Clerkenwell, so he'll come in from the north.'

'I thought you said you hardly know the guy.'

'And you should never have used my name back there. If Freddy has his head screwed on, he will blame Jack when Speke shows up. Speke can't get to me, billeted in the Tower, but he knows where Kitty lives.'

'You should have warned me.'

'Yes, I should,' said Jack through his teeth.

'Well, thanks for nothing. What are we going to do with these sacks?'

'Get them to the Regimental Purser, for his bookkeeping,' said Jack. 'Trot on!' he called to the horse.

'Gee-up!' said Terry, giving Jack a nudge, and Jack rolled his eyes.

Along Hosier Lane and over Holborn Bridge they clattered, down Shoe Lane to Fleet Street and the Strand. After the anarchy of last night, the West End was quiet and the mare made good progress.

From Charing Cross they passed into Pall Mall. Halfway down, Jack saw exactly where he would have laid the caltrops, if he had been Speke. You could bottle up the entire cannon train, with no road exits on the south side and St James' Square to the north, the perfect holding pen for an ambush, with attack points a third and two-thirds down the line. The mob only had to wait for the tail to pass St James' Street. Then, strung out, hobbled at the front, unable to stop at the back, let alone reverse, Colonel Shere's column would have to surrender or be cut to pieces, outnumbered ten to one in hand-to-hand combat.

St James' Palace was open and unguarded, as far as Jack could tell. The cart made good speed and they slowed slightly for the gentle rise through the green fringes of the grounds, towards the corner of Hyde Park, with Knightsbridge beyond. Even this slope would have played in Speke's favour, thought Jack. Coming down it, we would have had our full momentum as we ran into his trap.

Shortly after half past eight Terry slowed the cart and they pulled up at the first of Colonel Shere's defensive rings. 'Pity,' he said, 'I was getting used to civilian life.'

'It's just another uniform,' said Jack.

'I know,' said Terry. 'But a soldier grows to thinking he couldn't survive without his sergeant major to tuck him up in bed at night. At least now I can chuck it in and become a carter.'

The sentries knew the Colonel's orders if two civilians and a cart were spotted and they were whisked to the command tent.

Sir Henry was briefing his officers. Jack and Terry crept in at the back. 'We are such a force as is never seen,' the Colonel was saying. 'Our kinsmen fear us more than anything on earth. Irrationally, of course. But more than we fear them. We can use their fear to keep the peace if we stick together, march as one, play the part. Our orders are to get back to the Tower. That is what we are going to do.' He looked around with a ferocious eye, and they all believed it.

'Gentlemen, remember there will be no waving to sweethearts, no idle chatter in the ranks. Every man must stare ahead. To the populace, we must appear another type of matter, beyond flesh and blood, something out of a dream. Something both magical and repellent, from their worst nightmares.'

Then he spotted Jack. 'Lieutenant Wilson,' he shouted. 'Are we safe to go?'

Jack called back. 'Yes, Sir.'

'Good. Gentlemen, pass the word, we march at ten. No, make that half past nine. In forty-five minutes. Let's get home for lunch. Lieutenant Wilson, Corporal Jones, stay behind. Everyone else, dismissed.'

Jack and Terry led Sir Henry outside to inspect the wagon. 'What have you got in these sacks?' he asked.

'Caltrops, Sir. Two hundred and fifty of them.'

Shere looked puzzled, unfolded a pocketknife, walked round the side of the cart, cut a hole in a sack, and lifted out one of the newly-minted foot daggers. 'Good Lord. I've only ever seen these in Tangier. Why didn't we think of that?' He shook his head. 'And you got them all?'

'Yes, Sir.'

'Lieutenant Wilson, return to uniform and see me here in fifteen minutes. Corporal Jones, take this lot to the quartermaster. Show him what £10 can buy in the way of improvised weaponry on the street these days. Convey my request that he sort things out with the purser for me. Then get yourself ready to march back the way you just came. Both of you, try to look smart. Shave if you can. Dismissed.' He kept the caltrop he had removed.

Terry trotted the mare and cart away and Jack ran over to his troop's campfire. They had struck canvas, but his kitbag was out and his uniform laid over a limber in anticipation of a last-minute return. An ironic cheer went up at the sight of him.

'Thanks guys, what would you have done if I hadn't made it?' said Jack stripping off and filling a basin.

'If you didn't show, you had either deserted or were dead. Sergeant Bull had an eye on your boots. Others reckoned on burying your stuff, with full ceremony. So, what's the story?'

'With luck, we have foiled an ambush. Sir Henry says there's to be no talking in the ranks. And he wants a report now. Incidentally, we are marching at half past nine, not ten, to be home for lunch.'

'There go my morning prayers,' joked Bull.

'Someone's pressed my shirt,' said Jack.

'We didn't want you to disappoint your womenfolk.'

'You have no idea,' said Jack. 'Oh, and no smiling or waving to admirers. Forbidden. We have to be made of matter beyond flesh and blood.'

Back at Sir Henry's tent, his three senior officers had joined the Colonel to hear Jack's report.

'At ease, Lieutenant,' said the Colonel. 'Evidently a worthwhile little outing.' He held up the barbed iron device he had taken from the cart. 'Tell us about it.'

'The second of my letters leaked, Sir. News of our approach reached a ringleader of the rioting yesterday. He had an idea to stop us with caltrops. He had two hundred and fifty made last night and was due to collect them from the blacksmith first thing this morning. But we beat him to it, paid for them and brought them out safely.'

'So, the advantage of surprise is lost?' asked the Major.

'Yes, Sir. However, only among their leadership. The rank and file have not been told that a cannon train and a regiment of fusiliers is coming. The idea is probably too frightening.'

'The print apprentices were already hatching something?' asked Willoughby.

'Probably for weeks, Sir. They have held at least one election and put hotheads in the driving seat. Their headquarters is a pub at the northern head of London Bridge, a long way from this front. I don't know what that means.'

'This is more than just a riot. And how does the King being gone affect things?' asked Shere.

'They see it as an opportunity. One said that the publisher of the *London Gazette* would be begging them for favours by tomorrow night. I think they plan to take control of the City, before the Dutch arrive.'

The officers looked amazed.

Jack continued. 'King James leaving for France would have at least doubled the size of the mob. But the instigators hadn't reckoned on our artillery train returning. So, we are now their main threat. They seem to want us not to reach the Tower. But that part, about the importance of the Tower, is another mystery. Make of it what you will, Sir, even the ringleaders' closest lieutenants don't know that the cannon train is coming.'

'Strange indeed,' said Shere. 'As you say, the troublemakers may worry that talk of us would frighten their followers off. If so, the element of surprise is not lost.'

'I find it hard to believe that our presence here is widely unknown in the City,' said Captain Exe.

'Why not?' said Sir Henry. 'We only got here last night. We are deep in a 600-acre park. No one but Wilson and Jones have left camp. There was nothing on the road coming in. The apprentices have closed the newssheets by taking to the streets. And the citizens have their own preoccupations.'

Jack said, 'I traced our entry route in the cart, Sir. The two obvious places for them to use the caltrops were Temple Bar, or three-quarters of the way down Pall Mall. Each is the neck of a funnel, but Pall Mall has least chance of escape to the sides. The mob would marshal in St James' Square, out of sight, until we were stopped in confusion by a cordon of caltrops, then fall on our open flank. Our train would have picked up speed down the slope from the park and the back end would ram straight into the chaos at the front. With two side streets from St James' Square, they would cut our line in three, with us having no chance to advance or reverse, and them having huge superiority of numbers at the attack points.'

Captain Exe coughed. 'Are we to imagine that we are dealing with some kind of military genius behind this rabble, Sir?'

'Well, he nearly out-thought me, with these caltrops,' said the Colonel. 'So, if he's stupid, what does that make us?'

The other officers grimaced.

'Another thing, Sir,' said Jack. 'I mentioned the publisher of the *London Gazette*, Edward Jones. I met him. He had spent all afternoon at Guildhall, where some version of the Privy Council met yesterday. They are trying to run things without the King. They struggled to find a leader, to the extent that they left it to the Mayor and Aldermen to formally invite the Prince of Orange to come to London. But they will reconvene every day until he gets here.'

'We must send them a message to say we are here and are proceeding via St James' to the Tower. Draft that now for me to sign, please Adjutant.'

Jack continued. 'Mr Jones said to tell you, Sir, that if you have any advice on tactics, to get word of it to Guildhall this morning. They meet at ten.'

'Well,' said Sir Henry, and paused again. 'That is rather a good idea. I would say that if the Council has any troops to command, put them in St James' Square. It is the key to St James' Palace and the park behind it, which is the soft underbelly of Whitehall. Prepare for a battle royal with the mobile. If I know the Marquess of Halifax, he will chair that Council today. And he lives in St James' Square. So he will appreciate the logic. The only question is, has he already left home for Guildhall? Views?'

'Seems a bit wild, Colonel,' said Exe.

'Major?' asked Shere.

'You are a step ahead of me, Sir,' said the Major. 'How do we know they will concentrate in St James' Square?'

'It's what I would do,' said Shere. 'The French Embassy, a royal mass house and supposed royal pleasure palace. Rich pickings. And there are a dozen ways into Whitehall Palace through the park.' He turned to Exe. 'Captain, we have not a moment to lose. You and the Lieutenant mount up and ride like the wind to Halifax House. You have your horse outside. Lieutenant, take mine. Tell Halifax that the fulcrum of his line should be his own front door. Say to expect a mob of five or ten thousand. I recommend he puts all his best soldiers and cavalry into that square, with orders to fight. I mean kill. They will be hugely outnumbered. So, fix bayonets, draw sabres and fire with bullet – otherwise those troops are dead and we'll have weeks of street fighting on our hands, not to mention one angry French King with a looted embassy, and a furious Prince of Orange with two sacked palaces and no coin to pay his troops. If this mob gets a taste for palaces, it will be Somerset House next, and we may never pull the fat from the fire.'

Jack was relieved that the Colonel saw it his way.

'However,' continued Sir Henry, 'if the rabble somehow beats us to control of the Tower of London, all bets are off.'

No, thought Jack. That's not it. Not even Spike would want the Tower.

'So that's still where I'm going. Adjutant, have you got that note for me to sign?' Sir Henry asked impatiently. 'Captain Exe, if His Lordship has already left home, ride on to Guildhall. Halifax will want cannon. Say we will send him some, once the Tower is secured.' The adjutant handed him the note. He glanced through it and signed. 'Here's the letter to the Council to make it all official. Deliver it as appropriate, Captain. Lieutenant, you will come back to me. While you are in St James' Square, have a good look up and down Pall Mall, to be sure no new barricade is being built. If they are to block us with furniture in time, they will have started by now. I don't want to change route down Piccadilly and the Haymarket, because of the corners, but we still can. So, bring word back to me. And Captain, if you get to Guildhall, stay with Halifax until you hear from me. Dismissed.'

Exe and Jack saluted and ran for the horse line. In moments they were galloping out of the camp, yelling warnings ahead and sending soldiers leaping to the side. Jack led. It helped that he was on Sir Henry's grey, the only one in the regiment – the sight of it seemed to give the men a split second longer or a sinew more to spring out of the way. But he was aware that this mount would draw attention in town, even if his uniform did not. For Exe to try and reach Guildhall so conspicuously mounted would be suicide.

From the corner of Hyde Park, down the gentle slope of green they flew, into the entrance to Pall Mall and to St James' Square. A Privy Council carriage stood outside Halifax House, the front door was open and Spray was waiting on the top step. Jack dismounted in time to take Exe's reins. The Captain strode up to the doorman to announce himself.

Then a voice came from the carriage.

'Can I help you, Lieutenant Wilson?'

It was the Marquess, with a younger man, about to set off.

'Good morning, My Lord,' said Jack. 'The Captain has an urgent message for you from Colonel Shere.'

'Then he had better get in with us. My son and I are departing for Whitehall and cannot wait.'

Captain Exe turned to Jack, 'Take my horse back to camp Lieutenant, and tell the Colonel it's not Guildhall anymore, but Whitehall.' He opened the carriage door, removed his hat so that his blond hair fanned out, and pulled himself up and in.

'Yes, Sir. See you at the Tower, Sir,' said Jack with a smile, thinking what a buffoon the man looked.

Exe glared, 'Drop the complacency, Lieutenant. Pall Mall may look clear of barriers, but we are a long way from making your plan stick.'

'Drive on,' shouted Halifax, tapping the roof with his cane. The coach trotted away past Ormonde House.

Jack sighed. The Captain was right, but his dismissive tone rankled. At such moments, officers needed to keep clear heads and anticipate, not score points.

He would take a moment to look over this prospective battleground before hostilities commenced. He led the two horses into the middle of London's newest and grandest residential quadrangle.

St James' Square was larger than he had realised, not the size of Lincoln's Inn Fields, but almost as big as Horse Guards' Parade. It was hard-packed, unpaved and treeless. Fine mansions were set back on three sides, while the fourth presented only the ugly backs of shops and houses that faced onto Pall Mall. A big space, but still too enclosed for unwieldy cannon, thought Jack. Such bulk could not be positioned, protected, manoeuvred or operated, in-the-round, so to speak. Breech-loading swivel-guns would do it, but only the navy had those, to sweep enemy decks at close quarters. He imagined sailors repelling boarders.

This coming fight would be almost the same. The mob would fight Halifax's soldiers hand to hand. Pistol, musket, sabre and bayonet, outnumbered many times over by sticks and stones. Quite an even match. Victory would be down to discipline and organisation. Fusiliers to fire in three ranks. It would be as fatal to the defence if all were reloading at once, as it would if the rabble captured some of Shere's ordnance in the morning. He thought again of the artilleryman's dream, a big gun that can advance facing forward, but now modified in his mind to have a swivelling turret.

The first bands of rowdies were beginning to swing in to the square, chanting and swearing. They radiated a sense of invincibility, remarkably fresh, drawn onward by the prospect of ever greater prizes. It was clear the artillery train was not expected. They jeered at him from a distance but didn't approach.

Jack led the horses to a mounting block, put his left foot in the grey's stirrup and swung his right leg over. As he did so, he glanced up at the first-floor windows of Ormonde House. Elizabeth Forrester, dressed in black, was looking down at him. He raised his hat with his right hand, held it out to the side and bowed gracefully from the waist. Yes, he thought, no cannon in this fight – too many innocent parties in the surrounding buildings; and to damage such handsome faces would be unconscionable, not to mention the facades.

Then he spurred the grey, and raced the two horses back to Hyde Park.

In his absence, the cannon train had formed up, four across. The Colonel was seated on a roan, between the Adjutant and the Major, behind the pipes and drums. At the sight of Jack, he broke his horse out of the formation and dismounted.

'Well, Lieutenant?' he said, returning Jack's salute, while the regiment strained to hear.

'We caught Lord Halifax leaving for Whitehall, Sir, not Guildhall anymore. He asked Captain Exe to join him in his carriage and brief him on the way, as time was short.'

'Excellent. Any sign of the rioters?'

'Gathering, Sir.'

'Barricades?'

'All clear, Sir. No preparations. Captain Exe also confirmed that was his view. We are not expected.'

A groom from the baggage train ran up and took the roan and Captain Exe's mount.

'Well, let's try to keep it that way.' Shere checked the grey's girth, then said, 'Give me a leg up, would you? Thanks, Lieutenant. You may rejoin your troop.'

Jack walked back to Terry, Bull and the boys at the front of the line of well-travelled field guns.

Then the Colonel rode his steaming mount into position and shouted, a previously unheard-of call in the Royal Ordnance, 'Train, quick march.' It was echoed down the line. The musicians struck up *Sir Edward Nowell's Delight* and, like a spine in which every vertebra cracks in turn, the convoy moved off.

Elizabeth, 07:00

Elizabeth Forrester had slept well. After lying in each other's arms for a comfortable while, William had collected their things and they had dressed each other. Drizzle had shown his lordship out while Elizabeth blew a goodnight kiss from the stairs, across the coffin. Back in her own room she had stripped again, washed, pulled on a nightshirt and dropped off shortly after.

Now that she was awake, she still had no qualms. She had wanted to know. And now she knew. She was glad it was with a married man, he would not cling, indeed, he would do everything to hush it up. She was glad that only Drizzle was aware, he could be trusted. And she was glad for her own sake; Elland's pleasure at her hands, and hers at his, had quite astonished her. The world seemed clearer – it explained much that had been confusing, about mistresses and extra-marital pregnancy and bastardy, about men, even about her own father's rakish reputation. She wondered how Emelia would have reacted to this development. The Dowager Countess would have seen it in forgiving terms of bloodlines and hierarchy. A future Marquess, not bad for a first attempt, even if he was already married.

She reflected on the strangely self-fulfilling hostility of Lady Elland. William had murmured that his wife was driving him to this. Elizabeth wondered what it was they had done last night that Elizabeth Elland wouldn't, or couldn't, do. She felt curious, were women not all the same? How could anyone have a husband like William and not satisfy him? Perhaps now Elizabeth Elland would make an effort. Or perhaps she deserved sympathy. Would M'lady go into an even steeper decline? Elizabeth would wait and see.

She closed the lid on that topic and thought of the coming funeral. The clothes she would wear, the prayers she would say over the Ormonde crypt, the weight of immortal souls of those buried in Westminster Abbey, and whether she had done permanent damage to her own with last night's amour. It certainly did not feel like it.

Gradually, an unfamiliar nervousness set in. Today had many moving parts. If everyone remembered their roles, their exits and entrances, it would all go fine. She thought of Henrietta, an orphan. She thought of a mother being buried after giving birth eleven times, with only one of her children able to attend, or even aware that she had gone. She thought of the once mighty beauty laid to rest without a single old admirer present. A coffin in the hall, straddling three dining room chairs. It was pathetic.

Elizabeth, she told herself, snap out of this. She jumped up, did her ablutions, dressed in her funeral weeds and joined the household. Hendriksen came to her with a good question. How many staff should be left in the house, given last night's rioting? And did this tally with the number of seats available in the cortège?

'Twelve places for staff,' she said. 'Six in the second coach and six in the third. And we are only ten. The problem is not seating space, but guarding the house.'

Elizabeth suggested Hendriksen call the household together. Henrietta sidled in, looking vulnerable.

'Dear Henrietta, come and stand with me,' said Elizabeth. To the staff, she began. 'Big day today. I hope everyone slept well and has since eaten. You all look smart and would have made her Ladyship proud. Unfortunately, due to the rioting last night, two will have to stay behind to guard the house.' There was a general groan from around the room. 'I can ask for volunteers or I can draw lots. And bear in mind that Hendriksen must go. So, there is a chance that you won't. How shall we do this? By age, by length of service, by seniority, or by lot?'

'Draw lots', said Modesty. 'It would be a strange person who volunteered.'

So they drew lots and Cook and Drizzle lost. They took it in good part.

'At least you'll have a decent lunch when you return,' said Mrs Cross.

'And I'll try to keep the riff-raff out in the meantime,' added Drizzle.

At nine o'clock Elizabeth faced going into the salon, which held such fresh and pleasant memories. She stood at the window, keeping half an eye out for the hired cortège. A carriage pulled away from Halifax House. Then she saw a soldier in Royal Ordnance uniform lead two fine chargers into the middle of the square. He was facing away from her and she thought how dashing and reliable he looked. She wondered why he needed two horses – that grey in particular was as fine a steed as Elizabeth had seen on the London streets. And then she recognised him.

He seemed preoccupied with the square, while the horses followed meekly. She saw the first rioters enter from the direction of the Haymarket, and how they barracked Jack and he ignored them. Then he appeared to resolve a question and walk over to a convenient mounting block.

'Go on. Look at me. Look up, Jack,' Elizabeth said quietly. As he mounted, Jack did indeed raise his eyes, see her, smile, doff his hat and bow deep in the saddle. It was a thrilling sight, the white horse, the Lieutenant's uniform and the elegant gesture, like something from a tourney in the age of chivalry. When he wheeled the grey and spurred away to west, she could see what a good seat he had and how well he understood his mount. She wondered how long fate would take to bring them together again.

She turned away from the window. Henrietta was standing in the centre of the room on the Aubusson. 'Can I ask you something?' said the fourteen-year-old. 'It's rather private.'

'Certainly,' said Elizabeth and walked over to shut the door.

'It's just that you and Lord Elland made some noise last night. My room is above this one and I couldn't help hearing. I wonder why you would do such a thing, on the night my mother died.'

'Oh Henri, there was something mad about yesterday. I needed to know about it. Have for a long time. I'm not sorry. In fact, it was perfect.'

'Do you think it is death, the darkness getting into us, that makes us do mad things? Like me dressing up in mother's clothes when she was barely cold in the next room. People would say that was creepy. But it felt like saying no to death.'

'Yes, saying no to death.'

'I thought you were dying last night, but then I heard you laughing and talking in between, and I realised what it was. As if happiness and sadness are part of the same thing.'

'Some tastes are acquired. Cheese and coffee and beer. And what a man and a woman do is like that, all the better for being all the worse.'

'Would you say it was a popish thing to do?'

'Heavens no. These things are pre-Christian, not anti-Christian. Dressing to depict monsters and ghouls, frightening ourselves in the dark, lust even, is about proving we are alive in the presence of death. These tropes have been around as long as war or plague or famine – group madness comes with any of these.'

Henrietta nodded.

Elizabeth thought, how much I have learnt from one night, and continued. 'It is our primitive side showing through. It has nothing to do with the love that Jesus taught, and lots to do with fear of the abyss. The Catholics call it a *dance macabre* but it surely was happening before Christianity.'

'Do you admit you are in temptation?'

'Yes, I do.'

'So am I. Are we secretly Catholics?'

'Henrietta, Protestants and Catholics are not divided by whether they fall into temptation, or into moments of madness. It is true that the Latin Church has carnivals and dressing up and images of walking skeletons and tortured saints. But Protestant countries also have their uniforms and cults, witch-hunts and Hell-fire preachers – they're nothing to do with Jesus' love either.'

'I hope this *dance macabre* passes soon,' said Lady Henrietta, standing before one of the tall windows. 'Look at that. The rabble is filling the square. And here comes the funeral party to collect us.'

'You know you can always talk to me if you are frightened, Henri,' said Elizabeth. 'But please don't discuss my visitor last night with anyone else. Particularly not with your brothers and sister.'

'I promise,' said Lady Henrietta.

'And now we must secure the house before we leave it in Cook's and Drizzle's hands.'

They went downstairs to greet the hearse. As the coffin was borne shoulder-high out of the hall and cautiously down the front steps, the staff went round closing the shutters, moving more furniture and rolling the rugs away from the windows. It was as if the soul of the house was departing and the rooms were putting on mourning.

At half past, Lady Pembroke did not appear.

'She is frightened avay by ze mobile,' said Hendriksen.

The pallbearers held the horses heads, the staff stood in the hall, and everyone waited while the mood in the square grew uglier. After ten minutes, William Russell came in to say, 'The crowd is making the horses restless. The sooner we go, the better, Ma'am.'

'She won't come now,' said Lady Henrietta.

'Well, zen,' said Hendriksen, 'Let's be off.' He led the staff out and began filling the back two coaches.

'Look after the old place, Drizzle, and thank you,' Elizabeth said. 'See you for lunch in a couple of hours, Cook. Remember, no supper needed for me tonight. I will be at my parents' from this afternoon, back tomorrow.'

Last to leave were Lady Henrietta and Elizabeth, taking the first coach to themselves. Drizzle stood on the top step and waited until Russell had shut the door of their carriage. He wept as the cortège rolled forward, led by the hearse, with the coffin-bearers seated three ahead and three behind. Then he closed the front door. Through the open carriage window, Elizabeth heard him throw the bolts.

It occurred to her that this mob was timed to meet the Artillery Train. The thought did not alarm her. The artillerymen would come down Pall Mall, drawing the troublemakers from her side of the square. Hopefully the sight would quell their wilder instincts. Her little procession still had plenty of time to reach the Abbey, more than an hour.

However, the crowd slowed the pace of the cortège. It took them five minutes just to cross the square. At first Elizabeth was oblivious, as Henrietta continued her precocious questions.

'Do you think Mama was secretly a Catholic? Because her old mistress, the Dowager Queen Catherine certainly is, and the late King Charles converted on his deathbed, and Mama was close to both of them, wasn't she? And to remain lady-in-waiting for twenty-five years, five of those after Papa had died… What was her secret? She and the old queen must have spoken of it.'

Elizabeth was happy to pursue this line of enquiry. She felt a maturing in Henrietta which she had known herself, for the same reason, when almost that age. 'Yes, I wondered about that, too. Your mother had a love of life. She had known hardship growing up in Holland. And again, in losing so many of her own children young. She was tolerant. She helped others and was a delight to be around. She was perfect for a merry monarch. Men particularly appreciated her company. Partly her uncomplicated optimism, partly her refreshing beauty, but also her integrity and wit. She smoothed any social gathering. She was always loyal to your father, but after he died, she was in great demand. That was why she employed me.'

Henrietta nodded. 'Go on. I like to hear about her.'

'The Emelia I knew was out to prove that her achievements were hers. She appreciated her good fortune in backing your father at the court in exile. But she also felt she had taken the risk and deserved the credit. She had married for love, not for one of the greatest dukedoms. As for religion, she respected whatever the King did. She fitted in with what people wanted. She feared God and never saw church attendance as a chore. I think she hoped to see again in Heaven the children she had lost along the way. But, for preference, she was closer to the pope than to Oliver Cromwell.'

'Do you think girls grow up to be their mothers?' asked Henrietta. 'Surely there must be something of their fathers in them too.'

'Henri, such searching questions! No. Only men who hate women say that girls grow into their mothers. We are different from our mothers. Nothing is predestined about how men or women grow up. You, for example. Knowing hardship as a child, as you now do, being orphaned young, has an impact on how you will view the world. Also, few people, men or women, are born with the beauty we all crave. Even if they are, tastes change. King James likes women to be thin as sticks, while his older brother wanted us curvy, with big noses. Self-confidence comes from within, and that is what most people respect.'

'But you are beautiful and self-confident,' said Henrietta. 'I am neither. Mama always said I have my father's looks and temperament.'

Elizabeth thought, I must not contradict anything her mother said, those memories are too precious. I owe that to Emelia. She answered, 'Your mother loved your father. She was paying you a compliment. I never knew him, but he married, in exile, as a man without prospects, one of the most beautiful, most vivacious women of the age. He must have had something going for him. If you have that quality, you need never worry again.'

The carriages had worked their way to a side street into Pall Mall, but seemed to be held up. The rabble around the ladies' coach began to grow abusive, rocking it on its springs.

'Don't react,' said Elizabeth. 'They will weary of it. We will get through this. We must just stay calm.'

Then, above the murmur of the crowd she heard pipes and drums. The front coach moved forward and the ladies' coach followed. 'There, you see,' she said. But then she realised it was only that the mob had led the horses out into the middle of Pall Mall and stopped them there. The crowd on her right had parted and a long military column, stretching back to the Palace gate tower, was coming straight at them, four abreast. The hearse too had been stopped across its path, ahead of them, completing a wheeled barricade. The formation marched at them with an unstoppable determination, at a fast pace, not slowing or deviating, as if the soldiers were more than flesh and blood.

'We must do something,' pleaded Henrietta, but remained frozen to her seat.

Elizabeth pulled down the little window and looked up at the driver. He was remonstrating with the men who held the horses, to no avail.

'Use the whip', she shouted. But perhaps he didn't hear her.

It was too much. She wanted to scream at him, tell him to lash out whatever the cost, but her mind locked in doubt. Perhaps this man sympathised with the mob.

Turning to Henrietta she said, 'It's no use, brace yourself for an almighty smash.'

Kitty, 08:00

At home in Blackfriars, Mary was quick to question Kitty at breakfast. The sack of the Printing House the day before, and the apparently noble intervention of Simon Speke, had reawakened in her an enthusiasm for Kitty to find a young male protector – and the sooner the better.

'I was married and pregnant with you by the time I was your age,' she declared. 'And this Simon fellow sounds decent enough.'

'Mixes with the wrong sort,' contradicted Johanna.

'He sounded authoritative,' insisted Mary. 'Like your father, Kitty. I know an orator when I hear one, and leadership quality when I see it.'

'You've never met him, or ever even seen him,' said Johanna. 'And as for oratory, the man only spoke one sentence: *This house is locked up, nothing here, boys, let's head on to the rendezvous at Lincoln's Inn Fields.* Hardly one for a prize in public speaking. In fact, it sounded hollow to me.'

'Well, if not him, then who? Kitty needs to step into life, instead of this sitting around sketching plants for the Apothecaries. What about that nice Nicholas Staphurst. Your father seemed to get on well with him.'

'Because the man is older than Edward,' said Johanna. 'Do you want to condemn her to decades of widowhood? Imagine what she'd have to put up with over breakfast, if she had to live with her son, like I do, and her son were to marry a stupid girl.'

Kitty thought it best to intervene. 'Please, Grandmother, Mama, I have a tongue in my head, and a mind of my own. Talking over me is not going to help. And Staphurst is probably married.'

'Well,' said Mary. 'What about that soldier who came to call last night. Edward says he wrote to you behind our backs. Seems odd that he wasn't in uniform. But you went off with him willingly enough. What about him?'

'Both Simon Speke and Jack Wilson have made advances. However, neither are remotely suitable. The former is a regular anarchist, if such a thing is possible; and the latter is a bigot, obstinately and unreasonably wedded to his Protestantism. Neither loves me for what I am, and both would make a disastrous marriage.'

'Well, it takes a bigot to see a bigot,' said Mary.

'Such cant,' said Kitty. 'It sounds clever but isn't. I need a partner who talks sense. But that does not occur to you. Anyway,' she continued, trying to smile, 'I remember only two days ago you and Father telling me to take things more carefully than you did. To enjoy life. *If no one around here has caught your eye, then a change of scene would do you good.* Those were Papa's words. What has changed since then?'

'Oh, I don't know,' said Mary. 'I just worry about you and want to see you settle down.'

Kitty felt her anger rising again. 'Down is the right word, Mother. You want to drag me down to your level. You can't bear to see me spreading my wings, flying with the eagles.'

'If you plan to get high and mighty with me, Catherine Jones, you can go on bread and water for a week. Me, who suckled you and wiped your arse and rocked you to sleep and taught you the Ten Commandments. What happened to honour thy father and mother? And if you think an afternoon with an apothecaries' librarian and an evening with a gunnery lieutenant is flying with eagles, you are stupider than I thought.'

'If you want a reason for a girl to marry, what about getting her mother out of her hair?' Kitty shot back.

'Kitty, dear,' said Johanna. 'That's enough of that. And Mary, it is true that only two days ago Edward was encouraging her to see things differently. I suggest that we kiss and make up until my son comes home, and then we can have a balanced discussion. Now, you and I must get ready to go up to the market and see what has happened to the price of a loaf in all this kerfuffle.'

So Kitty and her mother called a truce, neither of them quite knowing why they had fallen out. The two older women set off into the City with their empty baskets and Kitty waited for the post.

Back in her workroom, she felt more herself. On reflection, the row had been about men. She had broken well with Jack. Far from acting the prize bitch, she had paid him every compliment. She had kissed him, a first for them both, and had even managed to tell him the truth, well, part of the truth, the Catholic bit; she had spoken of love at first sight and even hinted at them not knowing her. Her mother would have been proud of her, had she known. But conversations with parents about affairs of the heart were impossible. The suggestion that Simon Speke sounded like a suitable mate for life had been the final straw. She had begun to look down on her mother, and Mary knew it.

As for Jack, he was attractive, and he had thought fast when the cart had been stopped last night. But his prejudice against Catholics was absurd. Did he not know his Bible? In Matthew 16:19 Jesus gives St Peter the keys of the kingdom of Heaven. The laying-on of hands in the Catholic Church went in a direct physical line back to Peter and the early Christians in Rome. What was Jack's problem with that?

She knew what it really boiled down to. Hatred of all things un-English. People had a chip on their shoulders about any foreign sophistication, the brilliance of German music, the light in Italian paintings, the New World wealth of Spain. What would Jack make of the Versailles orangery, with its thousand trees and secondary layer of glazing? Or wine and cream in his cooking? Or a 22-year-old woman writing and publishing music for the harpsichord?

As for Spike, did he really think that Catholics in Rome were now controlling England? As if Rome controlled the Catholics in Paris! Could there not be patriotic English Catholics too? Take back control! It was all nonsense, deliberately got up by muttonheads to hide their own shortcomings.

Eventually the postman appeared. He apologised – the riots last night had caused delays. Kitty gave him his usual tip. She was dismayed to see that all the letters were for her father. No word from James. Then she realised that a letter posted the night before last from the south coast would only arrive tomorrow.

Remonstrating with herself for her foolishness, Kitty wrapped up warm and went out to ask Nicholas Staphurst at Apothecaries' Hall who the Ranelagh apartment James was. She passed through the Society's modest portico, under the shield showing Apollo wielding a bow and arrow, astride the serpent of disease, supported by two golden unicorns. Alas for him, although medicine is his invention, love cannot be cured by herbs. *Hei mihi, quod nullis amor est medicabilis herbis*, woe is me, for no herb can cure love.

The place seemed as abandoned as before. Apothecaries, like everyone else, were staying at home rather than risk the streets. Nevertheless, she found her way up to the library, which seemed to be the remains of an ancient gallery, so narrow that books lined only the north wall. Men were gathered around a windowsill in the middle of the south side, three listening respectfully to the fourth, who was seated. Nicholas Staphurst was one of the quiet ones, with his back to her. The speaker was the King's apothecary who had come to Ormonde House yesterday. The other two she didn't recognise. As she approached, the man on the seat stood up. Nicholas turned to see why, and smiled when he saw her. The senior apothecary looked irritated to have been interrupted. He didn't recognise her.

Nicholas said, 'Master, Miss Catherine Jones, our budding illustrator. Catherine Jones, our revered Master, Dr James Chase. Also, Captain Robert Knox of the East India Company, and Edward Lloyd, with the new coffee shop on Tower Street.'

Kitty said, 'Master, forgive me for interrupting. We met yesterday at Ormonde House under less happy circumstances. Captain Knox, I have heard your name as an expert on eastern herbs. Good day to you, Mr Lloyd, I understand you cater for sailors, merchants and ship owners. Nicholas, I must pick your brains on a small matter. But perhaps I should come back another time?'

'No, no,' said Chase, 'do stay, Miss Jones. I remember you now. Poor Countess, before her time, but mercifully quick.'

At the name of such an important connection, Knox and Lloyd also relaxed.

The Master of the Worshipful Society of Apothecaries continued. 'We were discussing the much-needed preservation of our books, Miss Jones. This south-facing aspect and the narrowness of the room means we have a problem with bleaching from the sun, worse in the winter months, when the rays are low and strike the bookshelves square on. I was suggesting stained glass for the bookshelf doors.'

Nicholas continued the explanation. 'The same light which plants draw on to grow, turns out to be extraordinarily destructive to textiles and leather. We had this problem with the old library, before the fire, and already it is back.'

'And yet a library needs the light to read by,' said Lloyd. 'There are few things more pleasant than sitting in a window seat, with the winter sun streaming in and a good book in one's hand.'

'Well, Nicholas,' said the Master, 'as chemyst and archivist the problem remains with you. I am sure you will think of something. Meanwhile, Rob, you must tell us the conditions for growing these delightful seeds. And find a name for them. Otherwise, the confusion will last for ever. And not bangue, for Heaven's sake! This is no laughing matter.' All but Kitty chuckled. 'Now, I must be off. Rob, come with me. Good day.'

Lloyd and Staphurst bowed, Kitty gave a dip.

'Miss Jones,' said Nicholas, after Master Chase and Captain Knox had gone, 'to what do we owe this pleasure?'

Kitty was unsure whether her question about physic garden James was a private matter. If she asked to be alone with Nicholas, it would betray her feelings for the man. On the one hand, she would prefer not to feed gossip to a coffeehouse owner, let alone one so famously reliant on the latest news. On the other hand, what was the *Gazette*, if not also in the news business? She decided that this was a contact to cultivate.

'When we were at Lord Ranelagh's on Monday,' she said to Nicholas (and she saw Lloyd prick up his ears), 'who was the gentleman with him? He was kind enough to write, but I only caught his first name, James.'

'Let me think, now,' said Nicholas. 'Kitty, walk this way with me while I try to remember. Edward, we must part. I will call by your establishment as you suggest.'

'And you must come and see it too, Miss Jones,' said Lloyd.

'I will, Sir,' said Kitty.

Nicholas led her away at a stroll, out of the library and down the stairs. He opened the door to a room barely bigger than a broom cupboard.

'Come and sit in here,' he said, 'This is the librarian's den, my own little kingdom.'

Jars were heaped on the desk and shelves, as well as the floor. Two chairs were armrest deep in papers. Nicholas moved a pile and settled in one, while Kitty did the same for the other, intrigued by the sudden sense of mystery.

'Forgive me, Kitty,' said Nicholas. 'If the Duke has written to you, it is not something you broadcast. And Lloyd is one of the worst for name dropping.'

'The Duke?' said Kitty.

'King James' bastard son.'

'I'm sorry, I don't understand,' said Kitty.

'Queen Mary is the King's second wife. His first wife, Anne Hyde, was the one who turned him Catholic. She died of a breast tumour while he was still Duke of York. Duchess Anne had a lady-in-waiting, Arabella Churchill. Arabella bore the then Duke, now James II, four bastard children, all of whom he was pleased to recognise. Their eldest son is James. James FitzJames. Last year the King made him Duke of Berwick and some other titles I don't remember.'

Kitty was glad to be sitting down. The room seemed to whirl for a moment. 'I see. King James' bastard son. Which explains Lord Ranelagh's remark, *Who says they have no Tudor in them*? I had been wondering.'

'But surely you knew. Ranelagh introduced you.'

Kitty thought of a term Jack had used last night. 'Nicholas, have you any idea how hare-brained a girl can become, when being introduced to a handsome young man?'

'Well, at least you see why I wanted to be discreet.'

'But why have I never heard of him?'

'Berwick grew up in Catholic boarding schools in France. He is as Francophile as Louis XIV himself, and more papist than the Pope. As of the King's departure yesterday to France, he is also the most toxic man in England. And you say he wrote to you?'

Kitty nodded, 'I wonder when he will hear that his father has fled.'

'If he has any sense, he will leave too,' said Nicholas.

Simon, 07:15

Spike set off from Clerkenwell Green. It was not yet light, so he left Ike to sleep in – if indeed he was at home – the man would need his wits about him later. Spike felt good. Mrs Holmes had reheated a broth and fed him a rich breakfast. He hoped his day-shift rioters and Spartans would have as much sense. The militia's absence yesterday meant the forces of law and order would be fresher today than he and Ike had planned.

Spike had started in plenty of time, determined to walk at a measured pace. He had noticed that he had taken to marching everywhere, and he despised this martial look. Partly it was rage, partly lack of time, and partly a sense of superiority. And why should he not be angry, hurried and superior? Walking was a terrible waste of valuable minutes. Again, he dreamt of a fine carriage, horses and footmen to transport him while he grappled with higher matters. How much more could he achieve, if handed the levers of power? It was ridiculous, for example, that he had to run this errand to pay a blacksmith and a carter; and that he had to worry where the petty cash was coming from.

It occurred to him that he wouldn't have enough. The bag at the Physicians had nine pounds seven shillings and sixpence for Freddy, but what about the two pounds for Terry? He would rather not have to murder the poor dupe and steal his cart. That was more Ike's way of doing things. Probably one of the looters would have the money.

Spike cut south via Cow Cross and over the open space at Smith Field. He saw that the cooked food bars were doing good business. Freddy the blacksmith was opening up shop and, most gratifying of all, Terry and his cart were already there. He almost went over to say hello, but Spike preferred to have the money on him, before announcing himself. So he skirted round and into the courtyard of the Royal College. He bounded up the steps and pushed on the front door. It was locked.

Baffled. He was a printer's apprentice, not a doctor. He could not make a scene and demand admittance. A hundred windows were looking down at him from three sides. He could not break in. When would the doorman open up? How long after that before he became distracted? Would there be an early morning delivery, something to cover a stealthy entry? What about the rear? As far as he knew, the Royal College backed directly on the Roman city wall, with the Sessions

Courthouse in Old Bailey on the other side, so no way in there. Who was the Master of the Physicians? He racked his brains. Scunthorpe? No. Scarborough? Yes, Sir Charles Scarborough. Time was running out. He wished that he had spoken to Terry just now, so that he would wait beyond the eight o'clock meeting time. On the other hand, most people would dawdle a while for two pounds.

Spike was unsure whether to loiter in a corner of the courtyard for the straightforward solution, or to go on a long detour looking for a side entrance. Better the frontal assault, he decided. The minutes ticked by. The clocks struck the three-quarter hour and still he waited.

The front door opened and was fastened back and all was again quiet. Nothing ventured, nothing gained, Spike told himself, and he strode in. Once more, the entrance booth inside the door was unattended. He turned into the oak-panelled cloakroom, went to the dark corner and reached under. He felt the bag, quietly slid it out and placed it under his coat.

'Can I help you?' said a deep voice from behind.

'Thank you so much,' said Spike standing and turning to face his discoverer. 'Inspection complete. Please give my regards to the cleaners. I will report favourably to Sir Charles. Keep up the good work.' He walked past the speechless porter. 'Constant vigilance, constant vigilance,' he shouted over his shoulder and was gone.

Turning the corner back into Warwick Lane, Spike allowed himself a backward glance. The man was still standing on the top step of the entrance, hands on hips.

Spike ran on up under Newgate and on to Smith Field. But the cart was nowhere to be seen. He sprinted across to Freddy's forge.

'Hello, Simon, I wasn't expecting to see you.'

'What do you mean? We agreed eight o'clock. Or is this smithy humour?'

'Your lads picked everything up five minutes ago. Gave your name, paid in full. They said you might drop by. I was to ask you what words you had really used about minding my own business.'

'But I gave no such instructions. They tricked you, you idiot. My God! What did they look like?'

'They paid, so as far I'm concerned they tricked no one. And how would they know your name, or indeed know all about the deal, if not from you?'

'A guy with a horse and cart? Sleepy fellow? Welsh?' asked Spike.

'Yes, and his friend. What did he call him? Jack.'

'Jack? Jack Wilson?' asked Spike. Freddy shrugged. Jack Wilson, thought Simon. Surely not. But how? That Kitty Jones. How else? I'll tear her limb from limb. 'Freddy, where can I get a cab?'

With his unspent bag of shillings and half-crowns, Spike now had the mobility he craved. He gave the driver two crowns and hired him for the morning. As they trotted through the streets, Spike saw many signs of petty looting and burning. Acts of revenge, old scores settled under cover of darkness and the pretence of rooting out traitors. He called by Lincoln's Inn Fields. The bonfire was still smoking. By daylight the previous night's work looked even more complete, although Lord Powis' house had not been attacked, which might have been expected. This mob had not yet really found its teeth. He drove on to Weld Street, where the Spanish Embassy had become a similar hole in the terrace and the looting had spread to surrounding shops. They turned down to the Savoy, past the smouldering remains of street fires, and looked in on the Jesuit school he had seen attacked the morning before. That too had been carted away for building material. So far, the rioting had gone as well as he had hoped, but no further.

All the while he was thinking. The artillery train must still be stopped in Pall Mall. If only he could find the means…

At the bottom of the Haymarket he directed the taxi up towards the Italian embassies of Florence and Venice. He smiled at the evidence of disturbance outside both, more rubble and bonfires. Both legation chapels had been pulled down and heaps of sacerdotal paraphernalia were still ablaze on the street. Gorgeous vestments, tapestries, curtains, wooden ornamentation large and small, church furniture, paintings and picture frames, candelabras and chandeliers, canopies and rugs, flagpoles and processional banners, even things that would never burn, pots, ewers and vases, had been heaped in the flames or had rolled out, still smoking, on to the paving stones.

A dead body lay in the street, the head and torso covered by a cloak. Sticking out were the britches, stockinged calves and silver-buckled shoes of an officer of the London militia.

Spike spotted Ike in a doorway, looking fearsome in his long black coat, ignoring a small foreign gentleman who was remonstrating with him. Spike leapt out of his cab and strode over, crying out, 'Ichabod, I thought you'd still be in bed.'

'Hi Simon, no, it's Nat who's gone to bed. I couldn't sleep. Here, meet Francisco something-unpronounceable, Florentine Ambassador. I have half a mind to stick this in him to shut him up.' He drew his stabbing blade and turned it in front of the man's tear-streaked face, which did indeed silence him.

'What happened there?' asked Spike, gesturing to the corpse in the road.

'I didn't see. The lads heard there were some barrels of powder in one of these blow posts. Apparently, the captain of the trained bands took it into his head to try and defend it. He formed his men up in front and ordered them to fire on the rabble. In the first volley, a reservist shot him in the back. They are saying it was an accident. All I know is that the militia then dismissed themselves and some joined us in sacking this place. The mob has already been back once, and some have gone for ladders to take the lead off the roof. Fabulous pickings here, and up at the Venetian embassy. You'd think they were getting ready to finance a revolution. But no gunpowder.' He gave a sarcastic little grin. 'Who spreads these rumours?'

'Come with me, man,' said Spike. 'We need to get to St James' Square. I have a carriage and we can talk.'

Ike sheathed his dagger, pushed the ambassador backwards down his own steps so that he fell heavily, and walked over to the cab with Spike.

'I thought we were both going to get some rest for tonight,' said Spike.

Ike laughed. 'Fresh and uninformed. While you were asleep, I have been newsgathering. The King's army has been disbanded – unpaid.'

'No!' Spike was amazed. 'Including the Irish regiments? Still armed?'

'Exactly. It will double the impact of our rumour tonight. The Irish really could be coming, slitting throats. Also, that Council you saw gathering yesterday at Guildhall, it has asked the Prince of Orange to come into London as soon as possible. Fortunately, we planned for his early arrival. So that is also fine.'

'No. The Council of Peers dithered. It was the Mayor and Aldermen. But it reduces our likely support.'

'Timing, Spike, timing. The Council has issued a proclamation. It's being printed tonight and distributed tomorrow.' He spoke more quietly. 'You haven't told anyone about the artillery train?'

'No.'

'So, we should still see a good crowd at St James' Square this morning. The lads who missed out on the Italian loot here, gagging for action.' Ike climbed into the cab and dropped his voice further. 'How are you going to stop the cannons?'

'I still don't know. I had a plan, but Jack Wilson and a fellow calling himself Terry Jones fouled it up. I'll think of something. It may just be that we drag furniture out of the houses. *Le meglio è l'inimico del bene*, as Cousin Hugh would say.'

Ike frowned. 'Meaning?'

'Perfection is the enemy of good.'

'Can you believe it?' Ike changed the subject. 'We said the militia would shoot their officers and join us, and they have.'

Spike shouted 'St James' Square' to the cab driver and continued, 'Not really, Ike. The militia so far just haven't shown up. But this disbanding order explains everything. I had wondered why we hadn't seen them, or any troops. Not in any numbers. But it won't last. The Hierarchy will gather them back. And they will be fresher than us. Today will decide everything. If the Council gains control by tonight, then our rumour will make the people run into their arms, not ours.'

'If the cannon train gets through, I will not attack the Tower. It would be pointless. Too strong.'

'If we can take St James' Palace today, we may not need the Tower,' said Spike.

'We still need the Tower, mate. The storming of the bastion will be the symbol of our revolution. Down the generations our republic will be celebrated on December the twelfth.'

'Just so you know, Ike, even if the cannons get through, I *will* fight on. One-man-one-vote, common land returned, regular parliaments, free education for all and reforming the universities. While there is any chance, I will not give up. At moments like this, fate turns, and turns, and turns again. And my Spartans will fight on precisely because they are unaware of the artillery train's importance.'

'Spartans?' said Ike in a teasing tone. 'Is that what you are calling them?'

'I thought you coined it.'

'Well, they may die for you. But much as I like you, I won't. I will die for a vision I can imagine succeeding. Along the way I'll enjoy looting and killing as much as the next man. Particularly if it encourages the next man. But if I don't see how this plan works out, I am stepping back. If we haven't taken the Tower by tomorrow morning, we are doomed. Even if we do get it, I am not sure, without holding the King, and with the army disbanded, and with this Council in the way, that we can get to the negotiating table, let alone win. But at least if we have the Tower, I'll give it a shot, and die in the attempt if necessary.'

Spike and Ike's arrival together was a moment of high satisfaction for all concerned. The conspirators were delighted by the size of the crowd, and many in the mobile were excited to see them. Spike told the cab to stop in the middle of the square. As he alighted from the carriage he was hailed by his Spartans. He gathered them round and the mob saw it and jostled forward. He climbed on the roof of the cab, while below, the cabbie held the horse's head and Ike watched.

'Brothers, sisters, neighbours, friends,' he shouted. 'Behold the French Embassy. What weapons is Louis Quatorze holding in there? We have our reasonable suspicions. Will the ambassador arm the Catholics when he gets the signal?' Then he turned and threw an arm in the other direction. 'And yonder is St James' Palace. That is our target this morning. If we get that, we can finish things over at Whitehall too. Today, the twelfth of December, is the day that freedom takes flight, that the oppressed stand, that monarchy dies.'

The crowd cheered mightily.

'Yes, we can destroy a popish chapel, even loot a king's palace, but that is just a bit of fun. What we have to do is much more serious than that. This is about making you all burgesses in parliamentary elections and then, with our own members, reforming the law on common land, on education; and the Hierarchy knows it. They will send troops against us, but we will not run away. The troops want what we want. They will join us.' He pointed down. 'This is the ground we must hold today. This is where we show our mettle. From here we build our republic. This place will henceforth be called Freedom Square. This is where, every twelfth of December, our great-grandchildren will celebrate, grateful that the future lies in their hands, the hands of the free people of England. Tremble, you lords, landowners and lawyers! We will break your infuriating self-confidence, the arrogance of your sons, the entitlement of your daughters. We will rout your forces.'

The speech was welcomed with more hurrahs.

Spike jumped down and called his disciples around him. While he had been speaking, he had spotted a funeral cortège outside the largest house, on the north flank of the square. The coaches had moved off and turned his way. They seemed to be heading for the side road to Pall Mall. An idea began to form.

'I have a little job for you lads,' said Spike to the huddle. 'Right now, there is a funeral procession coming across the square. A hearse and three carriages. I want to use it as a rolling barricade to block off Pall Mall, in about ten minutes. Can you quietly surround it, slow it down until it is in that exit road and then hold the horses until I give the word? I will meet you there. We are going to lay an ambush, slit some throats and grab some real weapons.'

'Ambush who, Spike?' asked a printer's devil who knew him from Henry Hills'.

'You'll see,' said Spike. 'The rest of you spread out along the street towards the palace gate, check your knives, get your blood up and be ready to pounce. When the chaos starts, when the trap is sprung, charge in screaming and slashing. Then the palace will be ours. Take the mob with you. Surprise is on our side. Seize what weapons you can. This will be the first of many victories today.'

The square had filled with a huge crowd, much bigger than yesterday's in Printing House Square. Maybe ten thousand, thought Simon. The Spartans melted away. Under their influence the throng began moving towards the south and southwest exits. Spike spoke to the taxi driver. 'That will be all, mate. It's early but you are free to go. I'll be here for the next few hours. Come back at three o'clock if you happen to be free and want to earn another quid. I should be looking for a lift.'

'This exact spot?' asked the driver.

They were in the square's dead centre. 'Yes, or as near as dammit.'

The cabbie whipped up and drove back east, through the remaining crowd. Turning to Ichabod, Simon said, 'Stick with me Ike. We both need to see this, to talk about it when we are old and venerated.'

The friends worked their way south through the crowd to the junction with Pall Mall. The mob there was chanting, working itself up for its juiciest target yet, undecided between the French embassy or the Chapel Royal.

Spike knew he had five minutes to kill and asked Ike the question which had puzzled him yesterday. 'Forgive me mate, I understand what gets these boys out of bed, but what is it with Rosa? Why is she quite so crazy?'

Ike leered, 'Rosa and Carl's adoptive mother died. Mrs Luxmoore. Their child mistress, Lady Charlotte, was to be wed to some silver spoon Henry as soon as they both reached puberty. So, aged thirteen Lady C duly married a boy of fourteen. The couple took Charlotte's servants into their household. Charlotte produced their first child a year later. While she was still recovering from giving birth at that young age, the Henry, now first Earl of Lichfield, made advances to Rosa. Of course, Rosa wasn't interested. With no mother of her own to turn to, she consulted the boy's grandmother, Anne, Countess of Rochester.'

'That was a mistake,' said Spike.

'Indeed. The old Countess was a dragon at court and dangerous as Hell. She had lost three brothers to the Royalist cause in the Civil War, and had herself been widowed twice. Her second husband, Henry Wilmot, a dashing Cavalry commander, had rescued Charles after the battle of Worcester and shepherded him for six weeks.'

'Hiding up oak trees and all?' asked Spike.

'That's him. Once in France, Charles made him Earl of Rochester, but Henry died and after Charles regained his throne, Anne Rochester exploited his sympathy to the full. She never hesitated to falsify records, lie, perjure herself, and generally milk all the privileges afforded the English aristocracy. She hated servant tell-tales and anyone with dark skin. Anne told her grandson to accuse Rosa first of those very things he had tried on her. Rosa and her brother were dismissed, supposedly for exploiting their mistress' incapacity, and warned to lie low or be jailed. For the second time in their lives they were out of a home, in just the clothes they were wearing.'

'What about the sea captain?' asked Spike. 'Couldn't he help?'

'As a widower, Henry Luxmoore sought adventure one last time. Thinking the children safely employed, he had sailed off on a two-year quest. Rosa and Carl tried for a boat to Ceylon, to rejoin their mother and face down their stepfather. They stowed away on an East Indiaman, and hid in a locker until well at sea. But this time the English captain was having none of it. He marooned them on the Barbary Coast.' Spike frowned but said nothing. 'Morrocco. Aged sixteen and fourteen. Rosa saved them again. Amazing what you can do if you are literate, numerate, trilingual, play five types of musical instrument, and can shuffle a pack of cards in one hand. They made a new start in Tangier.'

'Clever girl,' said Simon. 'But it didn't end there, did it.'

'A few years later the English pulled out. Colony abandoned. Everyone who spoke nicely got free passage home with the Royal Navy. The cadaster records were a mess. Rosa had the good sense to forge some land deeds before the army blew up the whole place. She took the compensation and settled in Southwark.'

'And the brother?'

'With the East India Company now. Madras and Bombay, and he speaks Tamil, which is better than nothing. He's a factor's assistant.'

'Does he ever come back?'

'I've not met him yet, but she's seen him a couple of times. She's proud of him. Anyway, since the age of twenty-one she's been living off her winnings at cards and dice south of the river – Southwark, Bermondsey and Lambeth. In fact, she's a bit of a legend down there, in her red Phrygian cap. She's like us, got an appetite for power. Rather enjoys it. Being looked up to, giving the orders, and she's good at it too. Better than most men, and they know it. Never rigs a game and her heavies enforce legitimate debts. She only needed to lop off a few top-joints to get a reputation. She would do it personally, with a meat cleaver. Don't you love that?' Spike grimaced and looked at his forefinger. So it was true. 'Anyway, around the time she met me she had bought her own home.'

'Over London Bridge, with your fear of heights,' teased Spike.

'She hooked me in no time. You know she gave me this?' patting his blade.

A shout came from the western side of the crowd. The sea of heads swivelled.

'What can you see, Colonel?' Spike asked Ike.

'A military column, in the distance.'

'Pick me up,' said Spike. Ike lifted him to see over the crowd. 'They are earlier than I expected, but we've got them now.'

Gradually, the crowd silenced from the palace end.

'Is that music?' asked Spike, as Ike put him back down.

'Sounds like a quick march. Pipes and drums. They've got a cheek. This isn't the Lord Mayor's Show.'

'Stick with me, Ike, when the killing starts. I'm not built for the hand-to-hand stuff.'

'I'll cover you, mate,' said Ike.

The music was closer. The chanting to the east had also stopped. Spike could see nothing, but he knew where things were from the sound of the bandsmen. He went up to the two Spartans holding the black-plumed horses of the hearse. 'All right, boys, you can move them forward now. Just stand this wagon in the street, facing towards the wall. We'll bring the next one up behind you and block off these musical clowns.'

The hearse team walked forward, along with the slice of mob hemming them in. Spike said the same to the men holding the second carriage and they followed. In it, he was surprised to see the ungrateful bitch from Maiden Lane, Elizabeth Forrester, and another of about fourteen, both in black, white-faced, a pretty contrast. Elizabeth did not recognise him. Well, he thought, we only met that once, but she had this coming.

'Enough!' he said to the disciples leading the next carriage, containing six older funeral guests. 'Keep them here in the side street. Ike, stand with me here by this lot and we will have a front row seat.'

The mob to his right had begun cheering. Spike's mouth set in a grimace. He sensed his nemesis. Someone had counted on the crowd responding as patriotic crowds always did. Jack.

'How far would an artillery train need to stop without the back crashing into the front?' asked Ike.

'I doubt anyone has worked it out,' said Spike. 'But more than they have left now.'

'Are they blind? They aren't even trying,' said Ike. 'What the Hell are they thinking?'

The mob parted. Spike's view of the scene opened up. Behind the pipes and drums, next in the column, were three mounted officers. Two had drawn pistols pointed to the sky.

Elizabeth, 09:55

The mob parted. Elizabeth could see every detail of the front row of the regimental formation bearing down on her. It seemed that a crash was inevitable. The men holding the horses ducked under their necks and out of the way. Then Hendriksen was running past on the crowd-free side, heading for the hearse and shouting, 'Vhip up, drivers, move. Move! Move!' He dealt a stinging blow to the rump of the lead horse. Both carriages sprang forward and turned left. The back wheel of Elizabeth's coach slipped out of the pipers' path with just feet to spare.

From the other window, she saw how the mob was taken aback, stripped of their barricade. The soldiers were upon them, with three mounted officers, two with pistols drawn, and the long cannon train right behind, cheered on by their own crowd further up the street.

The nearest apprentices were punched back as if by an invisible hand. The truncated funeral cortège was in clear space. The leading pair of horses reared, twisting the hearse's central shaft so that the driver dropped the reins and the pallbearers clung on for dear life, while the whole contraption bucked. Then the horses forged into the mob, which recoiled like a flock of starlings or a school of mackerel, trying to escape this snorting, black-plumed vision from Hell. The hearse horses broke into a mad gallop and the girls' carriage followed closely.

Bodies went under or were flung aside. Nothing would stop the force of those death wagons now, and the crowd's panic was absolute.

Elizabeth, in the seat facing backwards, had almost fallen into Lady Henrietta's lap as their carriage sprang forward. In the rear window, the two staff coaches which should have followed had vanished. The mob was forming a respectful avenue for the troops to pass along. Rioters who had been knocked down by Emelia's bier were being dragged from the soldiers' path. Out of chaos, something like order formed. It was as if the hearse and two carriages had revealed a bigger spectacle. A military march-past of England's finest. Thousands of thrill-seekers, who had come for a different kind of show, nevertheless liked what they saw.

As the hearse reached Charing Cross, its driver managed to regain control. He turned down Whitehall, steel rims skittering sideways over the stones. Elizabeth's carriage followed. The horses slowed of their own accord as they passed the Banqueting House and under the Holbein Gate, which was open and unguarded.

In the calm of the Inner Street, they saw Lord Halifax's carriage and several other Privy Council vehicles alongside the checkerboard topiary of the Privy Garden. Past these, the little cortège came to a halt. The black horses were flecked with white foam wherever their harnesses rubbed. The drivers jumped down to hold and reassure them.

'Can you believe that?' said Elizabeth.

'*Dance macabre,*' said Henrietta.

Up ahead, William Russell stepped down from the hearse and walked back to uncurl Hendriksen, who was crouched on its backplate, still gripping the handrail for dear life. Elizabeth and Henrietta climbed out.

'Is my mother all right?' asked Henrietta.

'Yes, M'lady,' said Russell. 'We screw the coffins between mounts. Not that we expect anything like that. May I suggest we pause here for a few minutes to regain our composure?'

'Mr Hendriksen,' said Henrietta, 'would you do Elizabeth and me the honour of completing the journey with us?'

'Villingly, M'lady.'

Elizabeth thought how proud Emelia would have been of her daughter.

Jack, 09:45

The Artillery *sans* baggage swung out of Hyde Park at the novel pace. Quick march. They took the gentle downhill curve through the green park towards Pall Mall. Jack was in prime position to see ahead – the regimental band, with their thin screen of fusiliers, marching to a merry tune. Between rode the Adjutant, the Colonel on his grey and the Major, three abreast, pistols in their belts. In courtiers' mansions overlooking the park, windows were being opened to watch them. The vanguard reached Henry VIII's brick-built entrance tower to St James' Palace.

What had not been rehearsed for, now presented itself dead ahead. A street filled with a rabble of Londoners, stretching as far as the eye could see, apparently intent on entering the palace by force and now starting to look their way. It was a heart-stopping sight. To march into such a melee had been Jack's idea, which made him almost freeze in his boots. But the music played on, the soldiers tramped, the wheels rumbled and somehow the trance held.

How easily the opening came. It was like running your thumb down the seam of a ripe bean pod. Except no seam was visible. An apparently homogeneous crowd individually knew which way to jump. As they did, those behind saw the troops coming and jumped too. The music penetrated ahead, faster than the train marched and soon a channel formed for a hundred yards, down which the troops could tramp. Jack's hopes soared. This was surprise as he had conjured it. That the crowd would part like the waters of the Red Sea. But he had not imagined that they would start to clap. He almost believed the plan was going to work.

But he also knew his enemy. Jack felt him out there. Simon Speke had not finished with him yet. And indeed, at that moment, from the left side of the crowd, in the distance, where it had just parted, a funeral cortège pulled across the wide street. The black horses wore matching plumes on their heads. The drivers were uniformly in black. The black carriages were topped with black feathers and the front one contained a black casket. He remembered the under-takers arriving at Ormonde House last night and understood. Shere's column was marching into some diabolical theatre of death. The crowd now saw it too. On either side, Jack caught flashes of dagger blades emerging from under jackets and scruffy coats. He saw the adjutant and the major draw their pistols and look towards Shere. But the Colonel just gazed straight ahead.

The leading bandsmen were now almost upon the carriages. Even back where he was, Jack could see the fuzz of the plumes, the detail of the carved black rails around each roof. Then a portly, middle-aged man, also dressed in black, sprinted out from the crowd, gesticulating up at the drivers and slapping a lead horse on the rump. The funereal vehicles sprang forward. The fusiliers and bandsmen did not miss a stride. It was as if a secret panel had slid open. As the hind carriage turned, Jack spied Elizabeth facing backwards, grasping the sides, trying not to fall into the footwell.

The funeral horses took the bits between their teeth and were away, carving a channel for the train, but no longer neatly, leaving bodies scattered in the road, which friends pulled clear. As Jack passed the side street from which the hearse had appeared, he saw two other black carriages, with identical black-plumed horses, held back by the crowd.

Kitty, 10:00

Kitty walked unsteadily from the Apothecaries' Hall to Glass House Yard. Her world was rocked. James a duke? James a royal bastard? *The seed of the adulterer and the whore,* as Isaiah put it. The most toxic man in England, in Nicholas' words. And about to leave the country. Thoughts heaped on thoughts. She despaired of what people would say. Her 'love' would now be interpreted as ambition, treachery, in the worst possible taste. If James FitzJames left England, then so should she. Could she bring herself to fly the nest? Then she thought of poor James himself. Abandoned by his father. A king who had fallen from such a height, from excess to exile, his income cut off, his estates attaindered, his supporters proscribed, an object of mockery, of pitiless derision, leaving his bastard son to fish for a wife in the puddle of continental cast-offs.

On the other hand, James FitzJames was healthy, intelligent, at the start of his life, good looking, multilingual, steady, experienced beyond his years, well-connected, educated – many would envy him all that baggage.

'Papa,' Kitty called as she walked back into the house.

'Here, darling daughter,' came from the sitting room.

'Are you free for a moment?'

'If it's quick. I'll be setting off for Guildhall shortly. Come and sit with me.'

She settled beside her father on the banquette and put her head on his shoulder.

She asked, 'Have you ever heard of James FitzJames, Duke of Berwick?'

'Well, of course I have,' said her father.

'And what do you think?'

'Who's asking?'

'Only me,' said Kitty.

'Well, if it's only you, I will be frank. It is a pity King James didn't marry Arabella Churchill when Anne Hyde died in 1671. James FitzJames was a tiny baby and could have been legitimised. He'd have made an excellent Prince of Wales. His father only admitted to Catholicism in 1676, three years after marrying his second wife, Mary of Modena. He may have been Catholic before that, but Arabella would have steered her husband and his son to her Protestant faith. The boy is only Catholic because his wicked stepmother wanted him so, and out of the country, and had him packed off to the Jesuits in France. Maybe his long childhood exile toughened him up – men and women are schooled by youthful adversity. Maybe, if he had lived in the English Court as Prince of Wales, he would have grown into a spoilt brat. Maybe Monmouth, his older bastard cousin, would have cowed him. But James FitzJames came back from the Continent with more energy in his fingertips than most of our supercilious aristocratic trash have in their entire bodies. More charm and courtly manners, more poetry, more humanity, more dash. Henry VII's great-great-great-great-grandson. There's a touch of the Tudors about him.'

Kitty was tempted to say that Lord Ranelagh had expressed the same opinion. But she also realised that she needed more time to digest all this. It was too soon to bare her heart, even to her father.

Edward said, 'I have something serious we need to discuss.'

'Can we do that now?'

'No, because it needs time and I must get up to Guildhall to linger in the anterooms and catch this *Declaration* printing contract when it pops up.'

'Can I come with you?'

'Good idea. You might glean some hard news for the *Gazette*, and I may need someone to run errands. But let's give ourselves an hour tomorrow to think seriously, once the Council's *Declaration* is out.'

'No need for me to change,' said Kitty, putting her scarf back on.

They bid farewell to the mistresses of the house and set off on foot for Guildhall.

'These dark December days,' said Edward Jones looking at the sky. 'I'm not surprised the King ran away.'

'How can you even joke about that, dearest Papa? To be born to such privilege and then feel so sorry for yourself that you run away from your responsibilities. It is just disgusting.'

'He didn't ask to be King. God made it happen.'

'Yes he did ask,' said Kitty. 'Maybe not at first but, in a way, that's worse. As a young man in exile, he was happy to be invited back as Duke of York. His older brother would have legitimate children. That would be fun without the responsibility. However, by the time his brother's wife proved unable to bring a pregnancy to term, he had grown big-headed enough to angle for the succession, even though many wanted him excluded.'

'That's not true. The Stuarts were always great believers in family. Charles I called his two sons together before the end and drummed that into them. The Duke of York was to obey his older brother the king and back him up at every opportunity.'

'Well, the Duke may have been loyal,' argued Kitty, 'but he got what he wanted in the end, to be King. He built up a court that relied on him, only to let them down and run away when things grew too tough.'

'I'm surprised at you, Kitty. You stick to your guns on religion and he is sticking to his. He finally has a legitimate son whom he, in good conscience, wants to bring up Catholic. In this bigoted country of Protestants, he knows that a Catholic cannot currently be heir. He also knows that one day such things will not matter. Whether that day is four years away or four hundred, who can tell. He finds that all his efforts to accelerate the change come to nought. So, rather than accept a humiliating compromise or step aside for his Protestant daughter by his first wife, Mary, he runs away. To live to fight another day, perhaps. You would probably do the same.'

'Leaving the field in the possession of the enemy. It's a recipe for disaster. He supposedly sent carriage-loads of gold ahead with his wife and son. And will probably receive support from Louis XIV. But he will never be able to mount and execute an invasion of England like the Prince of Orange has. Not even a tenth of one. He should have stayed in Whitehall and faced down his accusers.'

'Ireland is Catholic. Scotland is Stuart,' said Edward. 'He is still king in both of those. Maybe he thinks the English will tire of their Dutchman, as they did of Cromwell; that he, James, can still turn the tables, as his brother Charles did.'

'Neither of those countries have the population or temperament to conquer England. Perhaps if they tried it together, but their aims and attitudes are so different. They wouldn't trust each other that far. No, he has made his bed and now must lie in it.'

Father and daughter skirted the scaffolding around the still-rising St Paul's and reached Guildhall Yard. They passed the arched entrance to the cloth market, Blackwell Hall, on the right, the new fire station on the left, and approached Wren and Hooke's grand entrance, flanked by the office of the City Comptroller and the steps down to the coal holes.

Kitty thought Guildhall almost as dignified as the Tower of London, and the finest non-ecclesiastical building in the City. The mayoralty had not escaped the fire twenty-two years before, but its medieval walls, end gables and stone tracery windows had survived. The magnificent space had since gained a new pitched roof, with high, suspended coffered ceiling. Its volume was second only to Westminster Hall.

The edifice was strangely silent. A doorman was allowing the few petitioners and hangers-on into the Great Hall. Some made themselves comfortable on the benches of the two Sherriff's Courts, under the large west window. Others sat with their legs swinging off the side of the hustings dais, a stage running the full width beneath the matching east window. Keen petitioners stood on the steps leading up to the Mayor's Court, the Aldermen's Court and the Council Chamber, tucked away behind the north side.

Edward was careful not to push through.

The men in front of them were discussing the previous night's riots. 'Did you hear about the Spanish Ambassador's place last night? Rich pickings, they say.'

Rather than engage in the rights and wrongs of diplomatic immunity, Edward turned to his daughter and kept up a whispered commentary. 'Since the Fire, the Mayor and Corporation have been gradually buying up neighbouring plots. There's an unusual shape to the street plan either side, where Basinghall Street and Aldermanbury bulge away from each other. It makes for an exceptionally large city block. When the Corporation has bought up the whole site we'll find out why.'

'But surely they'll keep this hall,' said Kitty.

'As sure as we can be of anything. But times change and so do tastes. Until the Fire, the canopy over there' (he pointed at the eastern hustings) 'had two huge, ancient, wooden carved statues of giants. Gog and Magog. They were supposedly to remember two barbarians, or maybe barbaric tribes, which Londoners are said to have defeated. I would love to see someone replace them. But fashions change.'

'No one believes in giants, or fairies or sprites any more, Papa. And if they do, it's idolatry.'

'Well, they'd been there since before recorded history. They were a reminder that little people can bring down the mighty. London's David and Goliath story. I see no harm in that.'

Kitty felt irritated with her father, or perhaps she was more generally disappointed. The whole place felt oddly deflating. A parochial council, she reflected, rather than the spinning hub of history.

When they reached the front of the queue, Edward told the gatekeeper at the top of the ceremonial steps, 'We've come for Secretary Gwyn, Council of Lords Spiritual and Temporal.'

'Not here, squire,' said the man. 'The Lords are back at the Privy Council Chamber in Whitehall from now on. It was agreed when they stopped sitting yesterday.'

'Wrong place!' Edward pressed his clenched fists to his brow. 'But we must fly. We can still make it.' He almost ran, Kitty certainly did, and within a minute they were in a cab heading back towards Ludgate.

'This is Halifax's doing,' said Edward, settling in his seat.

'You're obsessed. He wasn't even at the meeting that changed the venue.'

'Maybe. But the Mayor and Aldermen are close to the Prince of Orange's party. The peers won't let Guildhall be the seat of power. Not that the Aldermen think like that, or want it to be. Oh, we have wasted a valuable hour. They might have told me they had changed.'

'You are whining, Papa, and it's not becoming. It was for you to find out. That is what the *London Gazette* does. News. These people hardly know what's going on themselves. They see the rabble as a problem for the sheriffs and trained bands, but it isn't. Something else is afoot. It's as if there are two revolutions, the one we talk about and the one we don't.'

'Until the one we don't talk about does something worth talking about, it's not really there, is it?' said Edward.

'By the time it does something worthy of the *Gazette*, it will have won. You people in charge need to understand what the unenfranchised want. You need to adopt the good bits before frustration boils over into something much worse. What if some of it *is* reasonable? Surely the *Gazette* should look into that and report both sides of the argument.'

Edward sighed. 'That would get us shut down and me thrown into prison for sedition.'

'Will you even report these riots?'

'It depends on what the Council gives me this morning. It they take a full front page, then no, I will have no space tomorrow. Issue 1,409 will be historic anyway, without adding your kind of news about revolution from below. The Spanish ambassador's fate, which we overheard just now, is news, told in a diplomatic way for our foreign readers. Sacking an embassy. That's something every court in Europe cares about.'

'I would have thought an attempted citizens' revolt would interest other monarchies,' said Kitty.

Edward conceded. 'If we have only a column or so from the Council, then, yes, I promise to mention it. An interesting stop press on page two.'

The cab pulled up outside the Banqueting Hall in Whitehall. Thirty-nine years before, from one of these tall windows, King Charles I had stepped out to the scaffold to be decapitated for insisting on his divine right to rule as he saw fit. The place still felt like a shrine. The crowd on that distant morning had feared, if the King was God-given, that the ground would open and swallow them for such defiance; or they would be struck by lightning. As it was, the day had gone on like any other. Retribution only came eleven years later, after the Restoration, when those most complicit in regicide, and still living, had been punished. Sixteen were hanged, twenty-five imprisoned for life and a similar number frightened into permanent exile, where one or two were murdered.

Edward led Kitty through a warren of passages deep into the palace. 'No guards. This is awful. Look, the Lord Chamberlain's Office, empty, stripped of ornaments..., the Lord Keeper's Office likewise, all pictures and mantel decorations gone.... Here we are.'

The Council Chamber lobby had double doors into the Chamber itself, and one of these was ajar. Outside, in Whitehall's Privy Garden they saw a soldier in captain's uniform pacing the gravel paths. He looked fine in his sweeping, broad-brimmed black hat, haystack-yellow hair with matching crescent moustache, and his blue and scarlet tunic flowing under steel breast and back plates.

'Papa,' Kitty whispered. 'That man is in Lieutenant Wilson's regiment. Shouldn't the *London Gazette* talk to him? For our readers?'

'Later,' said Edward. 'He'll still be here when we are done. He has no hope of getting back to his unit dressed like that with the streets the way they are this morning.'

Well, thought Kitty, if he had any sense, he'd take the cab that dropped us off. But she changed the subject. 'What's happening in the Council Chamber, Papa?'

Jones looked through the crack. He gave it a small push so that more of the inside could be seen, nodded to the chair, then returned to her side. 'Most of the Privy Council are here, plus other members of the House of Lords who happen to be in town. The council secretaries, Richard Collings and Francis Gwyn, are taking the minutes, there, at the end of table. Old Collings has done this for thirty years, a frightful gossip. Not to me, but I hear things back from Pepys, and from Morrice, the Presbyterian journalist. Tight-lipped Gwyn is the coming man, a Somerset Welshman and currently MP for Cardiff. Rich, forty years old and too busy to marry.'

'You mean too busy to get married? Or too busy for me to want to marry him?'

'Yes, yes. Very funny. The man in the chair facing us is the Marquess of Halifax. Just back from negotiating with the Prince of Orange. He wasn't there yesterday up at Guildhall. The Archbishop of Canterbury chaired that Council. Interesting, Dr Sancroft has not come back. Although I see the Archbishop of York.'

Edward sat Kitty down in a corner of the lobby where they could watch the door, but still talk quietly. This was a game they loved, where she picked up stuff, the way the World worked, the meaning of life, and would bat it back to him, sometimes hours, sometimes weeks, sometimes even years later.

Edward kept up his commentary. 'Lord Halifax is that rare creature, an intelligent man who can think on his feet, speak beautifully, and remain moderate. The King dismissed him as President of this Council for wanting to retain the anti-Catholic Test Acts, and for resisting the standing army. He's trusted by both sides, just now. Usually, he drives at least half of them mad. He tends to move his weight to support the weaker voice in any given debate.'

'Halifax,' said Kitty, nodding. 'I've seen his pamphlet, *Character of a Trimmer*. Trimming in the sense of balancing a boat to get the best speed out of it. Full of the usual typos, of course. The world just gets sloppier. Why don't these authors use proper proofreaders, instead of leaving it all to their public? It's almost as if a few typographical errors are the new sign of authenticity.'

'Spoken like a true printer's daughter,' said Edward. 'As George Savile, Halifax was a member of parliament for eight years after the Restoration. He rose on merit, and was elevated by Charles II, must be twenty years ago. He saved King James' chances of succeeding his brother, but then was demoted and fired from the Privy Council when James became King, only to be recalled and now dismissed again.'

A movement in the Chamber silenced them. Documents were brought to the Chairman, then passed around, different council members signing different ones. Then Francis Gwyn came through to the lobby and called for Edward, 'Mr Jones, Printer at the Savoy.'

Kitty and her father stepped forward. They had made it in time.

'Here are your instructions, signed by sixteen members of this Council.' He gave Edward the note and held up a second paper. 'This Declaration will be your lead story in tomorrow's *Gazette*. Four hundred words and twenty-nine signatures. And here is a third document. It is the order from this Council to Lords Pembroke, Weymouth, Culpepper and the Bishop of Ely to take this Declaration to Prince William. They went first thing this morning with a report of yesterday's proceedings at Guildhall. I want all three published together, single-sided, posters and handbills – two reams of public notices – usual procedure for Declarations. When can I have the galleys?'

Kitty saw that Edward's victory had rendered him speechless for a moment. She stepped in to clarify their instructions. 'The posters and flyers – how many variations? What paper?'

'Two sizes,' said Gwyn to Edward as if Kitty had not spoken. 'Say, hand and royal hand, have you that in stock? I want the larger ones legible from a window or news wall.'

Edward recovered. 'Hand and royal hand are in stock. So, two settings, medium and large, standard font. Plus the *Gazette* front page. Hmm.' He thought for a moment. 'All back here by half past three. My daughter will bring the proofs. When can you sign off?'

'While she waits. Fifteen minutes to proofread all three, if no mistakes.'

Edward asked, 'What rates do we charge for the posters, and to whose account?'

'Rush rates, Privy Council account.'

'Mr Secretary Gwyn,' said Edward, 'with the greatest respect, this will be double-rush rates.' Francis Gwyn looked sceptical, but open to reason. Edward continued, 'You heard what happened at the King's Printing House last night.

Few printers are functioning today, what with all apprentices being on the streets. My shop will have the *Gazette* out in the morning; and we'll do your posters and handbills, even if we have to work the spare press through the night ourselves. But the labourer is worthy of his hire – the rate must be fair for the circumstances.'

'Double-rush rates it is, Mr Jones. Don't let me down. With Hills off the park, there's more where this came from. I look forward to seeing you or your daughter.' He turned to Kitty for the first time, 'How do you do, Miss Jones? Three-thirty today, or earlier if possible. I can arrange cash on delivery – to the booksellers, not here.' Francis Gwyn turned on his heel and resumed his own double-rush job.

'Kitty,' said Edward beginning to walk to a different exit, 'I will start the typesetting. Please go home and tell your mother we need all hands on deck, code red, then join me back at the Savoy.'

In the courtyard behind the Banqueting House, he tipped the surprised doorman. 'Roly, there's no guard on the Holbein Gate entrance.'

'We haven't the staff, Mr Jones, Sir.'

'And remember this face. My daughter, Kitty Jones. Kitty, this is Constable Roland de Luge, you will not meet a man with a better memory for faces. Roly, let her in from now on, it's for Mr Secretary Gwyn.'

'Yes, Mr Jones, Sir, day or night,' said de Luge,

'And we need a taxi.'

The watchman placed forefinger and thumb to his mouth and, with a screech that sent the crows flapping off the rooflines, whistled up a cab.

The blond-haired officer whom Kitty had seen pacing earlier, had positioned himself close at hand. He made her shiver, in a reptilian way, like the snake in the Garden of Eden. As he passed, he caught her eye, or maybe she caught his.

She wanted him to know that she had recognised his uniform, and that she was not just some court decoration. 'Did Jack get the caltrops?' she called after him, which stopped the captain in his tracks. Immediately, she regretted it.

Edward continued talking to Kitty, 'Bring your mother in this coach, you won't find another, so pay him to wait.' They climbed in. 'And please fetch my mother too, gently; and food, and refreshments. We have cots there. This will take all night and I don't want mother alone with the rabble up like this. Here's money, just get them and you to the Savoy to help; and certainly in time to bring these galleys back here to Mr Gwyn by three-thirty.'

The blond captain was at her window. 'Thank you, Miss, yes. A sweet night's work, damn his handsome chops. Though I can imagine sweeter,' he said, and he raised an eyebrow and gave a twist to his blond moustache.

'Savoy, Blackfriars, then wait, then back to the Savoy,' shouted Edward, and with a shake of the reins the hackney cab was off.

Kitty flared inwardly at the captain's words. Who did he think he was? Evidently a close colleague of Jack's, perhaps his immediate superior. What had induced her to provoke him like that? And why did he have to insult her? But the caltrops were safe. A sweet night's work. She could not have put it better herself.

Simon, 10:00

Spike's world was rocked. All around him, the mobile was cheering, even his Spartans were caught up in the new mood. What a splendid thing the Royal Ordnance was, a national treasure, so long as it was marching past you, not aiming at you. Spike hated that. It showed the fickle heart of the mob. He must be patient while they enjoyed the spectacle.

What uniforms! What music! What flintlocks! And above all, what mighty cannon, dealers of death, heading for something more important than a mob of 10,000. So professional, so unperturbed, so physical; fit, honest, martial. What men! Anything else suddenly looked trivial. Childish. Infantile. So, you have sacked a defenceless embassy? Grow up. So, you want to fight me? You cannot be serious. As for one-man-one-vote? Why not join the army instead?

Spike had grabbed Ike's sleeve as the first cannon passed. 'Those two. The tall lieutenant and the little corporal. That's them who've done this. Remember their faces. Jack Wilson and Terry Jones. They took my caltrops.'

'Got it. Except for the caltrops bit,' had said Ike.

Simon held on to his sleeve to keep his eyes from wandering back to the march past. 'Caltrops. Speke's spikes.' He tried to make a four-spike shape with the fingers of one hand. 'They position faster than hearses, and do not move thereafter. Two hundred and fifty of them. I will be avenged. Did you see those men, Ike? If I don't make it, you'll avenge me, won't you?'

'Yes man, I saw them. I'll remember those ugly mugs. But I'm sorry, Spike. The artillery and fusiliers will now reach the Tower of London. My soft target just became impregnable. You know what that means?'

Spike sagged but did not answer.

The train passed and the majority of the rabble began to disperse, laughing and slapping each other on the back. The Spartans had an inkling that something had gone wrong. That this was bad. They gathered around Spike looking for a lead. He needed to pick them up quickly. He searched for the spark within himself. Had he lost the war, or just a battle? However, he had spotted something more distant – history turning.

'Hey,' he shouted to his disciples, 'those fools missed us. They fluffed it. They could have dispersed us, but they didn't. They are like a runaway cart blindly following the kerbstones. Their last order was probably to go home and that is all they can do.' He continued more quietly, and those near him hushed to listen. 'What kind of revolutionaries are we if we forget our cause at the first pretty little military parade? Remember our age-old grievances. Remember these extraordinary times, this is the one chance to change things peacefully for many generations.'

A murmur of consent ran through his audience.

'Spread the word. The Royal Chapel and the Palace are still on. But first we need to secure our flank. Now they have seen us, they will try to come back. Foot guards, militia, maybe horse. That means we need to hold this square against all comers. The militia joined with us at the Spanish embassy last night; they shot an officer and came over at the Florentine embassy this morning. And that was before they knew that the King had disbanded everyone. All the more likely they will turn to us now. Some government troops, here and there, will stick together, like the gunners we have just seen, but they too will have no fight in them.'

'Yes, Spike, that's more like it, they've no fight in 'em.' The mob was getting its fire back. 'We're with you, Spike.'

'First, I need a few of you to scout out the side streets. We need warnings of any attacks.'

His usual acolytes stepped forward.

No sooner had he spoken than the ground shook and a troop of twenty cavalry swept through out of Charles Street, charged across the middle of the square and disappeared into King Street. They had not drawn sabres, but a handful of late-rising rioters or early drinkers had stood in their way and now lay concussed and bruised in the dirt.

'See what I mean? Get scouting,' yelled Spike, clapping his hands, and a dozen Spartans trotted off.

Spike's mind was racing. The rump of the funeral cortége was released. He needed fixed defences, furniture from houses. The nearest and softest targets were the homes along the south side of the square, unshuttered and easily entered. 'There's your barricade,' he shouted, pointing to the terrace of dwellings. 'Pull bulky stuff out and start building a fence in the middle of the square. A circle, a ring, minimum perimeter, minimum weak points.'

But the pickings came slowly and were thin – dining room chairs, kitchen dressers. 'We need wagons and carriages we can tip over,' said one of his lieutenants. 'The barricade group has those for tonight, but in the city. Even if we had some way to get them here, they can't be spared, they have barely enough as it is.'

'Nonsense, there's plenty here. Beds, cupboards, washstands, dressers. I want not a stick of furniture left in any of those houses. Move.'

Nevertheless, Spike felt another wave of nausea. He had forgotten the barricade group. The barricaders could not close the yawning gap in the southeast corner of their line caused by the loss of the Tower. The Royal Artillery would shoot down on them from the walls. So, how far back should they hold such a line? Downstream of London Bridge, that was for sure. Holding London Bridge could still be an asset, depending on their support in the south. Ike knew Southwark, but the place was a law unto itself.

For the first time, Spike sensed that feeling which must creep over the captain of a sinking man-of-war. He must go down with it. But this would not happen for a while. It was still too early to call 'abandon ship'. He must give fate another chance, let time deal him more cards, to twist luck the other way. Who knew, a proverbial shot into the magazine, or in his case another mutiny among the militiamen, might still win the day. His troops were still thirsting for a fight, the latecomers had seen no booty, and the earliest were already back for more. However, in his heart he knew that from now on they would be fighting out of anger, or for booty, or just for the sake of the fight, but not because they could hold the balance of power if they won, not even because they might win.

Ike had evidently been thinking the same thing. While the rioters warmed to their new task, he took two of the barricade chairs to one side and sat Spike down.

'What's up, Colonel?' Spike asked him.

'Why are we fighting?'

'Because we might win.'

'Before the cannon train we were ten thousand. Now we're five. If we don't quickly start looting the embassy, the palace and the chapel we will be one thousand. How are we going to win?'

'We need one more mutiny. Supposedly, the army has been disbanded. So, regular troops will hesitate to fire on us. The militia may even join us – they hate the idea of a standing army as much as we do. And we still have tonight's rumour about the Irish coming – unpaid, still armed, insane.'

'And if the rumour backfires and people are so panicked that all rioting stops?'

'We have six hours before the rumour. That's long enough to cause a mutiny. After that, the Council won't dare send more troops.'

'All right, so paint me a picture, mate. I want to believe. The Council sends the militia, the militia shoots its officers again and we all go and loot the palace. Tonight, the rumour spreads and the barricade group seals off the city.'

'But with a gap around the Tower.'

'Exactly. Then what?'

'Would we have the Council at our mercy?' wondered Spike. 'No, because we don't have the Tower. Meanwhile, the Tower has twenty-six more cannon and four hundred more fusiliers than we'd planned.'

'Could we assassinate the Council?' asked Ike, fingering his dagger.

'Or kidnap them?' said Spike.

'Poison?' mused Ike.

Simon saw that the central circle of household furniture was forming into a respectable barricade. 'Do you know any poison makers?' he smiled. He was turning the corner. This was the part he loved about conversations with Ike. Conspiracy for its own sake.

'Apothecaries?' said Ike.

Spike's face darkened. He conjured a luminous auburn-blonde turning away into Apothecaries' Hall. 'You know who else is responsible for this mess? Apart from the officer and the corporal? Kitty. She's the only soul I mentioned caltrops to. I thought it would go over her head. I was trying to show off and of course my vanity has been punished a thousand-fold. But she deserves to die for that. If I don't make it, Kitty Jones, Jack Wilson and Terry Jones must all die.'

'You'll make it, Spike,' said Ike. 'Anyway, the caltrops weren't infallible. They had their own risk.'

'Like what?'

'Like the artillery train suspecting a trap, anticipating an ambuscade. They only came on because they knew they had foiled your plot. Why else would they have risked it?'

Spike smiled again. 'We did well to conceal we knew they were coming. Meant the lads behaved naturally beforehand, for the Royal Ordnance scouts, didn't it?'

'That was my idea, but I was wrong,' said Ike. 'We should not have kept it to ourselves. We gave their colonel back the advantage of surprise. And God, did he use it. Only a London mobile could change its mood like that. I might have foreseen it. But it would take a genius to bet his regiment on it.'

'Are you saying their colonel is some kind of military genius?'

'Well, he out-thought us. If he's stupid, what does that make us?'

'All professional soldiers are stupid.'

'Maybe their philosophy of life is stupid,' said Ike. 'Support the landowners against the labourers. Help big countries to eat up small ones, to finance more war, to gain even more markets, for the benefit of the owners. But unless a soldier is killed or maimed, he has quite a good life. The officers get to throw their weight around. Some even study the art of surprise and ponder battlefield control. And the cockerel's plumage pulls the hens. No, professional soldiers may be hateful, but they are not all stupid.'

Spike shook his head. 'If the choice is between a barracks and a school dormitory, between a parade ground and a playground, between a regimental cook or a seminary servitor, give me the school every time. Let's have education for all, child literacy, free school meals. A literate, numerate, productive population is surely the best defence any country can have.'

'So, today we fight and die for an impossible utopia,' said Ike. 'Why don't you and I keep that little secret to ourselves too.'

'It is not impossible. Ike, you are forgetting yourself. This century or next. This millennium or next. It will come. All we can do is try to speed it up.'

'And get our names in the books those students read,' added Ike.

Three scouts ran in from Charles Street on the east side. 'Soldiers, Spike,' said the first to arrive.

'Looks like Colonel Baggot's Foot,' said the second.

'The Horse went up thataway,' gesturing north and east, 'round Piccadilly and down the Haymarket, getting ready for another pass.'

Spike called the rabble round him. 'Listen, comrades. Regular troops are coming. This is good. The foot soldiers are bringing what we need, which is muskets and bayonets, maybe pikes. With bayonets and pikes we can stop the horses. If the cavalry comes through first, stand back, let them go. Only jump out when you have the footguards' flank.'

'Where do we get the bayonets and pikes, Spike?'

'From the foot soldiers. We must mob them before they can form up. Ambush them when they are just into the square. Get over there, either side of the Charles Street entrance. All right, go!'

A hundred listeners ran off to the east side of the square, collecting more as they went. At the same time a scout from the west ran up and said quietly to Spike, 'The Royal Ordnance baggage train is still in Hyde Park, with little guard.'

'Good to know, but let's not get distracted,' said Spike. 'We may feel their collars a bit later.'

Of course, he thought, they decided to run two convoys to the Tower, the faster, more valuable one first. Next convoy will be slower. Probably via Oxford Street. Let's see how things go here.

As Spike had foreseen, the cavalry came through, east to west again, and the rioters stepped back into the corners of the square, or behind the barricaded ring in the middle, watched them fly past and let them go. Then came the infantry column. The mob in the corners held well, letting them parade into the square, before attacking from both flanks. The section of foot numbered barely a hundred and were unprepared for a close fight. A hand-to-hand scuffle against fearsome odds was not what they had trained for. Some soldiers fought bravely, others threw down their muskets and ran away. In short order, the company was overwhelmed and their captain surrendered.

Spike walked in and received his sword. A loud cheer went up. The rabble was back in good heart.

'Disarm the prisoners and take their jackets to show they are now neutral,' said Spike. 'If they won't join us, take their boots as well. Then release them. No prisoners and no unnecessary killing. Quickly. The next wave will be here in a moment. Scouts, go back out and find them.'

The mob was having fun. About a quarter of the soldiers switched sides, and from the rest a pile of boots grew near the front porch of the French Embassy. As the captain, his three lieutenants and their remaining men shuffled away in their stockinged feet, Spike was lifted shoulder-high so that the mob could see him.

'Now we need two groups,' he shouted. 'A smaller one with the captured muskets and bayonets, and a bigger one for infighting. Muskets that side of me. Infighters this. Quickly, we have very little time.'

As the crowd at the Crown Tavern had the morning before, a narrow gap appeared down the middle of his audience.

'If you have a musket and bayonet, fix the bayonet and get into the barricade ring. Prepare for the next cavalry attack. When it comes, stay low. Crouch under the furniture. Keep out of reach of the sabres. Aim for the horses. I want those horses shot or stabbed in the belly if they jump over you. Lose the bayonet if you must. Keep your heads clear of the hind hooves. The next time the cavalry comes through must be the last. Either their mounts will be dying, or their riders will be too afraid. Keep the ring small. Don't let chargers gather in the middle. If they get in, swarm them, club them, pull them down, like we did last month in Clerkenwell. Drive them out. Off you go and have fun.'

He turned to the majority who had remained.

'You infighters are for the infantry. Rule one is stay out of the way of the cavalry. Let them through to the barricade. While they are in the square, tuck into the corners, where they can't manoeuvre. Rule two is to arrest and disarm, rather than kill. Keep in the shadow of the buildings until the foot soldiers are alongside. Repeat what we just did. Jump out only when you have their flank, no earlier. And not so late that they can form up and fire. We must assume that their tactics will improve. So, I want four groups, one for Charles Street, one for Duke Street, up by Ormonde House, and one in between, ready to go either way, or down to the bottom of the square, if they come on three sides. Soldiers, welcome to the party. Please share yourselves between the groups. We need your discipline and skill. And someone fetch those malingerers in Pall Mall and get them up here. This is where the action is. We will all have our booty soon enough.'

Another cheer went up.

'So, four groups please, you know what to do.'

Scouts shouted, 'Cavalry, Duke Street'.

As a flock of pigeons bursts in different directions, so the rabble ran for the corners of the square, mainly by Ormonde House and Halifax House. In the central ring, the bayoneters crouched under their low barricade. A waterfall of sound came into earshot, first a whisper, then a roar, as hundreds of horseshoes on hard earth, many tons of horseflesh, washed down from Piccadilly.

The ground shook.

Elizabeth, 10:05

In the calm of the street within the Palace of Whitehall, beside the clipped parterre of the Privy Gardens, Lady Henrietta took Hendriksen by the arm and said in her mother's tongue, '*U heeft het goed gedaan, beste heer Hendriksen.* You have done well, my dear Mr Hendriksen.'

'It vas ze moment to act, M'lady,' he said, looking down.

'It was indeed. You did great service to my mother's memory, and to me.'

Elizabeth added, 'And to this city. Did you see the knives out? They were ready to slit throats.'

'It seems we have two revolutions,' said Henrietta. 'William of Orange's and the people's. Why else would they try and stop soldiers, rather than just do their looting somewhere unguarded? They want to take control.'

Hendriksen said, 'Zey care for power zemselves. Ze King has gone, ze Orange revolution has yet to come.'

Elizabeth nodded. 'Kitty Jones tried to warn me yesterday that the Spekes had hatched something. Henri, it's a revolution within a revolution.'

The drivers rubbed down the horses, the passengers stretched their legs. When all was calm again, the pallbearers re-embarked. 'Please Ladies, into our coach,' said Hendriksen. 'Ve have grievous business to attend.'

The procession, if two vehicles could still be called that, trotted on to St Margaret's Westminster. Before that modest edifice, they turned right, under the vast cliff of Westminster Abbey, and finally round to the unfinished western facade. Its central gothic-arched window and elongated statues of twenty saints overwhelmed the single pointed doorway below. The convoy stopped and the oak double doors opened inwards. Only when Bishop Sprat and two vergers stepped out and were dwarfed by the entrance, did the building snap into scale.

The mourners alighted. Henrietta, Elizabeth and Hendriksen stood to one side while Russell's men unclamped the casket and slid it off the hearse.

The Bishop approached and said, 'I will take the service from our 1662 Book of Common Prayer. What the choir does is up to them. They have been well paid.'

He greeted the black coffin with, '*I am the resurrection and the life, saith the Lord: he that believeth in me, though he were dead, yet shall he live: and whosoever liveth and believeth in me shall never die.*'

He then led the procession into the cavernous Abbey. The space inside was dim. The floor was as sparse as an open deck. A double row of massive, fluted columns rose from its surface, marching into the distance and soaring up to bear the rib-vaulted roof. The architectural style was deeply unfashionable – Wren had rejected the pointed arch as 'Saracen'. However, Elizabeth felt the intended effect, an irresistible impulse to turn the eye upwards to Heaven, to tilt the head backwards, to drop the jaw. Peerless piers, she would have said to Jack, and he would have laughed.

A plain paved stripe led straight through the chevron pattern of the flagstone floor. Down this the procession slow-marched in silence, led by the Bishop and vergers, the pallbearers and coffin in the middle, the three mourners behind. In such a void, the group barely seemed to progress, and yet around them the vessel had its own dynamic, as if hurtling through a spiritual realm quite disassociated with the earth it sat on. Centuries of constant prayer and worship had powered it up to be an ark for the ages.

After the tumult of their journey from Ormonde House, the silence affected Elizabeth more than any music could have. The sense of approaching something holy rose to a pitch she had not imagined.

It took well over a minute for the party to reach the empty choir stalls. As they began to pass between the bare pews, an unaccompanied solo alto, out of sight in the north transept, led off the first notes of what might have been a Latin requiem. The music was from another time, again deeply out of fashion, probably even illegal, but the effect was so stunning that the party simply stopped.

The sound grew into four voices, but sung by a full choir, with no musical instrument involved. Half now came in from the south transept, visibly bound to the north by the precentor, conducting from the pulpit. The acoustic dimensions matched the vastness the eye beheld – polyphonic English counterpoint, harmony with discord, splashing off the walls, floor and vaulted roof from two directions – and the aural effect was ravishing.

Bishop Sprat tiptoed back to Elizabeth. After a moment he breathed in her ear, 'I know this is wrong, being written by a Catholic. But...' What he was about to say was almost too awful to utter. He swallowed, 'It may be the last time Byrd is ever sung in this place and Emelia loved him so.'

Elizabeth saw he had tears running down his face. She looked around, so did Henrietta and Hendriksen.

'We must go on,' she said quietly, and the Bishop signalled for the pallbearers to continue.

The little coffin passed the high altar, moated by its vast, swirling, Italian mosaic, already four hundred years old, and along the north ambulatory, winding round the shrine of Edward the Confessor. Just as Emelia herself had on Sunday, her coffin turned up the steps to Henry VII's Lady Chapel. To the opening bars of the *Gloria*, the Bishop led them past the tombs of Queens Mary and Elizabeth, and round the slab marking the resting spot of their grandfather, Henry Tudor.

Now they were in the presence of family. The Ormonde crypt lay straight ahead and the capstone had been lifted. Steps led down into a candlelit space where the coffins of Henrietta's grandfather, grandmother, father and little niece lay. The men lowered their burden on to trestles. The choir reached its superb, sophisticated 'Amen' and Bishop Sprat launched into his tribute.

He spoke of the small wager he and Lady Emelia had taken only three days before, as to where they would each be by that time next week. Had he but known then what he knew now, he would have answered differently. He recalled an early encounter, when he was a young prelate finding his feet at court.

'She used to say, "If you can, in your lifetime, touch the stars just once, don't hesitate." Emelia and her equally beautiful sister were among the shooting stars of the Restoration, but Emelia was the most genuine of all of them. She had married in exile, for love, before any prospect of power and wealth could have put her motives into question. After her came a different kind of lady courtier, superficial, bad-tempered, extravagant and promiscuous. But she was the real thing, lovely all the way through. The encouragement she showed me, and others around her, and later particularly the younger generation, was genuine. Having borne her beloved husband children, and lost many young, she also spoke of tragedy from experience.

'Emelia did touch the stars. People ask, where is Heaven? What is Heaven like? Emelia was a little slice of Heaven, just as this morning the choir also touches it. We must follow their example. What an ungrateful world, what a distracted time, that such a beauty, with such gifts of intelligence, generosity and good humour, held in affection by so many, should be laid to rest by so few.'

His voice trailed away. The small group stood in silence. Then Bishop Sprat gave a signal and the pallbearers took up the coffin. Russell removed the trestles, stepped to the front and, walking backwards with his hand up against the front of the box, helped his crew down the steps into the spacious crypt. From the transept came the gentle, embracing *Sanctus.*

Elizabeth felt Henrietta's hand reach for hers and clasp it tightly. She was glad the Bishop, the vergers and they themselves would stay above. She should have thought this part through, she told herself, anticipation is protection. This tomb might one day receive Henrietta's earthly remains. It was almost too sad to bear.

The distant choir was still. As the bearers came back up, Bishop Sprat spoke the timeless words from the book:

> *Forasmuch as it hath pleased Almighty God of His great mercy to take unto Himself the soul of our dear sister Emelia here departed: we therefore commit her body to the ground; earth to earth, ashes to ashes, dust to dust; in sure and certain hope of the Resurrection to eternal life, through our Lord Jesus Christ; who shall change our vile body, that it may be like unto His glorious body, according to the mighty working, whereby He is able to subdue all things to Himself.*

After the Lord's Prayer, the Collect and the Grace, the service concluded. The choir closed with *Agnus Dei* and its luminous prayer for peace. The party turned, broke into informal pairs and threes, and walked respectfully, but at a normal pace, back the way they had come.

'They skipped the *Credo*,' said Bishop Sprat, matter-of-factly, to Henrietta.

'It was a perfect service,' she replied. 'You did your friend proud. Please thank the choirmaster and choir.'

When they reached the west door, William Russell came up to Elizabeth. 'Will you require the carriage home, Ma'am?'

She looked at the leaden sky, 'Thank you, Mr Russell, which way do you go?'

'We live in Petty France, but we can go home round the Park.'

Henrietta and Hendriksen shook their heads, while Elizabeth said, 'The weather is holding off and the walk will do us good.'

'But I insist you three join me for lunch,' said Bishop Sprat. 'Everything is arranged, the table is laid.'

'No, no. We must get back,' said Elizabeth. 'The mobile may turn again.'

'I'm sure Her Ladyship would have approved of you staying,' said the prelate. 'And we have much to discuss in these uncertain times. Please, do me the honour. Come this way. The meal is served and a chance will not arise again.'

He began to steer them towards a small entrance in the south wall of the courtyard.

Jack, 10:05

The artillery train was soon at Charing Cross but its fast pace was unnecessary and probably dangerous, even though it was easy, even for troops who'd had regular exercise for a month. Also the fusiliers must slow to a normal speed if they were to march straight back to fetch the baggage train and bring it home today.

Jack had been so focused on running the gauntlet of the rabble that he had not considered what to do if his ruse succeeded. The question of Temple Bar had likewise barely been discussed. It seemed to Jack that the Colonel, the Major and the Adjutant were having similar thoughts. They would need to stop, if only for ten minutes. Also, that bottleneck needed scouting out.

All three turned in the saddle and looked back, trying to judge if the tail was now out of sight of the Pall Mall mob. Jack could see them thinking it through.

Communicating forward to the band and leading fusiliers required firing the pistols for an emergency stop. But there was no emergency. So the Major passed the word to expect the alarm when the vanguard approached the Savoy. It would take that long for the warning to reach the end of the column, by when it should be clear of Charing Cross and visible down the Strand.

The senior officers duly fired their shots. The band ahead fell silent but continued marching for forty paces, as they had rehearsed, slowing their stride by increments. More shots echoed down the line. The cannon train came easily to a stop. The Colonel and his two immediate subordinates rode out to the left of the column and up to the front. The Major went on ahead, evidently to Temple Bar to check that the coast was clear. Shere and the Adjutant worked their way down the caravan, reloading their side-arms and repeating the message that they would restart at a normal pace.

To Jack's discomfort, it did not escape the Colonel's attention that a bunch of matrons was also walking down the column on the other side, whistling and hooting to their various sons as they espied them. Jack's mother was among the group and was quick to spot him. 'Jackie, Jackie, it's me, Mum,' she yelled, her cup of joy quite overflowing. Then she added in a lower but still clarion voice. 'What a poppet you are to arrange to stop for us.'

Several other victims were exposed to maternal welcomes, otherwise Jack would surely have died where he stood.

Just as Jack was cursing himself for having forgotten about his note to his mother, a horseman came up the line calling for Colonel Shere. 'Urgent message from the Council at Whitehall,' Jack heard him shout.

Whatever the advice or instruction was, the original plan stood. The Major cantered back from Temple Bar, announcing that the coast was clear. After the promised ten minutes Shere bellowed, 'Train, forward march.' The drums rolled, the musicians struck up again and the column soon dropped into the easier rhythm. The senior officers took their positions just ahead of Jack's troop.

'Nice one, poppet,' Terry said under cover of the first creaks and every trooper within earshot spluttered.

The column crossed the Fleet bridge with alacrity and barely noticed the incline of Ludgate Hill, which normally tested the horses. Near London Bridge they were puzzled by the sight of at least a hundred ne'er-do-wells gathered outside the Boar's Head, who looked at them in astonishment. Then they were approaching Tower Street and the officers were firing their pistols for a final halt.

Never had the Tower of London looked so beautiful, thought Jack.

While the Royal Artillery regiment wound into the fortress, Colonel Shere ordered the fusiliers to draw up in two bodies on the open ground toward the Tower Hill scaffold posts. He then inspected them, thanked them and asked Major St Clair to take half of them back to fetch the baggage train. They were to follow the northern route via Newgate, Holborn and Oxford Street, staying well out of harm's way. This would bring them to the wagons from the northeast corner of Hyde Park. If all was well, they were to return by that same route, for the same reasons.

Before all the cannons were through the defile, Shere called Jack to the residence of the Lieutenant-Governor of the Tower. Jack knew what it would be about. His apprehension was confirmed by the severe look Shere and the Adjutant gave him as they broke off their conversation.

After Jack had saluted, Shere said, 'Gentlemen, we seem to have a moment before the conference in the Governor's room to plan out the next few hours. Mr Willoughby, please keep an eye out and let us know when the Tower authorities are all there. Meanwhile, Lieutenant Wilson, do you have any idea how a flock of Royal Ordnance mothers came to know the exact time we would be passing the Savoy?'

Jack's answer made him shake his head.

'Lieutenant, I should be congratulating you on a few days' excellent service to the regiment, His Majesty and the country. However, your passing of critical details to civilians could have done grave harm and been a court-martialable offence. I accept that you wrote to your mother before I stopped all correspondence and that you reported three leaks, eventually, although investigating only two. Furthermore, you mitigated a serious consequence by capturing the caltrops and proposing a formation which correctly anticipated the behaviour of the mob. And lastly, the fifth commandment entitles mothers to a certain deference. I wish my own mother had been there to see us, God rest her soul.'

Jack felt a prickle behind his eyes.

'On balance, the bad deed is cancelled out by the good. As to whether it is entirely cancelled, I reserve judgement. Do you agree with me, Mr Willoughby?'

The Adjutant looked away, temporarily inconvenienced by coughs.

'Are they ready for us?' Shere asked.

The Adjutant opened the connecting door, glanced in but shook his head.

'Lieutenant Wilson, since you are young and fit and seem to have more lives than a cat,' continued the Colonel, 'take a look at this order I received from Whitehall.'

Jack read:

> *Order to bring the Traine of Artillery to James' Parke*
>
> *Whereas Wee, the Peers of the Realme, with some of the Lords of the Privy Councill, have received a letter from you, dated this day, giving us an Acc.t that you are marching up with the Traine of Artillery under your care, guarded by the Regim.t of ffusiliers towards St James' Parke, Wee have thought fitt to signifie unto you, that we approve thereof, and accordingly Wee doo hereby direct you to bring the said traine of Artill.ry to St James' Parke, where you are to expect such further Orders, as shall be sent unto you. ffrom the Council Chamber in Whitehall the 12th day of Dec.r 1688.*
>
> *To S.r Henry Shere Kn.t L.t Gen.ll*
>
> *of the Traine of Artillery*
>
> | | | | |
> |---|---|---|---|
> | *Halifax* | *Tho. Roffen* | *Anglesey* | *Vaughan Carbery* |
> | *Kent* | *Tho. Petriburg* | *Berkeley* | *Crewe.* |
> | *Mulgrave* | *Chandos* | *Nottingham* | |
> | *Ailesbury* | *North & Grey* | *Newport* | |
> | *P. Winchester* | *Carlisle* | *T. Jermyn* | |

Jack passed the paper back.

'Well,' said Shere, 'they had my note but Exe forgot the verbal bit. Had I obeyed, the Tower would not be secured. And who ever tried to turn back a 165-yard cannon train, four abreast, in a city street? Or to march one through a mob twice in a morning? As for this Lieutenant General Shere they are writing to – it's obviously code to ignore the whole nonsense.'

The Adjutant said, 'They are coming in, Sir.'

With a smile, Shere stood up. 'Still alive and still together. We should be grateful for that. Lieutenant, in Captain Exe's absence, please come through to the Governor's conference chamber. Gentlemen, let's agree the rest of our day.'

In the larger room they found Lord Lucas, his Captain of the Tower Garrison, Thomas King, and the Captain of the Fusiliers, deputising for Major St Clair.

After everyone was introduced and seated, Sir Henry said, 'My Lord, with your permission, I would like to go over to Whitehall immediately and assure the Council of our loyalty. Do you wish to join me? I imagine that Captain Exe is still there. We could bring him back and hear the latest news on the way.'

'You are most kind, Colonel,' said Lord Lucas, 'but they already saw me this morning. While you were on your way to Salisbury the King replaced me with Mr Skelton, but the Lords chaired by Dr Sancroft reversed that yesterday. Here's the warrant, twenty-seven signatures.' He passed over a large sheet of parchment, scattered with surnames in an exotic variety of hands. 'I have promised to show up every day for morning prayers, but otherwise to be here. Certainly *you* must call on them as soon as possible. And if I were you I'd leave your captain there for the afternoon, and maybe also send him back to observe tomorrow and the next day. He can liaise with troops who trickle in, direct urgent messages to us, and in the evenings report in person on the day's events.'

'Agreed,' said Sir Henry.

Lord Lucas continued. 'From you they will want cannon on the street. What troops can we promise them?'

'Captain?' asked Shere. 'Each gun will need sentries from your department.'

'Whatever guard we offer, we will need to change it every four hours, six at the most.'

After much debate, it was decided to dispatch rotations of sentries from the Tower. Each company would stand watch four hours, taking an additional hour to march there, and another hour back.

'And the artillery, Sir?' asked the Adjutant.

'Ah yes, thank you,' said the Colonel. 'Still necessary, I fear. I propose one cannon only, with canister, at each palace, Whitehall and St James'. So that's two guns, six men per gun, eight-hour shifts. But let's not have them traipsing in and out from the Tower. We'll put them in tents in the park, so three shifts each a day. How many gunners are we talking about, Lieutenant?'

Jack said, 'That sounds like thirty-six of us based in the park, Sir, at any one time.'

'How long would you leave them out there, Adjutant?' asked the Colonel.

'Three nights, sir. We have enough men for four tours, so three nights out, nine in.'

'Heavens,' joked Lord Lucas, 'if it's going to take twelve days, we might as well build them a barracks. I'm amazed we don't have one around there already.'

Colonel Shere continued. 'Lieutenant Wilson, you will be acting Captain. Get yourself a hat and sash. And please talk with the Adjutant about which men and guns to take. Choose two cannon you wouldn't mind spiking. You will lead the first contingent in St James' Park. Mr Willoughby, please arrange written orders to load and fire at their Captain's discretion, but I want those two cannon kept unloaded until he gives the word. So, Acting Captain, have them stand by with canister, manned by six men each, day and night.'

'We will need the tents from the baggage train, Sir,' said Jack.

The Colonel nodded. 'Adjutant, get a message to Hyde Park and tell the Quartermaster to pitch tents in St James' Park on his way home; and bedding for thirty-six gunners; and for the Bridging Master to send some pioneers to dig latrines. Go by Oxford Street.'

'Suggestion, Sir,' interrupted Jack.

The Colonel signed to him to speak.

'Double the number, Sir. Easiest done now. Best to be ready for trouble.'

'Adjutant, I need to be able to sleep twice the number, in three rotating shifts, you work it out. Acting Captain Wilson, Captain Exe will relieve you with a new force on Saturday morning. The camp will become his. Adjutant, come with me, you can cut on through St James' Park and reach the baggage train before the fusiliers. Tell the trainmaster, quartermaster and cooks what is happening and get all our remaining rations into St James' Park by nightfall. Of course, it won't be enough. Also, when the fusiliers reach Hyde Park, invite Major St. Clair to give our new forward base some cover until the guns arrive from here. Nothing extravagant, twenty men should do it. We don't want to frighten the ducks.'

'Can I put that in writing, Sir?' said the Adjutant.

'Be quick, I'm not waiting. But don't mention the ducks.'

Turning to Jack, he said, 'Captain, please would you brief Major St. Clair when he returns. Together make a plan for protecting our guns and gunners. I want them guarded, particularly if they have to open fire. We'd better limit the great guns' powder and canister, in case the rabble captures them. Suggestions?'

'Six shots each, canister,' said Jack.

'You'll never get off six,' said the Colonel. 'Three. Six altogether. Then spike 'em and run back here.'

'To summarise,' said Lord Lucas, 'we offer their Lordships continuous protection, day and night, until further notice, by a gun at both palaces, each with three shots of canister, crewed by gunners based in the Park and guarded by Fusiliers based in the Tower. Pretty thin gruel. I hope they have more troops up their sleeves elsewhere.'

Shere and Lucas exchanged a shrug.

'Talking of gruel,' said Lucas, 'what about feeding arrangements? You will need a mess sergeant and cooks. I'll sort that out with my people. The Beefeaters know a thing or two when it comes to vittles.'

He stood and the meeting was ended. 'Gentlemen, we know our tasks. I make the time now, noon. We will reconvene here at five o'clock. All but Mr. Wilson.'

Kitty, 12:30

Kitty was at home in Blackfriars trying to persuade old Johanna Jones to leave home for a night at the print shop.

'My daughter-in-law,' her grandmother declared to Kitty, as if Mary was not in the room, 'may have chosen a dislocated lifestyle when she married Edward, but uprooting his mother is a different matter.'

'But it's a crisis,' pleaded Mary.

'It's always a crisis until it isn't,' Johanna said. 'Have you learnt nothing from twenty years being married to a printer?'

'I'll go,' said Mary to Kitty in desperation. 'You stay and look after Grandmother.'

'Papa was clear, and I'm sure he has his reasons,' Kitty replied. 'Really Mama, one moment you complain that he is not here to protect us, and the next you want to split us up. Anyway, I am better than you on the presses. Why deny him his best helper?'

'Well, you persuade your grandmother! I'm sure she won't listen to me. But someone has to go.'

'Come on Grandmother' said Kitty. 'Think how you felt after your brush with the parapet upstairs, even if you only imagined it. This will be fun. And you will be helping Papa. You know how good he is to you. Well, now's your chance to return the favour.'

'I am in no way in debt to that boy,' said Grandmother.

Eventually, Johanna passed that point where the pleasure of irritating her daughter-in-law was less than that of pleasing her granddaughter. She said, as if talking to a person the others could not see, 'The charms of a grandchild are hard to resist – particularly a feisty one with her life in front of her. Truth be told, once I've stirred myself, I would follow Kitty into a jungle, just to see how the girl got on. So what is a theatre of war to me?'

As she began to round up her toiletries, she even admitted, 'I do feel the years fall away with all this.'

Fifty minutes after the cab had arrived, it set off again, somewhat heavier with three generations of Jones women, their overnight bags and assorted treasures from the larder. The lone horse hauled them to the top of Blackfriars for the descent from Ludgate. However, its passage up Fleet Street was blocked by a small military column proceeding westwards even more slowly. Kitty was conscious of the deadline to deliver the proofs to Secretary Gwyn. Mary was not amused either. She knew time was tight and she hated to be late on one of the rare occasions when her husband asked for her help. Under the Temple Bar they crawled. When the soldiers pulled over in the wider space after St Clement Danes, Kitty saw two cannon with accompanying tenders and baggage carts, three dozen gunners and half as many fusiliers. She was horrified when her mother leaned out of the window to dispense bile over the troops for having hogged the road.

The cab was a stone's-throw from the gunner captain walking at the head of the column. The man turned and called back, 'The pleasure is all ours, Mrs Jones.' He doffed his broad black hat with a gallant bow. The cabbie stopped.

'Heavens, Mary,' said Grandmother Johanna. 'How will we ever live this down? It's the nice young man from last night!' And she gave Kitty a wink.

'And it looks like he's had a promotion,' said Kitty. 'I'll walk the last few yards.'

She reached through the open window to turn the door handle from the outside and began to step out just as Mary shouted to the cab driver, 'Press on, press on.' The cab jerked forward, the door swung shut and Kitty fell into her mother's lap.

Scowling with frustration, Kitty pushed herself away. The taste of blood was on her tongue. She had bitten the inside of her lip. Regaining her rearward seat, she looked through the window. A senior soldier on horseback had appeared from the direction of the Strand and was in conversation with Jack. Kitty knew better than to try and outrank a colonel.

'Mother, this is a small town, you cannot go shouting like a fishwife in the street.'

'And you cannot go throwing yourself at anything in uniform.'

Past Somerset House they went, Kitty struggling to maintain an air of insouciance. She dabbed her lip and remarked that the guard on the Dowager Queen's gate had been doubled.

The cab turned in under the entrance arch to the Savoy, past the scant remains of the Jesuit school, and pulled up in front of the printworks. Her father must have placed a watch, for his clerk was on the flagstones to take down their bags as soon as the cab came to a halt, while he himself went to pay the driver.

'One hour and three-quarters,' said the cabbie.

'Make it two,' said Edward.

'And a weight surcharge.'

'Yes, yes. Here, take this. Can you come back in an hour?'

'Where would that be to, Squire?'

'Whitehall.'

'Not worth the showing up for, small job like that. And I've got a young gent who pays well at three.'

Kitty came round to listen. 'I can walk to the Privy Council almost as fast as a cab, Papa. Or we could find a waterman from here to cut the bend.'

Edward called over the clerk. 'Paul, what's the tide doing in an hour's time?'

'High tide at two, Sir.'

'Yes,' said Kitty, 'That's too soon. Let's not tie up this gentleman any more. I'll have the proofs there in a trice.'

'As you wish,' said Edward.

'Thanks for the business,' said the driver. He clicked his tongue to the horse, tapping its rump with his whip, and pulled away.

Edward fussed round his mother. He took her into his office, ensured that she was settled with refreshments and her knitting, then led Mary and Kitty to the shop floor. It was too quiet, only a dozen or so staff on hand. Worse still, in the last hour they had achieved almost nothing.

'The front page is set on forme one,' said Edward. 'We are going to start on two and three. The flyer is for you two. Once you have it right, the lads can run in the poster. I want them the same. The poster just scaled up, so, same baselines, same font, leading, tracking, everything except the point size. Please could the two of you focus on the frame for that flyer? The *Gazette* proof off forme one is on the wall by the windows, where the light is good.'

Kitty took down the proof. She regretted the narrow *Gazette* format, full of hyphenations, but the words still had an appropriate ring of solemnity:

> *The DECLARATION of the Lords Spiritual*
> *and Temporal, in and about the Cities of*
> *London and VVestminster, assembled at Guild-*
> *hal, 11.Dec. 1688.*
> *VVEE doubt not but the World be-*
> *lieves that, in this great and Dan-*
> *gerous Conjuncture, We are hearti-*
> *ly and zealously concerned for the*
> *Protestant Religion, the Laws of the*
> *Land, and the Liberties and Properties of the*
> *Subject. And We did reasonably hope, that the*
> *King having Issued His Proclamation and Writs*
> *for a Free Parliament, We might have rested Se-*
> *cure under the Expectation of the Meeting : But*
> *His Majesty having withdrawn Himself, and as*
> *we apprehend, in order to His Departure out of*
> *this Kingdom, by the Pernicious Counsels of Per-*
> *sons ill Affected to Our Nation and Religion, We*
> *cannot, without being wanting in Our Duty, be*
> *silent under those Calamities, wherein the Popish*
> *Counsels which so long prevailed, have miserably in-*
> *volved these Realms. We do therefore unani-*
> *mously resolve to apply Our Selves to his Highness*

the Prince of Orange, who with so great Kindness
to these Kingdoms, so vast Expence, and so much
hazard to His own Person, hath Undertaken, by
endeavouring to Procure a Free Parliament, to
rescue Us, with as little Effusion, as possile, of
Christian Blood from the imminent Dangers of
Popery and Slavery.

'There's a typographical in line twenty-eight, Papa, possile should read possible,' shouted Kitty, but she wasn't sure anyone heard.

And We do hereby Declare, That We will, with
our utmost Endeavours, assist His Highness in the
obtaining such a Parliament with all Speed, where-
in Our Laws, Our Liberties and Properties may
be Secured, the Church of England in particular,
with a due Liberty to Protestant Dissenters, and
in general the Protestant Religion and Interest over
the whole World may be Supported and Encoura-
ged, to the Glory of God, the Happiness of the
Established Government in these Kingdoms, and the
Advantage of all Princes and States in Christen-
dom, that may be herein concerned.
In the mean time, We will endeavour to Pre-
serve, as much as in us lies, the Peace and Se-
curity of these great and populous Cities of Lon-
don and Westminster, and the Parts Adjacent,
by taking Care to Disarm all Papists, and Secure
all Jesuits and Romish Priests who are in or about
the same.
And if there be anything more to be performed
by Us, for promoting by his Highness' Generous In-
tentions for the Publick Good, VVe shall be ready to
do it as occasion shall Require.

W. Cant.	*Craven.*
Tho. Ebor.	*Ailesbury.*
Pembroke.	*Burlington.*

Dorset.   *Sussex.*
Mulgrave.   *Berkeley.*
Thanet.   *Rochester.*
Carlisle.   *Newport.*

and running over to the top of the second column:

Weymouth.   *Chandos.*
P. Winchester.   *Montague.*
W. Asaph.   *T. Jermyn.*
Fran. Ely.   *Vaughan Carbery.*
Tho. Roffen.   *Culpeper.*
Tho. Petriburg. *Crewe.*
P. Wharton.   *Osulston.*
North and Grey.

Then came the announcement ordering four emissaries to Prince William.

'Where is the part I'm proudest of?' Kitty asked, approaching her father. 'The instruction to Edward Jones, Printer at the Savoy, to publish all this.'

'That goes on the flyer and poster only. My name is always on the *Gazette*, so that would be a waste of space.'

Mother and daughter clicked into a familiar routine to set the flyer. Kitty laid out an eye-catching headline, D E C L A R A T I O N, and below that the sub-titles, perfectly symmetrical, varied fonts and points. Meanwhile her mother picked an elaborately carved wood block for the opening W of 'Wee doubt not…' one they also had in a larger size for the poster. Then Kitty called the words and Mary found the type, which Kitty set, justified to both margins, with as few hyphens as she could. The *Gazette* had been only slightly affected, but for the flyers and posters they were seriously short of capital Ws. So Mary fed Kitty a stream of Vs – VV being almost as good.

When they were halfway through, they ran off a first galley so that Edward's two regular typesetters could get to work copying it for the poster.

In the absence of the apprentices, the old hands joked about feeling young again and who needed those rascals around anyway? Spirits were high. They all knew that this *Declaration* issue, number 2,409, would become an instant collectors' item. A keepsake to be handed down from grandparent to grandchild. But still the rush was on, the buzz of any pressroom as news deadlines approach.

Elizabeth, 12:00

The hearse and carriages departed. Bishop Sprat took Lady Henrietta's arm and steered her off for lunch. Elizabeth and Hendriksen followed. They headed to a portal in a low castellated building tucked under the Abbey's western facade. As he unlocked the door, the churchman said, 'One of my predecessors had this little entrance added for just such moments. So that we Deans could pop home for sustenance.'

Inside was a long, narrow room beneath a ridged timber roof. The low stone fireplace midway down radiated heat, evidence that its blaze had been well fed since dawn. The Bishop paused to warm his backside and gestured at the long oak table of great age. 'From this fine refectory board the translation of the King James Bible was overseen. Some of it, anyway.' His arm swung upwards. 'The Jerusalem Chamber. Built in the reign of King Richard II. So, it's three hundred years younger than the Abbey. King Henry IV died on this very hearth – beneath my feet, so to speak. He had been praying in the Abbey about setting off on a crusade to free Jerusalem from the Turk. To atone for his treachery. Having usurped the throne, as you know. But he was struck with a sudden apoplexy. They brought him here, unconscious, and laid him in front of the fire to keep him warm. He woke and asked where he was. They said Jerusalem, so he would die a happy man, believing his sins forgiven. And he did. Maybe they even were.'

'And then they took him back next door to bury him,' said Henrietta.

'You might think so,' said Bishop Sprat. 'But he is in Canterbury Cathedral. He had snatched the throne from his cousin, so he wanted to be buried in the holiest place in the Kingdom. Next to Saint Thomas à Becket. Few people in those days could go to Rome. But they believed in the unction of pilgrimage and went to the shrine at Canterbury. Henry was hoping for legitimacy and peace by association. It didn't work, of course. His great-nephews and nieces went on fighting among themselves.'

'Did someone mention lunch?' asked Hendriksen.

'Yes, yes,' said Sprat, and he led them on. 'How was your journey this morning?' he asked as they walked through a parlour and into a corridor.

'We were separated from the rest of the household by a mob,' said Elizabeth, and she explained how they had been held in the path of the royal artillery train and that, but for Hendriksen, they would have been run down by it. They rounded an inner courtyard and entered the Deanery dining room. Fresh logs crackled in the hearth. A servant removed surplus place-settings.

'I wasn't sure how many we would be,' confessed the Bishop. 'Now I understand the absences. I saw the flames last night and Lord Lucas told us at the Council it was still going on. At least the four of us should now have enough to eat.'

The servant returned with a slow-roasted haunch of beef and all the trimmings. The Bishop said grace and they were served.

'So,' said Henrietta. 'Doubting Thomas is buried in Canterbury.'

Bishop Sprat laughed but Elizabeth raised her fingertips and said in her softest voice, 'Thomas Becket is not in the Bible, Henri dear. That's why we don't talk much about him since the Reformation. He was just a courtier five hundred years ago who was made Archbishop of Canterbury by a king, and then was murdered when he wouldn't do what his king wanted. Sainted by the Pope.'

'But,' added Sprat, 'you are right, that his name is from *the* Doubting Thomas. Thomas à Becket was born on the feast of St Thomas the Apostle. It comes round again in a week's time, on the winter solstice, and we shall remember them both'.

'Vhy vas he murdered?' asked Hendriksen, spooning vegetables.

'The endless squabble over control between England and the Continent,' said Bishop Sprat, helping himself to sliced beef. 'It's what's happening now. Who controls England? Who makes the top church appointments? Who takes the church revenues? Where is the ultimate court of appeal against a priest? An English king, ordained by God, or a foreign pope, God's representative on Earth who has never been to this country and can't speak English? Should the Church pay taxes to the English Crown? Is the pope a puppet of other monarchs, the French, the Spanish? What happens to all the money going to Rome? Is the papacy corrupted by its wealth and power? Why should church services be in Latin, a language no normal person can understand? Miss Forrester, let me fill your glass.'

'And vhy vas he murdered?' repeated Hendriksen.

'Ah yes,' said Sprat, scolding himself. 'King Henry got drunk and appeared to order it. "What dullards are you," he challenged his courtiers, "to let your Lord be treated with such contempt by a low-born clerk?" Something like that. Anyway, three lickspittle knights went down to Canterbury and did the job. Against the high altar. An archbishop in his own cathedral. Another exact spot you can stand on. It's even more spellbinding after dark. You imagine yourself alone, before that vast, strangely steep and crooked nave. An absurd emptiness. Then torches flicker in the distance, below, among the pillars, as they come for you. It fair makes your hair stand on end. Even now, in this era of horrifying fiction, false press and news that runs twenty-four-hours a day. How much more was the impact on a thirteenth-century pilgrim. It would change their life.'

'So it vas like Henry VIII vanting a divorce. And this invasion by Prince Villhelm. Alvays trying to be a bit more in charge.'

'Yes, yes, But I am neglecting my duties. Dear Sir, let me top you up and we'll make a toast to Lady Emelia, and all other life-changing experiences.'

They drained their glasses, Lady Henrietta too.

Elizabeth said, 'My Lord Bishop, are you trying to get us drunk?'

'Have you not heard of a wake, Miss Forrester? This humble fare is my attempt to do justice to the memory of one of the muses of the age. I will take it seriously amiss if we do not blow away some cobwebs.'

'But what about the rural deans at three o'clock?'

'The rural deans will take it seriously amiss too. Do you know the topic on our agenda? Freedom of conscience. Government policy, until yesterday. The King's Declaration of Indulgence. To be preached from every Anglican pulpit in the land. Even for Jews, Mussulmen and pagans. We are discussing whether freedom of conscience for Catholics and Dissenters could ever work. It's all a bit hypothetical now, since His Majesty has departed these shores. Whether freedom of conscience for Catholics and Dissenters could ever *have worked* is now more apt. Was it a trap? Some said the policy would lead back to papist domination, that once they were in power, the Catholics would steer us to Rome. Others that freedom of conscience was the same as no conscience – that it would be the end of religion itself. That people would stop going to church on Sundays because lying in bed, lazy atheism, is too seductive. If it's pouring with rain and the river is up in between, and you have two country miles each way, would you bother? But my point is that a discussion like that, on top of an emergency Council in the morning, and a Duchess' funeral before lunch, can make a man a dull host. If we are to resolve anything in this vale of tears, we will need our sense of humour.'

'No, Sir,' said Hendriksen. 'Ze immortal soul is no laughing matter. Zat vay lie ze fripperies and vanities of Satan.'

'Good heavens, man. You must join our debate this afternoon. The Lollard view is under-represented.'

'But surely,' said Henrietta, 'these matters cannot be debated. The Bible tells us and there it is.'

'Not even the Puritans follow Christ's teachings to the letter,' said Sprat. 'They own property. Look at the New England settlers. They do not hold all things in common. You say, the Bible tells us and there it is, but you are in the hands of the translator. If you just read the Good Book in your own language the debate starts. Was Isaiah's prophesy that *a virgin shall conceive, and bear a son*, or was she *a young woman*? The Hebrew is *Almah*, which equally means young woman. Two hundred years after the calamity of Thomas Becket's murder, an Oxford professor organised the first English translation of the Bible. John Wycliffe. Printing had not been invented. Each volume had to be copied out by hand. Writing out a whole Bible, Lady Henrietta, can you imagine? But Wycliffe's Bible was enough to start the questions. Fifty years after his death, the Pope had his bones dug up and burnt. We have been executing heretics and traitors in England ever since.'

Elizabeth was intrigued. 'Freedom of conscience is like freedom of choice. God does not force us. We have the choice between good and evil, to love him or not. Forced love is not love.'

'Indeed it is not,' said the Dean Bishop. 'As some of our church leaders today have learnt the hard way. We are all human, Elizabeth.' He looked at her with a raised brow, as if asking for her confession. An image of Lord Elland, naked and aroused, flashed into her mind.

'I don't know what you mean,' said Elizabeth, glancing at Lady Henrietta, who was blushing deeply.

'How is your mother, Elizabeth?' asked Bishop Sprat, appearing to change the subject. Without waiting for an answer he continued. 'I knew her slightly at Oxford. Miss Isabelle Foley. She was magical, irresistible, the centre of any mixed company. Of course, she was only interested in boys older than me. Oh, how she could dance, barely touching the ground. She was *la belle du bal* – Henry Compton had his eye on her, indeed, that is why he left without graduating. Had to.' And he shook his head.

'You were at Oxford with the Bishop of London?'

'Oh, yes. We're both Queens' men. But he was a third-year and I had only just gone up. He had no thought of taking holy orders in those days, whereas I was already set on the priesthood.'

'And what happened with my mother? She remembers Queens with affection.'

'I have said too much already. I thought you knew. Forgive me.'

Elizabeth's eyes widened. 'You thought I knew what?'

'Nothing happened. Henry Compton left the country. He went abroad for a few years.'

'He never graduated?'

'Well, only ten years later, after he had tried the Continent and then been a cornet in King Charles' Cavalry. But he went back. Oxford and Cambridge, Doctor of Divinity, and it has been upwards ever since.'

'And why did he leave Oxford in such a hurry?'

'Do you know him?'

'Yes, he's a friend of my mother's.'

'Ah well, my dear,' said Sprat. 'Then you can ask him yourself.'

They ate in silence for a while.

Hendriksen took up the conversation, 'It is interesting, vhat you say about knowing the scriptures in your own langvage. In a vay, the more knowledge you have, the less you know.'

'Precisely,' said the Bishop. 'Knowledge is like inflating a bladder, pumping all the facts inside. The larger the surface, the more it touches the unknown outside. The mysteries just become more mysterious. Look at the wonders of this century. The telescope. The microscope. I have not used either, I only know they have transformed our ideas about creation. Clouds of stars. Hairs on the legs of fleas. But imagine what is still to be discovered. It is so easy to speculate on the next advance – for example, if we could put a telescope or a microscope to each eye, not just the one.'

'I can imagine that,' said Henrietta, shutting one eye and then the other. 'It is the sort of question my mother loved. Much more interesting than fripperies and vanities.'

'But you say that because you are your mother's daughter,' said Bishop Sprat.

'In the sense that she brought you up to have a questioning mind,' added Elizabeth. 'You and me.'

Henrietta continued, 'If intelligence was the only thing, God would have given us bigger heads and weaker bodies. But our bodies are good for dancing and hunting and fighting too. The size of our brain is limited by the skeletons we have – we are a balance between a child-bearing skeleton and a dancing, hunting and fighting one.'

'The human mind is our form of plumage,' said the Bishop. 'Your mother's wit and humour were what people loved. I suspect Prince William doesn't listen to women. But in the Stuart court, a beauty without wit would not have survived as Emelia did, nor been as loved as she was. If you marry someone beautiful and stupid you will discover after a few months that you have made a huge mistake.'

'Beautiful and stupid is better zan ugly and stupid,' said Hendriksen.

'I doubt that,' said the Dean. 'A beauty may be stupid enough to be disloyal.'

'Beautiful and witty,' said Henrietta. 'And loyal. And well-bred? Certainly rich.'

'And healthy?' asked Elizabeth, 'And creative? And patient?'

'Not too patient,' said the Bishop. 'What about decisive? Charismatic? Energetic?'

'Loving?' asked Hendriksen.

'But not spoiling or indulgent,' said Henrietta.

'Exactly,' said Elizabeth. 'Beyond indulgence lies addiction.'

'Or smothering, overprotective,' said Henrietta. 'When they don't let you grow.'

'The best defence against fraudsters, imposters and extortionists is to have been brushed by their corruption, without succumbing,' said Sprat.

'What good parents we would make!' exclaimed Elizabeth. 'But would our children be as good parents as us? You know what they say, clogs to clogs in three generations.'

'And lying?' asked Henrietta.

'No lying,' said Hendriksen. '*Zou shalt not bear false vitness.* Commandment number nine.'

'Closely related to false witness, is spreading false news,' said Sprat. 'This *Third Declaration of the Prince of Orange.* I hear he has disowned it. So, someone made it up. What kind of a sin is that, to go to such lengths, just to drive a venomous wedge into society? To frighten people into taking extreme views, when they are inclined towards compromise and moderation?'

'But ze King vent vithout a fight. Does zat not justify ze lie? I suppose if you have a view, ze end justifies ze means?' asked Hendriksen.

'That is the revolutionary approach,' said the Bishop. 'Throw everything in the air: it cannot land any worse than it currently is. But many people may be harmed. Many lives ruined. No. The key lesson from Good Queen Bess is that stability beats decisiveness. Little by little, twenty years of procrastination with the King of Spain led to life being twice as good as it had been, for normal folks. Her decades of indecision are remembered as a golden age. Jesus certainly understood that. *Blessed are the meek, for they shall inherit the earth.'*

'And yet Jesus' message was itself revolutionary,' said Elizabeth. 'Depending on the translation. We are back where we started.'

The clergyman sighed. 'I like to drink a little coffee after lunch, and I will need it if I am to stir up my rural deans.'

The servants cleared the dishes, the guests finished their wine, and Bishop Sprat led them to his parlour, which overlooked the Dean's Yard. After they had sipped the stimulant and admired the cloistered orderliness, Sprat led them back through the Jerusalem Chamber to the outside world. Elizabeth stroked the table as she passed. To have touched the workbench of the Authorised Version, that most settling and aural of translations, gave it a new perspective.

'My dear young lady,' the churchman said to Henrietta as they parted. 'I have seen your mother in you. You will do her justice. Do not stay away too long. I expect your brother will be home very soon. Please tell him that we did right by his mama.'

'You have done all that and more. More than anyone expected, under the circumstances. And you were right to ask us to lunch, My Lord Bishop,' said Henrietta. 'Thank you.'

'That is most gratifying,' said the Bishop. 'Well, your household will be worried. And I must go and find my debate.'

Simon, 12:10

In St James' Square, the sound of hooves grew louder. Colonels Spike and Ike watched their streetfighters crouch under the low barricades and squeeze back into the corner angles. Morale was high and there was a palpable sense of superiority, of intelligent restraint, of springing the trap on the prey at the perfect time.

Spike saw spectators at a couple of salon windows, although most were shuttered or blank, even at Ormonde House. He thought, the bitch Forrester is still at her funeral, how apt.

The Horse Guards came in from the north. Eighty cavalry chargers whirled clockwise round the central defensive ring with its bayonets sticking above the domestic furniture, looking for a weakness to jump across. It was an obstacle to be removed by cannon not cavalry, and they knew it. Indeed, they were so hypnotised by the conundrum posed in the middle of the square that they did not seem to care about the softer targets huddled in the recesses. It was impossible to hold a tight curve at full gallop and in changing stride some horses lost their footing on the hard-packed earth. After the first couple went down, almost immediately followed by another three riders, and as chargers swerved to avoid the fallen, their captain led them out, again down King Street.

Not a shot had been fired. Fallen horses were quickly up, apparently unharmed, shaking their manes and trotting off after their fellows, leaving five cavalrymen on the ground, bruised, winded and defeated. The bayonet holders sprang out to grab their sabres. The soldiers were brought to Spike. All refused to join the rabble and in short order were deprived of their helmets, cuirasses, backplates, jackets and boots. Laughing apprentices prodded them to limp off to the west.

The shiny metalwork and five pairs of black knee boots were tossed on the heap at the French Embassy door. Spike saw Ambassador Paul Barillon at a window, looking down with a pensive air. After eleven years as Louis XIV's eyes and ears in Whitehall, Barillon was known for his excellent English and unmatched proximity to the later Stuarts. Today's action would be reported back to Paris, a curiosity rather than a lesson, since nothing like it could ever happen there. The diplomat's expression set Spike to thinking how his new English republic would deal with the Sun King's France, the epitome of monarchy. He had no doubt that England's republican cause would be feared and vilified across the Channel. But in the end France would reform, perhaps to a parliamentary monarchy, avoiding such scenes as this. London and Paris both had bastions and neither could be stormed.

Ambassador Barillon must be expecting his residence to be ransacked. But that would expose their rear. What if, Spike wondered, his Spartans' display of battle discipline was followed by an equally disciplined search of the French Embassy? It would be a trick to match the Royal Artillery Colonel's with the mob, to show haughty mercy while awakening their worst fears. It would also be hard for French commentators to fit it into their propaganda about a London revolution.

A handful of scouts ran in from York and Charles Streets shouting, 'Columns of foot from north and east.' The tramp of soldiers grew louder and the rioters crept out of the corners.

The infantry showed the same intentions as before: march into the Square, deploy in three ranks and fire on the rabble. The mob pre-empted them as before:

offered the chance to change sides, removed the boots of those who would not, and added to the revolution's stock of modern weapons.

'They will get wise to this,' said Ike. 'And they will keep coming back. It's the Privy Council, they and the colonels egg each other on.'

'Damn the King for running away,' said Spike. 'If we had captured him, we wouldn't have this council of peers playing God. I tell you, for the next battle we need a miracle. We need their troop morale to collapse.'

All the while, he felt Barillon watching from behind his elegant sash window. Now Spike walked up to the pavement below and signalled that he wanted to talk. The Ambassador reacted with a shrug, pushed open the window and leant out.

'What do you want, Commander?' the Frenchman shouted.

'Good afternoon, Your Excellency,' said Spike. 'Do you have any weapons or gunpowder in your house?'

'Good heavens, no. Am I mad? What would I be doing with such things?'

'I regret that we will have to inspect your premises, Monsieur. It is not that I disbelieve you. Indeed, I do believe you, which is why I encourage you to let me and my captains search the house for weapons and explosives. If you have nothing to hide, you will let us in. If we find nothing, you will be unmolested. If you do not let us conduct a peaceful inspection, I cannot answer for the consequences. Which will it be?'

'That is outrageous. Protocol protects diplomatic missions. If you enter here, you are invading France, Monsieur.'

'Not if you invite us in. Then we pass as if we were guests. I repeat, Your Excellency, which is it to be?'

'How many tourists do you propose I invite to France, Monsieur?'

'Six. Me and five others. You will attend us and open any room, cupboard, cellar or attic we ask. We will not handle your goods unless you refuse to assist. Which is it to be, Excellency?'

'This house is full of valuables. Are you saying these will be untouched?'

'Yes. Which is it to be? Do you want me to rouse this rabble to demolish your house to its stones and joists? You will have heard what they did in Wild Street. These citizens also hate France and think I can walk on water. Or will you open your door and invite me in?'

'Gather your five men, Monsieur. I wish to see them.'

Spike walked over to Ike. Someone had obtained lamp-oil and was pouring it over the confiscated uniforms to make a bonfire. The spectacle drew part of the mob. Ike fired a pistol at close range into the sodden heap and up went the flames, the cloth smoked while the oil burnt clean.

'Good diversion,' said Spike, taking Ike to one side while the mob hooted and cheered at the pyre. 'I want to play the French embassy differently from the Haymarket or Wild Street. It could do us a favour down the line.'

'He'll have a Mass House in there. And God knows what for bribes and inducements.'

'I know mate, but if we win today and tonight, we are going to need some diplomatic credentials with France. With no King James on the ground and William of Orange not being an option for King Louis, they may prefer someone more neutral. Can you bring four of our original Spartans? I have talked Barillon into letting us search his house for arms and powder.'

Ike chose four of the lads who would have been on the Tower gambit with him and the group of six stood under Barillon's window. The corpulent old ambassador leant out. He looked at the distracted mob dancing around their bonfire and at the six apprentices and made his decision.

'I will bolt the front door behind you after you have entered. There will be no rough behaviour. I will show you every room, from the attic to the *cave*, and my servants will open every cupboard, desk and drawer you ask. But you must touch nothing unless it is a weapon or gunpowder. Is that understood? Since there is no such item in this house, that means you touch nothing. In particular you touch nothing in my chapel.'

'We agree,' said Spike. 'But if you are lying, this guarantee is void.'

Barillon closed the window and shortly afterwards Spike heard bars being lifted from behind the front door.

'Lads,' Spike said to the others. 'I am deadly serious now. No harm comes to him, the house or his chattels, so long as we find no arms. No pilfering, no pocketing, no touching. You may admire, but you may not touch. Understood?'

'We've got it. Choristers all,' said Ike, the former altar boy.

Barillon's door opened, his butler stood back and the six filed in. Barillon personally greeted each one as the servants dropped heavy bars back into their cradles on either side of the door.

Spike felt as if he had stepped into a slice of Versailles. All surfaces had been decorated by French craftsmen in the style favoured by Louis XIV, cream walls with symmetrical plaster scrolls of gold foliage. In the curl of the stairs was a fine marble bust of a man with flowing locks and a jutting chin, his head half-turned to his right, which Spike guessed was the Sun King himself.

'We don't have long. The next wave of troops will be back. Where would you hide an arsenal of weapons in a house like this?' Spike asked Ike.

'Top of the house or cellar,' said Ike.

'Fine. Ambassador, we need to see the attics and cellars. Attics first. Please lead on.' To his fellows he continued, 'There may be a false wall somewhere, everyone knock on walls and keep an eye open for proportions which don't add up, marks on the floors, anything that doesn't make sense.'

The apprentices had never been in such lavish surroundings. The residence was centred around a formal staircase that led up three floors and was hung with portraits of past foreign ministers and ambassadors. Facing down the first flight was a full-length portrait of Louis XIV on his throne in a ridiculously long brown wig, holding a victor's crown of laurels and a sceptre. A shapely, white-hosed leg showed through his ermine-lined cloak of dark blue velvet which, like his footstool, was covered in golden fleurs-de-lys. It was an image of unutterable arrogance and wealth and, for a moment, Spike wavered as his blood boiled. But he turned away and said, 'Show us the servants' stairs.'

The house had two rear wells of bare stone steps. Moving fast, the search party went up to the attics, then down to the cellars. They looked under eaves, tapped walls and jumped on floors, but found nothing suspicious, let alone any hard evidence.

In the cellar the Ambassador showed them his strongroom, which contained a fortune in small, bejewelled keepsakes and gold and silver coin. But no weapons. Spike noticed Ike fingering his sheathed dagger and put his hand firmly over his friend's. Wordlessly they glared at each other, before Ike rolled his eyes and closed them, conceding.

Spike whispered, 'I know what I'm doing.'

They hustled through the formal rooms, asking for tapestries to be lifted forward, chests to be opened and desk drawers to be pulled out. In the chapel they tested the ornate mosaic for hollow spaces, looked under pews, behind curtains and around the altar. Opulence, yes; excess, certainly; a theatrical superficiality, as in the wings of a playhouse, absolutely. But no weapons. Not so much as a pistol. Not even a decorated sword hilt or painted powder flask.

Ike said, 'It makes sense. Why would an ambassador to the mightiest king on Earth keep arms in his own house? If he wanted to stockpile weapons he would find some barn deep in the country.'

'Particularly this man,' said one of Ike's trusties. 'If all diplomats paid as promptly as Ambassador Barillon, London tradesmen would welcome Catholic missions with open arms.'

'He's joking,' said Ike to Barillon, knowing he was not.

'Your famous English humour,' said Barillon, speaking for the first time.

As they returned to the hall, Barillon continued. 'We understand each other better now, gentlemen. This embassy, like your mobile, is more subtle than the others. Your colleague mentioned that I pay upfront for my groceries and settle all other bills immediately. Why should I not? My royal master is no miser, and neither am I. We preach a better way to run a country, a sure way to peace and justice through absolute monarchy.'

'Neighbours,' said Spike, 'we are wasting our time. We need to be back outside.' The Ambassador signalled for the horizontal bars on the front door to be lifted. 'Monsieur Barillon, you have passed the test. No weapons. So have we. No violence. Your house is intact, as is my reputation. Please report this back to Paris so King Louis learns something to his benefit. We look forward to dealing with you once our revolution has succeeded.'

The six passed back into the street, to find the mob gathered rowdily outside. Ike shouted for a little silence.

Spike addressed them. 'Ambassador Barillon has no weapons, we have searched thoroughly. Our dispute is not with him, nor his with us. He has been a good customer to many, he owes none of us a debt. The Kingdom of France and the Republic of England will need to respect each other once we are running things. Now, let's get back to our places, our next victory will settle things.'

The mob dispersed to their previous positions.

Ike turned to Spike. 'That was a mistake, mate. If we win, your business with Barillon may prove to have been clever. But if we lose it will have been another grave error. Barillon will say he compounded with us to go away, and our memory will be a laughing stock, if we are remembered at all. We should have thrown open his front door and let the mob in. Then the message of the people would have got back to Paris and shaken their complacency. Now, if we lose, the monarchy of France postpones its own day of reckoning. The longer you dam up history, the bigger the flood when it bursts. When the mob really goes mad – I mean for months and years – who knows what depths it could plumb? Your games in there may lead to something much worse in Paris. Had you let me kill that bastard after he showed us his money, we might have steadied a see-saw and saved many lives.'

'Come on Ike, you just wanted to get rich quick,' said Spike.

Scouts came running in from the southeast, 'New attack. Mixed cavalry and infantry.'

All debate about the French Embassy was forgotten.

The professional soldiers had evidently been thinking. This time they came from three sides, with foot soldiers advancing at a jog, shielded by trotting horses. The rioters had assumed their previous positions, but there was no stopping this new multi-pronged, mixed force approach. The barricade ring was reached by the infantry and taken. Spike's bayonet wielders scampered out through a hastily opened exit. Not one of them threw down their weapons. None were killed and, although some tripped and were grazed, they all made it out to Pall Mall. But they had lost the centre ground.

The cavalry withdrew, but the tables had been turned. Foot soldiers were inside the barricade ring. The besieged had become the besiegers and turned to Spike for direction. He stood on a wall on the north side of Pall Mall to give them their new orders. Five thousand people hushed to listen.

'The problem with a musket is how long it takes to load,' he shouted. 'The problem with a mob is that it forms an easy target. So, we spread out as much as possible and don't give them time to reload. That means, when we go back into the Square, we do it from all five entrances. We stay back, against the houses, once we are in, and spread out into a ring. Don't bunch up. Put a yard or two between each of you. We can probably make three rings. When I whistle, start walking in. If we walk up to them, they may not fire. We are their countrymen and they are not cold-blooded murderers. If they do fire, that is the moment to charge. Most of them will shoot high. Yes, a few of us will be hit, but we knew that when we started this, and our few fallen will be venerated by our children's children. But the simple fact is, you cannot keep a mob at bay with musket fire if it charges as you reload. Reloading takes twenty seconds, particularly if you are flustered. Most of us can sprint a hundred yards in twenty seconds and the middle of that square is only seventy yards away. When we get into the barricade the object is to disarm and dismiss, not to kill. We outnumber them ten to one. More. Just sit on them until they see sense. Tell them to come and join us in looting the palace. Their colonels will not send soldiers again after this defeat.'

The mob roared its approval. Spike waved for silence.

'You have ten minutes to form the rings. Then I will whistle,' Spike put his fingers in his mouth and gave a blast any market stallholder would have been proud of.

'*Lilliburlero*,' came a shout from the crowd.

'Yes,' shouted Spike back. 'We'll sing the *Lilliburlero* as we walk up to them. They will never fire at that. When I whistle, start to walk and sing. Now go and have fun.'

'My, God,' said Ike, 'The wisdom of crowds. This might almost work.'

'After this, the palaces,' said Spike. 'And we start the Irish Night rumour.'

Already the mob was humming. It was a catchy tune, jolly, upbeat, a piper's dream. They all knew the words of the anti-Catholic anthem, mocking how the Irish army had been packed with Catholic officers; and making fun of the prophecy of the Emerald Isle's independence, supposedly found in a peat bog. Since every English army unit had just been purged of Catholics, they would be playing to the gallery. But would the officers give the order to fire? And if they did, would they be obeyed?

The mob took a while to trickle back into the large square, via the streets and lanes. Eventually, and without a shot being fired from within the barricade, Spike had his three-ring encirclement. The mood was purposeful and unhurried, with the different sections of rioters humming the *Lilliburlero* out of time with each other, a ragged cannon, a swampland chorus. To the waiting troops it must have been disconcerting. Then Spike's whistle shrieked out, the humming clicked together into a single song and the mob stepped forward.

Jack, 13:10

Jack Wilson passed St Clement Danes at the head of their little column of two cannons and escort. He heard a woman shout from a passing cab, looked round and recognised Mrs Jones. Without breaking step, he removed his hat and gave a sweeping bow. The cab stopped. A hand came out of the open window and turned the handle. The door started to swing open. He knew who it would be. He was unsure how to greet her. She smiled at him and was about to jump out. Then the hackney cab lurched forward, the door swung back and she fell inside.

It could have been worse, Jack thought. A second later and she would have been swinging on the open door, with her mother trying to pull her in. Then he chuckled, at last he could laugh about Kitty. It was a relief. But whether it meant he was less in love with her, or more, he could not tell. They were still marching, the cab was just ahead, when Colonel Shere rode up from the Strand and came alongside Jack.

Jack greeted the grey as it slow-marched beside him at cannon-train speed. He could tell the horse recognised him.

'Any sign of the rioters up ahead, Sir?' he asked.

'Captain, you are in charge and I wouldn't want to interfere, but you should already know that. Or at least have scouts out. But since you ask, no, nothing between here and Whitehall.'

'Thank you, Colonel,' said Jack, feeling bad.

'Have you worked out your watches yet? I may drop by and inspect your camp in the morning.'

'No, Sir,' said Jack, feeling worse.

'Well, that is something else to dwell on between now and Charing Cross. It should take your mind off pretty girls falling out of cabs.'

'Yes, Sir,' said Jack. So the Colonel had seen his bow.

'Please arrange to be available in your mess tent this time tomorrow. What is it, a quarter past one?'

'Yes, Sir.'

'Well done, lads, keep going,' Shere shouted at the column. Then he continued in a normal voice. 'Captain, the peers want six gunners serving three guns this side of Whitehall Gate. They seem to think there are two gunners to a crew – despite Patch Mews being there. They agree on one cannon in front of St James' Palace.'

'Maybe Bishop Mews stepped out. We will do all we can, Sir. Which is this.'

'Agreed. Whitehall will have to make do with just these two for now.'

'Do you trust them, Sir?' The Colonel gave him a look, as if to say, where did that come from? 'I mean, Sir, to use wisely the deadly power we are putting under their control?'

'It won't be just us. The army seems to be getting a grip, Captain. Colonel Villers and old Captain Symmonds have brought them one hundred and sixty horse of the Household Cavalry. Colonel Selwyn of the Duke of Grafton's Regiment of Foot has four hundred men at arms. And Colonel Baggot of Prince George's Regiment has four hundred. They are sending eighty of the Horse to St James' Square as we speak, and two hundred of the foot are following. This is about keeping the peace, if necessary, by force. I trust them to seek peace. And they trust us to achieve it.'

'So the palace should be safe by the time we get there,' said Jack.

'It will be touch and go. But extreme danger focuses the mind. If ever you needed an example it's this Council of Lords Spiritual and Temporal. All rivalries laid aside. Like the prophecy of the holy mountain, *The wolf shall dwell with the lamb, the lion shall eat straw, the weaned child shall put his hand on the cockatrice's den.*'

'Isaiah,' said Jack.

'Chapter 11,' said the Colonel. 'Tories and Whigs united in one aim – to hold back the tide from below. I told them about the caltrops. They sense a pattern, but have no idea what it is.'

'First the chapels, then the embassies, then the palaces, then the Tower.'

But the Colonel was still musing on his glimpse of the holy mountain. 'Lord Rochester and My Lord Bishop of Winchester, royalists both if ever I saw, signing orders with gusto alongside hardened Williamites like Lords Crew, Culpeper and Montagu. Others standing back, giving their blessing but signing nothing: Lords Middleton and Feversham and Viscount Preston – men as much in shock as if they had just lost an arm or a leg. Dr Sprat trying to be everywhere at once, hurrying off to officiate at Lady Ossary's funeral.'

'That was her cortège the mob tried to block us with this morning, Sir.'

'Yes, Captain, I know that now.'

'And I know Simon Speke, Sir. He is not finished with us yet. He is resourceful and relentless. And he wants power.'

'Naked self-interest on both sides. Speke and his henchmen on the one, the established state on the other. Both will fight to keep their power. And it will be you and me who decide how quick and how deadly that fight is. We will speak tomorrow. Carry on.'

The Colonel returned Jack's salute and wheeled back towards the Tower.

Jack marched at a cannon-train crawl, but his mind raced – Simon Speke, insurrection, the difference between fighting for a monarch and for a cabal of barons. Stop that, he told himself. Soldiering and sentiment don't mix.

The Savoy was coming up, his mother's home. Would she spot him again? This time he must not break concentration. His promotion increased the chances that someone would die because of him. The trick was to care enough to prevent it, but not so much to hurt you if you didn't. Sometimes you could only choose the lesser of two evils. Sometimes your mind would wander, as his had just now, with men trusting that you were alert. No scouts! He could kick himself. The chances of a fatality had soared. The skill in soldering lay in anticipation. Shere had rammed that home. Well, not all the skill, but more than they admitted.

When he had asked if the Colonel trusted the Council, he might better have asked if he, Jack, trusted himself. This much he knew: he would fire on the mob if he had to, in defence of those he was supposed to protect, including himself. But he would not punch canister into barricades put up by countrymen with whom he agreed about so much. As regards the absence of scouts, he would make a virtue of it with a surprise dash for this side of St James' Park now. The Colonel's report reduced the chance of being ambushed in the streets. He would not stop at Charing Cross, but double his speed, head for the open space of Horse Guards' Parade and pick his campsite before the pioneers did it for him. He might not find a raised position with a good field of fire, but he would still do things his own way. He would only send out scouts from his next halt.

If the immediate coast was clear, he would plant the first gun team and sentries at the gate in Whitehall Palace. Colonel Shere had said the cavalry and foot were already there. So, although the long riverbank was porous to sneak attacks, a mob could not infiltrate through Scotland Yard. Finally, if the Pall Mall rioters had gone, he would deploy in front of St James' Palace. From there sentries could patrol as far as Hyde Park, to be sure of not being outflanked.

While he mulled on all this, the guns passed the Savoy with barely a wave from the townsfolk. We're yesterday's news, thought Jack to himself. Typical hard-bitten Londoners. He passed word back that the column was to switch to quick march on his command; and that the tail-end corporal was to run up and repeat the message to him when he had received it.

A minute later the man appeared. 'Ready for the order to quick march, Sir.'

Jack took his courage in his hands, turned and yelled, 'Column, quick march. Left-right-left-right.'

He bellowed the beat, heard the fusiliers take it up, the clip-clop of the horses sped up. He glanced back. Two guns, thirty-six gunners and half as many fusiliers were still with him. Wonder of wonders, so were the Tower's mess sergeant, cooks and supply wagons.

They turned into Charing Cross but the double gates to the Park were just out of sight. Were they open or closed? He could not risk it. He stuck to the left and led the way down Whitehall. The traffic stopped when it saw him coming, a crowd began to form, but then the train was through the open entrance to Horse Guards and under the tunnel. Jack called a halt on Horse Guards Parade.

The guns and their soldiers remained in a column. Jack ordered them to stand easy and gestured his officers together. He sent out the sergeants on scouting parties, to report back in fifteen minutes. Lieutenants Swarbreck and Webster were to take a group each and decide which of them would man the Whitehall station.

Jack took an ensign and two artillery horses and rode into the Park to choose the best campsite. In the glade behind the first plantation of trees was a long mound of spoil, residue of King Charles II's canal, dug roughly east-west. The water feature converged with a tree-lined avenue at an acute angle on the distant Arlington estate. The ground on the brow of this mound would be dry and the field of view west better. The canal would cover his back while the carriageway would give sentries a line of sight across the northern front. He marked a spot for the central watchtower by sticking the ensign's pennant upright in the ground and sent him hurrying on to Hyde Park to tell the Bridge Master and to lead back whomever they sent. He repeated Shere's request for everything the Quartermaster had – firewood, fodder, braziers, lanterns, posts and all the duckboards.

Trotting back to Horse Guards, Jack saw three figures approach from the Abbey, dressed in black. He waited as they rounded the canal towards him. Yes, it was Elizabeth Forrester with the man who had cleared the roadblock that morning, and a younger maid he didn't recognise. He jumped down from his horse and led it towards them. He was pleased to see Elizabeth. The trio stopped.

Elizabeth spoke first. 'Hello Jack. What a perfect day for a march-past.'

'Or a funeral,' he said.

'If any day is, for burying one's mother,' said the girl.

'I meant no disrespect, M'lady' said Jack, realising who Henrietta was. 'I should have said what I meant: Even on days like today, we need to retain some sense of humour, or we will all go mad.'

'Zat is vhat ze Bishop thinks,' said Hendriksen. 'If ve are to resolve anything in zis vale of tears, ve vill need our humour.'

'Gallows humour,' said Elizabeth. 'It binds together the living, otherwise we are helpless in the face of death. Henrietta, this is Jack Wilson of the Royal Artillery, whom I mentioned at breakfast the other day. Jack, Lady Henrietta Butler.'

'Delighted, Ma'am,' said Jack and gave a bow.

'And this is Mr Hendriksen, who saved the day,' said Henrietta. 'You seem to have come just in time.'

'The Royal Ordnance aims to please. We are setting up a small camp here.'

'So qvickly goes it?' asked Hendriksen.

'By nightfall. We are putting one gun under the Holbein Gate and one at St James' Palace under the tower. Both manned from here, day and night, until this disorder has stopped.'

'Do you think the rioters are still in our square, Lieutenant?' asked Henrietta.

'The Council has sent eighty cavalry and two hundred foot to St James' Square,' said Jack. 'Whether that will clear a crowd of hotheads like we saw this morning, I have my doubts.'

'Elizabeth calls it is a revolution from below. From what you saw this morning, would you agree?'

Jack nodded. 'Yes. The Prince of Orange is here to replace one elite with another. The mob wants more. They are literate in this age of print and have opinions but no voice. They feel the system is rigged against them. This religious hatred masks something deeper. The attacks on property, the thieving, they reflect a sense of unfairness.'

'But the mobile is the mobile.'

'No. Something is different. They are disciplined and well led. And a long way from their beds.'

'They seem to have picked on our square,' said Henrietta.

'They may still be there tonight Ma'am. But everything done so far has been within bounds, no serious bloodshed. It can be forgotten, as if it didn't happen. Even the sacking of the Spanish Ambassador's house will be just a diplomatic incident. No one died. However, if the Artillery is asked to fire on even one barricade, or if the mob tries to storm the guns and we reply with canister, that will be in the citizens' memory for ever.'

Elizabeth smiled at Jack and put her hand on the sash across his chest. 'Have you changed your uniform since I saw you this morning, Jack?'

'Acting Captain Wilson at your service, Ma'am,' he replied with a smile. 'Did we see each other this morning?'

'You remember well enough, Captain. You were on a white horse in the square and doffed your lieutenant's hat to me. If you are going to be based around the corner from us for a few nights I hope we will see more of you. For now, we must be heading home. The household will be worried.'

They exchanged goodbyes and walked on.

Jack watched them go longer than he should, until they had left the Park. Elizabeth had planted a hope in his heart. Or perhaps it had always been there, ignored because he feared rejection. He remembered the fifteen-year-old girl who would sneak into Harvey Court through the back way to give carrots to the chestnut gelding. What was he called? Orion. Losing her might hurt even more than being turned down by Kitty. Not because she was a baron's great-niece, but because she had an outdoorsy wild side which fitted his.

He looked at the sky. It would be a cold, dry night. The wind must have turned northerly. Singing came over the rooftops from beyond the King's Garden, the direction which Elizabeth, her charge and the butler had taken. Jaunty notes carried on the breeze. The *Lilliburlero* if he was not mistaken. He mustn't dawdle. The scouts would be back at Horse Guards Parade by now.

A tremendous volley of musket fire rang out from towards St James' Square. Seconds later, bullets pattered on the ground around him and into the canal behind. Jack felt a strong urge to gallop after the trio. But now was no time for private investigations. Duty before curiosity. He must stop dithering and place his cannon. He might already be too late. As he spurred back to Horse Guards, he tried to calculate the ballistics. If a level musket shot was still lethal at three hundred yards, what angle would the troops have fired at to have dropped musket balls only four hundred-odd yards from St James' Square? With a gentle tailwind, the soldiers were aiming almost straight up.

The scouts were back. The troops had formed two groups. Jack called his lieutenants together. 'So, which of us is for Whitehall?'

Lieutenant Webster stepped forward. 'We are Sir. You heard the shots?' Everyone had recognised the musket volley from the north west.

'Indeed. Sir Henry said something was going on in St James' Square. Any other signs of attack?' he asked the officers who had led the scouting parties. Only to the north, apparently, where troublemakers were baiting a body of troops around the

Haymarket. Pall Mall was almost empty and St James' Palace deserted. 'Then let's have Webster's cannon under the Holbein Gate. I'll come with you.

'Lieutenant Liddell, I need you to oversee the Pioneers setting up our camp. Ensign Lehman is bringing them from Hyde Park. His pennant marks the spot between the carriageway and the canal. Put in a watchtower. Lieutenant Swarbreck, if it's safe, take the second gun carriage through the park and the King's Garden and set up under the tower of St James' Palace. Have a scout establish the route. Move as quickly as you can, otherwise wait until I rejoin you.'

Liddell asked, 'What are the rules of engagement, Sir?

'Load when in doubt. Get the first shot off quickly. A determined mob can cover a hundred yards in the thirty seconds it takes us to reload. Aim low, just in front of them, so the shot fans off the cobbles, losing speed and causing leg injuries rather than deaths. Half-powder only. Then sponge and reload. Barrel still relatively cold. Aim left or right of the injured, whichever side comes on strongest, fire our second round, same charge. Reload immediately. If that hasn't stopped them, fire the third shot the other way. Spike the touchhole and leave the hand-to-hand stuff to the foot soldiers. We are anyway out of canister. That is all. Let's get these guns rolling.'

Jack was with Webster laying the line under the Holbein Gate, looking up Whitehall to Charing Cross, when the Lords began to reconvene for their afternoon session in the Council Chamber. The Marquess of Halifax and the younger man from this morning strolled past. They recognised him and came over.

'Lieutenant Wilson, or should I say Captain now?' said the Marquess with a glance at his larger hat and sash. 'What do you make of things?'

'I hope this is only for show, My Lord,' said Jack.

'This is my son, Lord Elland. You may speak freely. If you need a warrant to fire live shot, you only have to ask, Captain. Our last two orders this morning were for just that – *to use utmost endeavours to quell and disperse the rabble; and in case of necessity, to use force, and fire on them with bullett.* Something like that. But make no mistake, you are here to fight, not only for show.'

'Yes, My Lord. Colonel Shere has been crystal clear on that.'

'You have ammunition?' asked Lord Elland, indicating the near-empty limber.

'Three rounds of canister, Sir. The Colonel is keen that we do not arm the mob. Did you hear the volley of musket fire from St James' Square between quarter past and half past two?'

'From home? No,' said Lord Elland. 'There was a volley?'

'Perhaps two hundred muskets.'

'Good Lord. Mother,' said Elland, while at the same moment, Halifax said, ''True'.

'It's true, Sir?

'Gertrude, my wife,' explained the Marquess. ''True.'

'It sounded like the rabble may have met their match,' said Jack, trying to sound reassuring.

'Only one volley?' asked Halifax, looking puzzled. 'That could have been while we were inspecting the Banqueting Hall cellars. It appears at least the royal wine was overlooked by the pilferers.'

'Yes, My Lord. Possibly to scare them off. I believe it was fired deliberately high.'

'And if the mob comes for us?' asked Halifax. 'Here in Whitehall? Will you fire high?'

'We'll take no risks with your Lordships' safety. We'll load at the first sign of trouble. And hope to get off three rounds between the top of the Close and here.'

'Impressive,' said Halifax, with raised eyebrows. 'And how many dead? No, I mean, what casualties? How many rioters down?'

'Well, Sir, as you say, immobilised. Maybe a thousand down, so four thousand to run away. It is almost impossible for untrained civilians to advance over wounded bodies, to physically propel their legs and move forward, across open space, under fire of canister. They look down and their resolve evaporates. No discipline. At least, that is what the gunnery sergeants tell us. I doubt it has ever been tried on a street mob in the British Isles.'

'And if they rally and charge again?'

'Then the Palace of Whitehall will be in flames, Sir. A mob that survives such a beating will give no quarter in return.'

'It makes no sense,' said Lord Elland. 'Why do they fight? If they held the Tower, or the King, or had something to bargain with, I might understand. But the way things are, their cause is hopeless. The mob cannot take and hold this city.'

Lord Halifax and Jack exchanged a look as if to say, will you explain it, or shall I?

'They moved one day too late,' said Jack.

'Less,' said the Marquess. 'Twelve hours.' He seemed on the verge of saying more but did not.

'Then it would not have been spontaneous,' Elland said.

'You said it for me,' replied his father. 'And it wasn't.'

So, Halifax knew.

'Correct, Sir,' said Jack. 'This was organised in advance.'

'We must be getting along,' said Halifax with a frown and they parted.

A few minutes later, Kitty Jones marched up in great haste with a scroll of documents under her arm. Jack's heart missed a beat at the sight of her under full sail. She had regained all her composure and more. The fusiliers challenged her, but she was clearly on Council business. Jack waved her through.

He handed over to Webster, fetched a sack of pegs and a mallet from the cavalry barracks, remounted under the arch and crossed Horse Guards Parade. He was angry with himself. Through the gloaming he galloped, down the crosswise avenue of bare trees, turning into the wide carriageway of the Mall towards Arlington House. The coincidence was too much. Fate was mocking him. Elizabeth and Kitty, within yards of each other in the space of twenty minutes. Two sides of the same coin. Could a man go mad, strapped to the mast of duty between such sirens? Passing, he saw Liddell's torches, but where had the pioneers to set up his camp? He urged his mare to jump the low hedge into the King's Garden and slowed at the back of St James' Palace.

Swarbreck had the cannon set up in the entrance, as neat as for an inspection on Tower Green.

'Situation, Lieutenant?' asked Jack.

'They've gone, Sir. Vanished. I scouted up to the square to have a look.'

'Who's gone?'

'The mob, the Foot Guards. All of them, Sir, arm in arm, heads down, just melted away.'

'Who are those people with furniture?' asked Jack.

'Just householders reclaiming their looted chattels from the barricade the mob built.'

'There was a barricade?'

'Earlier today in the Square, apparently.'

Simon Speke, thought Jack to himself. But if Speke had won, why had he not finished the job? Why had the rabble not stormed the Palace? Not for fear of one puny cannon under the gatehouse, that was certain.

Elizabeth, 14:00

Elizabeth led the trio out of the park, across the King's Garden, under the gate tower and into St James' Street. They were in time to see the mob filter back up from Pall Mall into St James' Square. She tacked north and then east, past hatters, vintners and cobblers to the nobility, through an alley and into King's Street.

No one noticed them. The rabble was prowling forwards quietly, an enormous pack focused on some common endeavour. It was as she imagined the end of the world, the crowd all walking one way, at one speed, with one light in their eyes, upright, evenly spaced from each other, humming the same tune, as if towards the risen Christ. From the west side of St James' Square, she watched them filter sideways, begin to form three rings around the centre, the outer one pressed back against the buildings. In the middle of the square was a barricade like a fourth ring, a heaped jumble of common household furniture – bedsteads, bookshelves, tables, dressers, here and there an upturned rocking chair. Inside this defence, some hundreds of Foot Guards formed a fifth ring, with bayonets fixed, prickly as a scarlet porcupine.

A piercing whistle rang out and the humming from the mob slipped into song, a single sound from five thousand throats. The *Lilliburlero*. Such a catchy little tune, silly, upbeat. Hendricksen was tapping along. But to her stupefaction the rings of rioters began to constrict around the scarlet thorn-pig. She watched as bayonets dropped to the horizontal, and troops nuzzled their musket stocks to their cheeks. She felt Henrietta grab her hand, she grabbed Hendriksen's, and together they ran away, seeking the nearest cover in King Street, ducking low.

'It's too far,' shouted Elizabeth. 'Down.' They threw themselves to the ground. The singing grew louder. A volley rang out. She heard the whistle of bullet, the awful, soul-ripping cry of a shot man. She looked back into the Square. Most of the mob had survived. They had abandoned their three rings and were sprinting towards the barricade. Very few bodies lay on the ground.

Lady Henrietta was up first, approaching the nearest casualty. Elizabeth and Hendriksen followed. The boy was lying on his back, his right hand on his chest, his life blood squirting from a neck wound. He looked glassily at Elizabeth and said, 'Ah, Miss Forrester.' Elizabeth recoiled. It was the apprentice from St Paul's Churchyard. The lad who had talked her mother down from the scaffolding on the new cathedral and brought her safely home. Surely this was one angel who did not deserve to die. She circled around, unable to approach such a ghastly injustice.

The stink of spent gunpowder was in the air. Henrietta was kneeling, pressing her bare hand to the side of the young man's neck, trying to staunch the huge wound. He beckoned weakly with his hand, towards his mouth. Henrietta leant forward so he could whisper in her ear. When she sat up the blood had ceased to spurt. He was dead. Henrietta started shaking uncontrollably.

'Come avay ladies,' said Hendriksen. He pulled Henrietta to her feet and guided his two charges to Ormonde House. Elizabeth was in a daze. As they passed Halifax House, she saw faces in the first-floor windows, women, perhaps Lady Elland, perhaps the Marchioness. But mainly she was bewildered by the contrast, the young hero's death and the sight of rioters and soldiers fraternising in the middle of the square. It was too awful. The troops had joined the rebellion. Now no one would be safe. The only question was whether the mob would come for the noble mansions on the Square now, or go straight to the palaces.

Hendriksen banged on the drabbed-down front door of Ormonde House. He shouted their names. She heard bolts being drawn back. The portal opened, Drizzle snatched them in. Two footmen slammed the door, slid home the bars and re-wedged long shelves from the library against it. Elizabeth saw the entire household standing in the hall, armed with pokers, fire irons, even rolling pins, ready to fight off the mob. One or two knives were lashed to broom handles.

'Lord be praised,' said Cook, and ran to hug Henrietta. 'But you are wounded, my little bird, all this gore.'

It was true, the daughter of the house was trailing blood along the stone floor. It dripped off her black funeral cape and skirts. Red does not show on black but now it was on Cook's white apron and everyone could see how much there was. It seemed to come from nowhere.

'No, Mrs Cross, I am fine,' said Henrietta, who had stopped shaking. 'It was a little apprentice, but I couldn't save him. I would like to have a bath. Please.' She looked at Modesty, who nodded and hurried off to brew up the hot water tank.

'So, you all got back safely,' said Hendriksen.

'We missed you,' Elizabeth said, closing the lid on what she had just seen. 'It was a lovely service. Afterwards the Bishop gave a wake in the Deanery, expecting you all, far too much food. Sorry we weren't at lunch here.'

Drizzle had been peeking through a crack in a boarded-up window and said, 'The mob has retaken its barricade in the Square.'

'Ve don't really have ze time to tell you all about it,' said Hendriksen. 'Ve will account it in ze opportune moment. For now, please, two or tree of you go to upstairs vindows and keep vatch. Others stand by in ze downstairs rooms tovards ze square and report any sign of ze boards being removed from outside.'

Henrietta said, 'Elizabeth, please help me out of these things. We don't want blood on the rugs. The rest of you, please do as Hendriksen says,' and she began taking off her gore-soaked clothes in the hall where she stood.

Drizzle finished bracing the door. 'After the hearse and your carriage got through the mob, we heard music and the mood seemed to soften. But we saw nothing from here. I understand they parted for the troops, even cheered them.'

Torrance, the youngest footman said, 'But they were never going to let us follow you to the Abbey.'

'Such a crowd,' said Cook. 'I was just saying. Do you remember when the Old Duke returned from Ireland in eighty-five, how many went to meet him on the road? Such a train followed him into the Square, I don't know as how they all fitted in, the multitude what greeted him. And the shouts and cheers.'

A lookout called down the stairwell from the first floor, 'The rabble is dispersing.'

The staff in the hall gave it a few more minutes. Modesty brought a gown and slippers and Lady Henrietta, careful to spare the carpets, traipsed upstairs for her bath, while her clothes were taken to the laundry. Others went down to the servants' hall. A few disappeared to return their weapons to their normal roles. A maid mopped the blood off the marble floor, where yesterday the coffin had stood.

Elizabeth was left alone. She felt exhausted. Then a new fear seized her. She must hurry over to Covent Garden to check on her parents.

Ichabod, 14:05

In St James' Square, Ike saw how the rioters tightened on the central circle of the barricade. Behind the wooden ring the infantry officers yelled, 'Take aim'. The redcoats levelled their flintlocks. The senior officer growled, 'hold – steady – wait – wait until you see the whites of their eyes.'

But then the miracle happened. The *Lilliburlero* grew louder. The troops began to sing along with the mob. One by one they put up their muskets. In haste their captain yelled 'fire', but almost all shots went up over the rooftops. The mob cheered and rushed forward. The soldiers could never have reloaded in time – were unwilling even to try. They threw down their weapons and greeted their compatriots with shouts and open arms.

Nevertheless, a few had fired into the crowd. Officers had discharged their pistols on the level. When the mob reached the barricade it knew so well, and pulled it apart to climb in, some scuffles and punches ensued. The odd fanatical defender was taken down in a struggle. Sympathetic soldiers assisted, crying out, 'Huzzah for the revolution.'

The way to the palace was clear, thought Ike. The Council of Peers would not dare send troops after this. It was the crowning triumph for Spike's battlefield tactics. Looking around, Ike failed to see him. 'Where are you, you bloody genius?' he cried. 'Come to me.'

Then a dread crept in. The open space beyond the mob was dotted with three or four casualties, moving on the hard earth, trying to pick themselves up. Ike looked back to the clear area of the Square behind him, where he and Spike had walked towards the barricade together. He saw a body laid out on its back, its right arm across its chest. He pushed his way out of the melee and ran over to it.

Spike was there on the ground, the side of his neck shot away. Stone dead.

Ike cradled his friend's head, then lifted his corpse, now impossibly small, out of its pool of lifeblood. He carried it back towards the barricade. As he approached, that side of the mob began to fall silent. A way through opened in front of him. He reached the centre of the crowd. The only chatter now was from soldiers, babbling with relief, then even that died away.

Ike was stiff with misery, his voice died in his windpipe, tears streamed down his face. He had no fight left in him.

He laid the body down and stood back.

One by one Spike's Spartans stepped to the front, forming an inner circle around their fallen leader. Those who had known him best crouched down, stroked his brow and walked away. As they left, others came forward.

'They're putting a cannon in front of the gatehouse at the Palace, with gunners and fusiliers,' one said.

'It's over,' said another.

'Call off Blackie Lockyer and the barricades,' said a third.

The crowd began to drift eastwards, back to their homes.

Ike felt the same. Denied two aces, the King and the Tower, the revolution had already been riding on a wing and a prayer. Now it had sacrificed the third ace, Spike's oratory and battlefield flair. That left just him and Nat Brazier. Ike's lack of sleep crashed over him. He knew he did not have what it would take. He might be more cold-hearted than Spike, but he was no Caesar, no Alexander, no ace. Nor was Nat. Maybe the other side had the fourth ace.

In his bitterness at himself, in his pain at losing his best and perhaps only friend, his constant co-conspirator, Ichabod looked up to the heavens. Then he remembered. For a moment the old rage flared in him. He stood up, tall in his greatcoat. His voice came back. 'Warn them,' he bellowed, 'warn everyone. The Irish are coming, cutting throats!'

Immediately a whisper ran through the mob. 'The Irish…' Now the distraught rioters were angry again, they began to disperse more quickly.

Ike was alone with his dead gladiator in that amphitheatre of wealth and power. He stooped to straighten the cadaver's clothing then took off his coat and laid it down its length. He crouched beside the corpse and whispered, maybe to himself, maybe to the bundle, maybe to the gods, about revenge. After five minutes or thirty, he heard a horse's hooves. A carriage creaked to a halt behind him. He looked up. It was the hackney cab from earlier this morning.

'Three o'clock', said the driver. 'Gent said I should come back now, if I was short of work. Nice fellow. Seen 'im around?'

'He's here,' said Ike, pointing to the shape under the coat. 'Give me a hand and we'll get him up to Clerkenwell Green.'

'Lord, what 'appened?'

'Riot. Musket ball through the neck.'

'I don't want no blood in my carriage,' said the driver.

Ike stood and drew his dagger. 'You can help me, or I can leave you under this coat and drive my friend to Clerkenwell in your cab myself. Choose.'

'Easy, mate, easy,' said the cabbie. 'We can do it. They say these things is washable for a reason. It's just that, so far, I've avoided them that'll, y'know…'

'Let's get him in then,' said Ike, sheathing the knife. 'We'll put the coat under him. He's pretty well bled out but his britches are soaked.'

'You're quite a mess yourself, guv'nor.'

They lifted Spike's body into the footwell. It was so light it almost floated in by itself.

Ike reached into Spike's jacket and removed the moneybag.

'Where to, guv?' asked the driver.

'Clerkenwell Green. I'll show you when we get there. Take us up by Holborn and Hatton Garden and over the bridge at Mutton Lane.'

The taxi set off at a sedate pace. At St Giles the traffic was halted by an advanced guard of fusiliers. The baggage train of the Royal Ordnance came from the Tyburn Road and crossed into High Holborn on its way to the Tower. It took many minutes to pass, during which time Ike perceived that it was guarded by the self-same soldiers who had run his gauntlet in Pall Mall that morning. He regretted missing such a soft, almost undefended target in Hyde Park, while Spike had focused on breaking the hard one, the flower of the elite Guard in its proudest square. Yet it had been Agincourt all over again, the underdog triumphant. He also regretted not looting the French Embassy. That would have gone down in folklore – if only for the pickings. Instead, he was not even going to be rich by the end of this.

It dawned on him that he would have to tell Hugh Speke how his cousin had died. As far as he knew, Hugh was Spike's only relative in London. He must try to find him, once he had got his friend home. Ike looked at the bloodless, grey face and his heart broke again. Rage, pain, rage. And still the baggage train passed in front of him. Wherever the rioters had retreated to, they were being flanked right now. Out-manoeuvred. Spike would have known what to do.

So he sat there in his hackney cab, facing the underbelly of his enemy, fingering his Moroccan blade, devoid of tactics, afraid, unable to strike. Then a small thought occurred. He realised it wasn't much. Nat Brazier would still be fired up. The other mob, from last night, would have some heart. Bloomsbury was still a target, and the mobile south of the river would not take this lying down. Even Tower Hamlets might have some fight left in them. For him personally, Southwark would offer a shred of self-respect. It wasn't revolution, or even a strategy, but it was a revenge of sorts. It would make the story slightly harder for the hierarchists to paint out of history, to sweep under the carpet. Tomorrow he would go down and see what Rosa could organise for Friday. And this time, no sanctimonious ideas about saving the future Republic's international reputation.

Kitty, 15:00

Kitty worked fast, her hands flying over the type, wedging, locking up, moving down the forme. She was conscious of the earlier wasted time. Gwyn's witching hour of half-three was approaching. However, the old lads were also fast, so that they set the *Instruction to Edward Jones* at the same time she did, and whizzed off the last line ahead of her. She shook her head in feigned dismay. They patted each other on the back in mock delight and delivered some affectionate banter, 'You're showing your age, Miss Kitty' and 'You'll make one of us yet.'

The clock was on the half hour as the papers were damped, the formes inked, the tails pulled and the finished galley proofs scrolled together. Kitty strode off round Charing Cross and down Whitehall. Passing Scotland Yard, she was glad the Tideway has been against her. Otherwise she would have missed what was happening in the streets. She was impressed by the scores of horse and foot soldiers drawn up. Straight ahead, a cannon with limber, a full complement of gunners and twice as many fusiliers faced her from under the Holbein Gate. She walked boldly in among them. One of the gunners was Jack.

She was determined not to embarrass herself again. 'Pleased to see you, gentlemen,' she said. 'I'm afraid I can't stop.'

'What's the hurry, Miss?' asked the senior fusilier.

'Privy Council business, I have an urgent delivery,' and Kitty tossed her hair, smiled her brightest smile and patted the scroll. 'Roly de Luge will vouch for me.'

'Step on through, Miss Jones,' said Jack.

The fusilier relented. 'Ah, so you know the Captain. Why didn't you say? Bring us some news if you come back this way, Miss. We're always the last to know what's going on.'

'That I will, Sergeant.'

De Luge opened the side door of the administration block without a word and she was back in the anteroom, looking out over the Privy Gardens. She was told to wait. Two gardeners were still at work in the setting light, pruning the shrubs on the parterre. She thought of another garden in this winter light, and a handsome young man, who had turned out to be James FitzJames, Duke of Berwick. Tomorrow morning she would have his second letter. Did she doubt that? No. But how would she feel? She seemed to spend her life waiting.

It struck the hour, she was thirty minutes late. She put her head round the double doors. Francis Gwyn looked over, nodded and held up a palm with five fingers splayed, to signal that he would be with her shortly. Turning back into the waiting area, she jumped. The blond, moustachioed officer from this morning was at her shoulder.

'Miss me?' he breathed.

'Forgive me, Sir, have we been introduced?'

'Horace Exe, Captain, Royal Artillery, at your service. And you?'

'Johanna Catherine Jones, the *London Gazette*. Anything we should be putting in tomorrow's edition?'

'How about: *Mobile foiled – How I knew about the caltrops?*'

'I can't print that. No one can print that. Ever.'

'How about: *Spanish Ambassador takes royal apartment in Whitehall Palace after night of Hell?*'

Kitty's ears pricked up. 'No, we can't print that, although others could.'

'*Gazette gains from rival's misfortune?*'

'That's not news. Not even *King's Printing House Sacked*. No, tell me something vital which everyone needs to know tomorrow.'

'Only if you give me something consequential back.' He lingered. 'Not now, I'm on duty, but soon. I claim your company on a tour of the crown jewels.'

Kitty saw he knew a story. She sighed. He seemed intelligent and, after all, she had cast the first fly with her caltrop barb. 'Yes, I agree we will speak again.'

'*Lord Chancellor Jeffreys has been sent to the Tower*. That's why this delay. The Council is just signing it,' said Exe. 'To keep him safe prisoner until further notice.'

Yes, the *Gazette* should run that, Kitty thought to herself. That's news indeed. 'You mean His Majesty left Judge Jeffreys behind?' She laughed, the beast deserved no less. Then she saw Exe's predatory gloat and quickly straightened her face. 'But he's still Lord Chancellor. They can't just arrest him. For what? If they lock him up that is open sedition. What happened?'

'He was disguised as a merchant, down in Wapping. Some say he tried to bribe a ship's master to take him to Hambourg, others to New Castle. But he offered too much. Forty pounds. Ten, twenty times too much. You know, these days people are jumpy. Others say he looked from a window where he was hiding and his wig slipped. Anyway, the mob dragged him out and roughed him up for a while. The militia came, which must have stuck in their throats – risking life and limb for the most hated man in England. They pulled him out and put him under heavy guard. With the mob howling for blood, they took him to his old flunky the Lord Mayor, for permission to lock him up.'

'That must have been a sight' said Kitty, captivated.

'I haven't even started. Sir John Chapman threw a fit. Literally, he fell foaming to the ground, to see his puppet master brought so low. This terror of the assizes, this monster who had stripped his City of its charter and then brought it back with lickspittle joy, this Lord Chancellor before whom all had trembled, shown to be as mortal as a mouse. It sounds like neither of them will live long, and good riddance to both if you ask me.'

'So, they brought Jeffreys here?'

'No, no. A messenger came. They have him in the Tower, but need authority.'

'This Council is locking him up in the Tower for his own protection?'

'That's not what it says on the order.'

'They are getting careless.'

'These are careless times, Johanna Catherine,' said Exe, with his blond eyelashes and serpent's eyes.

Francis Gwyn came out of the Council Chamber and exclaimed, 'Captain. You still here?'

'Colonel Shere's orders, Sir. I'm his liaison, your closest point of contact. To remain here until you call it a night.'

'Well, don't make yourself too comfortable. Miss Jones, what have you got for me? Come over, let's lay them out under the candles. So, these are all actual proofs? Yes, I like the layout of the handbill. Please congratulate the man who did this. And the poster copies it. Good, good, a sense of order and control.' He read in silence for a while. 'Captain,' he complained when Exe tried looking over his shoulder. 'May I ask you to liaise a little less closely? You will read it all in the *Gazette* in the morning. What's wrong with your paper's capital 'W's?' he added, as if Exe and Kitty were the same person. 'I see, I see. Standard practice to use 'VV' when the 'Ws' run out. Tell your father we are not a coffeehouse rag. But, yes, that will do.'

'Thank you, Sir,' said Kitty. 'Do you want to keep the proofs since there are no changes?'

'Good idea, yes, for the record. One less thing for the morning. What else have you got in tomorrow's edition?'

'News from abroad, Sir. Vienna, Ratisbonne, Liège, Francfert, Hambourg,

Cologne. I was wondering if we might mention that Judge Jeffreys has been taken in Wapping and sent to the Tower?'

Gwyn looked Kitty hard in the eye. 'Young lady, if that is all you print about the goings-on in London this day, I can live with it.' He added, 'Back page.'

'Then, Sir, Captain, I must be on my way. Thank you both, it's been gratifying.'

With nary a glance back, she sailed from the room and out of the palace. To her relief, Jack was gone. She took care to drop word to the remaining gunners and their lieutenant about their latest prisoner being held back at base, which caused at least as much merriment to them as it had to her.

News of Jeffreys' discovery, beating and incarceration had reached the Savoy printworks by the time Kitty returned. However, she had it 'By Authority', and who cared about it being on the back page? This was the stuff of newsmen's dreams. A crucial, uncensored story landing as the paper went to bed. They reset two of the back page pieces in the left-hand column, about Francfert and Hambourg, into smaller type, which let Cologne move up. Brussels could now start in the bottom left-hand corner. It looked less balanced, but made room for Kitty's two sentences half way down the right-hand column.

Thus it was that the *London Gazette* of 13 December 1688 carried Catherine Jones' first contribution:

> *Whitehall, Decemb. 12. This day the Lord George*
> *Jeffreys was taken at Wapping, and was sent to the*
> *Tower by Order of the Peers assembled with some*
> *of the Privy Council in the Council Chamber at*
> *Whitehall.*

'As a debut,' said her father, 'that is a gem. Pure journalistic serendipity. Had you delivered the galleys on time, you would not have been at the Council when that story broke. But now we have a nationwide exclusive. No rival can run this before us, with our presses starting this minute, even if they try. What chance the *London Gazette* catching a story this big, by authority, as we go to press, when we only appear every three days?'

Kitty said, 'Isn't this what our job should be all about?'

Her father nodded. 'What is more, the piece is just hilarious. It will have everyone, but everyone, laughing, if not dancing in the streets.'

Jack, 16:00

Captain Jack Wilson was back in St James' Park before Blood's Pioneers and the Quartermaster's wagons arrived from Hyde Park Corner. It was his first time with a commission to pitch a camp and the past month's experience came in handy. In fact, he thought, it was possibly the first time any gunnery captain had been left with so many resources and the freedom to execute a campsite plan. Normally, the specialists would be all over such an opportunity. Out would come the Provost Marshall's rulebook about how many men could fit in a tent, the Bridging Master's fixation with straight lines, and the Major's passion for rank. But for once none of them were there to make a mess of things. The senior officers were preoccupied with the bigger risk of running into the mob; or were distracted by their room allocation when they returned to barracks.

Jack had deliberately left his questions about the camp unasked and now he had the chance to apply his own ideas. He would erect more sleeping accommodation than regulations required, partly because he did not believe two cannon would be sufficient for the job in the eyes of the Council, and partly because, until such time as that proved correct, he did not want to be sharing – he had never liked someone else using his bed while he was on watch. Also, he would build in a circle to minimise the perimeter to guard if they came under attack and to reduce walking within the camp. Point-to-point speed might be essential. The only doubt was the mud. It was bound to rain, sooner or later. That was why he had asked for duckboards.

At the top of the mound he would construct a lookout platform. Around this would be the assembly area, mess tent and cookhouse, the places with the most tramping. The slope would help with drainage, not just outside, but also to keep tent floors dry within. Wind direction was important for shielding canvas entrances, and to be upwind of smoky kitchens, themselves upwind of the latrines.

With the mallet and sack of wooden pegs, he paced out the ground, marking where the various tents would go. No rain now meant he could keep bedding, the stores, fodder and firewood dry. This would transform morale when it came.

He centred the sleeping accommodation in a quarter-circle north-west round the cookhouse and mess tent. The baggage wagons he put to the south and the washhouse and latrines to the east. Through the camp and on the lower ground routes in and out, he laid out lines for duckboards, as far as they would stretch in the direction of Charing Cross and to the two palaces. He marked space for sentry satellites in each direction and at a few key viewpoints. The canal helped with security but was too brackish to drink. When the supplies began to arrive, he sent two carts to fill water butts where the River Tyburn divided before running into the top end of the ornamental trench.

He inspected the canvas the Quartermaster had sent. The man had done as Jack asked. With much more than he currently needed, Jack could reject anything torn and threadbare, and still have fabric to double-cover the mess, a tent within a tent, an idea he had long dreamed of. The Pioneers grumbled – they had reckoned on being home by now. But in midwinter, while the weather held off, they all saw the point. And Captain Blood led from the front.

Darkness fell on Jack's campsite, but the lanterns helped. The Quartermaster had sent all the lamps and oil he had, the whole wagon, possibly six dozen lanterns. The tent crews had pitched so often and so recently that they joked they could finish the job blindfold anyway. Jack encouraged a sense of competition between them and they took this blatant motivational trick in good spirit.

By six o'clock the canvas was up, the first Pioneers marched off to the Tower and the Quartermaster's men moved in. Next, was to fire up the kitchens. The camp would eat shortly, with stout beer all round, and the cooks from the Tower must not forget the second sitting for Swarbeck's and Webster's troops. He had put himself on the graveyard shift from eleven until seven in the morning, at least for tonight, to set an example. It also meant taking the St James' Palace watch for himself, assuming that would be the scene of worst trouble. Before then, he needed a good meal and a few hours' sleep. It was clear the campsite was on track and Jack felt able to tour his two outposts. He trotted a workhorse back to Whitehall and spent twenty minutes with Webster and his gun crew, picking up their finer observations and suggestions. Then he cut back west to St James' Palace and did the same with Swarbreck's boys. The silence was eerie and Jack could not believe they had seen the last of the rioters' masterplan. Since the close shave with the hearse roadblock, everyone knew the attacks were co-ordinated.

He returned just before seven, ready for several helpings of hash and beans with the off-duty contingent. While they tucked into the seasonal brew, he stayed on mugs of Tyburn water to keep a clear head. Thus fed and irrigated, he asked the mess sergeant to wake him at half past ten and repaired to his tent. Someone had even made a bed for him. He pulled off his boots, stuffed them with paper, applied his customary layer of grease to their seams and soles, and lay back. An image swam into his mind of Elizabeth in black, with her warm brown eyes looking up into his, patting his chest. Then he was out.

Kitty, 16:50

Edward Jones' workshop in the Savoy was up against it. Not only did they have to print tomorrow's *Gazette* and the Council's *Declaration* in handbill and poster formats, but the boss had chosen to increase the *Gazette*'s print run, expecting a surge in demand.

When Kitty had reminded her father they were short-staffed with their apprentices out on the street, Edward only shrugged.

'That's business,' he said. 'Our setup costs are the same. The extra thousand will triple our profits and raise our reputation to boot. With double-rush rates from the Council, we can buy a seventh press on the back of tonight's work. We'll be on our way to transforming the firm.'

Such deadline alarums were part of the job. Kitty had witnessed her fair share – it was when they roped her in. As the minutes on the workshop wall clock ticked away, excitement leached into the limbs and flowed like a humour under the skin. Fuelled by this miraculous, own-made sanguinity, the staff would do the impossible. It was the alchemy of creation.

'Shouldn't we just admit defeat?' she would ask.

'It'll all turn out well, you'll see.'

'How?' she would ask.

'It's a mystery.'

She had seen a similar theurgy at the theatre. It was why audiences went. Aside from the plot and the *mise en scène*, a pagan force was evident, each night another little miracle. No wonder the Puritans had banned it. Edward Jones knew this. So he pushed the boundaries. He would set to and his loyal printers would roll their eyes and follow. As did Mary and Kitty this evening. With a mountain to climb, soon every press was in full swing.

The old hands reckoned on one hundred and twenty single pages from one press each hour. The *Gazette* was double-sided, so in nine hours two presses could run off a thousand copies, one doing the front while the other took that output and printed the back. The *Gazette*'s usual print run had been two thousand, using four presses, with two in reserve or being serviced. The first deliveries of the new issue would leave the workshop after three hours, at nine o'clock that night; the last at three in the morning. But Edward wanted an extra thousand copies for this landmark edition. Normally, the two spare presses would deliver that, with the apprentices working overtime. However, tonight the back-ups would be producing the flyer and poster of the *Declaration*. Indeed, that was the prime task and took precedence over the newssheet in the eyes of the client. If either press broke, then their type would barge the *Gazette* off another. But if all went well, Mary and Kitty could set extra type for the *Gazette*, front and back, once Paul, the clerk, returned from the paper wholesaler and could relieve them on the posters. These presses would then tackle some of the extra thousand *Gazettes* once the *Declarations* were done. Thus, God willing and with all hands on the newssheet, the extended run could be out of the door by five in the morning.

Kitty had been immersed in the printing world from birth. She knew the process front-to-back and back-to-front. Once the rhythm of inking, placing, sliding, pulling, releasing and removing had settled, the operators would begin to chat. Kitty was paired with her father on such occasions, for propriety's sake, and the ensuing long conversations were among her happiest memories. This evening she was able to reopen the subject she had hinted at two nights before. Love.

'Papa, do you remember that I have something I need to discuss?'

'Ah, yes, the man. You said there's a man.'

'We have to talk, is now a good time?'

'Yes, a perfect time,' said Edward, leaning over the poster-sized typeface, patting out the corners to ensure an even coverage of ink. 'So, who is he?'

'I first saw him that afternoon I went to the Chelsea Physic Garden. I thought he was an under-gardener or an apothecary's apprentice. He's only my age. I admit I was a bit smitten, but we didn't speak.'

'So, who is he?'

'I'm coming to that. Don't rush me,' said Kitty as she put both hands on the handle or devil's tail and pulled back.

Her father gestured with his free hand in apology, to show that he could see this was sensitive stuff.

Kitty continued. 'But then came a miraculous second meeting. He was at Lord Ranelagh's apartment in the new hospital, when Nicholas Staphurst and I dropped by afterwards. One of his carriage horses had gone lame on the King's Road.

Lord Ranelagh helped without question, indeed he was delighted to see him. He asked him to keep me company while Staphurst and he talked politics. I was introduced, but was too flustered to catch his full name, only James. So we spoke as equals. We had tea together in his Lordship's library. The face seemed vaguely familiar. He was tall and slim and moved with grace and self-assurance. He spoke perfect French. He was attentive, modest, witty. I was, well, attracted to him. That's an understatement. It was magnetic. He seemed to feel the same about me. No, I am sure he felt the same. He did not need to speak, but when he did, it only made things better. I felt I had to warn him off, but it became more perfect.'

She removed the printed sheet and placed a blank one on the tympan. But Edward Jones had stopped. Instead of beating the ink balls on the type, he was looking at his daughter with a rapt expression.

'You told him?' he whispered.

'Yes, I told him. And he said he was too.'

Edward went to work with the ink balls, padding away at the metal surface until the distribution of the sticky black film was perfect. Then he said, 'Family is more important than business. No family, no future. I don't want to get in your way but, by God, I don't want to lose you to some bastard, either.'

His words stung Kitty, far more than he could have known. She recoiled and he saw it, 'I'm sorry, my darling. Of course I trust your judgement.'

'But what if he is a bastard, Papa?' said Kitty. 'In the sense that his parents never married.'

Edward tried to hide his expression. Kitty watched him struggle to find the right face, the right words. She closed the frisket over the type and he roused the coffin under the platen. She pulled the lever and neither spoke. They went through several cycles before Kitty continued. 'Though I didn't know that then. He asked if he could write to me, and I said yes. The very next day, yesterday morning, I got this letter from Hampton Court. I didn't open it until the afternoon.' She reached into her pocket and handed her father James' note. He held it without opening it. 'I went to Nicholas at the Apothecaries' Hall to ask who this young man was and he told me that, as of yesterday, he was the most toxic man in England.'

'So that is why you asked about the Duke of Berwick. I had been wondering.' He read James' letter. 'Has anyone else seen this?'

'Just you and me. And the author, of course.'

'Let's keep it that way. Please don't show your mother.'

'If you say so.'

'And he hasn't written since?' he said, handing the letter back.

'We will know tomorrow morning. The post from out of town often takes two days.'

Kitty had said her piece. The die was cast. She loaded the next paper on the tympan, closed the frisket and was ready to pull again. Her father pummelled away with the inking leathers, rounced the coffin and she put her back into another pull. And so it went.

Eventually Edward spoke, '1 Peter 5. *Be sober, be vigilant; because your adversary the devil, like a roaring lion, walketh about, seeking whom he may devour.* Also, 1 John 3, *For all that is in the world, the lust of the flesh, and the lust of the eyes, and the pride of life, is not of the Father, but is of the world… These things have I written unto you concerning them that seduce you.*'

Now it was Kitty who looked at him hard. Her knuckles were white on the devil's tail. She felt herself swelling with resentment. Cruel words were on the tip of her tongue, perhaps the harshest she would ever speak to her father.

A yell came from the doorway of the workshop. It was the clerk, Paul.

He shouted across the workshop, 'The Irish are coming, cutting throats.'

'Come,' said Edward to Kitty.

They ran to the entrance. Work had stopped. The printers hurried over.

'What do you mean?' Edward asked Paul.

'The town is in uproar. I was at the paper merchants when they heard. I came straight back with our delivery. We must defend ourselves.'

'But what do you mean, man, *The Irish are coming, cutting throats*? Why would they do that?'

'It is their revenge. Disbanded without pay. They want to punish us. Maybe they think it will bring the King back. They are men of the bog, with no respect of property. They kill without a thought. Their duty to the Pope is to wipe us from the earth.' The clerk checked himself and looked around at the ashen, fearful faces of his colleagues. 'Sorry.'

'I will go and see,' said Kitty. 'It sounds like nonsense, more false news.'

Edward nodded. 'It makes no sense to me, either.'

'Be that as it may, we must think of ourselves,' said Johanna.

'And others,' said Edward. 'Neighbours? What about the Forresters?'

Kitty said, 'Elizabeth won't be there. A panic like this could push Mrs Forrester over the edge. We should get them from Covent Garden and bring them here. Is that agreed, Father?'

Edward understood. 'It would be better for the Forresters to be with a larger group like us than sitting at home worrying.' He turned to his loyal crew. 'Men, Kitty will investigate this tittle-tattle, and bring in a nearby couple who are vulnerable to such gossip. We will know more when she gets back. Now, let's not stand around gawping. Paul, team up with me on the *Declaration* posters please. You ink and I'll pull.'

Brushing off Mary's protests, Kitty threw her father's cloak over her shoulders and set off into the night. In the Strand, citizens brandishing torches were swearing that they would stand together against the foe. She spotted the boy who had led the destruction of the Jesuit schoolhouse, swollen with new self-importance in the opposite role of defender of the peace.

She took her courage in her hands and went straight up to him. 'What is happening?'

'The Irish are coming, cutting throats.'

'Who says?'

'A horseman cantered through, covered in blood, yelling the news.'

'But it was dark. Did you see him?'

The boy hesitated. 'No.'

I don't believe it, Kitty thought, but said, 'What other proof do you have? He might have been a madman.'

'People have heard volleys. The lookout saw explosions in the night sky from the direction of Uxbridge.'

'What lookout? Where is he?'

'He has gone on to the Boar's Head to warn the Committee.'

'Did you speak to him?'

'Yes.'

Kitty was still unconvinced.

'It only stands to reason,' continued the angry ringleader. 'Those Irish were brought here to enslave us to Rome or die in the attempt. They are your madmen, not us. Fanatics – the Fian bands. Killing is in their blood. Papists are all the same.' And he spat on the ground to emphasise his disgust.

'My friend,' said Kitty, 'I think you are wrong. However, I cannot take the chance. What is this about a Committee?'

The bully looked closely into her face. Sweat reeked off his clothes and his downy beard glistened in the torchlight, 'You'd better get going, whore's breath, or I'll string you up for a papist myself.'

'I wasn't planning to stay,' said Kitty as she turned and marched away.

Propelled by her fastest walk, carving round moving obstacles as if they were stationary, she was soon on the corner of Maiden Lane and Half Moon Street. She paused for a minute to let her breathing settle, then knocked on the door.

Elizabeth and Kitty, 15:20

Elizabeth had warned Cook she might sleep at her parents', mindful that Wednesday was Hurlstone's night off. What she had seen in St James' Square made her all the more determined to do so. Before she could go, she sat down with Hendriksen to list which Ormonde staff would post watches through the night, and where. Those not on lookout were to bed down with a weapon to hand. Since Hendriksen refused to open the Duke's gun cupboard, the sentries would make do with the improvised spears they had brandished earlier. Elizabeth also ensured that every room and every member of the household had candles, the means to light them, and a basin of water to douse flames.

As she was leaving, Drizzle took her to the Duke's private cloakroom and said, 'For the streets of London,' as he selected a fine walking cane with a straight ivory handle, the upper half of which was shaped to fit the hand before widening to a dome at the top. The pale white horn was decorated in the French style, with tiny silver pinheads in crosslets and rosettes. Along the sides, the argent studs intertwined into elongated Cs.

'It's beautiful, but…' began Elizabeth.

Drizzle held up a hand. 'Miss, this was given to the Old Duke by the Old King during their exile in France – or maybe it was Holland. Look, it has a locking spring catch and…' With loving care, he withdrew a slim, blued, single-edged blade, the best part of three foot long, from the shaft of the walking stick. Concealing the sword again with a click, he held the innocent-looking staff out to her with a little bow. 'Take it with you in case, Miss. The streets after dark will be no place for a lady tonight.'

Elizabeth accepted the swordstick and examined the hilt, haft and latch. She saw how the grip flared to one side ever so slightly, like a pistol butt, orientating the palm and fingers to the direction of cut. She slipped the lock and gently extracted the steel. She held the blade up to the candlelight and saw how keen-edged and needle-pointed it was.

'What a beautiful, deadly thing,' she said.

Then she aimed it low front of her as she had seen swordsmen do in displays. She felt the balance of the killing instrument, a perfect weight for a woman, with the hilt waisted as if for her. With a flick and turn of her wrist she slashed an X in the air and the concave, triangular-sectioned blade whistled. She slid it gently back into its scabbard, then drew it as fast as she could, to see how quickly it would come to her defence. It was up and in her eyeline in an instant.

'Drizzle, I can't keep this.'

'It was made for you, Miss. The Old King would have insisted. He had a place in his heart for a damsel in distress, of which he,' Drizzle searched for the word, 'helped not a few. Nor would the Old Duke ever have let you venture forth on such a night, defenceless.'

'But its history, its pedigree,' she objected.

'Don't worry. The Ormondes have many such possessions. I have heard His Young Grace say the stick is unmanly. You know how fashions change. He was at a loss what to do with it.'

'Drizzle, you are an angel. I will bring it in the morning… or as soon as I can.'

The half-hour walk to Covent Garden in the midwinter gloom was strangely quiet. The mob had drawn back as does a mighty wave after it breaks. But would it return? *Reculer pour mieux sauter*, thought Elizabeth, to step back for a better jump. Or was the force spent, the roar silenced? She reached Maiden Lane without incident and the swordstick remained sheathed. Elizabeth was relieved, if slightly disappointed in herself for being so.

The Forrester household greeted her with seasonal cheer. She placed her cloak on the hall chair and leant the Duke's walking stick beside it. Her father pressed a hot toddy into her hand. Her mother kissed her. Hurlstone asked after her health. Rogue, the spaniel, licked her hands and would have reached her face had she allowed him.

Shortly afterwards, Hurlstone went out for his night in the pub, leaving the three of them to discuss events since Sunday. News of Lady Emelia's death had spread through London that morning. Major Forrester was keen to opine on the cause and much else that must be related: the formation of the Council of

Peers; the looting of the Spanish Embassy; and the return of the artillery train to the Tower.

Elizabeth had her own anecdotes: arranging the funeral with the Bishop and Mr Russell; writing to the Dowager Countess' family and friends; the mob trying to stop the train of ordinance, using her carriage with Henrietta and her in it; the service in the Abbey; lunch in the Deanery; and the troops' mutiny in the Square. She kept to herself Lord Elland's visit and the death of the apprentice who had been so kind to Isabelle.

She and her father chewed over these extraordinary events, while through it all Mrs Forrester sat with a puzzled look. From time to time she would raise a finger and the two would stop. But then she would put it down with a shake of her head, as if she had already forgotten what she wanted to say. Rogue would jump on to her knees at such moments, the sympathy of the dumb. She would wipe her eyes with her kerchief and settle into stroking the lapdog's delicate head and silky fur until she was calm. Then he would slide off to investigate a sound in the house, or a sight at the window.

As Elizabeth summarised the events, she sensed in her gut that she must stick with the Ormonde camp to advance through these enigmatic times.

'This is not Roundheads and Cavaliers, Papa,' she said, 'or even Whigs and Tories. It is not Catholics and Protestants. Or Anglicans and Dissenters. This is the elite against the left-behind. The mob I saw today has no vote. They have no education, beyond Sunday School perhaps. Their prospects are fenced in by royal monopolies, guilds and long apprenticeships. They live from hand to mouth, without certainty of job or health. Quite simply, if they break through to power, the hierarchy will pay.'

The Major agreed. 'We'd be doomed, robbed blind. It would be the Ranters and Diggers all over again, but this time they would be in charge. Rank would be a death sentence and property a millstone. The world would be turned upside down. The King was wrong to go, but now he has, he's dropped us in it. Parliament is no protection. The dice are rolling. Pandora's Box is unlocked and about to open.'

Elizabeth felt her courage melting away at the picture her father painted.

'It must be kept shut,' he said. 'And you think the Marquess of Halifax has realised all this?' She nodded. 'Thank God,' he continued. 'How could those scoundrels all have the vote? It would be pure populism. A race to the gutter. No direction, no strategy, unworkable. Education for all!' he snorted.

Isabelle raised her finger and said, 'Tax.'

Major Forrester and Elizabeth looked over, surprised. But when no more came, the old soldier incorporated her comment.

'As Isabelle says, taxes would soar. Free health care? People would take advantage, demand every cure, cost the earth, just to die anyway. Employment paid when sick? People would claim illness on any pretext. Unemployment insurance, likewise. Why work? Production would collapse. The populist, supposedly democratic rulers would need to go to war just to stir some pluck into the people, if not to cover up their own failings. Stupefy the masses with patriotism – which is the refuge of the rascal. We would be back to dictators, as in ancient Rome, with bread and circuses and triumphal parades.'

He was interrupted by a knock on the door. Rogue barked and Elizabeth went with him to answer.

'Who's there?' she called, glancing at the swordstick.

'Elizabeth. It's me. Kitty,' came through the heavy panel.

Elizabeth opened to find her friend slightly out of breath.

'Heavens, Kitty. Come in, come in. What's the matter?'

'My parents and I are at the Savoy workshop and we invite you to join us for the night.'

'Dearest friend, it is far too late for that. But come in and say hello anyway. We were just contemplating revolution from below. Look, Rogue, it's Kitty Jones.' Kitty picked up the enthusiastic spaniel and he seemed in no hurry to be released.

'Mrs Forrester, Major, Elizabeth,' Kitty began. 'I am sorry to disturb you at this late hour. However, my father has reason to believe that your lives are in danger, and I have checked. Unfortunately, it's true. You should come over and join us at the printing house, at least until the alarum has passed.'

'What on earth are you talking about?' said Patrick.

Kitty explained. Patrick argued. But she persisted. Elizabeth was the first to be won over. Their visitor was in deadly earnest and she trusted her judgement. Elizabeth could find little harm in the idea, and plenty of advantage. The presses would be in full swing. That would be a sight to see. She might even be allowed to work one. Patrick sensed which way the wind was blowing, and followed Elizabeth's lead. As a retired soldier, he rather doubted anyone would cut his throat before he cut theirs, but he had the Persian rug and his womenfolk to consider.

Isabelle was another matter. She saw no point. She understood the need for safety in numbers but if the Irish really were coming cutting throats, would she not rather die in her own home? Why make the long and perilous expedition at night, hundreds of paces across the Strand, to reach an equally spurious safety? Then there was the challenge of what to pack. However, by carrying the dog Kitty unwittingly held the ace of trumps. Isabelle eyed the happy animal. She would follow Rogue anywhere. Rather than call to him, or complain further, or burst into tears, Isabelle announced that she had been persuaded.

While Kitty helped assemble some overnight things, Elizabeth wrote a note for Hurlstone saying where they would be and suggesting he follow if he wished. Half an hour after Kitty's knock at the door, the pair led the way along Maiden Lane and across the Strand to the Savoy. Kitty gave Isabelle her dog to carry, which soothed her, and took the little spaniel's basket. Elizabeth had her walking stick. The entire route was lit, a candle in every window. Families huddled, shaking on their doorsteps, submitting to the end. The mood was terrified, without a trace of resistance.

Elizabeth said, 'It wasn't like this when I came home. What a difference three hours make.'

'They can't take any more,' said her father. 'This has been building for decades. The Great Plague. The Great Fire. The Dutch in the Medway. Dr Oates touring London with his ruffians rounding up innocents in the King's name for his spurious Popish Plot. We Forresters only saw the aftermath, when he was pilloried and whipped through the streets. People didn't know what to think. Still don't. Was there a plot to kill the King? Or did a score of innocent men suffer judicial murder, before his lies were exposed? Then we had the Hilton Gang, again dragging the monarchy's name through the mud, protected by that awful Sir Thomas Jenner who kept the fines for himself. And then Judge Jeffreys and his extortions, until this very week.'

Halfway there Kitty steered them up the Strand, to avoid the fluff-bearded ringleader.

'All the while fed by this print revolution,' continued the Major. 'So much information – not the *Gazette* of course, Kitty – but so much of it vicious, anonymous. Misinformation, false news. How on earth can ordinary people spot the truth among all that? Whom do you trust? This drip, drip, drip of fanaticism, fabrication, injustice and disaster has burnt like vitriol, to the bone. The King's going is just the latest drop.'

'No, Papa,' said Elizabeth. 'The final straw was his disbanding a Catholic army next to a Protestant capital.'

'Not even that,' said Kitty. 'This latest rumour is what has broken the people. *The Irish are coming, cutting throats.* The Irish troops are probably sleeping in their tents as we speak, waiting for someone to sort out their pay. But the rumour started somewhere. So glib. The Irish are coming, cutting throats! Hordes of migrant brutes panting for holy vengeance. It is just too perfect to be an accident.'

After that they were silent and made it unmolested into the Savoy precinct. Again, candles at windows. Again, exhausted neighbours awaiting their doom. Only after the little group had entered the print shop, did life regain a forward movement.

The creaks and squeaks of the presses, the drumming of the beaters, the grunts of the pullers, the low conversations within two-man teams, and louder calls for more paper, more ink, or for relief men to take over. Rogue was spellbound.

Kitty pointed out the three production lines of newssheet, leaflet and poster; and the proprietor back to inking the press with the posters. At the sight of him, she remembered their severed conversation about James.

'Five minutes,' Edward shouted to the newcomers when he saw them.

Mary was already on her break, and she and Johanna came over to welcome them. 'Isabelle, Patrick. I am so glad you came,' she gushed. 'And Elizabeth. Such a surprise. How lovely to see you. It has been too long.' She embraced each in turn. 'What terrible times. We heard from Kitty about poor Lady Emelia. And now this awful business with the army. You will be safer here. You won't get much sleep, of course. It's a working night. We are about a quarter of the way in. Come and watch how it goes. Kitty will be back on a team, I'm afraid, at the next changeover.'

'And me,' said Elizabeth. 'On a team, I mean. I wouldn't miss this for worlds. What are you printing?'

Kitty fetched copies of tomorrow's issue and the *Declaration* handbill, while her mother told the Forresters about the doubled workload and the absence of apprentices. Major Forrester read the *Declaration* with the greatest of interest.

'Look,' Kitty said to Elizabeth, turning over the *Gazette*, 'my first piece of journalism.' She pointed proudly to the short paragraph about Judge Jeffreys on the back page. Elizabeth read it out loud.

'But that is just wonderful news – and *you* broke it,' said Elizabeth, and hugged her. 'Kitty, the investigator, the journalist. You're amazing!' And she meant it.

What a girl to have on one's side, she thought. She saw the respect on her own father's face, and even Isabelle seemed appreciative.

Kitty sensed the change in attitude to herself. But she also felt a fraud. Even in this moment of excitement, she doubted this life was for her. The real Kitty, with her twin secrets, and her father's harsh reaction to the second, weighed on her heart.

Edward rang a handbell for a pause and called across the workshop floor, 'Tea break, lads. Come and greet our guests and hear what's up.'

Ichabod, 17:20

The hackney cab carrying Spike's corpse stopped on Clerkenwell Green. The place was dark and quiet. Ike opened the door and climbed down, careful to prevent Spike's legs slipping out behind him.

'This'll be my last job tonight,' said the cabbie. 'I'll not be taking anyone else, with my floor messed up like that. I hope you'll consider that, Mister.'

Ike ignored him. He had three options to house the body: the church of St James'; his mother's coffee shop; and Spike's landlady, Mrs Holmes.

'Round here to the left, into the side street,' he said to the driver. 'I'll lead the way.' He shut the door and walked ahead down the lane behind Spike's lodgings to where the vicarage stood beside the church in Clerkenwell Close. It was a double-fronted house with small wings protruding either side of the entrance.

'Wait here, please,' said Ichabod to the driver.

'I'm hardly likely to run off, mate.'

'Exactly. So less of your lip, shithead.'

He knocked on the front door.

The position of vicar of St James', Clerkenwell, was elected by the parishioners, not gifted by a patron. Accordingly, he had closer than usual ties to his flock and a politician's memory for monikers.

Ike had had few dealings with this priest. He had known a previous incumbent, having been volunteered by his mother as an altar boy for a while, before he rebelled. He could not recall this man's name and felt at a disadvantage. He also realised, too late, that the vicar would have set views on Spike.

The cleric held up a little lantern and recognised the son of a loyal parishioner. 'Mr Kingston, Ichabod, isn't it?'

'Thank goodness you're at home, Vicar,' Ike began. 'There has been a tragic accident. One of your young parishioners has been killed and I need somewhere temporary to lay the body, while we sort out burial. Would the crypt do?'

'My goodness, how awful. Who is it?'

'Mrs Holmes' lodger, Simon Speke.'

The vicar stiffened. 'Not one of my flock. How did he die?'

'Bullet through the side of the neck.'

'Violent. Whose bullet?'

'I don't know,' said Ike, which was strictly true.

'Well, were you there? Tell me the circumstances.'

'It was in St James' Square. The soldiers opened fire on some troublemakers. Simon was an innocent bystander.'

The vicar held the lantern close to Ike's face – well above his own. The side of his mouth twitched. 'I am sick of shot rioters being dumped here, after last month. My church will have nothing to do with that man. He flouted the legal requirement to attend during his residence in this parish. Worse than that, he tried to turn people against us. He flaunted his atheism, and mocked me personally to anyone who would listen, usually when drunk. For him, it is too late.' He lowered the lantern. 'As for you, coming lying to me about what he was doing, I hope you will repent, Ichabod Kingston. St James' Square is a long way from home and from Printing House Yard. If I recall correctly that was where Mr Speke was employed. An innocent bystander, you say. Do you take me for a fool? Troops don't just open fire with bullet on peaceful Londoners. I shall have words with your mother about this. Go and make your peace with her, before I get there. And come again when you are ready to repent.'

The vicar stared up at Ike, showing no sign of wavering, or even of going back into his house. Ike was on the verge of apologising, but then his heart hardened. He spat on the ground to one side, turned and walked back to the taxi.

The driver had heard every word. 'Where now, Icky?' he asked, with sarcasm.

The dagger across Ike's breast pocket seemed to heat up and tremble. He pressed his hand over it and growled, 'Back to the Green, a hundred yards, I'll walk it.'

He led the horse out the way they had come and down to his mother's. Again he told the cab to wait. A candle was burning in the upstairs front room. The rest of the house was dark. The rumour had not spread this far. He gathered himself, took his key from his pocket, found the keyhole, opened the front door and entered.

He fumbled for the steel and tinderbox kept on a shelf by the entrance. The charcloth flared and he tipped the candle to light the wick. He left the candlestick on the table, went back to the taxi and called up to the driver.

'This is the end of the road. Give me a hand with the body into the house and I will pay you.'

They slid Spike's corpse out onto the road. Then Ike took the armpits and the cabbie the feet and they walked crabwise up to the coffee shop. Mrs Kingston was standing in the entrance. As soon as the cabbie saw her, he dropped Spike's feet.

'You'll be wanting your greatcoat,' he said to Ike, and retrieved it for him.

Ike lowered the heavy end of the corpse, paid the man from Spike's purse and watched the cab trot away.

'What in the name of all that's holy are you doing, Ichabod?' said Mrs Kingston.

'It's Spike, Mum. Simon Speke.'

'Dead?'

'Well, yes, obviously,' thinking, you old cow, and then, to his own amazement, he began to cry. All his shattered dreams, all his admiration for his friend, all his yearning for a father, his desire to be mothered, welled up in him, and he stood sobbing in the dark street. An awful, animal howl broke from his throat. He felt something burst inside him. He needed to be hugged.

But his mother was having none of it and hissed, 'Do you want to wake the neighbourhood?'

Ike felt the dagger do its thing again.

'Have you stopped snivelling?' she asked, once Ike had recovered himself.

'We can't leave him in the gutter like this, Mother.'

'Well, you are not bringing that little heathen in here. What on earth were you thinking, coming to me? This is a respectable establishment, not a morgue. Take him to St James', the vicar will know what to do.'

'I was just there. He washed his hands of us. I'm bringing him in.'

'Then you can have two dead bodies to deal with. If your squitten little friend doesn't deserve a Christian burial, at least I will. Anyway, who killed him?'

'He caught a stray bullet when we charged the barricade in St James' Square.'

'What was he doing there?'

'You don't know anything about him, do you, Mother. Or me.'

'You are both print apprentices and very naughty boys. I'll have no rioter's corpse in my house and that's final.' Mrs Kingston went inside and shut the door.

Ichabod heard the latch turn and through the window saw the light fade as the candle was carried up the stairs. Across the Green, another shone in Mrs Holmes' lodging house. Putting his coat over his shoulder to keep off remaining body fluids, he took Spike's arms, lifted him, crouched forward and hoisted him up.

He knocked on the guesthouse door and Mrs Holmes called out, 'Who is it?'

'Ichabod Kingston, Mrs H. I've got Simon here. There's been a terrible accident.'

Ike heard the bolts draw. The door opened. The landlady stood there in her coat and nightcap.

'He's dead,' said Ike.

Mrs Holmes looked him in the eye, unflustered. 'Come in, come in. Put him on the parlour table.'

'I think it would be better in his old room, just for now, Mrs H.' said Ike.

'Well, if you can get him up there, yes, that would be better for everyone. Top floor on the right.' She opened the door to the stairwell. 'Here, take this candle.'

Ike trudged up two flights bearing Spike's corpse, careful to keep the smelly flame away from the cloth. He opened the attic door and stepped into the garret. He saw at once how frugally Spike had been living. Ichabod stooped and, rather than soil the mattress, laid the wet corpse on the bare floor between the washstand and the bedstead, catching the head as it fell back. He put his overcoat on the neighbouring boards, then rolled the cadaver onto it. Unsure how to leave, he gabbled, wholly out of character, 'The-Grace-of-our-Lord-Jesus-Christ-and-the-Love-of-God-and-the-fellowship-of-the-Holy-Ghost-be-with-us-all-evermore-Amen.' Then he took the candlestick and returned to the ground floor.

Mrs Holmes had re-lit the parlour fire. She thrust a tumbler of sweet sherry into his hand. 'Here, drink this. Now sit down and tell me what happened.'

So Ike sat. He found it easy to unburden himself. As he talked, his sadness and shock eased and his hot, flowing anger cooled into a hard ingot. When he reached the part where the vicar turned him away, Mrs Holmes raised her hand.

'I've been thinking about that. Do you know Highgate? I grew up there. My brother is still the landlord of the Red Lion.'

'I've never been. An hour or so's walk north, I believe.'

'No matter,' said Mrs Holmes. 'The point is, the old nunnery up there has its own little park, and they've an area where the nuns and abbesses were buried. It's why I live here, really. Highgate was a daughter house of the old St Mary's Nunnery here in Clerkenwell. Deconsecrated at the Dissolution. I have heard of people being laid to rest there, who've been denied holy ground. Suicides, convicts, known atheists. I could get a message to my brother tomorrow and ask if that still happens, and if so, who fixes it.'

Ike produced the moneybag. 'Here's what was on him. I imagine it is all he had in the world. Please, take your due and spend the rest on the arrangements.'

A hair-raising cry came from the street.

'Alarm! Alarm! Wake up! Wake up!'

'What on Earth?' said Mrs Holmes.

Together they ran to the front door. Lights were appearing at upstairs windows around the Green. Ichabod saw his own mother across the road open the window and hold up a lantern. Three young ruffians, apprentices perhaps, stood in the centre of the little square.

'What's the matter now?' Mrs Kingston shouted down to them.

'Save yourselves,' came the reply. 'The Irish are coming, cutting throats.'

Elizabeth and Kitty, 22:00

Kitty and Edward had been printing the *Declaration* poster for ten minutes. Her father pulled and Kitty beat. They had lifted the tempo of the whole shop to rather better than two sheets a minute.

Elizabeth observed them closely. Kitty felt her presence. It meant that she could not pick up the conversation she craved with her father about the dangers of lust as applied to James FitzJames. Edward seemed frustrated too. However, as he lifted another poster off the tympan, Elizabeth stepped forward, evidently hoping to take over from him.

'Mr Jones,' she smiled, and Kitty saw how she unconsciously batted her eyelids in supplication, 'your wife says the *Gazette* run is coming up for first dispatch. You'd be much better overseeing things. If Kitty doesn't mind, I'd like to try my luck at pulling – I think I've seen how it goes. Of course, I won't be anything like as fast.'

'Do a couple of cycles then,' said Edward, 'while I watch. We don't want you hurting yourself, or my press for that matter. Kitty, you be the judge.'

So Elizabeth set to. She made it look easy, particularly the paper handling. Kitty and Edward exchanged a nod and Edward thanked her and left them to it.

After a couple more sheets, Kitty said, 'I hope you don't think we are taking advantage, hooking you in like this. To be honest, Elizabeth, I thought you wouldn't be home and wanted to make sure your parents were safe. If this Irish rumour turns out to be true, they are better off here. Had I known you were with them, I wouldn't have worried. But then I saw you and I thought – Elizabeth could make all the difference to tonight's commission. That's typical of how things work out in this line of business. It's a mystery, but they always do. Going from fifteen of us, including Papa, Mama and me, but not Grandmother, to seventeen, if your father joins in later. That is a better than a one-eighth improvement. Which is all it takes when deadlines are so tight. And it is so much better for your mother that you are all here. You must take a breather and watch with her at some stage.'

'You do make me laugh, Kitty, dear,' said Elizabeth, 'with that mathematical head of yours. Tell me what is in your heart.'

But Kitty could not tell her. The whole kingdom knew that James FitzJames was Catholic. Even to make him sound like a plausible match would betray her family secret. James knew it, obviously, but he could be trusted. And Jack – she already regretted telling him. But at least if the truth leaked any further it would have come from him. If she told Elizabeth, both she and Jack could deny spreading it and Kitty would have lost two friends. Nor did she have another swain to whom she could allude. Jack was now free; she did not want to reopen that avenue, any more than start a hare running about Nicholas Staphurst or, God forbid, Captain Horace Exe.

'There's still no one, Elizabeth,' she lied, although she then sailed closer to the wind than she might. Out of friendship or perhaps from pride, she said, 'But I didn't tell you about my visit to Lord Ranelagh's new house in Chelsea.' She described how Nicholas had gone there on an impulse, taking her. 'Lord Ranelagh mentioned introducing me to his daughter, Lady Catherine Jones. Wouldn't that be fun, to meet one's namesake?'

Elizabeth thought it a capital idea. She had seen Lady Catherine in St James' Square, but they had never spoken. She thought her Ladyship was almost their age, rather younger, going on seventeen, certainly unmarried.

'What about Jack Wilson?' said Elizabeth, checking her own ground.

'Captain Jack, as of today,' said Kitty. 'We passed his troop as we were returning here. He was also at the Holbein Gate when I went to Secretary Gwyn to have the *Declaration* proofs approved.'

'Yes, I saw him in the Park this afternoon. Is he in the running for your hand?'

Kitty sighed. She remembered how Jack had written to them both, to make her jealous. 'Not my type, dear Elizabeth. That has been resolved and he has accepted it. Of course, he has the makings of a magnificent man. Intelligent, loyal, decisive, thoughtful, easy on the eye. And he says he is mad about me. But…'

'But what?' asked Elizabeth. 'What more could a girl want? Money? Rank?'

Kitty smiled. Jack, like her, was of printer stock, but that was not what Elizabeth needed to hear. 'He is born for the outdoor life. He loves horses and they love him. I am an indoors person. A printer's daughter. I know as much about fetlocks as he does about fonts. He would make a fine landowner, but I'd be pining for the double-glassed greenhouse at Versailles. I could read to him in French, German, Greek or Latin, but what would be the point?'

'Money and rank are important, too,' said Elizabeth. 'That is what could put me off Jack. I need a man who will carve a path in society. How else are we girls to grow the future leaders?'

'Jack will carve a path, Elizabeth, mark my words.'

Elizabeth worked the lever, putting her back into the final pull.

'I have discovered another factor too, dear Kitty,' she said, 'which might offend you. Physical compatibility.'

Kitty caught her eye. 'Go on.'

'Last night I did it. I mean I lost, you know. Oh, don't look so shocked. I had wanted to for so long, and everything worked out. It could have been grim but it was the opposite. And now I understand so much more.'

Kitty was unsure where to look. 'You don't regret it? I mean, you know what it says in Revelations: *And I gave her space to repent her fornication; and she repented not.*'

'Kitty, it was absolutely the most natural feeling of my life. I would try it again tomorrow. What I can't understand is that some wives apparently don't, well, enjoy it, the way I did. I think physical compatibility must be central to a marriage. Otherwise one of the partners will stray. It is just too tempting. Once you know the truth, the temptation would be much worse. Adultery must be worse than a little pre-marital fornication. And how are you supposed to know you are compatible, if you can't try beforehand?'

Elizabeth raised the tympan and removed and reloaded the paper, while Kitty beat the ink balls vigorously to wet the type.

'Was he a virgin too?' asked Kitty, thinking of Jack.

'Oh no. That sounds like a recipe for disaster. One of you must know what they are doing.'

So, it wasn't Jack, thought Kitty, irked to be so relieved. 'But what about the sin? *Behold, I will cast her into a bed, and them that commit adultery with her into great tribulation, except they repent their deeds. And I will kill her children with death...*'

Elizabeth shook her head. 'If it is done with love and intended to secure marriage, how can it be a sin? Is not God also the God of Love?'

'And if it leads to a baby?'

Elizabeth winced.

'Then surely you are ruined,' Kitty pressed home.

'You are right, a baby is a true test. The man must be responsible. And any husband of mine would need to be a good father. I suppose you should only try it with men who would marry you if you got like that, or at least own to the child. A married man might be safest, mightn't boast about it to their men friends, which bachelor men would.'

'Was last night a married man?'

Elizabeth was unsure how to answer. She waited for Kitty to slide the coffin home, then she pulled the devil's tail. After the whole cycle had completed and she had replaced the printed sheet with a clean one, she said, 'That's how I know about the physical compatibility problem. I would never have guessed. Actually, I am not sure I believe it. It could just be a married man's excuse to stray.'

Kitty was mystified by this idea. 'Surely all men are made one way and all women the other. So, what could be incompatible? It does rather sound like an excuse. And here's your father.' She dropped her voice to a whisper. 'Tell me if you find out more. I can't ask my parents about it.'

Patrick Forrester had come to watch. He seemed intrigued that just anyone could operate a press. The room had settled back into a single rhythm, rouncing the coffins and swinging the devils' tails at the same time. The workshop became a living, breathing organism, with presses consuming paper and ink and excreting newssheets and announcements at the rate of several a minute of each.

On their next break, while Johanna and Isabelle slept, Edward, Mary, Elizabeth and Kitty gathered round and asked Patrick for his first impressions.

'In one way it is sad. There is no skill involved. If you could find a way to drive it without human hands, it could all be done in the dark and much faster. But in another way, it is joyous. A spectacle.' The major raised his arms and turned like a Morris man. 'People moving in time with each other, in pairs. More village revel than palace ball. If you put it to music, I for one would pay to watch.'

Mary laughed. 'Dear Henry Purcell could make, what's the word, an opus. If you wrote him some words.'

Patrick picked up her theme. 'Opera. I hear he has written a *Dido and Aeneas*. Something for the continentals at court. It will never catch on over here.'

'Which King James wants performed,' said Mary.

'Wanted,' said Patrick. 'Dido will have to wait for her lament.'

'The mobile was singing Purcell's quickstep in St James' Square,' said Elizabeth. 'To the words of the *Lilliburlero*. It's a pity that missed the deadline, *Mob wins over troops in St James'*. But I suppose things are always missing deadlines.'

'Mutiny?' asked Edward.

'Well, it certainly wasn't a defeat.' said Elizabeth. 'Only one person was killed, and that a civilian. The mob charged the troops, the troops fired in the air, and then they all sang the *Lilliburlero* together.'

'The *Gazette* couldn't have printed it anyway,' said Kitty.

Edward expanded on the theme. 'There's enough news to go round. Someone will pick it up. Dick Baldwin says his *English Current* will do a second edition on Friday. John Wallis launched *Universal Intelligence* yesterday, up in Whitefriars. George Croom, down at the Blue Ball on Thames Street, is hatching a rag for this Saturday, the scoundrel. Only he can't decide what to call it: *London Mercury* or *The Moderate Intelligencer*.'

'He'll probably call it both,' joked Mary. 'The trouble with journalists is they want to have their cake and eat it.'

'I don't care who reports it, or no one,' said Elizabeth. 'Tomorrow's *Gazette* has the *Declaration* and Judge Jeffreys sent to the Tower, and that makes you cock of the heap for a long time to come.'

'I found this,' said Patrick, unfolding a sheet from his pocket. 'In the street coming over.'

Edward took the single sheet from Patrick. '*London Courant, issue number 1, today's date,*' he said. Turning it over, he continued. 'No printer's name, but here, it says *Henceforwards this Paper is intended to be published on Tuesdays and Saturdays.*'

'That's at least four competitors launched this week,' said Kitty.

'Don't you worry, daughter,' said Edward. 'The news will slow and they will tire. Some may try to adapt, to reinvent themselves, but the *Gazette* will see them off. We have the inside advantage with government sources and international correspondents. In time we will be the only survivor.'

'Until the next generation, with dailies,' muttered Kitty.

'Come on everyone,' said Mary. 'Back to work or it'll be time for bed. Edward – less posset and more beef!'

Patrick intervened. 'Let me take over from you, Edward. I can't have Elizabeth showing me up. Mary, may I have the pleasure of this dance, while he gets the dispatch out?' He took up the leather inking balls, one on each hand.

Mary chuckled, 'You can say you were at two balls tonight. Let's see if you can beat and talk at the same time, Patrick.'

Once her father was distracted at the other press, Elizabeth said, 'So, Kitty, if Jack Wilson is out of the frame for you, you won't mind if I make a move that way?'

'Oh Elizabeth, he's too good for you,' joked Kitty. 'But I thought you wanted money and a title and to entertain powerful people in a fine house, and to be invited back and sparkle on the circuit.'

'Yes, I do,' said Elizabeth with a sigh. She thought of Suffolk and where it would fit into such an ambition. It would be enough. But could she admit to Kitty the independence it gave her, and how she should marry a man who could share and enjoy it, give it his respect, his time, and his muscle? She had never talked to anyone of her own age or rank about Parham – neither about her way of managing it, nor her crinkle-crankle wall, nor speculated when she would move to live there. It was too complicated, with her parents in London and no eligible men in the Suffolk countryside. So all she managed in reply was, 'Don't you think we educated women have it hard? We are taught the wrong dreams, then loved by the wrong people, and finally achieve the wrong fulfilment.'

'*C'est dure, la vie d'une fille,*' said Kitty.

'I don't often pity myself,' said Elizabeth, 'but truly, in this life, I am the victim.'

That is just your cover for a devious mind, thought Kitty. Then for a laugh, she said it out loud.

Elizabeth gave her a look from under her eyebrows. 'Speak for yourself.'

Jack, 22:25

Jack's dream started in reality. He was seventeen again, on a visit to his godfather's farm. His mother, Ivy, had taken him down to be with Simon's parents on the anniversary of the boy Peter's death. The roads had been excellent. The Wilsons had arrived days before they were expected.

Ivy Wilson had often sung the praises of Cornwall, the Granite Kingdom she called it. Jack had never been. So, they had travelled past Tiverton into that ancient county, with its own proud but fading lore and language. Then they had spent their fortnight with Godfather William, with Jack sadly failing to recapture the joys of youth. On their last night, a fire had broken out at a nearby mill. Almost all their household had joined the bucket chain to try and put it out. The next morning, they heard how it had been started by black-hearted Simon, fratricidal Simon, who had even pretended to be a ghost, whooping 'Speke's Revenge' from the shadows as the neighbours struggled to quench the flames.

The dream then shifted to the farm kitchen. In the room next door, Simon was being whipped by his father. Jack had his fingers in his ears. Simon's mother, Barbara, was wondering how the fifteen-year-old could continue to deny the arson, yet fail to produce an alibi, although beaten half to death. Jack's mother had wept and winced at every lash. Of the two women, Ivy had been the more distraught. Jack had been unable to console her. All this was familiar, and true in some points – although not quite how it had happened.

However, tonight the nightmare took a novel course. The scene jumped back to the earlier funeral for Simon's twin. The interment was over. The family was keeping a twenty-four-hour vigil over Peter's resting place. Jack volunteered for the night shift in the graveyard. He took a firebrand and found Simon weeping on his brother's headstone. Simon accused Jack of starting the fire at the mill. They fought by torchlight and Simon pulled out a knife, mortally wounded Jack and ran away. While Jack lay dying, the church clock struck eleven and the ghost of Peter rose from the grave to say he too had been murdered, by Simon daring him to ride the stallion bareback, like Jack had. Then he had spooked the horse to make it rear up, again and again, until it had thrown him and he'd fallen head first and broken his neck. Now Peter thirsted for justice, so that his soul could be released. He warned that Jack's soul would be earthbound too, trapped, if he died now, until such time as Jack's own murder was avenged. But then Peter's ghost turned into Simon's ghost, also moaning for revenge and shaking him…

Jack woke in a sweat with the mess-hall sergeant standing over him. ''Arf pass ten, Sir. God's light, you aren't 'arf an 'ard man to wake.'

In a daze, Jack pulled on his boots, unsure what was reality and what not.

Both relief squads were present and correct on the assembly area. He dispatched the Whitehall contingent eastward, and led his six men northwest in the dark, through the park for the late shift at St James' Palace. He brought a firebrand. They arrived on the stroke of eleven.

Swarbreck had built a bonfire from packing cases in the street. That lifted Jack's spirits. We all need colleagues with initiative, he thought.

As soon as the old watch was gone, Jack went into the guardroom, found a candelabra and made a personal tour of the palace. He needed to know what he was defending, both in terms of other entrances, including the mews at the back, and of targets and valuables. Perhaps the building had already been robbed or vandalised. The mob had been kept out, but what about sneak thieves? Or the staff? These were good reasons to poke his nose into everything. In fact, although the shadows jumped and waved in the flickering candlelight, the place seemed untouched. Nevertheless, curiosity was satisfied. He would not often have a free pass to roam such a place, to slide down a grand banister, stalk a silent ballroom, or sit on an empty throne. He resolved to bring Elizabeth here as soon as he could, to share the thrill.

One surprise for Jack was that the complex had two places of worship. The main one was Henry VIII's Chapel Royal. This stood beside the entrance gate tower, aligned north–south. Its altar was at the north end, under a magnificent double-height English perpendicular window facing up St James' Street. The other church tucked in by the garden, a hundred years younger, but just as grand and infinitely more problematic, was the Catholic mass house, known as the Queen's Chapel. This had been built by Charles I for his French consort, Henrietta Maria, the current King's mother. Supposedly, it had been used as stables during the Commonwealth, but returned to its original function after the Restoration. Both Charles II and James II had Catholic wives.

Jack saw that the only way he could hope to defend both the gatehouse and the Queen's Chapel with one cannon was to position it out in the open, backed into Cleveland Row. This road was the stub by which the artillery train had entered Pall Mall from the park that morning. Pointing the cannon at St James' Street would have let the gunners shelter under the gateway arch and be out of the weather if it began to rain. But the mobile would not come from the north.

It was midnight before all this was settled. Nothing stirred. Jack went for a stroll westwards through the park towards the village of Knightsbridge. He looked up at the stars from the dark tranquillity and savoured the prospect of a quiet night. And yet the darkness was not complete.

The haze over London to the east was faintly aglow.

End of Book One

Afterword to the Glorious *trilogy*

How well the late seventeenth-century chimes with the modern era – the younger we are, the louder. We see the mainstream media grapple with upstart, tech-enabled businesses; and find the upstarts variously indispensable, or wise to avoid. Today, a new podcast blows down the proverbial street as frequently as first-issue newssheets littered the City of London in December 1688. And delivery has likewise accelerated to unheard-of speeds, at fractions of the traditional cost.

Now, as then, we struggle with 'fake news', 'alternative facts' and supposedly 'biased fact-checking'. We are showered with conflicting propaganda around events. We grapple with information overload. Irreconcilable partisanship overwhelms debate. Some of the national choices involved can be heartbreaking.

If a sense of *déja vu*, or more correctly *depuis vu*, peeks through in this narrative, one purpose will have been served. The parallels are not only intriguing, but also hopeful. *Glorious* sheds light on an earlier time English-speaking men and women survived extreme national division. But survive it they did. The coup of 1688 may have tipped the country into centuries of misogyny and warmongering, but it did not lead to dictatorship.

This book began life when I was a teenager. My mother's parents had died within weeks of each other, and I was asked to comb my grandfather's library for anything which might sell at auction to help pay two sets of confiscatory, 1970s death duties, with the rest to be given away. One volume stood out. Roughly A3 in size, slim and bound in yellowed, faded vellum, it had scrawled almost illegibly on the front cover: *The Peers Meeting at Guildhall from 11th Dec. 1688 and continued till the Arrival of the Prince of Orange. Fra. Gwyn, Secretary.* It appeared to be a manuscript minute book. I have since found (*Fortnightly Review* vol 40, p 359, Sept. 1886) that it had been purchased from a Dorset estate sale in 1846 by a great-great-great-grandfather of mine, Sir Thomas Coombe Miller, so let us call it the *Miller MS*. But back then it was just an anomaly. I requested the mysterious item as part of my small inheritance, thinking it might fit well with my future undergraduate (grad. student) history studies.

It turned out that *Miller MS* had companions. A partial draft was in the Cambridge University Library, minus December 14 and 15, bearing scorch marks and a burnt bottom right-hand corner (*Eee 12/15*). A longer version was in the

British Museum (*Stowe 370*), with a copy of *Eee 12/15* (*Egerton 3361*), both now in the British Library; and what appeared to be a copy of *Egerton 3361* was in Oxford's Bodleian (*Rawlinson A77*). So, the essential information was available. GH Jones had used *Stowe 370* in his biography of Middleton (1967), and Robert Beddard had mentioned it in a footnote in *Historical Journal XI Part 3* (1968). But that was it. The inside story of this upstart Council lay almost untouched.

Historians had accepted Lord Ailesbury's defence of the Council to the King, (*Memoirs* p 209) 'that your going away without leaving a Commission of Regency, but for our care and vigilance, the city of London might have been in ashes.' In hindsight, a French-style 'reign of terror' had been avoided ((Foxcroft (ed.), *The Life and Letters of Sir George Savile (1898),* vol 11, pp 33–4) due to 'the political instinct so characteristic of Englishmen' that '[o]rder, all felt, must be preserved at any cost.' However, they ignored the contradiction in those statements. Could 'All' feel that way, when so many had rioted? Had historians understood how and why the *mobile vulgaris* was rising?

The tercentenary of 1688 came and went, with a predictable flurry of new theories and evidence. In particular, Dr Beddard published a major contribution to the topic. At over 200 pages, *A Kingdom without a King* (1988) was a study of the interim council with a full, annotated transcript of *Stowe 370*. It transformed access to the source and appeared to be the final word.

But what about the sequence of rioting which *Miller MS* and *Stowe 370* helped illustrate? Two mobs had sprung up in London, independently but in parallel. One was anarchic, reacting to the news of the King's flight as it spread from Whitehall Palace, by sacking the nearby Jesuit seminary in the Savoy. But the City riots two miles away were well-led and systematic. Moreover, they seemed to have broken out before they heard that the throne was empty.

The Dutch Ambassador, Everard van Dijkvelt, had been watching this source of trouble for some time. He had reported the mobile electing itself three colonels on 16 November, the day before the King left to join his army in Salisbury (*BL Add MS 34510, Mackintosh Collections*, vol XXIV, f 177, p 252). The implications of an organised third force in December 1688 had still not been addressed. Prof. Tim Harris had admitted, 'there was a considerable degree of structure and discipline behind much of the rioting', although he saw these as 'law-enforcement riots' (*Revolution: The Great Crisis of the British Monarchy, 1685–1720* (2006), pp 300, 301). Beddard had noted that the marking of houses in Bloomsbury for attack on 14 December 'clearly indicate[s] an element of planning' (*Kingdom*, p 107). But I wanted to go further. This was not a disorganised opportunistic rabble, however ephemeral and apparently easily beaten by an alliance between the burghers and the landowners. Their rapid and co-ordinated attack on the morning of 11 December was too soon and too premeditated to be just a reflex reaction. London, it seemed, had been threatened by a revolution from below.

If the behaviour of the rioters was premeditated, the absence of the militia on 11 December and its reluctance to fire on the rioters in the Haymarket on the morning of 12 December had likewise been too lightly dismissed. The smoking gun, literally, was the report of a militia officer being shot for ordering his men to fire on the rabble attacking the Florentine embassy (*English Currant* No 2, 14 December 1688, p 2, also *Stowe 370*, top of f 18, *Miller MS*, p 12).

How close had the mob colonels come to success?

Again the answer was publicly available, if obscure. It lay in a letter dated 13 December 1688 from Colonel Shere, the gunners' commander, to Lord Dartmouth, Admiral of the Fleet, then in Portsmouth (HMC XI pt 5, vol 1, p 233, 1887, *Manuscripts of the Earl of Dartmouth*). This showed that a mighty convoy of artillery, the royal cannon train, had passed through the heat of the riot on the morning of the 12th, where 'there was so great a tumult that nobody believed we should have escaped a man of us'. However, it seems the mood of the rabble changed. The report in *English Courant* spoke of the train marching through 'amidst the loud Shouts and Acclamations of the People'. The rioters had been in St James' by then. So, the palaces of St James' and Westminster had been saved by a fluke. In my view that chance encounter, with its pivot from deadly threat to friendly acclamation, was a forgotten but seminal moment in English history. It also offered high cinematic drama, if correctly explored.

The third, and to me most fascinating discovery, was that the interim Council's minute book had been carefully falsified in real time by those at the very top. As a young student I only managed to spend a few hours with each of *Stowe 370*, *Eee 12/15*, *Egerton 3361* and *Rawlinson A77*. Photographing them would have been cumbersome and photocopying inconceivable. However, in those days I could bring the *Miller MS* with me for side-by-side comparisons.

Initially, the differences seemed to be small, slipped into *Miller MS* retrospectively and then transcribed word-perfect to *Stowe 370*. For example, in the *Miller MS* the imprisonment of Chancellor Jeffreys on the afternoon of Wednesday 12 December (p 10) has vindications squeezed in around as an afterthought. These are spaced evenly in *Stowe 370* with added apology. But thereafter, the sequence of events begins to be rewritten. On the chaotic morning of Thursday 13, as the King is found, the last order in *Miller MS* (p 13), to pay the troops, is annotated '1' in the margin and jumps to first of the day in *Stowe*. The gaps and changes in handwriting that afternoon in *Miller MS* become seamless, fawning extenuations in *Stowe*.

Most notably, the penultimate entry for Saturday 15, a letter from the Duke of Berwick submitting to the Peers and proposing to surrender Portsmouth, is numbered '1' in the margin of *Miller MS* (p 26) and appears in *Stowe 370* as the first new item that day (and first in Beddard's transcript, see p 352, below). The importance of this letter had been overlooked. It gave the Council the excuse for everything they had done. If James II's most trusted lieutenant, his own son, had offered capitulation of his strongest military base on hearing of James' flight, who could blame them for doing the same in the capital?

What historians were calling a 'clerical fair copy' (Beddard, *Kingdom*, p 7), began to smack of self-justification and whitewash.

Why make Berwick's letter more prominent? Why re-write a minute book recording 10 meetings, each with between 9 and 33 attendees, across a population of 51 participants putting in 231 attendances, recording 748 signatures to 122 documents? Why go to all that trouble? William of Orange had won.

The only moment when anyone cared was when, unexpectedly, James II was on his way back to London, between 13 and 16 December. The tables had been turned. The interim Council would want to appear in the best possible light, given the accusations of treason which they might be about to face. No one could undo the orders they had signed and which were circulating in the outside world, each bearing its date (e.g. BL Add. MS 22183 f 144 for the orders to Sir Henry Johnson 'to fire on them with bullett'). But within any particular day, they could change the sequence in which information arrived and action was taken. They could show themselves quicker to clamp down on the rioting, slower to accuse His Majesty's friends. Servants of the Crown had toiled through the night to forge a document that might save their careers, if not some noblemen's necks. It was a scene of pure theatre, to add to that of young apprentice-colonels hatching a revolution from below, and the insurgent mob briefly silenced by a passing show of overwhelming firepower.

Additional known elements had previously also been largely dismissed: the collective nervous breakdown of Irish Night, a nationwide panic, when a divided elite united at three in the morning on a false alarm; the muddled surrender of Portsmouth, which King James had reinforced with his most loyal commander and dragoons as a Plan B; the midnight attack by the Dutch Blue Guard on Westminster on 17–18 December, when foreign infantry marched unopposed across St James' Park with fuses lit and put an English king under house arrest; the ruling monarch being rowed away down the Thames the next morning in the pouring rain, downstream because of the ebb tide, under foreign escort, to imminent exile; and the exhausted, alien conquerors entering the bastion of the capital, the Tower of London, with its immense arsenal, Royal Mint and the Crown Jewels, again without resistance.

Comic, tragic, sordid, these scenes sat awkwardly with the 'glorious' epithet.

Worse than that were the consequences, an Hogarthian brutalisation.

The parliamentary reforms which Whig historians glorified chanced from William III's obsession with financial and military support against France, and lack of dynastic interest. His was a curiously Calvinist, cold-blooded world view. He was self-confident, self-disciplined, physically brave, tactical and strategic; but all this verged on the sociopathic. A man raised without parents or siblings, who had no children, and almost no interest in women, briefly gained more power in England than anyone since Henry VIII and possibly William the Conqueror. The gamble paid off, but with the consequence that the nation too became more confident, disciplined, brave, tactical, strategic, and verging on the sociopathic.

In 1688, England's elite had been so keen to reject papal religious or French diplomatic influence, or as they saw it, to retake control from continental powers, that they had overstated their popular mandate. Their coup crushed a dream which has since become daily reality, and ushered in an age of misogyny, squirearchy, slavery, and imperialist war. The echoes may be fading by now, but they are still heard in most corners of the Anglo-Saxon world, and not least in Celtic Ireland.

My challenge would be to bring this restatement gently but adequately to public attention. It would require topicality, and a passable yarn. Topicality we had in spades, with divisive European referenda in Spain, Scotland and Great Britain, to say nothing of the upheaval in American politics.

But what about the story-line? A rabble of villagers had looted the artillery train's baggage on Hounslow Heath on the morning of Sunday 9 December 1688, before it reached London (HMC XI, pt 5, vol 1, p 236, Gardiner to Dartmouth 18 December 1688). How had they been driven off, apparently without injury, let alone loss of life? A duke's dead mother had been transported from her town house on the north side of St James' Square for burial in Westminster Abbey on 12 December on the same day and crossing the very street where the great guns briefly cowed the mob (Chester J, *The Marriage, Baptismal and Burial Records of the... Abbey... of Westminster*, (1868) p 222). What if the two had clashed?

Moreover, such a long and comprehensive set of Council minutes could not have been transcribed from *Miller MS* to *Stowe 370*, by a single hand, with added clarifications, some of them a page long, all in one night. How had it been done?

Research around the topic revealed further unremarked aspects and unasked questions about the 'Glorious Revolution':

- The artillery train sent from London to support the King's army in Salisbury had covered less than half the distance before James II despaired and returned to London (HMC XV, pt 1, vol 3, p 133, (1896) Shere to Dartmouth 25 November 1688). Hartley Row is not even as far as Basingstoke. That must have influenced things, but how?

- King James failed in his first attempt to flee. On the afternoon of 11 December, his boat from hidden-away Elmley Ferry to France was stranded by the ebb. Why this strange embarkation point? What went wrong? How could such an experienced sailor miss the tide? Who was to blame? How come fishermen from Faversham arrested him twelve miles off in Sheerness? Here James II's own memoirs (Clark J, *The Life of James the Second, King of England* (1816) p 252), Morrice's *Entring Book* (2007, vol 4, p 389) and modern tidetables provided answers.

- The Duke of Berwick, King James' illegitimate son, whose submission to the Peers and proposed surrender of Portsmouth had been emphasised in the revised minutes, was a teenager. How much was naivety to blame?

- The Council forgot Bristol in its long list of port closures (e.g. *Miller MS*, p 23). Did any fugitives take advantage of this?

- Time lags in communications conspired against the King
  - Berwick submitted to the Peers and proposed to surrender, before he heard that the King had been 'stopped' at Faversham and was returning to London.
  - James returned to London, unaware of the loss of Portsmouth.

- The King held a Privy Council on the evening of his return. This was the moment when he could have offered concessions, as I depict, and kept his throne. What stopped him? Did he call for the minutes of the interim council? Perhaps he was shown them anyway, as would have been normal practice, but with the ulterior motive of highlighting Berwick's submission to the Peers. Did the King's resolve thereupon crumble? Might this partly explain the contrast: riding into town on such a high, summoning a meeting, and then issuing one, gutless Order to keep the peace, with an afterthought for Pepys to reopen the ports (NA PC2/72, p104). And what did that afterthought imply?

- The *Miller Journal*, a looseleaf account by Secretary Gwyn, tucked into the *Miller MS*, of life at the royal headquarters at Salisbury in November 1688, revealed a tension between the physicians and the apothecaries. King James was not only 'let blood ten ounces' (p 3) but also prescribed opium as a sleeping draught (p 6). This cast light on Dr Chase, his apothecary (notably not his physician, as one newssheet claimed), leaving for Faversham on 14 December (*Miller MS*, p 19), and on James' extreme mood swings over the previous and following few days. Did laudanum help explain why the King threw the Great Seal in the Thames on the night of 10–11 December; and demystify why he flunked his opportunity on the evening of the 16th?

- The Annals of the Royal College of Physicians for 1688 include a complaint by the Apothecaries (HMC VIII Part I (1881), pp 230–1). In their private war, were the Apothecaries overkeen to prescribe?

- The King's possible access to cannabis through the Apothecaries is suggested by a lecture given by Robert Hooke, 'An Account of the Plant call'd Bangue', to the Royal Society on 18 December 1689, reprinted in *Philosophical Experiments and Observations of the Late Eminent Dr. Robert Hooke* (ed. Derham W, London, (1726), pp 210–12).

- *The Gazette* of 20 December sent loyal regiments to the King in Kent.

- What about the phony *The Prince of Orange His Third Declaration* (NA SP8/2, pt II, ff 198–9)? Who wrote, printed and circulated it? John Oldmixon (1673–1742) suggested Samuel Johnson (*History of England during… the Stuarts* (1730) p 759), although Hugh Speke had laid claim to it (*Some Memoirs*, (1709) pp 59-60), Oldmixon said Speke was incapable of it. But what if Speke was telling the truth? Dalrymple, a keen Williamite, accepts the claim (*Memoirs*, vol II, (1790) p 215).

- What of the country-wide Irish Night panic of 12 December? Oldmixon was unable to attribute it, but admitted (*History*, p 761) '[it] was universal in one Night, and must have been concerted long before there was any thought of their [the Irish regiments] being disbanded in that manner'. What if Robert Ferguson was correct (*The History of the Revolution*, (1706) p 20, (1707), p 22), that the panic was contrived by the same Hugh Speke? In 1709 Speke glossed over other 'Strategems and Cunning Devices' (*Some Memoirs*, p 113), saying only that the end justified the means. However, in 1685 his uncle, William Speke, had uncovered a similar mailshot before Sedgemoor (Roberts, *Life of Monmouth* (1844, pp 214–15) quotes the Axe Papers in BM Harleian 6845). So the use of the Royal Mail for personalised, viral messaging would have been known to Hugh. And indeed, after the death of Queen Anne, Hugh did claim Irish Night as his (*Secret History of the Happy Revolution* (1715, pp 41–44), and explained how he did it, which I reproduce here. Speke was clearly a fantasist in other places, for example he casts himself as the chief cause of King James leaving Rochester on the second flight. However, that lie does not disprove everything he claims and again Dalrymple accepts it (*Memoirs*, vol II, (1790) p 215).

- The timing and placement of artillery at Whitehall and St James' Palaces on 12–17 December is accurate. However, given the round-the-clock threat, the gunners would have needed a forward camp to maintain readiness, rather than resupplying from the Tower, three miles away. How was this done? I have placed such a camp in St James' Park, on the high ground recently created by excavating the ornamental canal.

- Lord Craven's withdrawal of the Coldstream Guard is well documented. But what about the Royal Artillery? Were the cannons extracted at short notice? A pre-emptive withdrawal of the cannons to the Tower of London on the night of 17–18 December is one possibility.

- My invention of Horace's injury echoes that of Roger Dell, who 'received a Bruise in his Members, by which... not being able to make Urine, by reason of the Swelling, after some Languishment he died.' (*Proceedings of the Old Bailey, 5th–6th December 1688*, ref. t16881205-2).

Other small contributions to the historical record may be worth mentioning:

- A tide timetable for London Bridge for the year 1688 was published by the Astronomer Royal, John Flamstead, in the December 1687 issue of the *Philosophical Transactions of the Royal Society* (pp 429–432). This, combined with James II's detailed log of his escape attempts in his *Memoirs* (Clark J, *The Life of James the Second, King of England* (1816), pp 252, 275–8), and modern tidal data for the recreational yachting community, allowed me to model the ebb and flow in the Thames Estuary throughout the *Glorious* fortnight. The resulting tables (see fergusdunlop.com/glorious-sources) show the crucial importance of tides in both King James' plans for flight, and their subsequent failure or success. The contrast between how well the Monarch knew his river, and how badly he grasped his political realm, is one of the ironies of this tale.

- A visit to the Pepys Library in Cambridge revealed a misattribution of an eyewitness report of the Battle of Sedgemoor (Pepys MS 2490, *A Journal of the Proceedings of ye D. of Monmouth*). The drawings of the battlefield can now be assigned to the naval architect and international spy, Edmund Dummer. Pepys' cataloguer in the 1690s, Paul Lorraine, had misstated the author as an Edward Dummer. A forensic examination now corrects this (see online supplement, under Sources). That early slip had led to centuries of confusion among the experts and the creation of a separate personage in the literature. Edmund is now reconciled with himself.

- Records in the French Diplomatic Archives in Paris showed the erratic, extensive, coded *reportage* supplied by Ambassador Paul Barillon to Louis XIV (8CP volume 167, microfilm bobbin P438). This gave new insight to the rambling mind of a diplomat who developed so close a relationship with the object of his interest that he lost the wider picture.

- Research into the mill complex at Brimpton, Berkshire, which is recorded in the Domesday Book, identified it as a probable example of Roman hydrological engineering. The Roman road from Silchester to Cirencester, The Ermin Way, crossed the River Kennet precisely there, to meet the London to Bath Road at Thatcham nearby. Engineering the multiple water channels at this site is easier to attribute to the Romans than to England in the Dark Ages.

- Research into seventeenth-century Bristol shipping by Dr Richard Stone of Bristol University led me to the National Archives in Kew and the Bristol Archive. Kew holds the Port of Bristol overseas outward records (E 190/1149/1–2). No ship left Bristol docks for the American Colonies in December 1688, despite this thriving port being omitted from the Council's stop order of 15 December (*Miller MS* pp 22–23). The *Morning Star* for Barbados and Nevis had been loading since 3 December, with John Banks as master; and the *Martha & Gareth* for Jamaica since the 4th (E 190/1149/1 Folio 86). I have assumed that Christmas, coming on the heels of the Lord's Day of rest (Sunday 23), was enough for the *Morning Star* and the *Martha & Gareth* to finish loading on Saturday 22 and sail on the next daylight tide. Although no further overseas ships loaded, the docks did not entirely close for the festive lull, since two coastal boats turned around on Monday 24 (Bristol Archive Wharfage records SMV/7/1/1/16).

- Mrs Christine Stone's kind exchange of emails with me on the Colston family of Bristol, emboldened me to consider the intergenerational tenison between Thomas Colston and his nephew Edward, when the young bachelor was starting out in London. Edward has become a by-word for hypocrisy, being both misanthropist and philanthropist, of which we have examples among successful businessmen today. But how much was Thomas the true culprit, and how much Edward the victim?

The greatest blessings for me as a researcher in 1979–80 were the many volumes published by the Commission on Historical Manuscripts (HMC) a century before. Between 1869 and 2003 the HMC reproduced in print a small mountain of primary material from the archives of great houses, colleges, county councils and other institutions. Given the financial, social and political upheavals of two World Wars, not to mention the physical destruction, it was miraculous to me that predecessor historians could have had the opportunity and foresight to gather and publish so much endangered primary material relevant to my field.

Since 1978–9, things have only improved. Forty years of research have added to the colour, most notably the publication in 2007 in six volumes of the *Entry-Book of Roger Morrice*, edited by Prof. Mark Goldie. Morrice was a diarist to rival

Pepys, another Cambridge man, though less personable. However, where Pepys achieved high position as Secretary to the Navy, Morrice was an outsider, a vicar defrocked for his non-conformist beliefs, a manic collector of first- and lesser-hand political intrigue and a transcriber par excellence. His manuscript resides in Dr Williams' Library in Bloomsbury. As an undergraduate, I quoted it from tertiary sources, but had no idea that it was round the corner from the British Museum Reading Room, where I was beavering away on *Stowe 370*. That's how benighted we were.

Other primary sources are offered in ever-better consolidated and indexed collections. The catalogues of the British Library on London's Euston Road and the National Archive in Kew are many times more powerful than they were at the mighty, circular Reading Room and the old wrought-iron galleried Public Records Office off Chancery Lane, beautiful though I found those spaces.

Various projects to mass-scan academic collections now offer rare books and learned historical journals online, in a way and to an extent then unimaginable.

Wikipedia's encyclopaedic database continues to improve. Although sometimes still irritating, its links to the UK's *Dictionary of National Biography*, since 2004 the *Oxford Dictionary of National Biography*, and historyofparliamentonline.org are game-changers. Together they open an unparalleled chance for the armchair amateur – and in due course for artificial intelligence. The opportunity for a twenty-first century historical storyteller to connect the dots is limitless.

Most locations in *Glorious* are correct, as is the architecture. St Paul's Cathedral was still under construction following the Great Fire of 1666. Much of the City had been rebuilt, such as the Boar's Head Inn, the Apothecaries' Hall, the Old Bailey courthouse and St Clement Danes church. The Monument to the fire, which Kitty climbs to view the King's return, was already standing proud.

Only a few locations are speculative or invented:

- The Duke of Ormonde, the Marquess of Halifax, the Earls of Pembroke and Ranelagh, Ambassador Barillon and Sir Robert Southwell all had houses in St James' Square in December 1688, but I have guessed where (see Map 10 on p 374). As far as I know, not one of the original buildings remains.
- Lord Ranelagh's apartment in the incomplete Royal Chelsea Hospital is speculation. He did like the spot and acquired the neighbouring land after James II fled. Here he built a country mansion in the early 1690s.

- The *Third Declaration* was printed clandestinely. But where? What cheekier place than the King's Printing House in Blackfriars?
- Based on the monks' graveyard at Downside Abbey, I have imagined a late medieval graveyard for nuns in what is now Highgate Cemetery, but then were the grounds of a countryside manor belonging to St Mary's Nunnery, Clerkenwell. Since the Reformation, the land had become part of the Bishop of London's hunting forest.
- The Expectation tavern in Wapping is my imagined predecessor to the Prospect of Whitby public house.
- The ancient Cardinal's Hat on Bankside is authentic, although some say it was a brothel rather than the players' tavern I depict. The archive of former patrons' tabs, preserved in a dusty office upstairs, is my invention.
- John Milton's house in London is correctly located in Petty France, against the Park. However, I have imagined that this later became the home of William Russell, inventor of the term 'under-taker'.
- The Rising Sun pub on Bowden Hill was only a smallholding in 1688, but when I visited it in the 1970s as an undergraduate, before its extensive remodelling, it really was as miniature inside as I describe, with a countertop which lifted to access behind the bar. The Potter brothers were in charge, selling one beer from a tap in a cask, one cider and one brand of cigarettes, Craven A – and the landlords really were so short they would bend down to walk under the flap.
- My mother's parents, as small children at the end of the 19th century, saw the Christmas mummers perform in the two grand houses set back at either side of the road at the top of Bowden Hill; I recall my grandfather once entering the room saying, ''Ere comes oi, brave St Jarrge', which filled them both with nostalgic glee. Mummers still playact nearby at the Red Lion in Lacock on Christmas Eve. However, whether this happened in December 1688 is only speculation.
- Although the Maypole pub in Hanham offers indoor skittles today, and the pub existed in 1688, with the forge nearby, I don't know how old the alley is; the idea of a Bristol skittles league is also conjecture and probably, if such a league had had a waiting list, they would have organised a lower league too, though I have not gone that far.
- Bristol's Tolzey Courtroom was real; the skittles alley behind is imagined.

- Bristol had a Duck Lane behind the Horseshoe Tavern, but the Drake Inn on this street is my fancy.
- I have christened the otherwise unnamed fishing smack in which James II crossed to France, the *Harwich*. This resolves a problem which arises in the King's *Memoirs* (p 276), where James mistakes the name of Captain Trevanion's ship, HMS *Henrietta*, for *Harwich*. My assumption is that King did not pluck the name *Harwich* from thin air, but just mixed them up. However, this is only a guess.

As with the tides, we can be accurate to the hour – and sometimes even better – on the whereabouts of the major historical figures in the cast. The movements of King James, Prince William of Orange, Lord Jeffreys and Lord Halifax were of national interest and recorded in detail. Ambassador Barillon also gave his location in his daily encoded outpourings to King Louis XIV; while Lord Feversham, as Commander-in-Chief, and the Prince and Princess of Denmark, as son-in-law and daughter of the King, are easily traced.

A second group are correctly placed, so far as the record shows. We know some of the movements of the Duke of Berwick (e.g. King James to Lord Dartmouth, HMC XI, pt 5, vols 1–3, 10 December 1688, pp 225–6), Francis Gwyn, Edward Jones, the Duke of Ormonde, Sir Henry Shere and Hugh Speke. But nevertheless blanks have been filled in to suit the plot. For example, it is fair to assume that Ormonde hurried to London on news of the unexpected death of his mother, which took an extra day to reach him because it would have been sent to Prince William's camp at Hungerford or Reading, whereas Ormonde had gone ahead to Oxford, to prepare the Dutchman's reception. This section of the cast includes the fluctuating and ephemeral membership of the interim Council whose attendance (and absence) we know from *Stowe 370* and *Miller MS*.

I have found no further records on the movements of my third group of real persons. Knowing they were in England, and their ages, ambitions and loyalties, and often their addresses and marital status, I have tried to make them plausible. Time of day (including the shifting direction of the Thames tideway), day of the week, weather, season, an approaching Christmas and the behaviour of the main historical cast all help shape the picture, and often we have a subsequent fact to hand. Such educated guesses apply to Lady Henrietta Butler, Edward Colston, Viscount Cornbury, Edmund Dummer, Lord Elland, Henry Hills, Mary and

James Johnson, Increase Mather, Lord Norreys, Reverend Simon Patrick, Lord Paget, Lord and Lady Pembroke, William Penn, Lord Ranelagh, the Duchess of Rochester, William Russell, Henry Sidney, John Somers, Sir Robert Southwell, Nicholas Staphurst, and Sir Henry Winchcombe and family. Lord Cornbury, the first commander in James II's army to take his troops over to William, was later governor of New York, and evidently came out as a cross-dresser in that city after his understanding wife had died (Bonomi P, *The Lord Cornbury Scandal...* (1988)).

Epilogues for these and many more are provided at fergusdunlop.com/glorious – click on the 'Epilogues: Historical Characters' button.

My invented characters are also given on the website, over fifty in all. They include the six leading voices, Jack, Elizabeth, Kitty, Spike, Ike and Horace. Where I have alighted on a surname, I have tried to pick something likely. For example, the surnames Dummer, Potter and Light appear to be as old as the small community on Bowden Hill.

Several themes around historical figures in this story are also invented.

- Edward Jones, printer and publisher of the *London Gazette*, as far as I know was never a Catholic, nor had an only daughter called Catherine who died young. He and his wife, Mary, had a son, Edward junior – who survived him, as did she.

- Kingston's (or Kingson's) Coffee House was on Clerkenwell Green, probably as early as the 1680s, with a Ralph Kingston in charge by about 1703 (Lillywhite, *London Coffee Houses* (1963) p 318). But I have no evidence of a Mrs Kingston, or of her being a widow or proprietress, or of her having a son, let alone that he predeceased her.

- As mentioned above, Lady Emelia Ormonde was buried in Westminster Abbey on 12 December, at the height of the rioting, having died the day before. However, one report puts her death early in the morning of 11 December, which would have been before the news broke of King James' flight. The news that her son had gone over to the Prince of Orange was known at court on 27 November (e.g. BL Add MS 36707 B19, Harrington, f 49) and is unlikely to have only reached her that morning.

- Henry Compton, later Bishop of London, did go down early from Queen's College, Oxford, without graduating, to travel and soldier for some years on the continent. However, I found no evidence that this was because of a girl, let alone that they had an illegitimate daughter.

- I also have no evidence that the 24-year-old Leveller ringleader, Robert Lockyer, shot by firing squad in St Paul's Churchyard in April 1649, three months after Charles I was beheaded, had fathered a son.

- The invented characters of Carl Luxmoore and Caesar are based on servants depicted in the margins of two contemporary oil paintings. The former accompanies the young Lady Charlotte Fitzroy, aged 10, hanging in the York Gallery, England. The latter is in a joint portrait of her and her future husband, Henry Lee, in the National Gallery of Victoria in Melbourne, Australia. More details can be found in the online Epilogues.

- All the orders of the Council I have quoted are verbatim (e.g. the order to Colonel Shere to halt the cannon train in St James' Park). However, General Feversham's order to Colonel Shere to disband is imagined. Such an instruction probably existed, based on the contemporary record, but I have not found it. Something seems to have been lost or gained in hurried communication. Two submissive notes from Faversham to William on 11 December (*King William's Box, NA SP8/2 ff 75-6 & 79-80*) suggest King James II may have intended his troops to be disbanded with pay and to hand in their arms.

- What about the forgeries? The *Third Declaration* was real, meaning it existed, but was exposed within months as a fake. The manipulation of the Council's minutes was real, although only now has it come to light. The forged instruction to Lord Lucas, purporting to be from the Council, to send troops from the Tower to Southwark, is my fiction, and the text imagined. However, the source for such a fake, the discarded first passport for Ailesbury to go to the King, was real (*Miller MS* p 13; Thomas, Earl of Ailesbury, *Memoirs,* vol 1 p 202 (1890)).

- Secretaries Gwyn and Collings indeed missed James II's last Privy Council meeting. However, Collings probably did not suffer from epilepsy. And the CUL's *Eee 12/15*, the draft minute book with the burned edges, appears to be in Gwyn's hand, not Collings'.

- The horses of Colonels Shere and Solms probably did not match.

- Hugh Speke and the widowed Dame Anna Speke had sued and counter-sued over the estate at Hazelbury in 1683 (NA C 5/93/25, C 5/94/10) and Hugh lost. So he is unlikely to have fled there after his uprising failed.

- I doubt that John Somers met Lord Halifax on 21 December 1688, or at Halifax House, let alone for the first time.

- Oranges were being waved on swords, pikes and sticks by supporters of the Prince (e.g. *English Current #3*, 20 December 1688), which was odd because even today the season for Seville oranges to reach London is after Christmas; it seems they had been imported early, which must have required scenes such as I have invented for the Chivers family with Ichabod Kingston on 16 December.

- I have imagined Berwick passing through London on his way from Portsmouth to his father at Rochester, and visiting Barillon.

- Gwyn's command to billet Dutch troops in the Tower is also imagined. Someone must have ordered the surrender, and if not him, then who?

- The meteor shower on the night of 20 December is another of my conceits.

- The London-based bachelor, Edward Colston, may not have spent Christmas 1688 in Bristol, visiting his mother in Temple Street and his sister's family. It seems possible. We have no evidence either way.

- I have fostered the idea that *Stowe 370*, the 'clerical fair copy', is the actual document produced for King James to inspect if he so wished, on his return to London on 16 December 1688. This is possible, created in the way that I describe, but unlikely for two reasons. Firstly, the date in the title penned seamlessly on the flyleaf, 'From ye 11th of December 1688 to the 28th following 1688', would have to have been written after the King had seen it on the 16th, which seems unlikely. Secondly, a clerical error in *Stowe 370* (pp 67–68), at the beginning of the day on 15 December and curiously omitted from the Beddard transcript (*Kingdom*, p 109), duplicates three items recorded the previous morning on pp 53–54. These are repeated 99% verbatim, pushing the crucial letter (see above) from the Duke of Berwick to the Council from position '1' on the morning of 15th, to position '4' in *Stowe 370*. I conclude that *Stowe 370* is 'a fair copy of a fair copy', and that the link between *Miller MS* and *Stowe 370*, made available for James II's return to London, is still missing. We will know it from the location of Berwick's letter in position '1' that morning.

- A more serious failing is my lack of evidence that the mob in 1688 sought electoral and other Leveller reforms, rather than just hating

Catholicism. History is happy with the gap between the thousands of Londoners recorded in Bulstrode Whitelock's diary for April 1649 as attending the funeral of the Bishopsgate-born Leveller, Robert Lockyer, shot for mutiny (see above); and the thousands of supporters of John Wilkes, the radical journalist and heir to their demands, born 75 years later in Clerkenwell. In both cases, plentiful printed evidence of their views exists. Why the decades-long silence between them? Perhaps it takes time to put demands into print, years in prison in the case of John Lilburne, whereas the mob colonels of 1688 were in operation for barely three weeks. Or perhaps, as suggested in *Glorious*, pamphleteering requires an individual with a passion for text, someone the mobile never threw up in 1688. Conceivably, the plotters disdained a written manifesto for security reasons. Whatever the explanation, I find it unlikely that the ideas of the literate, disenfranchised citizenry of the mid-1600s have no continuous submerged link with those same ideas in the mid-1700s, and did not bob up, albeit ineffectually, in 1688.

- My most controversial conjecture is the timing and course of the battle in St James' Square on the afternoon of 12 December. Doubtless something went on there, but the record is hazy. The reader must weigh the circumstantial evidence for themselves –

    o Dr. (subsequently Prof.) John Miller – whose *Popery and Politics in England 1660–1688* Beddard subsequently called 'the best introduction to the subject' – wrote in HJ XVI (1973 p 676) that Barillon's house was attacked 'seven or eight times' after 'the crowd came yet again', but without adequately referencing this;

    o Van Dijkveld (Mackintosh fol. 198, p 294) says that, '[the mob]… entered the house of Mr de Barillon, and searched diligently, to know whether there were arms or priests concealed in it';

    o Mazure claims two attacks on Barillon's house that evening being repulsed by '*la force des armes,*' (*Histoire,* vol 3, p 252);

    o *London Courant* #2 on the 15th noted on the back page an attack on St James' Palace chapel on the night of the 12th being 'forcibly repelled by some of the guards';

    o Luttrell reports of 12 December: 'That night the mobile… would have plunderd and demolisht the houses of several papists… if they had not been prevented by the train'd bands which were out; a party of horse were also out, who did at last disperse them.' (*Brief Historical Relation of State Affairs,* vol.1, p 486).

However, this is not the daylight set-piece which I have extrapolated. My battle is almost certainly a conflation of several skirmishes. But if there were several, that implies give and take, with temporary victories for the mob, as I depict. Here is a kernel of truth which history has completely overlooked. To make the point, I have taken it to the opposite, but still possible, extreme.

Why might such a battle, on the afternoon or evening of Wednesday 12 December, have gone under-reported at the time? I see five considerations.

First, much happened that day. It would be unreasonable to expect independent observers to hear it all, let alone tell fact from rumour and report it perfectly. Jeffreys was captured in the morning and Irish Night came only hours later, followed by the even bigger news of the King being 'stopped' in Kent. For example, Philip Musgrave, Clerk of the Deliveries at the Tower of London, writing to Lord Dartmouth, on the night of the 12th (HMC XV, pt.1, p 135), almost missed off the news of the return of the cannons, although Dartmouth, as Master-General of the Ordnance, would have been particularly interested in that. He writes, 'The distractions here have been so great that until this moment I know not what to write to your Lordship, the insolences of the rabble have been insupportable… If the prudence of the Lords here had not kept the soldiers that are about town together, all here had been 'ere this in fire and blood', only adding as a postscript, 'The artillery train is returned', leaving him to deduce the impact that had had in the west end of Town, and on the strength of the Tower.

Second, we are reliant on newssheets with a relatively slow cycle of publication, appearing as they did only every three or four days, with just two sides of space. Both *English Currant* and *London Courant* had rushed their issues #1 into print on the night of the 11th to report the King's flight and the rioting. Their issues #2 appeared respectively on the 15th and 16th. *London Mercury* issue #1 appeared on the 15th. By then, anything from the 12th was old news. Again, it would also have been difficult to tell fact from rumour. *English Currant* #3 on the 20th does attempt some detail on the artillery train, noting that its thirty-two-day (actually thirty-three) round trip was thought to have cost the King £7,000. However, it has the guns arriving on Hounslow Heath on the Monday, the day they left, and the Pioneers digging in on the Tuesday, when we know from *Stowe 370*, *Miller MS* and Shere's letters that the guns were almost back in the Tower by then.

Third, we see clear examples of self-censorship, playing down uncomfortable news, or even ignoring it. The *London Courant* #2 of 15 December says only that 'London. Decemb. 14th. For two or three nights last past, the heady multitude have committed many Outrages', followed by softened reports of thefts from the Spanish Ambassador's residence and the death of the captain of the trained bands in the Haymarket. The *English Currant* #3, with heroic hindsight, is silent on the crowd's reaction to the King's return to London on the 16th, but plays up Prince William's entry on the 18th as improRably triumphant ('The Roads for some miles were lined on both sides the way to the Townsend with Souldiers'). The perfidy of the *London Gazette* is seen in issue #2408 covering 8–10 December, which has no mention of the Prince of Orange even being in the country, while #2411, covering 17–20 December notes William's arrival on the afternoon of the 18th but omits the King's departure under Dutch Guard to Rochester only hours before.

Fourth, the explanation which I give in the novel is also possible, that senior commanders of troops acting for the interim Council issued a verbal instruction to deny and suppress all rumours of a temporary defeat at the hands of the mob, to protect their and the army's reputation. The pattern of military denial had already been set by the suppression of news of the artillery's baggage train being attacked on Hounslow Heath on 9 December, which surfaces second-hand and slightly garbled on 18 December in a confidential letter from the Tower Storekeeper, Thomas Gardiner, to Lord Dartmouth, but nowhere else (HMC XI pt 5 pp 236-7).

Indeed, no contemporary observer, and hence modern historian, that I have found has discussed in writing the impact (or lack thereof) of the cannon train. Despite a side-glance from Luttrell (*State Affairs,* vol 1, p 486), no one muses over its huge size and escort; or that such guns would have been better dispatched from Portsmouth, as before Sedgemoor; or its refusal to disband; or the timing of its arrival in London; or the psychological effect of its return to the Tower. Even Bryant, who quotes Shere's letter to Dartmouth on 25 November at length (*Pepys and the Revolution, (1979)*, pp 162–3), misses that it is written from a village less than half the way to Salisbury. Such blind spots remain to this day.

Last but not least, the afternoon of 12 December went unremarked because it could. The mob colonels were defeated and the hierarchy won. As Edmund

Dummer noted after Sedgemoor, although 'providence was absolutely our greater friend than our own action' (*Journal,* Pepys MS 2490, (1685) p 11) winning allowed the victors to paint it differently. After Sedgemoor, the 'friendly fire incident' was covered up (Tincey, *Sedgemoor 1685*, (2005) p 151). Likewise, in 1688 William of Orange wished the rabble to have been on his side. And since he had won, they were.

Purists will argue that I presume too much of the reader in mixing earnest historical reinterpretation with whimsical romantic invention. However, if the sticklers accept that the mob was already organising before the King fled; that the King at this juncture was dabbling with opium and had access to cannabis; that his reinforcement of Portsmouth with his most loyal commander and dragoons is evidence of a Plan B; that the cannon train's chance appearance in London dampened the riots on the second morning; and that the repositioning of Berwick's letter to the Council in its final minutes could have affected the King as I describe; then they are well on the way to reinterpreting events as I do.

Nor are the specialists my only intended audience. I would like to interest the wider, non-academic reader, which requires seeing events through young people's eyes. We know they existed, for example, the three colonels of the mob, but we know almost none of their names. To interest the non-experts we must scratch into the unvarnished passion behind the glossed-over narrative; and maximise the visual.

I have felt the historian's joy of uncovering new perspectives and the novelist's awe at disturbing their own muse. If the combination should fuse successfully, a clearer sense of that turbulent fortnight will emerge. 1668 was the first modern coup. As an illegal overthrow of one elite by another, its innovation was to play on public gullibility, claim a wider mandate than it had, exploit the grey zones of unwritten international convention, such as the rules of parley, and use the new media to cover its tracks. It brought ugly consequences, but dictatorship was not one of them. It certainly was not the end of democracy. May that message of hope reach those who will live to celebrate the 1688 Revolution's fourth centenary.

Whatever the historical background, men and women remain as alike as ever, ruled by ambition, imagination, attraction, rivalry, obsession, guilt and bias. But let's not forget love. Especially in turbulent times, if one can find love and hold on to it, things generally sort themselves out. Fate can still be cruel, but happy endings are also possible.

Acknowledgements

For constant support with this project over the years, encouraging, researching, proofreading and suggesting improvements, I thank my sister, Celina Dunlop.

I also acknowledge the invaluable contribution of Alison Shakspeare in challenging my slack thinking and sloppy prose, typesetting the myriad proofs and the seventeen maps which are here and online at fergusdunlop.com/glorious, and feeling our way together to a design for the covers.

Thank you also to my early readers, Jane Wheadon and Susan Gallienne; and the ultimate, or should I say supreme, cover artist, Peter Le Vasseur, along with his absurdly over-qualified technical assistant, John Fitzgerald.

At different stages of research I have benefitted in person from the expertise and aid of (in alphabetical order) Robert Beddard of Oriel College, Oxford University; C S Knighton; Martha Halford-Fumagalli; Darryl Ogier; Christine Stone; Richard Stone of Bristol University; Catherine Sutherland of the Pepys Library, Magdelene College, Cambridge University; and the management and staff of the Bristol Archive in Bristol, the British Library in Euston, the National Archives in Kew and Les Archives Diplomatique à la Courneuve in Paris.

To them all I offer my heartfelt thanks.

I still cherish the generous handwritten advice of the reviewer of my original undergraduate dissertation on this subject in 1980, the late J R Jones, Pro-Vice-Chancellor and Professor at the University of East Anglia in Norwich; and the ecumenical humanity of Cuthbert McCann OSB, then librarian at Downside Abbey in Somerset, both long since deceased.

Beyond them, the reader might turn to the list of printed secondary sources in my online Bibliography. When we consider the constraints our forebears worked under, we can only bow with respect to their diligence and genius in the field of historical research.

For all errors and omissions, I am solely responsible.

They shall bring forth fruit in old age.

Psalm 92 v 14

Epilogues for Major Historical Characters

(in alphabetical order; more at fergusdunlop.com/glorious)

Berwick, James FitzJames, Duke of, (1670–1734), and his father King James, landed in France at 03:00 on Christmas Day 1688 after a rough crossing. Berwick was stripped of his Garter knighthood by William III. Having failed with the Jacobite army in Ireland in 1689–90, he recovered to become a successful general for Louis XIV, and a Marshal of France; also for Louis' grandson, Philip V of Spain, and a Knight of the Spanish Order of the Golden Fleece. He is the only English commander of a French army to have defeated an English army in battle (the English were commanded by a Frenchman). In 1695 he married the young widow of his comrade, Charles Sarsfield, 2nd Earl of Lucan, Honora (née Burke). He treated Charles' and Honora's baby son as his. In 1698 Honora bore him a son of their own, to found a dynasty of Spanish dukes which continues to this day. However, she died in 1699. He remarried in 1700 – Anne Bulkeley, an English exile in Paris – and had eight further sons and five daughters, again founding a dynasty of dukes, this time French, which also survives. At the age of 63, he was decapitated by a cannonball at the siege of Philippsburg in southwest Germany.

Miege, The New State, not listed as a KG;
Berwick, Mémoires; Chabot, Le Maréchal de Berwick; W.

Butler, Henrietta, Lady, (c. 1674–1724), later Countess of Grantham, sister of the 2nd Duke of Ormonde and daughter of the Dowager Countess of Ossary, kept up her Dutch language skills and thirteen years later, at the age of 27, married her first cousin, Henry de Nassau, Lord d'Auverquerque, who shortly afterwards was created 1st Earl of Grantham. From 1718 she was Lady of the Bedchamber to the Princess of Wales. She died aged about 50, predeceasing her husband by twenty years. Neither of their two sons outlived her husband, or bore male heirs, and the earldom died with him. However, through her daughter, Frances, the Lordship of Dingwall in the Scottish Peerage survives today.

Journals of the House of Lords; EB, vol 20 p 354 CUP (1911); W.

Gwyn, Francis, (1648–1734), Secretary to the Privy Council, was returned unopposed to the House of Commons for the third time in January 1689 as Member for Christchurch in Dorset. On 5 February 1689 he was one of two

339

Commons' tellers counting the minority's votes in favour of the House of Lords' view that King James had not abdicated, and that the throne was not vacant. He was returned again in 1690, and for various seats in all subsequent parliaments until 1727, except that of 1715. In the last years of Queen Anne's reign, Gwyn was a Commissioner of the Board of Trade and then Secretary of War. In 1690 he married a West Country heiress, Margaret Prideaux (died 1709), daughter of Edmund Prideaux, through whom he gained his country seat at Forde Abbey in Dorset. Gwyn died at Forde aged 82, leaving sons and daughters. The *Miller MS*, with the diary notes from Gwyn's journey to King James' headquarters in Salisbury (*Miller Journal*), and some other Privy Council minute books from the end of Charles II's and James II's reigns, remained in his family's library until 1846, when the house was sold and its contents auctioned off.

Gatty, C, xlvi. 358–64 (1886); DNB, vol 23; W.

Halifax, George Savile, 1st Marquess of, (1633–95), was elected Speaker of the House of Lords in January 1689. He guided the Lords into accepting the proposal of the House of Commons that William and Mary be offered the Crown as joint sovereigns, and oversaw their coronation programme. He was made Lord Privy Seal and remained a Privy Councillor. However, having fallen out with both Whigs and Tories, he was soon blamed for the new administration's failures, particularly during King William's long absences abroad, and the military defeats of 1691–4. He died in office aged 61, from a rupture brought on by vomiting after eating an undercooked chicken. He was succeeded by his son, William, Lord Elland, and within a generation the marquessate was extinct.

ODNB; W.

Jones, Edward, (1653–1706), printer and publisher of the *London Gazette*, became the first English media mogul. He secured the royal patent from William and Mary, and raised the circulation of the *Gazette* tenfold. Every issue was translated into French. The news-sheet became required reading across the courts of Europe, and the staple source of news about the three kingdoms of England-with-Wales, Scotland and Ireland. In 1690 he had an office in Dublin. His mother, Johanna (née Griffin) died in 1693. He moved to Kensington, London, and died at the age of 53 after a lingering illness, much respected. His daughter in this story is fictitious (see online section on Invented Characters). In his will (NA, PROB-

11-486-485) he left a pension and chattels to his wife, Mary, while his business, along with one house in Albermarle Street, two in Pall Mall court, property in Windsor and fishing rights on the Thames, passed to his son, also Edward.

Timperley, p 592; Plomer, p 174; Glaisyer, 23(2) 1–25.

Ormonde, **James Butler**, **2nd Duke of**, **(1665–1745)**, voted against the claims that James II had abdicated (a voluntary action, with no intention of return); and that the throne was vacant (otherwise the monarchy would no longer be hereditary). However, he supported William once crowned. His sickly two-year-old son by his second wife, Mary, daughter of the Duke of Beaufort, died in 1689. Ormonde accompanied William to Ireland in 1690, and thereafter to the Netherlands, where he was promoted to major-general. He was captured and exchanged in a prisoner swap for the Duke of Berwick. In Queen Anne's reign he commanded the English forces in Spain and replaced the Duke of Marlborough as Commander-in-Chief in 1712. After the Queen's death in 1714, he was suspected of supporting the restoration of James III, was impeached for high treason and fled to France. His lands and titles were confiscated. His attempted invasion of England from Spain in 1719 was broken up by a storm. He retired to Avignon. Mary died in England in 1733, having had no contact with him for nineteen years. He died aged 70. His body was brought back to Westminster Abbey, where he was interred in the family crypt. The title became extinct.

Anon, *History and Proceedings of the House of Commons*, vol 2, pp 199–255; ODNB.

Ossary, **Emilia**, **Dowager Countess of, (née Nassau-Beverweerd)**, **(1635–88)**, also known as the Duchess of Ormonde, mother of the 2nd Duke of Ormonde and Lady Harriet Butler, was buried on 12 December in Westminster Abbey, in the Ormonde vault, alongside her husband (d.1680), mother-in-law (d.1684) and father-in-law (d.1688). The vault is at the apex (easternmost tip) of the Henry VII chapel. It had previously been used to bury Oliver Cromwell, three members of his family and nineteen of his officers – they had been disinterred by Act of Parliament in 1661, and the bodies of the Lord Protector and other regicides hung from Tyburn Tree. Today the side chapel above the vault is dedicated to pilots of the Royal Air Force who died between July and October 1940 in the Battle of Britain. Emelia was survived by four of her eleven children.

Cokayne, *Complete Peerage* (see under Ormonde); W.

Shere (Sheere, Sheeres), Henry, Colonel Sir, (c. 1641–1710), commander of the Tower artillery, retired and was succeeded by Sir Henry Goodrick. He was given a half-suit of armour by the Ordnance in 1691, a high honour. He remained devoted to King James and was twice arrested on suspicion of conspiracy in the 1690s, with nothing proved. During the 1690s he published: his translation of the *Historiae of Polybius* in two volumes, with a foreword by John Dryden; *A Discourse Touching the Decay of our Naval Discipline*; a poem prefixing Southern's *Oronooko*; and *An Essay on the Certainty and Causes of the Earth's Motion*. In 1700 and 1701 he edited two pamphlets by Sir Walter Raleigh (beheaded 1617): *A Discourse on Seaports* and *An Essay on Ways and Means to maintain the Honour of England*. In 1700 he was sent by the House of Commons as a trustee of King William's Irish grants, and in 1701 was recalled by the House of Lords to explain himself. In 1703 he published *A Discourse on the Mediterranean Sea and the Streights of Gibraltar*. He also part-authored a translation of Lucian, published posthumously in 1711. In 1703 he was bequeathed a ring by Samuel Pepys. He died aged about 70.

Miege; DNB, vol 52.

Speke, Hugh, (1656–c. 1725), petitioned William III for a reward for assisting his succession but was snubbed. He tried again with Queen Anne, and again with George I, even translating his petition into French to assist the latter. He lived off begging letters and the sales of two small books on the events of the Revolution (Speke, *Some Memoirs* (1709); *Secret History* (1715)). In these he claimed to have been the true cause of James II's flight in four ways: by exaggerating his reports to the King of William's forces in the West Country; by composing and circulating the forged *Third Declaration*; by masterminding the Irish Night panic which had catalysed widespread acceptance of William's coup; and by face-to-face force of argument to the King at Rochester. He was never believed. He died unmarried and without issue, in obscurity in the house of a friend in High Wycombe, Buckinghamshire, aged about 68.

EB, vol 25, p 665; W.

Stuart, James, King James II of England and Ireland, and VII of Scotland, (1633–1701), landed in France at 03:00 on Christmas Day 1688 after a rough crossing, accompanied by the Duke of Berwick. He was reunited with his wife, Mary of Modena, and infant son (The Old Pretender) at the Chateau of

Saint-Germain-en-Laye which Louis XIV had previously provided for Charles I's widow, Henrietta Maria. In March 1689 he landed in Ireland with a French army, where he remained until King William III arrived in 1690 and defeated him at the Battle of the Boyne. His last child, Louisa, was born in 1692. In 1696, a plot to assassinate William III failed, and in the following year King Louis made peace with William. Thereafter, Louis lost interest in James, who retreated into an ascetic life, dying at the age of 67 in 1701 of a brain haemorrhage. His body was placed in a sealed casket in a side chapel in the church of the English Benedictines in Paris, with various parts, mainly internal organs, donated to other churches. The tomb was desecrated during the French Revolution. His grandson Henry, the last of his legitimate descendants, died in 1807.

Clarke, *Life of James II*, vol III, p 275–80; Miller, *James II*; W.

Go online at www.fergusdunlop.com/glorious for supporting resources:
Maps
Epilogues of historical characters
Index of historical characters for the combined trilogy
Invented characters
Sources, including bibliography and tide tables
Miller MS
Miller Journal
Miller-Gwyn Papers

Maps for the Glorious *trilogy*

These maps illustrate events in Fergus Dunlop's *Glorious* trilogy
© Fergus Dunlop 2025 – www.fergusdunlop.com

Map 1. Southern England, with rivers and places mentioned in text

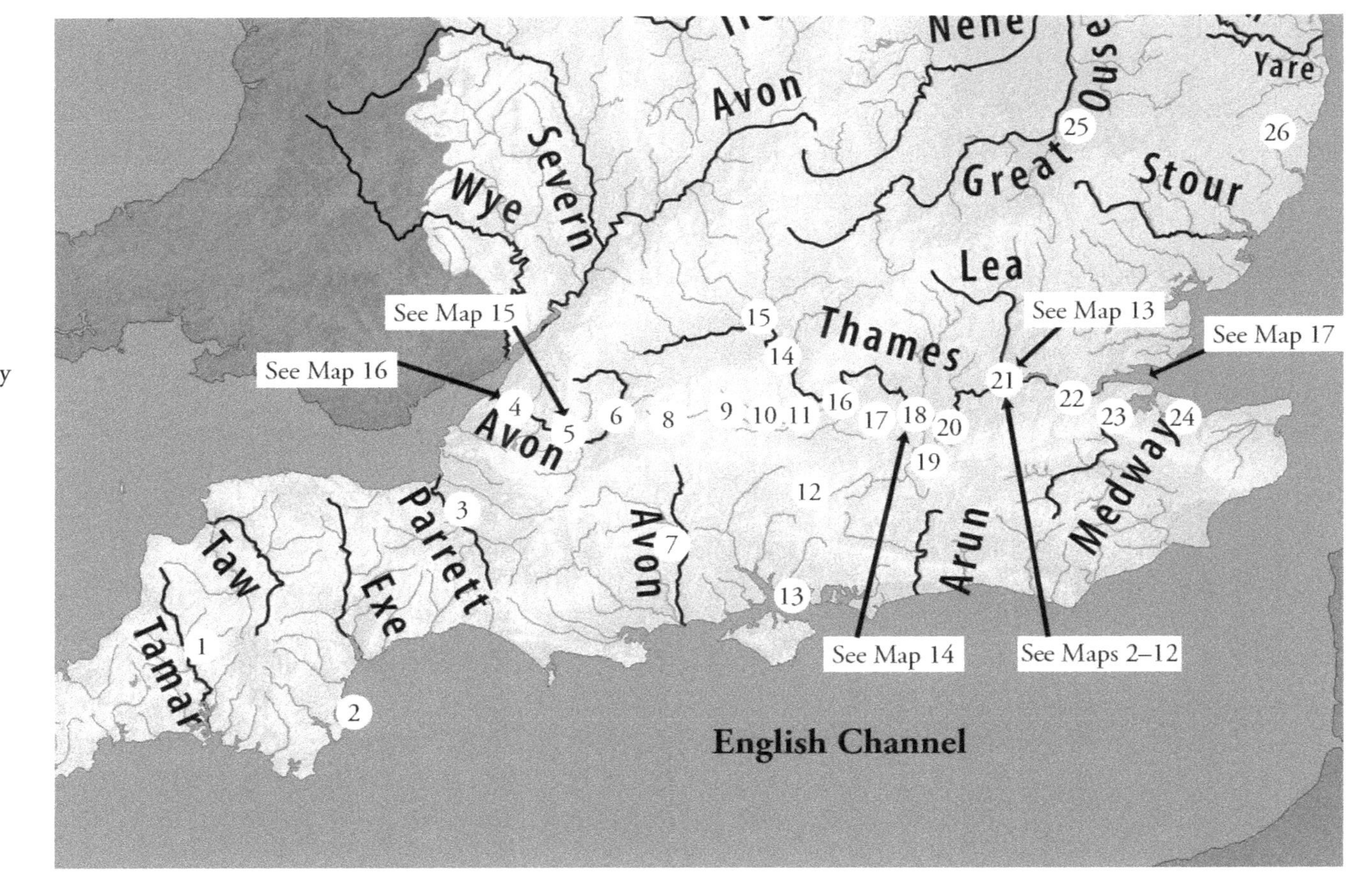

1 Tavistock
2 Torbay
3 Sedgemoor
4 Bristol
5 Bath
6 Lacock &
  Bowden Hill
7 Salisbury
8 Calne
9 Marlborough
10 Hungerford
11 Newbury
12 Hartley Witney
13 Portsmouth
14 Abingdon
15 Oxford
16 Reading
17 Wokingham
18 Windsor
19 Bagshot
20 Staines
21 London
22 Dartford
23 Rochester
24 Faversham
25 Newmarket
26 Saxmundham

Map 2. London in 1757, showing footprints of maps 3–12

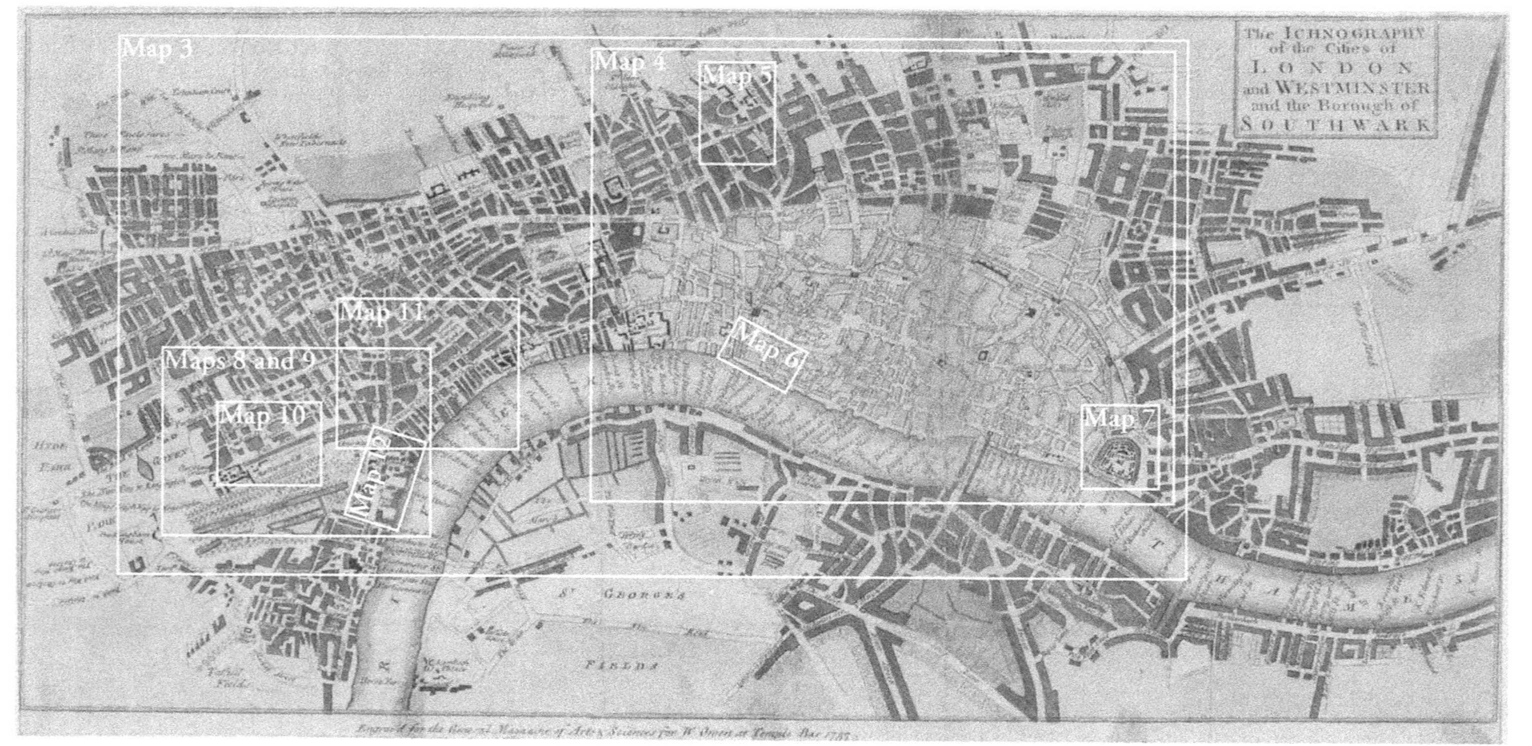

Map 3. Rioting in London, 11–12 December 1688

From Dunlop Dissertation (1980, p 42)

There were 2 mobs:

1. Savoy to Somerset House to Lincoln's Inn Fields, spontaneous on the news of the King's flight.

2. The Lime Street riot is correct. The Clerkenwell riot took place three weeks earlier. Newgate Market received part of the mob from Bucklersbury.

The Blackfriars mob found the Chapel at Lincoln's Inn Fields (3) already destroyed, and moved on to the Spanish Embassy (4) in Wild Street. Latecomers went to the Florentine Embassy (5) in the Haymarket. The next target was the Queen's Chapel in St James' Palace (6), but they met the cannon train coming home (7).

I could improve the map, for instance to show the Royal Artillery advancing north of the palace. But it is fun to show my original and it is also healthy to admit one's mistakes.

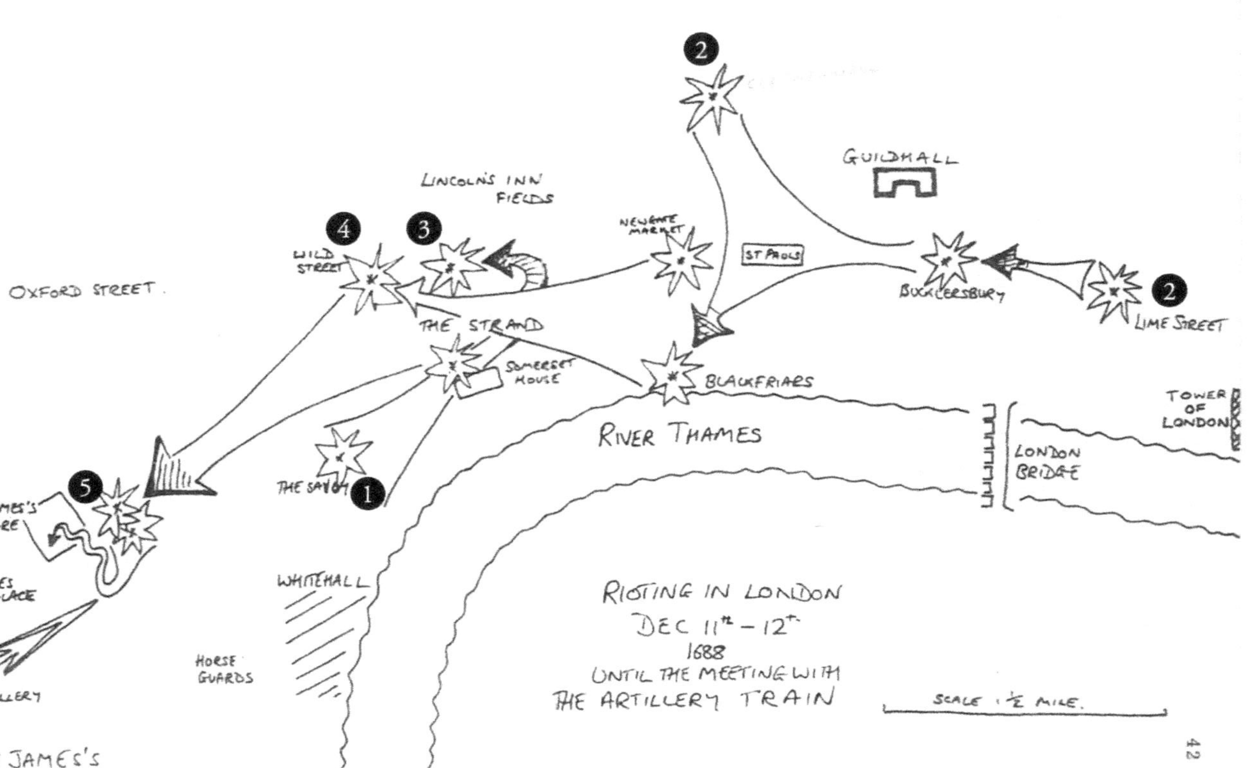

Map 4. A MAP of GROUNDPLOT of the City of London and the Suburbes thereof…

Wenceslaus Holler, 1666

1 The
  River Fleet
2 Apothecaries'
  Hall
3 Glass House
  Yard
4 King's Printing
  House
5 The Old Bailey
6 Physicians'
  Hall
7 Newgate Prison
8 St Paul's
  Cathedral
9 Cripple Gate
10 Guildhall
11 Bucklersbury
12 The Boar's
   Head
13 London Bridge
14 Southbank
15 The Walnut
   Tree
16 Lime Street
17 Crown Tavern
18 Lloyd's Coffee
   Shop
19 Aldgate
20 Thames from
   Syon
21 Thames to
   Gravesend

A GENERALL MAP of the whole City of London with Westminster

A St James' Palace
B Westminster
C Whitehall Palace
D Charing Cross
E Covent Garden and The Savoy
F Lincoln's Inn Fields
G Clerkenwell Green
H Smithfield
I Tower of London
J Tower Hamlets
K Wapping

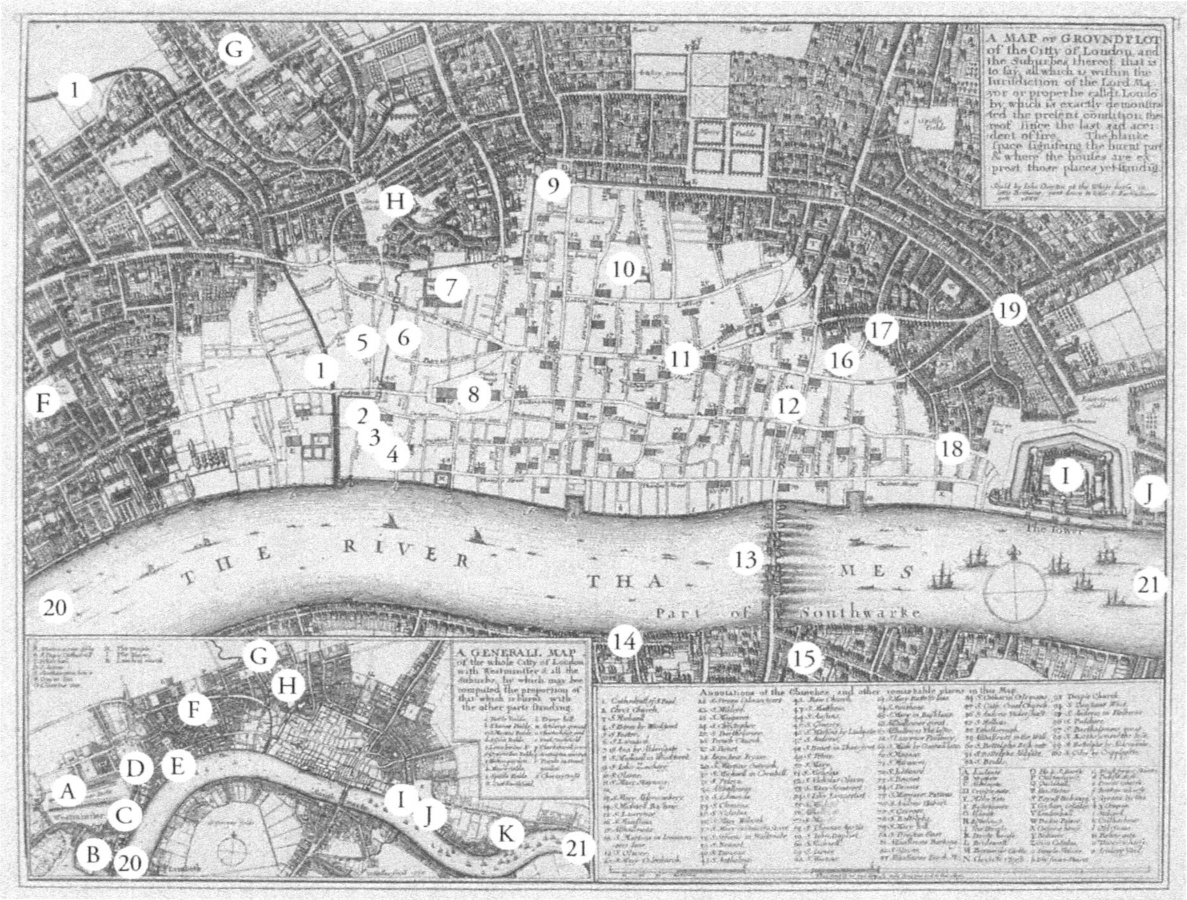

Map 5. Clerkenwell Green

Ogilby & Morgan,1676 (detail)

1 St James' Clerkenwell
2 Vicarage
3 'Mrs Holmes' boarding house', later
  site of Lenin's printing and editorial
  office, 1901–2
4 Kingston's Coffee Shop, later site of
  the Red Lion public house

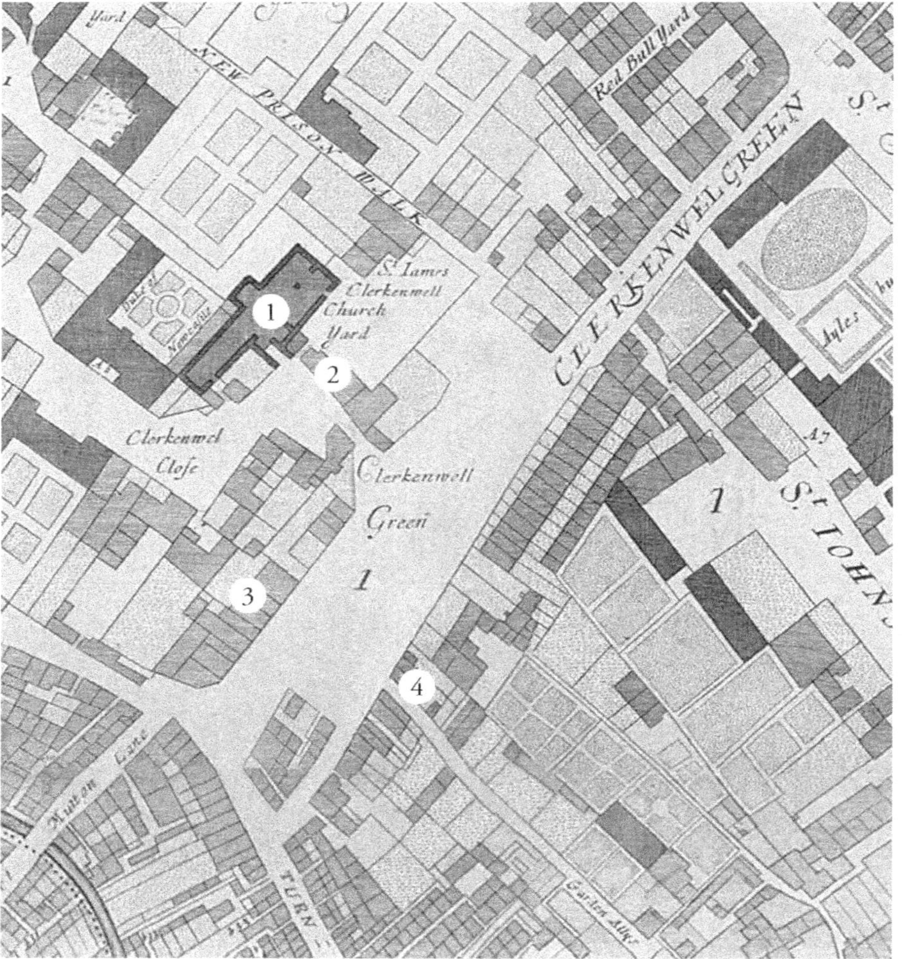

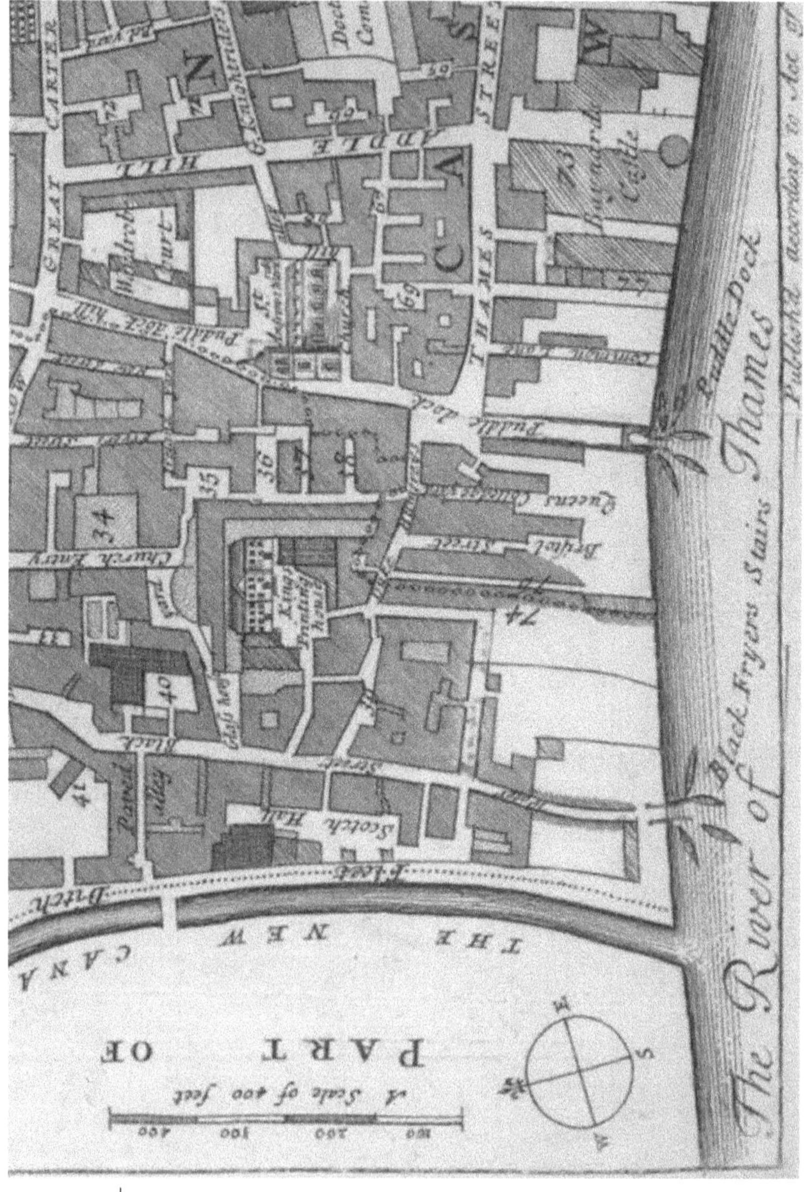

Map 6. Blackfriars

Detail from Farringdon Within and Baynards Castle ward, 1720. John Strype Map, John Stow

No 34 is the closed churchyard of St Ann's
No 40 is Apothecaries Hall

Map 7. The Liberties of ye Tower of London

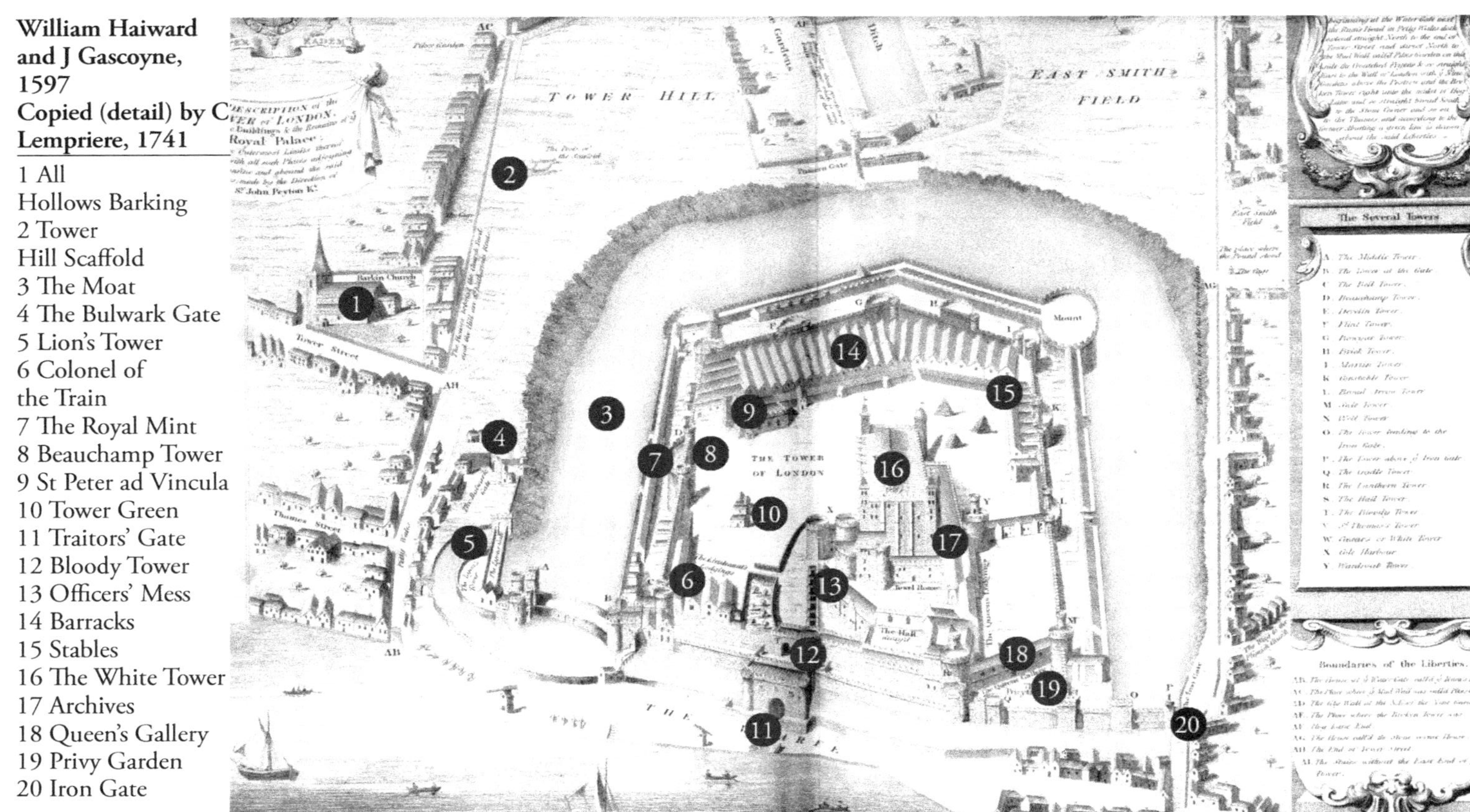

**William Haiward
and J Gascoyne,
1597
Copied (detail) by C
Lempriere, 1741**

1 All
Hollows Barking
2 Tower
Hill Scaffold
3 The Moat
4 The Bulwark Gate
5 Lion's Tower
6 Colonel of
the Train
7 The Royal Mint
8 Beauchamp Tower
9 St Peter ad Vincula
10 Tower Green
11 Traitors' Gate
12 Bloody Tower
13 Officers' Mess
14 Barracks
15 Stables
16 The White Tower
17 Archives
18 Queen's Gallery
19 Privy Garden
20 Iron Gate

Map 8. St James' Palace and Park, 1647

By Fairthorne and Newcourt, surveyed 1647, published 1657

1 The road from Knightsbridge to Charring Cross
2 The future site of Buckingham Palace
3 St James' Palace
4 The deer park
5 St James' Street
6 Piccadilly
7 The future site of St James' Square
8 The Haymarket
9 The Great Mews
10 Charring Cross
11 Whitehall Palace

Map 9. St James' Palace and Park, c.1700

Anon.

1 The road from Knightsbridge has been removed
2 Arlington House, future site of Buckingham Palace
3 St James' Palace
4 Petty France
5 Former house of John Milton
6 'The mound' protected by the ornamental lake to the south
7 Story's Gate
8 Horse Guards' Parade
9 Entrance from Charring Cross
10 Whitehall Palace

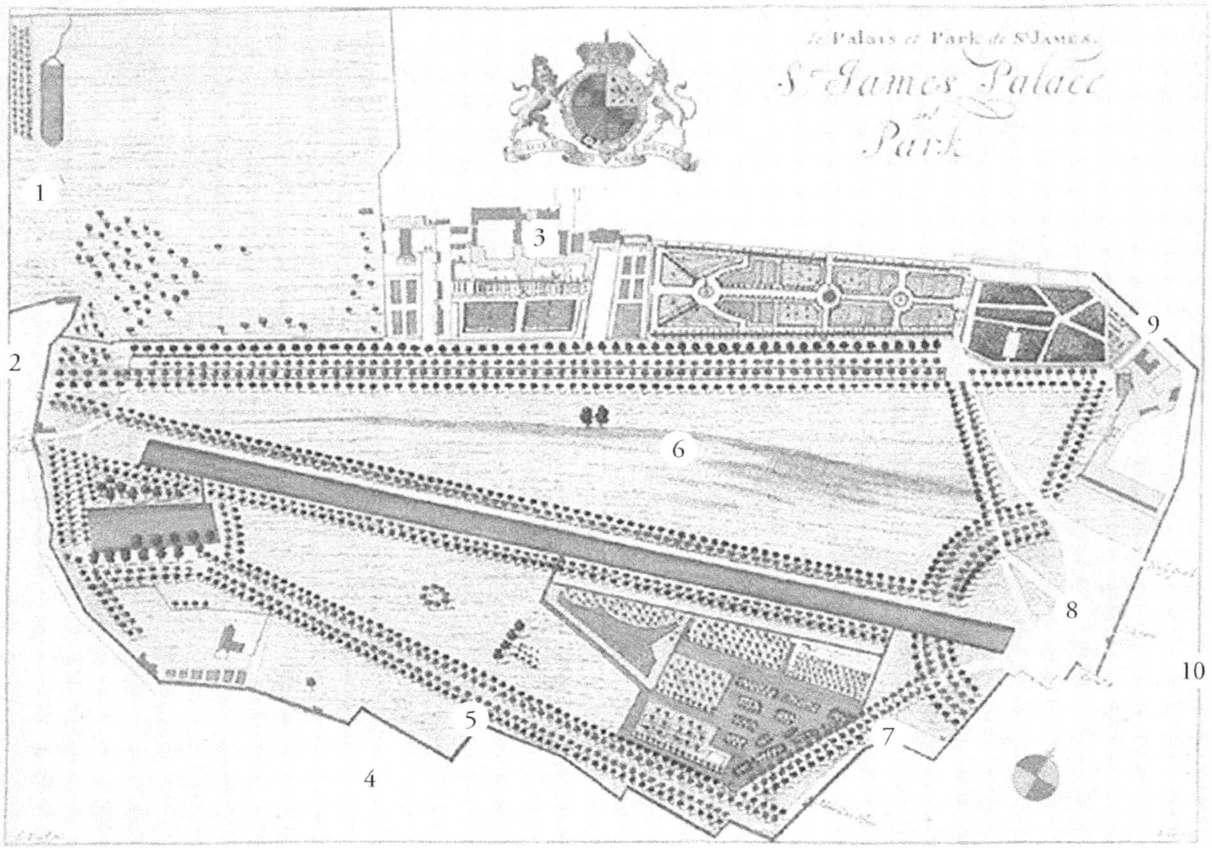

Map 10. St James' Westminster, London, St James' Square (detail)

Richard Blome c. 1695

1 Chapel Royal, St James' Palace
2 Queen's Chapel
3 'Halifax House'
4 'Ormonde House'
5 'Ranelagh House'
6 'French Residence'
7 'Where the funeral cortege was halted'
8 'Where Colonel Solms was halted'
9 'Florentine Residence'
10 To Piccadilly
11 To Charring Cross

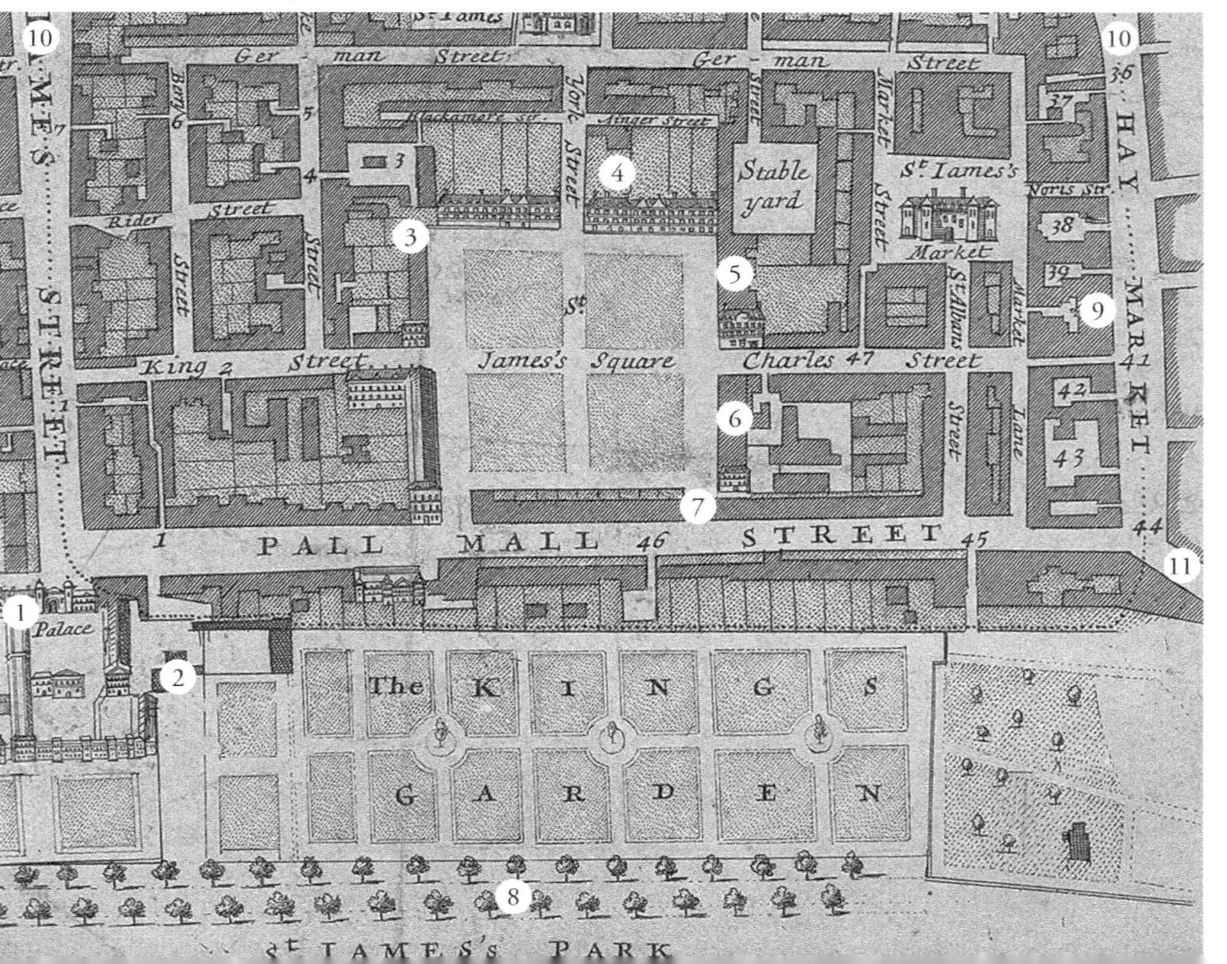

Map 11. Parish of St Martin in the Fields, London (detail)

Ston's Survey, 1755

1 St James' Park
2 Former entrance
   to park
3 Red Lyon Inn
4 The Great Mews
5 Charing Cross
6 Angell Court
7 St Martin in
   the Fields
8 'Jorrock's
   livery stables'
9 'Forrester home'
10 Rose Street
11 St. Paul's
   Covent Garden
12 Savoy Precinct

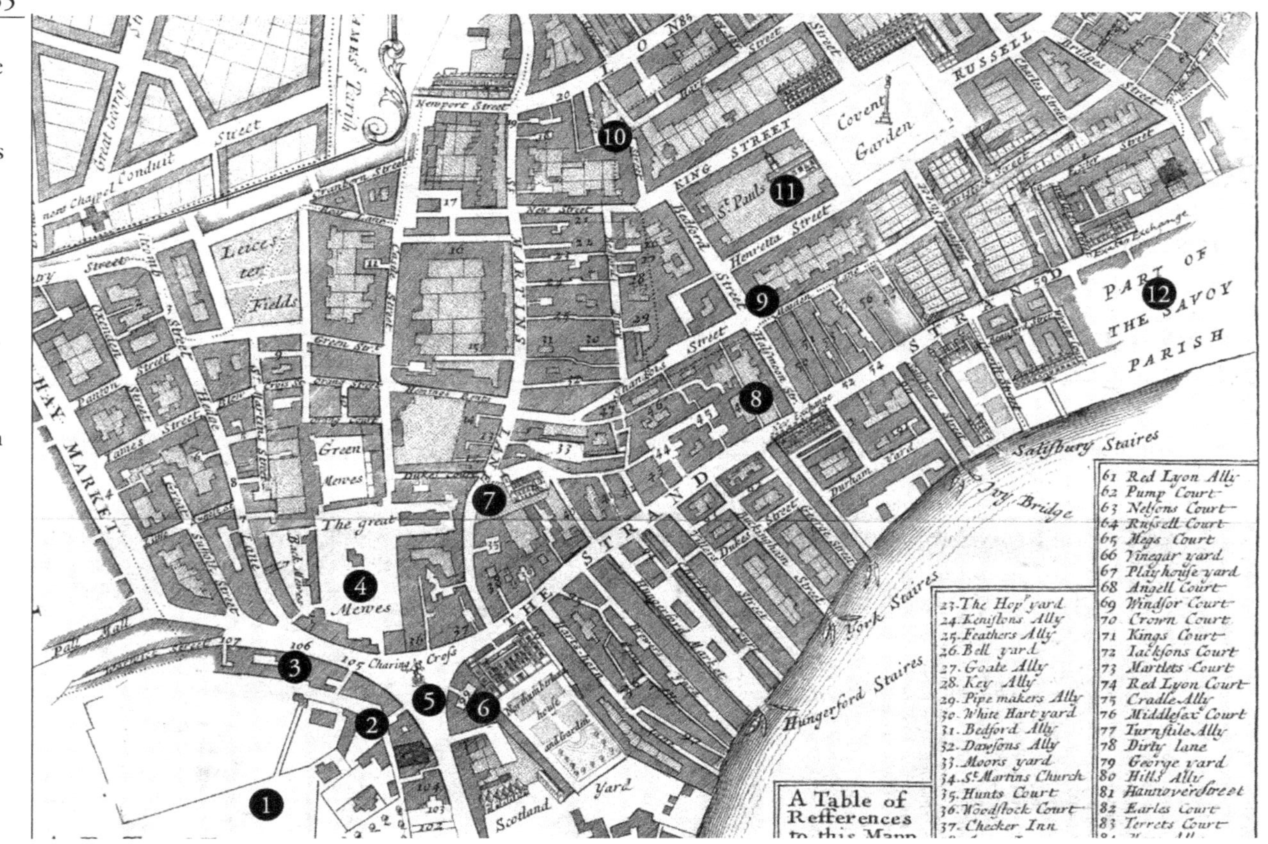

Map 12. Ground Plan of the Royal Palace of Whitehall, London

Fisher, 1680

1 King's quarters with
  internal courtyard
2 William
  Chiffinch's Room
3 The Privy Stairs
4 The Queen's room
5 Queen's Maids
  of Honour
6 Queen's Wardrobe
7 'Council Chamber'
8 Holbein Gate
9 The Chapel Royal
10 The Whitehall Stairs
11 Horseguards Barracks
12 To Westminster Abbey
  and Parliament
13 To Charring Cross
  and The Strand
14 River Thames from
  Syon House
15 River Thames to
  Gravesend

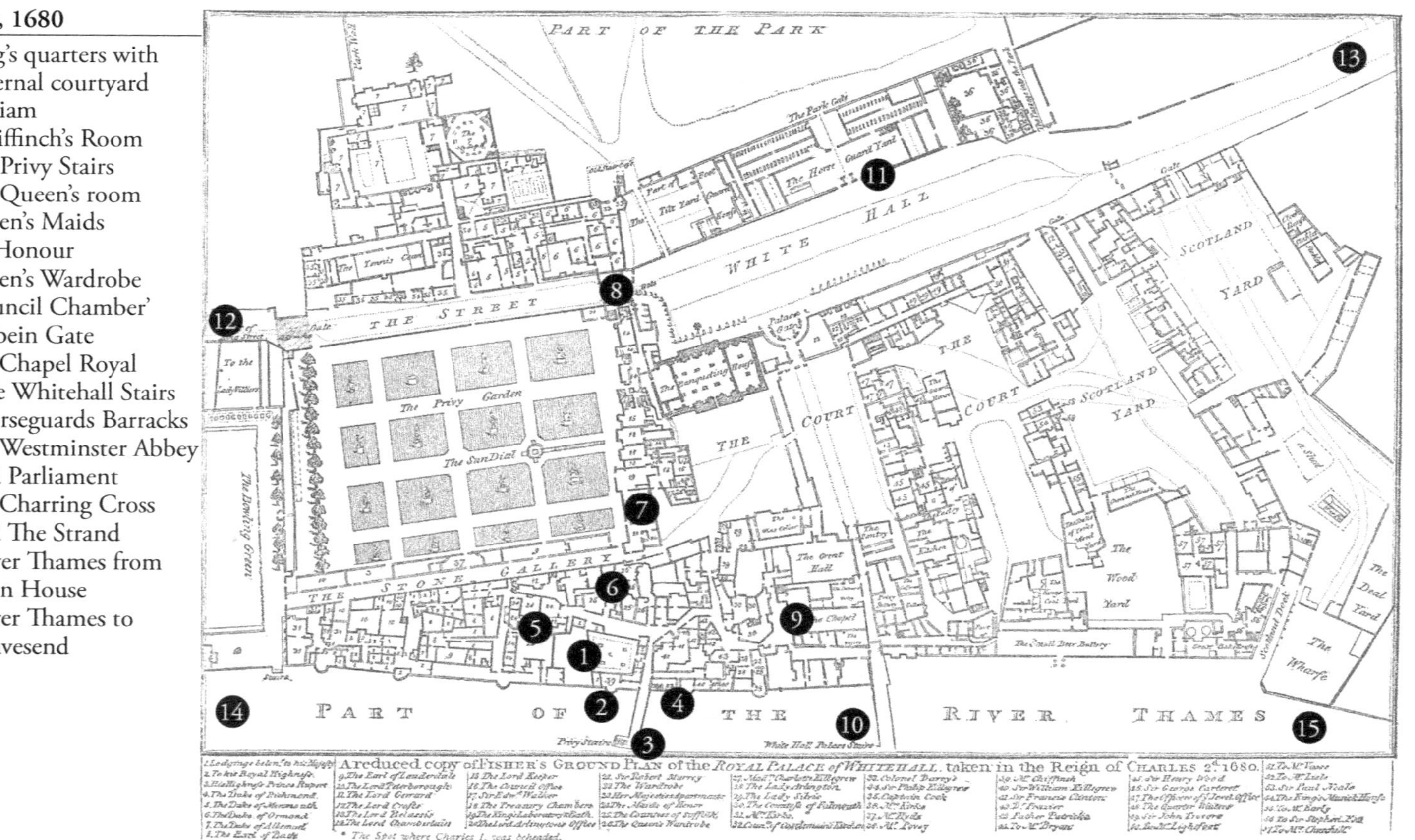

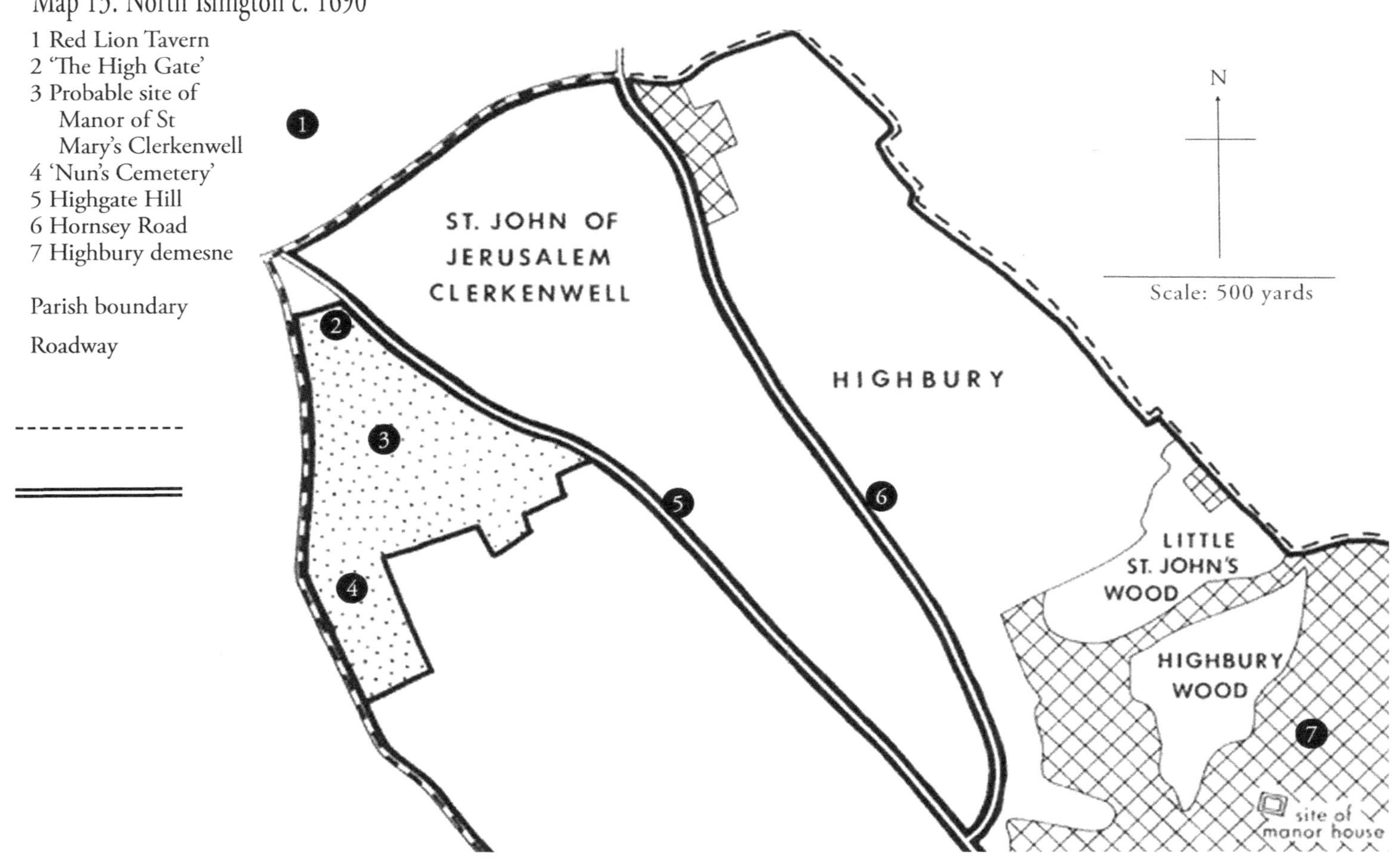

Map 13. North Islington c. 1690
1 Red Lion Tavern
2 'The High Gate'
3 Probable site of
   Manor of St
   Mary's Clerkenwell
4 'Nun's Cemetery'
5 Highgate Hill
6 Hornsey Road
7 Highbury demesne
Parish boundary
Roadway
Scale: 500 yards
N
HIGHBURY
ST. JOHN OF JERUSALEM CLERKENWELL
LITTLE ST. JOHN'S WOOD
HIGHBURY WOOD
site of manor house

Map 14. Windsor Castle and Prospect of The Castle from the S.E.

Wenceslaus Holler

Published in *The institutions,
laws and ceremonies of the noble
Order of the Garter,*
Elias Ashmole (1672)

1 The White Harte Inn
2 Clock on the Clewer or
  Curfew Tower
3 Castle Gate
4 South Porch to St
  George's Chapel
5 Arms of Phillip and Mary
6 Cloister and Tomb House
  entrance
7 The Round Tower
8 The Norman Tower
9 Stairway up to the Round
  Tower

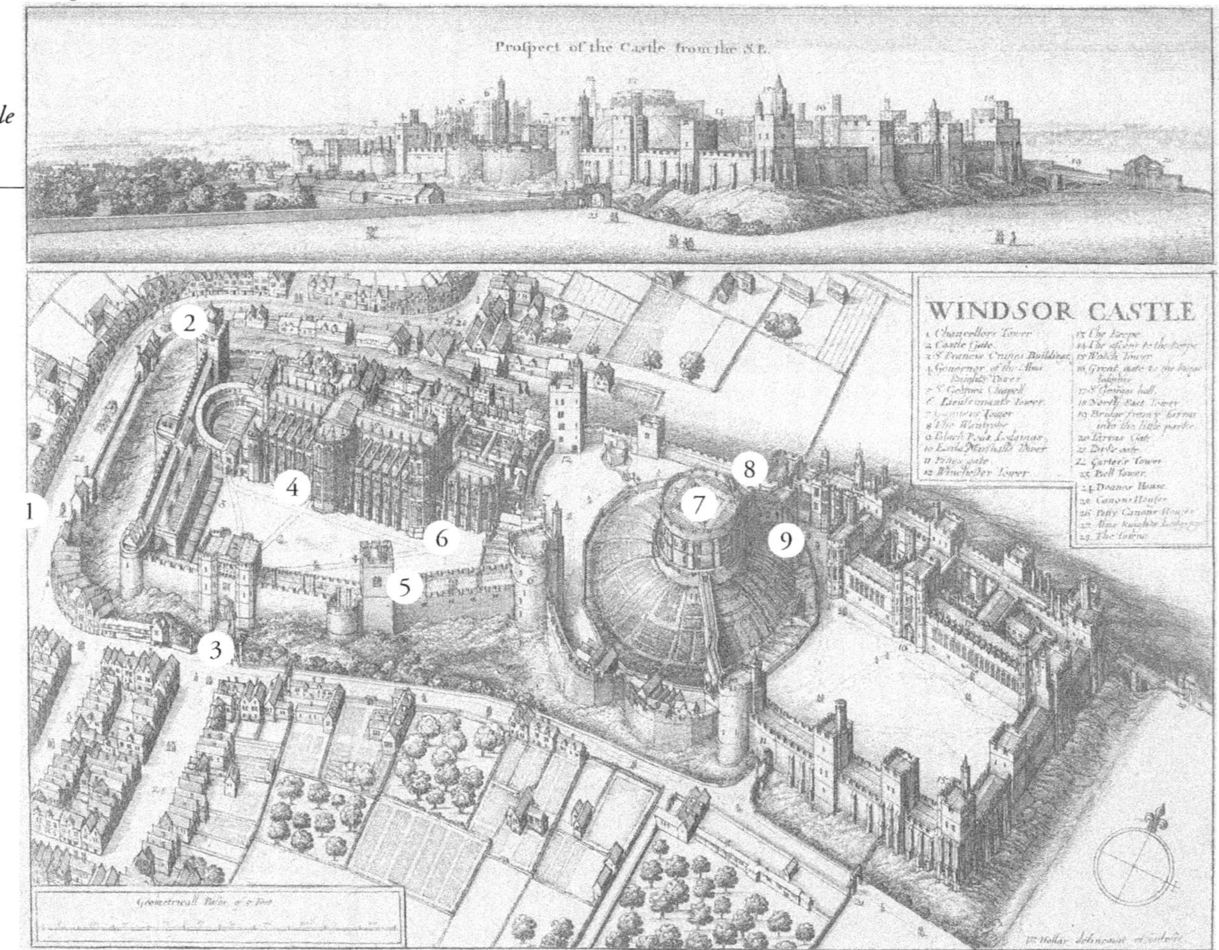

358

Map 15. City of Bath (detail)

Joseph Gilmore, 1694

Extracted by Dr Guidot out of his *Antiquities of Bath*, **1731**

1 River Avon to Bristol
2 West Gate
3 Road to Bristol
4 Bath Abbey
5 Prison (former St
   Mary's Church)
6 North Gate
7 Track along North Wall
8 Three Horseshoes
9 Road from London
10 River Avon from Lacock

NB the map is rotated 90°
   clockwise from the normal
   orientation to the north.

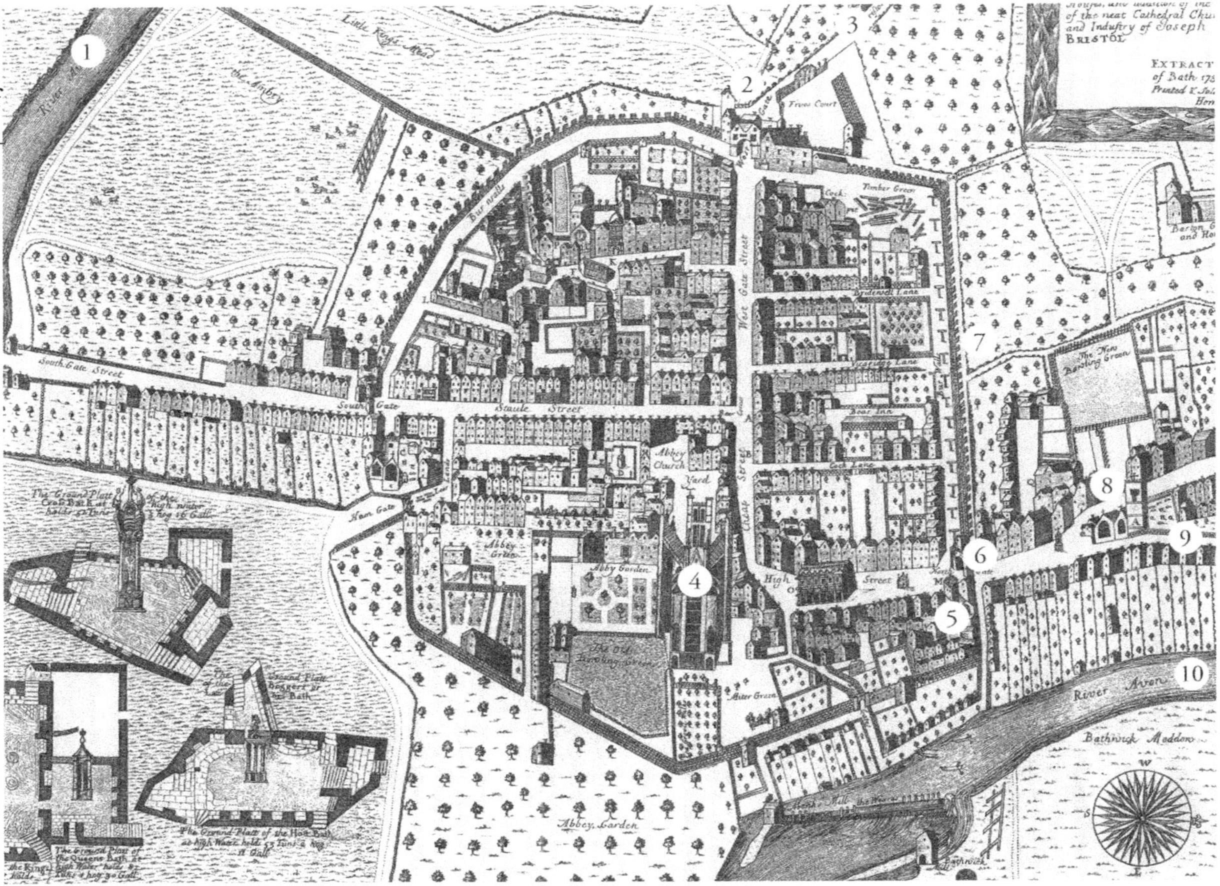

Map 16. An Exact Delineation of the Famous Citty of Bristoll and Suburbs

James Millerd, 1673
(Detail)

1 To the Avon Gorge
2 Brandon Hill
3 Cathedral
4 River Frome
5 The Gibb Shipyard
6 River Avon
7 Tower Quay
8 St Stephen's
9 St Nicholas' Back
10 Christmas Steps
11 Christmas Street
12 St John's Gate
    and Church
13 The Tolzey
14 St Nicholas Gate
    and Church
15 The Cross
16 Market House
17 The Swan
18 Temple Street
19 The Horseshoe
20 Duck Lane

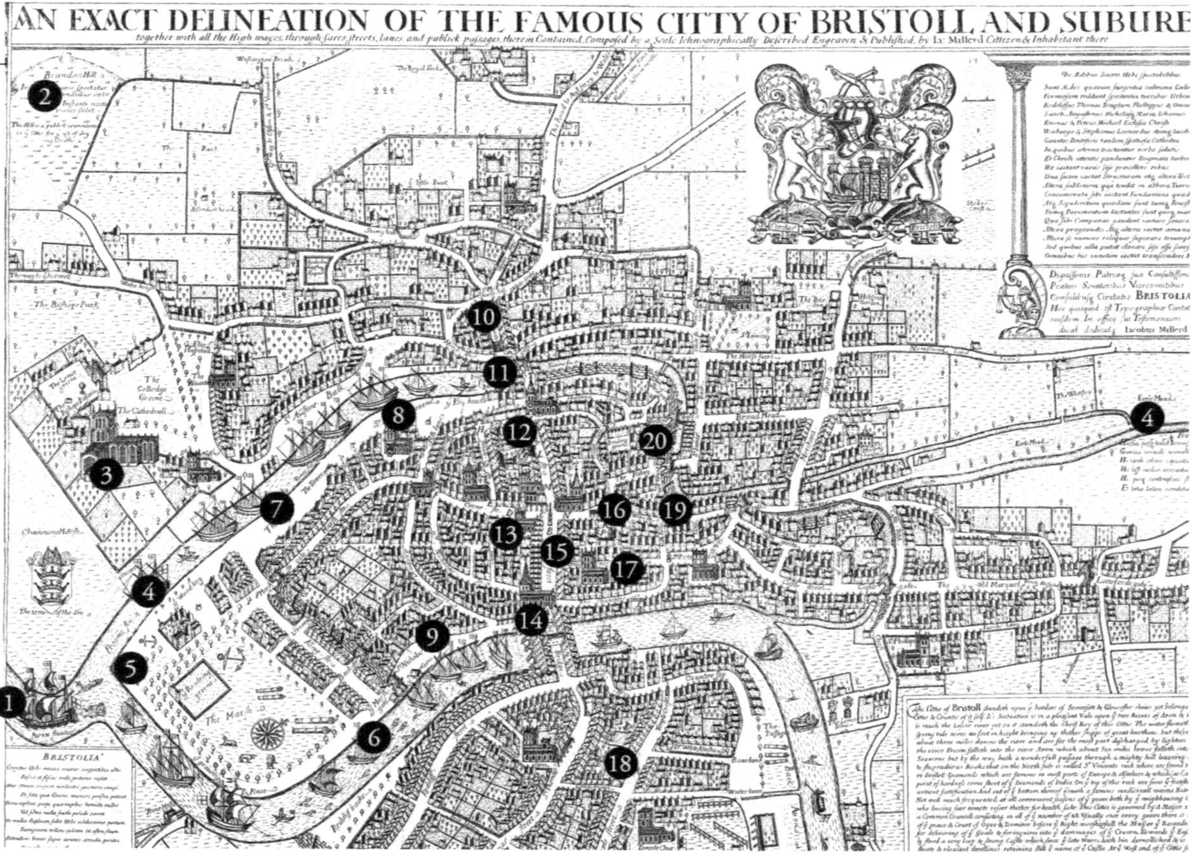

Map 17. Thames estuary, course of the King's 1688 escape attempts: 11 December (A–D); 24–25 December (1–7)

Anon., 1893

A Elmley Ferry, 12:00 Tues 11 Dec (the customs hoy)
B Sheerness, 15:00–21:15 (the hoy takes on ballast)
C Mouth of the Swale, 06:00 Weds (hoy waits for the tide)
D Faversham 12:00 Weds (hoy lands)
1 Rochester, 01:00 Sun (the shallop)
2 The Swale, 07:30 Sun (transfer to The Eagle, then 09:00 to the smack)
3 Southend Sand, 10:30 Sun (the smack)
4 Short of the Red Sand, 15:30 Sun (the smack)
5 Buoy of the Narrows, 10:00 Mon (the smack)
6 North Foreland Point, 10:00 Mon (the smack)
7 Top of the Downs, 14:00 Mon (the smack)

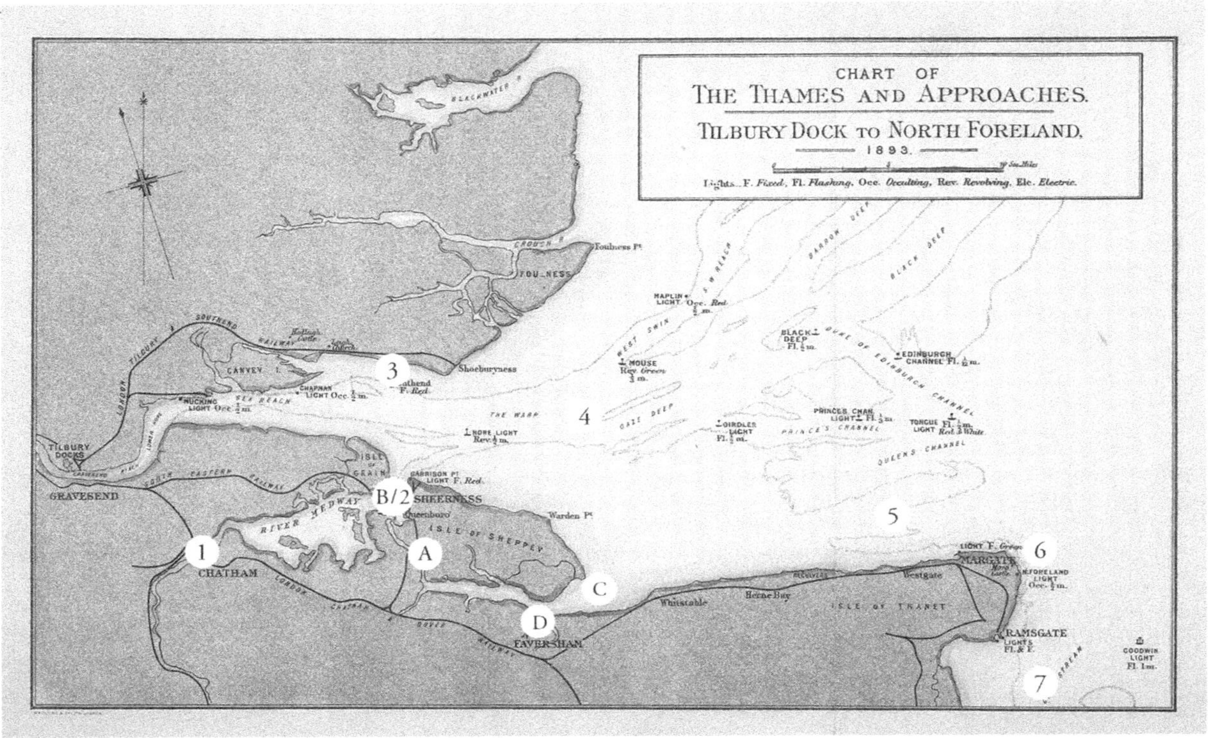

Index of Historical Characters

* Major historical character in online Epilogues